Abundance

A Novel

Jakob Guanzon

Graywolf Press

"If I Had Words." Written by Jonathon Hodge (ASCAP). Published by Finchley Music Corp (ASCAP). Used with permission.

This publication is made possible, in part, by the voters of Minnesota through a Minnesota State Arts Board Operating Support grant, thanks to a legislative appropriation from the arts and cultural heritage fund. Significant support has also been provided by the National Endowment for the Arts, Target Foundation, the McKnight Foundation, the Lannan Foundation, the Amazon Literary Partnership, and other generous contributions from foundations, corporations, and individuals. To these organizations and individuals we offer our heartfelt thanks.

This is a work of fiction. Names, characters, businesses, places, events, locales, and incidents are either the products of the author's imagination or used in a fictitious manner. Any resemblance to actual persons, living or dead, or actual events is purely coincidental.

Published by Graywolf Press
250 Third Avenue North, Suite 600
Minneapolis, Minnesota 55401

www.graywolfpress.org

Published in the United States of America

ISBN 978-1-64445-046-8

2 4 6 8 9 7 5 3 1
First Graywolf Printing, 2021

Library of Congress Control Number: 2020937597

Cover design: Kapo Ng

To my pa,
Nilo Pelea Guanzon

$89.34

$89.59

$79.00

$77.41

$0.00

$20.00

$77.41

$230.62

$17.41

$207.55

$17.41

$7.55

$16.41

$300.00

$16.40

$100.00

$80.00

$43.00

$11.40

$8,722.04

$8,622.04

$11.40

$50,000.00

$12.40

$0.01

$6.41

$0.00

$2.41

$12.22

$1.75

$9.04

$576.17

$0.38

$576.17

$0.38

$195.70

Abundance

$89.34

It's-a-girl pink. Too festive a color for the soap in a McDonald's men's room. Wrong color, anyway, just like it was eight years ago today. Michelle had been certain that the little boy now waiting outside for Henry would be a girl. So certain that she'd handed Henry a pink-ribboned cigar, right before lugging herself out of the truck and onto a stretcher.

Henry's thoughts scroll through a reverse inventory, its sum a taunt. The absentee list of birthday paraphernalia—balloons and streamers, candles and cake, a pile of presents, a pack of friends, a mother—seems to etch itself into the graffitied bathroom mirror. Henry's burned a gallon of gas to drive them three towns east of the boy's elementary school to this McDonald's in particular. Not only for its PlayPlace, but because there's no bus stop out front. No keypad code to access the bathroom. This is one of the nicer locations, even if passing squalor has left a few stains in here. Mirror all carved up with phone numbers, initials, *fuck u*'s. Smack center, one jagged message of encouragement says, *It gets better.*

Henry still reeks of the day. No chance to wash up. After he picked Junior up from school, they'd killed a couple hours at a park rather than inside the public library. When he unclamps an armpit reaching for the soap, a wet-leaf gutter musk seeps upward. The soap dispenser's porthole is a bloodshot cyclops. Tired and near empty. A weak sneeze of pink in his palm. He jiggers the pump till he's squeezed out every last driblet. The faucet is automatic, has a sensor but no knobs to warm the frigid gush. He's cavernous with hunger, and a shiver echoes through his bones. He works the soap into a sudsy film. Picks the crud from his fingernails, his cuticles, the cork of his palms. Before scrubbing his face and chest, he extends his leg,

3

presses his boot toe against the door. Wouldn't want to be seen like this, doing this.

Pinching the sternum of his crewneck, he fans air over his torso, then pats himself dry with a paper towel. His black hair juts upward, stiff with dried sweat and limestone dust, months overdue for a cut, making a boxy helmet around his face. He slicks it all straight back, then almost smiles. Thinks back to the singlewide, the first night in their new home. When Michelle had seen him like this, fresh out the shower, she covered her smirk with a fist, muzzling the dim contours of her incisors but not her trademark pre-insult, "Ha."

"What now, huh?"

"Nothing." She gave the bedsheet a little matador flap. "Just your hair like that? Dad wouldn't know whether you's a guinea or a spic."

"Fair enough," he said. "I'm still torn whether you're a redneck or plain white trash."

"Come here."

And so he did.

When he slides his boot toe off the men's room door, something jingles. A bright metallic note skitters across the floor tiles, comes to rest in the corner. A quarter. He squats to retrieve it, slips it into the front pocket of his jeans.

$89.59

The way Junior slouches by the soda fountain, jaw slack as his shoulders and awe stretching his eyes, he ought to be watching a rocket climb into the blue instead of this fast food menu. The park's dose of June sun has left a flushed, feverish slick on the boy's brow. When he finally notices Henry checking his forehead, the boy's posture snaps from languid to infantry stiff. Out of respect or fear, Henry can't tell. Can't help but wonder if the boy is still scared of him. Either way, he's proud of his son, but instead of saying so, he just squeezes the boy's neck, each vertebra a prizefighter's knuckle.

"Dad?"

"Pa."

"Pa, did you know Happy Meals are on the Value Menu now? Three bucks." Junior flashes that same frown of approval Henry himself often makes before saying, "Not bad."

It is, though—bad. Bad that Junior's already weighing dollars. Even worse is the oil slick of relief that runs over Henry as soon as that internal, automatic arithmetic crunches out a figure that's a third of what he's budgeted for this birthday treat.

"You order whatever you want." He steers Junior by the shoulders, settling them in line.

The clerk grips the cash register like a politician at a podium. His resemblance to Junior doesn't edge anywhere near uncanny, but close enough for concern. Similar almond tilt to their eyes, cheekbones lifted, craniums egg-shaped. Pigments hard to place but sure enough dark. What well-meaning white people like to call exotic.

Nothing exotic about the acne splattered over the clerk's face, so rutted and saturated that the boils down his neck look like runoff from the mess on his cheeks. Nothing exotic about the assembly-line hustle hard at work behind a geometry of stainless-steel panels and slots, glowing a fuzzy amber under heat lamps. Even though they've traveled a gallon east to celebrate at this one, a nicer one set on the final rung of the city's suburban orbit, the half-hidden machinery of these places never changes. Only the clientele, and with them the expectations.

Since getting out, the biggest change Henry's noticed is how everyone stares at their palms now, their heads constantly bowing to handheld screens as if in prayer. But when had they switched out all the overhead menus for plasma displays? Each time he looks back up, it seems he's just lost the Value Menu to dessert options or an inflated photo of a Big Mac, glossed up like a centerfold.

A manager is calling out order numbers, her accent curling digits into melodies. The top half of an employee disappears out the drive-through window. A sizzling metal basket is lifted out of the deep fryer, excess oil rattled off before french fries get dumped into a heat-lamped basin where they're sifted with a tool—half hand shovel, half funnel—and chuted into red cardboard sleeves. Even over all the commotion, Henry can still hear the salt sprinkling, and his nostrils fill with a scent that's got no name, only a color: gold.

Henry is now welcomed to McDonald's, asked permission to take his order. He can't bring himself to look at this acned, stretched-out version of his son, and such sour aversion to the poor kid's face only makes him feel worse. It's bad that he doesn't want a burger-flipping future for his son. Even worse that he thinks himself better than a greasy, minimum-wage job when he doesn't have even that. The last field of every job application. Check the box. Admit to convicted felon status. This bars him from so much more than nine-to-fives and food stamps.

Only after Junior confirms the price and orders a Happy Meal do Henry's eyes meet the clerk's.

"No," he says. "Make that a Big Mac, a meal. And Supersize it."

"No pickles, please," Junior says.

No pickles, Henry repeats, then orders himself a McChicken off the Value Menu. He scoops out a mound of coins and splashes them onto the countertop. His index finger slides coin after coin—four pennies, seven nickels, two dimes, eight quarters—across the counter. Turning over three singles and a fiver isn't exactly pleasant, but it's a relief to shed that heavy pocketful of coins, rattling after each step like tiny shackles.

$79.00

Henry sends Junior to wash his hands before squaring up at the soda fountain. He fills the cup with thirty-two ounces of Coca-Cola, takes two deep, fizzy gulps that tickle all the way down, then tops the cup off again. He peeks over his shoulder and—coast clear— heaps three greedy fistfuls of ketchup packets onto their tray.

This must have been one of the first franchises in the county to get refurbished. All the clunky, hard-plastic booths lacquered with that '90s paper cup color scheme of teal and purple have been ripped out, thrown out, and replaced with a stripped-down, pseudo-urban minimalism. Angular tables and chairs, booths arranged asymmetrically, all of it coated in a subdued palette of matte burgundies and Atlantic blues, despite the vast stretches separating them from both the eastern and western coasts.

The PlayPlace has been spared the facelift. Apparently interior decor trends have zero sway on the timeless functionality of tube slides and ball pits. In the glass cube extension housing the PlayPlace, only the furniture has been updated, looking like it'd been drawn up by some brooding Swede determined to undermine the wholesome American notion of warmth and plenty that those yellow arches outside not only embody but promise.

Instantly Henry realizes his mistake. Never should have tucked himself in the corner table next to the trash. From here he can see too much. A woman throws away a quantity of uneaten fries, burger bun ridges, and chicken nugget nubs that shapes his mouth into an appalled oval like the hole of the trash bin.

Once she exits the cube with her flock of kids, it's only Henry and a table occupied by two mothers, their daughters scuttling through the plastic bridges above. These mothers have got at least a decade on him, but they radiate health and comfort, arms muscled and lean from mornings at the gym, skin somehow sun-crisped yet silky at the same time. The prettier of the two—shrink-wrapped in athletic wear, her hair an asphalt-black wasp hive—catches him staring. His sights snap to Junior, before he can confirm whether the kink of her lips had been a sneer or a grin. He'd secretly disagreed with Michelle. Still thinks he looks sort of handsome with his hair slicked back like this. It feels good, if only for a second, to let himself believe this pretty mother might think so, too.

Patience. Too busy pacing himself, taking careful bunny nibbles of his McChicken, to monitor Junior. The boy now eyes his first bite into the Big Mac like a mistake. Henry dabs a fallen glob of mayonnaise off the wrapper, runs the flavored pad of his finger over his teeth. With his tongue, he presses the salt and serum into the membrane of his gums. No matter how slowly he eats, each swallow lands in his stomach with a distant thud, like a handball meeting the bottom of a dried-up well.

Junior sniffles. Puts the Big Mac down to smear at his nose. "Can I go play?"

Henry assesses the boy's progress. Half the burger gone, a divot dug into the fries. Not bad. This is the most the boy has eaten in a single sitting all week. Still, tonight Henry wants the boy stuffed to the backs of his eyeballs. Wants him waddling out of here, tummy swollen with enough nourishment to pad him for slimmer days to come.

Then again, it is the boy's birthday, and so Henry asks what day it is.

Junior cocks his jaw into that same defiant crook Michelle always had, right before dropping something snarky. "Tuesday."

"You know what I mean, smarty-pants."

Junior's neck sinks into his shoulder. That familiar, bashful hunch. The one Henry has been trying to wheedle out of the boy with pep talks on posture and confidence, the same one Papa had barked and skull-slapped out of Henry as a kid.

However essential it is to steel a son against the world's fangs, he still gets it, can't be too hard. A boy needs more than a father's hot ore to grow into his own, and so he now decides to do Papa one better. He tugs Junior's head close, kisses the whorl of his cowlick, and says, "The birthday boy can do whatever he wants."

And off Junior goes, before Henry can even mention tonight's surprise. What remains of the boy's dinner starts going stale under Henry's watch. Just moments ago, those fries were glistening, the steam casting a slight, woolly mirage in the air above them. Now they've got the same pallor and allure of a toppled stack of two-by-fours, more suited for construction than consumption. Even so, he wants some. Inside him births a craving so sharp it feels like the teeth of a rake, but something deeper tells him no. Not your son's food, not the boy's birthday dinner. Remind yourself of the consequences, the inpatient counselors had warned. Remind yourself, whenever you get the itch, of who you're going to hurt besides yourself.

The ghost of that fry, pressed square along the crease of his tongue, is all Henry sees and tastes when he closes his eyes, but he is a mountain of will power. He is serenity, in total control, Mahatma fucking Gandhi in steeltoes. If he were to deprive his own son of even a single fry, where would it stop? Look at what he's done, who he's been. Might have a lot to learn but he sure as shit knows that even a hairline fracture in the floodgates of his discipline can turn him right back into that greedy rat from the picture book—if you give a mouse a cookie, he's going to want a glass of milk, and if you give a mouse a glass of milk, he will so on and so forth, until Henry is coming to at three in the afternoon with his head wedged between a bathtub and toilet that's crusty with bile and blood from god knows who or what or when or how.

The why, on the other hand, is easy. The why is because he'd lost control.

At least there's free refills. No guilt for swigging soda to his heart's content. He gives a quenched, bubbly sigh. Without thinking, he reaches for the heap of ketchup packets, a reserve of sugar for later hunger pangs, but then catches himself. Wouldn't want to be seen. He risks a glance at the two mothers, who are now huddled over a phone between them. Sly as can be, he sneaks fistful after fistful of the ketchup packets into the pockets of his jeans, then tugs the hem of his crewneck over the lumpy denim bulge.

Is that why he hadn't sung "Happy Birthday" before digging into dinner? So he wouldn't shine a spotlight on this pitiful spectacle? He has been and will keep doing everything he possibly can, but all these two mothers would end up seeing is yet another deadbeat dad filling his kid with cholesterol and sodium and processed cheese and cancer and come on—does he really think this an acceptable way to celebrate? Pathetic. Cheap. Tacky. So unabashedly middle American, so irrevocably lower class.

But who's to say these women are any better than him? They're right here, too, feeding their daughters the same hot garbage.

Henry has stewed himself into a rage, alone, in a McDonald's PlayPlace, next to the trash. He collects himself with a deep breath. He exhales and opens his eyes: this whole mental tirade set off by a french fry.

The mouth of the tube slide produces two girls who dash across the padded floors, scamper up the steps, and belly-flop into the ball pit with two plastic splashes. From above, in a sagging cage made of stitched cargo straps, Junior watches the girls giggling and swimming through the ball pit. At such a distance, it might be a trick of the eye, but the expression on the boy's face is forlorn. Moldy with a despondent longing no eight-year-old should understand, let alone endure. If that wasn't enough, his son now reaches through the straps of the cage, and this whole prisoner metaphor is pretty much too much for Henry to bear.

What else to look at but the pretty mother? This time he strives for subtlety, glancing from the corners of his eyes with his chin aimed out the window, ready to act as if he's waving to someone pulling up in the parking lot, in case she catches him leering all over again. But studying her this time around, it's like he's scanning her for flaws. A sort of secret payback for everything he'd imagined she might have thought about him.

And so he decides she is wearing too much makeup—way too much for a Tuesday evening at McDonald's. Yet another prom queen past her prime, scrambling after the shrapnel of her bombshell days. Maybe she paints herself up like that because she doesn't see herself as beautiful as—he can't help but admit—she really is. The sharp arcs of her features and the oaky polish of her skin suggest some sun-bleached Mediterranean village, not a franchise grease pit here in fly-over country. She ought to be draped in white linen, not that waxy athleisure wear. Still, the elasticity of her outfit offers a lovesick-making display of her architecture, a form so deliberate in its bends and narrows, it's as if Henry himself had sculpted his ideal woman into breathing. She's got that spitfire air of a woman who isn't scared to tell a man exactly how she wants to be kissed, how she expects to be loved.

He is positive he could do precisely as instructed.

It's as if the crescendo of this imagined feast signals her. Those martini-olive irises, feline in their shading, now meet his. With the same shamelessness with which she'd taken him in his fantasy, her eyes now roll at him in reality, in this PlayPlace.

McChicken. Burger meat. Pig.

The tube slide coughs out Junior. Getting to his feet, he winds his shoulders a few times before locking them into the posture he's been taught. His belt cinches the waistband over itself, making ugly denim wads around his hips. His clothes, even from here, are visibly filthy. He flashes a sweaty, hold-my-beer grin at Henry, and marches toward the ball pit, the girls. A sense of purpose drives his twiggy-limb strut as he ascends the steps to the ball pit, one by one.

And then, just as Junior crouches to dive in, the pretty mother calls the girls. It's time to go home.

$77.41

A child should never stop smiling on his birthday, and so it's up to Henry to overturn Junior's grimace. Rivulets of ice cream streak off the cone and over the top of the boy's hand, a milky tree branching down his wrist. More of Henry's latest attempt to do his duty seems to coat the boy's arm than his tongue.

In the McDonald's parking lot sits their home for the last six months: Henry's trusty F-250. The truck's bed is lumpy with thirty-gallon Hefty bags full of clothes. Bolted flush under the rear window is a lockable, diamond-plated utility case holding the few valuables that hadn't been set outside in the frost during a last-minute, mid December yard sale. A few power tools and a plain white urn pin down a plastic folder with their birth certificates and old photographs.

Henry opens both the driver's-side and suicide doors. A narrow bench seat is littered with Junior's bedding, toys, school books, a plastic gallon jug for water, and Mom's bese saka–printed shawl. Lying tipped on its side is the heating crown, a metal, nest-shaped contraption Henry made by crimping and molding a wire clothes hanger to support the dashboard cigarette burner under a can of food. As of last night, their dinner stash is gone. All the tins scraped clean and fed into a machine for nickels to save up for tonight's surprise.

Before settling behind the steering wheel, Henry empties his pockets into the door's side compartment. On top of a prepay flip phone, its minutes long spent and battery dead for a week, he unloads all the ketchup packets. Duct-taped in the frame of the passenger's-side window is a layering of cling wrap as dense as a basement cobweb. When Junior closes his eyes, tilting his face to absorb the sunlight caught in the cling wrap, it reminds Henry of his own mother. Sad to think neither the boy nor his grandma would ever get to see just how similar they are to each other.

"Eat up," he tells Junior. "You're making a mess."

The boy scowls at the ice cream cone as if it's just asked a steep favor. To it he says, "My stomach hurts."

"You're full, that's all," Henry says. "Now finish it."

"I can't, Pa. I think I'm sick."

"Sick, huh?" He turns the key. "Guess your surprise will have to wait then."

The wrong part of Junior's face narrows. Henry wanted the boy's lips to seam with intrigue, not his eyelashes to zipper into suspicion. A familiar glare. Ever since November, the boy has grown stingy with his eye contact.

"What surprise?" Junior asks.

"Wouldn't be much of a surprise if I told you, now would it?"

Saying this, Henry is reminded of some thigh-slapping sitcom dad, and the comparison pleases him. To drive this wholesome image home, he tousles Junior's hair. It's stiff with grease and an odor follows, as if the rustle has released spores of unwashed scalp into the stale air of the truck cab. Very soon he wouldn't just bathe the boy, but scrub every last inch until Junior's hide was glowing, tender and squeaky-clean as a newborn.

They drive west and deeper into the dusk, a grand smudging of jackfruit and amethyst. The sky is so pretty it's noteworthy, and it's a shame he's got nobody to note it to. The boy is too busy chomping at the cone like he's been told to respond to Henry's nudge. Not sharing this sunset, not marveling in tandem doesn't make it any less pretty, though. Might even go so far as to call such a sight beautiful, and such an observation strikes him as strange. Out of character. Can't even begin to remember the last time he'd taken a moment to inject meaning into something as routine as the sun's daily retreat.

Best guess it's because tonight is different from the last six months. Not only thanks to Junior's birthday, but also the very real, within-arm's-reach prospect of comfort. The dose of hope for tomorrow's interview doesn't hurt either.

Last week, after opening the email invitation on a public library computer, he'd decided that the day before the job interview, Junior's birthday, they would splurge. They were owed a slender excess. Not quite sure whether it's funny or sad how sustained deprivation turns even the most commonplace amenities into luxuries. In a motel tub, they will bathe themselves, braise themselves under torrents of hot water for as long as they please, till they're pruney and choking on steam. They will have curtains to close and a deadbolt to lock, ensuring them a long, deep sleep on top of actual mattresses and bundled under clean sheets, undisturbed by the fear of a midnight *knock knock* against the truck's windshield.

The prospect of comfort. A crumb of hope. It's funny, not sad, he decides, that that's all it takes for him to wax poetic.

Hope might be a tall order, but comfort seems fair enough. He wonders if he someday manages to restore comfort to a constant, will he still observe his surroundings with a similar dopey awe? Or has this just been a fluke? A hiccup in the hard-times smear, a whiff of hickory smoke in the tundra. Will he end up like all those strangers—hollow-eyed in traffic, groaning in checkout lines, slumped over shopping carts—and bloat with entitlement? Will he fall into the ranks of their jaded herd? All of them shuffling after the only thing left: more.

If tomorrow pans out—and with all the practice and prep he's done, how couldn't it?—he swears he'll practice gratitude every morning. Make a sport of it, a part of his morning routine, like how that pretty mother must start her days with yoga or wheatgrass-fueled meditation. Even once they're back to living with plenty enough, there's a certain honor to this austerity, so he ought to strive to keep himself humble and coyote lean.

The earthbound scenery doesn't quite live up to the sky above. The landscape gets bleaker the farther behind they leave the city, each stoplight westward cueing a deeper shade of decay. They've already driven well beyond the town center's franchises and freeway exits. The main road slims from four lanes to two after they pass the last of the housing developments, their pastoral-corporate names as blatantly synthetic as the slopes the houses sit on.

This far west, boarded-up, single-story homes have crawled away from the curb and into the tree line, looking like cadavers abandoned midautopsy. Lonely stretches of scorched prairie in between them. A water tower's sprained leg. Bible verses on blistered billboards. From post to crooked post, power lines hobble and shrink toward the rigid horizon ahead. Soon they're passing a series of squat strip malls and empty parking lots, their surfaces bulging and broken like a wart under a microscope. Storefront windows are vacant and dusty, set off by the occasional mom'n'pop shop that's selling god knows what to keep the lights on and the debt collectors at bay. The few windows that remain lit look more like ashtray embers than invitations.

Laundromat.

Pawnshop.

Liquor & Wine.

Agricultural Supply.

Saint Jude's.

Nails.

Guns & Ammo.

XXX.

Bowling.

Check Cashing.

Then the strip malls and warehouses vanish into an empty swath of grass that's neither lawn nor pasture, before extending into a Walmart parking lot. At the end farthest from the store's entrance, a mobile shantytown assembles itself for the evening. The village centerpiece is a Winnebago. Scattered around it are vans and pickups rigged with makeshift campers of plywood and corrugated metal. A silhouette hefts a charcoal grill out of a sedan's trunk. Other than that, no sign of life. All those vagabond shadows are easy enough to forget.

Only hours ago, Henry'd popped into this very Walmart to buy a birthday present, right before picking Junior up from school. Walking in, he was greeted by death herself's obese cousin, wearing a blue vest that clung to her with the tenacity of a bungee harness. Behind her, that vast cathedral of plenty was pulsing with a fluorescent sneer. Henry didn't bother with a cart or basket. Waved away the proffered smiley-face sticker.

He'd deliberately parked on the opposite end of the store, away from the supermarket to spare himself the taunt of groceries, though this never squashed the question of how many hundreds of pounds of produce and meat and pastries and deli leftovers would wind up in the padlocked dumpsters out back. From this entrance, there was no avoiding the home and pharmacy sections to get to the toys. The main thruway to the back of the store was an obstacle course. Dazed, heel-dragging shoppers. Abandoned carts piled high with mundane loot. Signs shouting *Everyday Low Price* at every endcap and atop each squat tower of bargains that clogged the main lane. To the left, he passed domestic items he didn't need or want, but nevertheless couldn't afford.

To his right was the pharmacy section, aisle after aisle of makeup and soaps and shampoos and toothpastes and meds and shaving kits. By now his razor was so old its blade was brittle with rust and gunk, so over the last few weeks he's been letting his wispy beard grow unchecked into something between Fu Manchu and pubescent lumberjack. For Junior's sake, before falling asleep in the stuffy truck cab, Henry applies a nighttime coat of deodorant and has been going through Old Spice sticks at an expensive rate. He would need to replace that soon, too. Wanting to save his strength for tomorrow's interview, he hadn't arranged a Craigslist gig for tomorrow morning. There would be more cash to be made, not that it was ever enough. With any luck, once the paychecks started coming in and he'd paid off the remaining back rent, utility bills, association dues, sanitation bills, cleaning fees, and the New Year's Eve movers, simply having a home would remove purchases like razors and deodorant from the edgy plane of conscious budgeting.

The toys were way in the back. Henry coasted the aisles in a nauseous trance. Past an aluminum avalanche of bicycles stacked three high up to the ceiling. Through a hall of Nerf guns and Lego sets. Around a pigpen of bouncy balls. Without Saturday-morning cartoons, the action figure characters in the next aisle existed without context, except for the reboots of the G.I. Joes and Ninja Turtles he'd played with as a kid himself. But these plastic dolls were twelve, fifteen, others twenty bucks apiece—when had these fuckers gotten so expensive?

All it took was one lap through the toys until he hated himself. Rather than considering what gift options Junior might actually want, all his mental energy had been spent tallying and comparing price tags.

He went back to the action figures. Scattered on an ankle-high shelf was an assortment of toys on clearance: professional wrestler figurines. A failed series featuring the biggest stars from the sport-theater's heyday. The names of these steroid-charged pituitary cases were sure to be as meaningless to anyone born after the '80s as all the higher shelves' characters were to him.

A folding chair of nostalgia smacked him at the sight of his old favorite. Jets of sparks crackled and burst among stadium spotlights, an orchestra began marching through the opening bars of "Pomp and Circumstance," and Slim Jim peppers prickled his tongue. Maybe Junior would get a kick out of learning about his pa as a boy, flexing in front of a boxy, wood-paneled TV, turning furniture into turnbuckles and sofa cushions into archnemeses down for the count.

Plus it was only $4.97.

At the checkout counter, he asked for paper, double-bagged.

Outside he dropped the tailgate to make a workbench. At that point, only the Winnebago sat at the far end of the parking lot. From the diamond-plated utility case, he withdrew a utility knife and a roll of tape that was down to its last band. He slit along the seams of the brown paper, flipped the blue-ink logos outside in, then wrapped the gift up, careful to be conservative with the last shreds of tape. Sure enough, the tape ran out before he'd finished, leaving one flap of paper jutting out stubbornly. He doubled back inside to ask the greeter for a favor.

Junior isn't simply a smart kid. Inherited all his parents' skepticism but none of their lip, making him observant, perceptive, seemingly wise beyond his stubby eight years. Of course he'll sense Henry's excitement about this gift, will absorb the heat of his father's enthusiasm like a skillet over blue flames. Looking forward to something feels foreign. Awkward but thrilling, like the ecstatic angst of his first time with Michelle. Can't believe how much he still misses her, even now, after everything. Even though he hasn't quite forgiven her. Even though there's no forgiving him, either.

The boy's face is so soft it's all lobes. Hardly a hint of his mother's piercing features, for now at least. Searching for a trace of Michelle in Junior, Henry spots the mess of melted ice cream splattered down the boy's arm and hand, which he's now kneading into his navel.

Henry steers them onto the freeway, the asphalt and landscape ahead of them as barren as they are behind. Junior, sensing his father's gaze, swallows a wince. He turns away, staring out or into the cling-wrap cobweb. "It hurts."

"It's okay," Henry says. "Pa's right here."

$0.00

The wheelchair was overkill. A dramatic flourish, whether intended as a final act to flaunt the hospital's commitment to patient care, or else one last uppercut of deprivation—in this case, the simple dignity of walking—sixteen-year-old Henry wasn't sure.

The nurse barely looked up to tell him, "Hospital policy." Not that Henry had the energy to do anything besides comply, but still. With all the other inpatient kids gawking from the TV room, he would have liked to turn his back on them and march away on his own two feet.

Whatever. Any spit-in-their-face, teenage tough-guy resistance to authority had been smothered out of him by the end of the very first group session anyway. The fuse to his self-destructive streak had been extinguished, pissed on by all the horror stories of abuse, abandonment, rape, and incest that his circle mates shared. In that ring of junkies, survivors, psychotics, and the mousy girl with the shadow teeth, Henry's own grief shrank down to pettiness. A black marble, a child's plaything. His rebel veneer had stretched and ripped like cheap cellophane, exposing nothing but a lonely, bitter kernel.

Even the pretext for his two-week incarceration had been infantilized, sugarcoated in cliché. Rather than the accidental overdose of a tortured artist or feral rock star, the counselors had downgraded his brush with death to a cry for help. Henry'd been too exhausted to indignantly uphold his commitment to oblivion. Or maybe he'd kept his mouth shut because the demotion wasn't that far from the truth. He'd always had something to prove. All his partying—the chugging, snorting, freebasing—had been zealous to the point of theatrics. Maybe all his hammy thunder had simply been an attempt to dislodge that bitter kernel. Either way, it had certainly been bound to catch up with him.

Which it did, two weeks ago. A forty-eight-hour meth bender with the skinnies. After a pint of vodka had failed to steady, let alone slow, his marrow-deep tremors and molar grinding, a mix-and-match palmful of whatever painkillers and benzos the others were willing to part with seemed like a swell idea. A gulp. A wink. A minute, and after thirty more, the shivers went still and Henry went under.

If the stomach pump hadn't siphoned out who and what he really was deep down, then therapeutic captivity made sure to extract and exhibit all his sentimental goo. At heart, he was just another angry kid with no self-control. A self-medicating, self-sorry brat with a dead mother and an asshole immigrant father. Cue the violins. On with the pity parade. Alongside the other inpatient kids, each fully acquainted with abject suffering and god-nullifying cruelty, Henry had no right to complain. At least Papa'd been merciful enough to spare Henry monkey-wrench beatings or a cock in the mouth. So Papa was distant. Strict. Screamed when he had to, rapped Henry on the back of the head when he'd really fucked up, which, admittedly, he'd been doing plenty of lately.

Henry flopped into the wheelchair, his head dipped in surrender. He lifted two fingers in a wimpy wave to the others in the TV room, and then the nurse wheeled him around the metal detectors, past the steel-barricaded doors, and through the Pine-Sol–stinking entrails of the hospital. The nurse's tennis shoes squeaked on the salt-and-pepper linoleum, lending Henry's retreat a rubber-ducky drumbeat. All of him went slack in order to funnel any remaining strength to his right foot. Under his sock, between big and index toes, he clutched a precious shred of paper folded down to the size of a pebble. He held his breath as if that might keep it safer from detection.

Papa hadn't visited once since Henry got transferred to inpatient, hadn't bothered to bring a fresh set of clothes, so Henry'd been given a choice. Either get rolled out to the pavement in the same scrubs he'd worn throughout his sentence, or else change into the clothes he'd had on in the ambulance two weeks ago. He decided to change. A dramatic flourish of his own, a chance to showcase the aftermath of Papa's neglect. In a gallon ziplock bag his jeans were stale but fine. The t-shirt, on the other hand, was still crunchy with vomit, the bile's curry wafting out the instant he unzipped the baggie. But once the nurse wheeled him out into the sunshine, even the stench of his own rot was washed away by the spring air, sweet with lilacs and an almost maritime brine baking off the asphalt. The nurse stopped them under the shade of the emergency entrance awning.

Softly, Henry said his first words to the nurse. "Mind if we wait in the sun?"

"Good call," the nurse said, then released the wheelchair's brakes.

The hoarse thump of Henry's pulse echoed between his temples, seeming to fall into rhythm with the distant click of a cooling ambulance engine. All the colors out here popped with a new, vivid luster, from the emerald strips of freshly laid sod along the sidewalks to the mint and lavender of the scrubs worn by a row of nurses seated on a retaining wall as they released perfect tufts of cigarette smoke into the air. A gentle gust tickled the back of his neck when the nurse behind him pressed a contented sigh out his nostrils. Even if it was wordless, it felt nice, maybe even meaningful, to share this moment with someone else. After two weeks confined to that remote, monochrome wing of the hospital, its air fetid with adolescent body odor and bleak futures, relishing a sensation as simple and pure as the sun on his face satisfied an unfamiliar, animal need he'd never been aware of. Being Papa's son and reluctant heir to the old man's spleen and cynicism, he'd been trained to scoff at insipid pleasures like these. The advice to enjoy the little things had all the wisdom of Top 40 lyrics, he knew this, but still he let his thoughts meander freely, off to wherever they pleased. They stopped at his mother. Mom. How she used to pause in the middle of parking lots to close her eyes, then tilt her face to the heat above like a sunflower. Yellow. Serene.

Thank god she hadn't lived to see Henry like this.

He didn't have to open his eyes when Papa's truck pulled up. Henry would recognize the F-250's rusty thrum anywhere. All it took was one glance to see Papa had already calcified into his typical stony self. Miles from the tear-pulped version Henry encountered at the foot of the hospital bed when he'd stirred back into waking two weeks ago. His field of vision had been fuzzed sepia, his mouth coffin-dry and caked in the residue of some godawful cocktail of charcoal and dog shit. His tongue wouldn't obey, couldn't be pried from the back of his teeth to say everything he was supposed to.

Instead, something unexpected happened. Papa began saying the words that Henry couldn't. A slobbery cyclone of *I'm sorry, I'm sorry*, over and over, each apology winding and folding into the last. The downpour lasted all of one minute, abruptly sealed off with a gasp. Depleted, Papa let his head fall. Over the stiff hospital sheets a hand ventured toward Henry's but seemed wary of making contact. And so it was Henry's turn. Time to even the scales and heft all the guilt onto his lap, back where it belonged. But before he could muster language, Papa shuddered, then yanked Henry's arm so firmly that the IV tower jerked. The two waited as it swayed to a standstill, to silence. Papa's face was a single welt, chafed by fear.

"Don't ever make me come back here," he said, his voice puny. "To a hospital. I can't. Not anymore, not again."

Papa drew in a long, steady breath, but it failed to inflate him back to his normal posture, which made the next word possible. Smaller than a whisper came a syllable as unfamiliar to his lips as the brittle tone his voice had taken—*please*.

But the man now at the steering wheel was the Papa of ever and always. Not even a nod when Henry climbed into the passenger seat. Nearly pulled away before the nurse got Papa to sign the discharge forms.

Papa drove at a crawling pace in the rightmost lane of the freeway as if to prolong the torture of this silence.

"So," Papa said, finally. "Happy birthday, ah."

Of all the days to get released from rehab.

"Sixteen," Papa said. "How does it feel?"

"Lovely. Fucking splendid, *Dad.*"

The Americanism dug at Papa enough to make him choke the wheel tighter, snowcapping the peaks of his knuckles. Knuckles Papa had spared Henry, but not another child.

Although Henry'd been young, only twelve then, there were things Mom believed he had the right to know. Stories that might help explain why Papa was the way he was, for the years to come when she wouldn't be around to play arbiter. She'd been woozy with meds, stiff and stretched over the daybed where she'd spent her final months. From the belly down she was draped in a vibrant shawl that she used as a blanket, patterned with a shape he'd first assumed was a four-petal flower. A student from Ghana had given it to Mom, the young woman's economics professor, and explained the flower was actually a *bese saka*—a sack of kola nuts—a symbol of health and prosperity. Its color scheme had always seemed too bright for the circumstances. Irreverent, gaudy as a neon sarcophagus, but Mom still wore it every day. From where he'd been sitting, the elevated saline pouch perfectly obstructed the framed photo, tucked among the overflowing shelves of his parents' library, showing the three of them in Manila. Before starting the story, Mom made that wistful smile of hers. He would never understand how an expression that typically signaled contentment could dispatch such sadness.

Henry's dad—"your papa," she corrected herself—had come stateside for grad school. He only received partial funding, but, more importantly, his visa paperwork was taken care of by the university, which was where they met. A child of the plains, Mom had never met anyone like him, and, truth be told, her attraction could have been deemed problematic, after a colleague in the sociology department casually filled her in on the notion of racial fetishism. That skin, though. Those eyes. His papa had been so sharp, charming, tough. Even a little cocky, despite that bouncy, singsong accent of his. Adorable, really, but Henry had to promise never to tell Papa she'd said so, okay? A tremor ran under the bese saka shawl.

Plans changed when Henry came along. By that point, Papa had finished the master's portion of his degree, but duty overrode personal ambition. Instead of completing his doctorate like she had, he decided to teach high school to provide for the family. Figured he could continue working on his translations on the side. During the process of getting a teaching license, he was subbing classes, a real hit-or-miss gig. Never knew when a 6:00 a.m. phone call would send him scrambling out of bed and out the door. If the phone didn't ring, he would spend his days at the dining table doing his own research. Such discipline, such dignity, Mom sighed, then gave another sad smile. Although any aspirations of becoming a professor were long gone, his papa hadn't given up the look. Should have seen him in his dungarees and those elbow-patched corduroy blazers. Smoked Dunhills, for christ's sake. He wasn't a big man, not even for a Filipino, but he knew how to carry himself. Sturdy, self-assured, as if he could walk through walls. At least Mom had thought so. At least she'd fallen for it.

Papa lasted four, maybe five months.

Ever since they met, he'd been trying so hard to shake off those stubborn traces of his accent. Sometimes, midconversation, she would catch him repeating the sentence she'd just said under his breath, rolling syllables into place like a peppermint on his tongue. Always thought it a shame, all that effort to subdue something she'd found so endearing.

Some punk kid had found Papa's accent pretty cute, too. The student imitated Papa to the delight of a full and very white classroom. And so Papa put the child in his place.

Luckily the kid's parents didn't sue, but any chance at a license, here or anywhere else stateside, was out of the question, diminishing the value of his master's diploma to that of the card stock it was printed on. How were you supposed to feed a family with an English degree? After months of job hunting and then a few more of nothing, a cousin of Papa's made some calls and put him in touch with a contractor, and that was that. Got a job flipping run-down, inner-city properties commandeered by the nouveau riche. Kept a cassette player clipped onto his tool belt, audiobooks keeping him sane. His papa ended up yet another bitter man of letters, and—uh-oh—one with an arsenal of power tools.

"That was a joke," Mom said.

Henry waited. She turned to the dining table, where billing envelopes, coupon clippings, crinkled receipts, and a calculator had taken the place of Papa's novels, dictionaries, and typewriter.

"There's plenty in this world to be mad about, Henry," she said, "but not enough to be mad at it."

By now the silence between him and Papa in the truck cab had reached an excruciating pitch. Even worse now that Henry couldn't quite reassemble his mother's features according to the foggy schematics of who she'd actually been. The bulk of what he knew about his parents' lives pre-him came from that one afternoon. Mom's own past was a mystery, one Papa seemed to believe could only be preserved in the vault of his memory, as if exposure to daylight might send it fleeing, gone for good, like a caged rabbit released and skittering madly into the woods.

Henry cracked the window open, hoping the draft might sweep out some of Papa's palpable disappointment. Maybe the chug of air could clear Henry's mental canvas for Mom's face, but no. Instead, the wind started sculpting another's likeness into the guilty putty of his thoughts.

The mousy girl with the shadow teeth. Repeated contact with stomach acid had stripped the enamel from the back side of her teeth, leaving each one pronounced, almost fang-like. Her grin, which she covered with a fist whenever it escaped, reminded Henry of a wolf, carnivorous and cunning. Over the last two weeks, he'd never worked up the nerve to tell her how much he liked it. Then again, when could he have? On the long list of no-no's plastered on every corner and pillar of the youth inpatient wing, whispering was forbidden. So was touch, a rule enforced at the beginning of every group session with a mandatory elbow flap, ensuring everyone's personal bubble was safe from rupture. The cruelest rule prohibited patients from exchanging contact information, so they wouldn't get in touch and relapse together on the outside.

Bulimia, she'd explained, was about control. This had made immediate sense to him. There was something very deliberate and precise about her, from the arc of her left eyebrow to the way she spoke. That cool prairie drawl. The illness had ground every angle and bend of her to suggest, at least to him, a blade. Even her name, Michelle, reminded him of machete. Such a primitive, efficient technology. Its sole function to hack, which the thought of her did to him. It hacked at him, hurt him, but in a new way. A way that he welcomed and already missed.

Three days ago in the art room, Henry told her it was physically impossible to fold a sheet of paper more than eight times.

"Bullshit," she said.

The art room's posters and Crayola materials were more suited for kindergarteners than for teenage suicides and meth-heads. He'd hoped he wasn't the only one who found humor in their daily hour of Sesame Street crafts, before swapping horror stories in group during the two o'clock block of their schedule. Michelle's cuticles were raw, scabby, and when she went to squeeze the eighth seam, he reached for her hand, pretending to help. An excuse to brush fingers, to touch. That gasp of contact was all it took to get him hard.

A counselor reminded them of the elbow-length rule. Then, when he'd spotted their knees angling toward each other beneath the tabletop, he sent them to opposite ends of the art room.

No outbound phone calls, no cussing, no outside food or drink, no shoelaces, and absolutely no—zero, zip, nada—touching.

A half hour ago, when they'd returned Henry's ziplocked outfit, Michelle knelt beside him, helped thread a shoestring into the eyelets of his right sneaker. A chance to say good-bye, though they didn't say much of anything. Handing him the shoe was as close as they got to a handshake, let alone a hug. All she said was, "Eight folds," and then, slyly, she spread her fingers and dropped a pebble of folded paper into the shoe.

The paper Papa now stuck in front of Henry was only folded once. Longwise. A slender, pale green canoe.

For the first time since Henry'd climbed into the passenger seat, Papa looked at him directly. "Take it."

$20.00

"Happy birthday," Papa said.

Henry unfolded the bill. The crease left a bandit's mask across Jackson's eyes. Henry muttered thanks, while his mind weighed the bill's buying power. Two liters of bottom-shelf liquor, or a twenty-four-pack of beer. A half-eighth of weed, or, if he went through Al, he could score at least three points, maybe even a half gram of—

"Know what that is?" Papa asked.

"Double or nothing you're gonna tell me right now."

A skull smack. Henry'd asked for it.

When Papa's right hand settled back onto the steering wheel, his index and middle fingers remained extended, making a V.

"That," he said, "is almost two hours of my life. And before taxes, ah."

The bill turned to lead, sinking Henry's hands into his lap.

"Sixteen now. Time to get a job. That's your bus fare till your first paycheck."

Henry didn't say anything because what could he? Meanwhile Papa grumbled about hours, his time, his life, before the last couple breaths snarled into curses in Tagalog. Papa's right foot crushed into the floorboard, accelerating the truck to overtake other cars on the freeway. He was rushing them home, now that he'd said what he'd wanted, had taught what was needed.

$77.41

"Where are we, Pa?"

Henry calls it a hotel. Then he says, "Surprise."

If it hadn't been for a job repaneling a grain silo out here in the sticks last month, he would never have spotted this motel, thirty-some miles west of Junior's school, set off an unmarked service road and stapled at the edge of the pines. It is squat and wide with boxy, blacked-out windows, like some giant, unpolished harmonica. So remote and seedy, it surprises him he'd never come across this place back in the day. He knows all too well what goes on behind the doors of a place like this, but the sign out front—a sheet of plywood zip-tied to a stake of rebar—offers rooms for only $39.99 a night.

The parking lot is a dump truck's load of loose gravel raked out over dirt, making the tires crunch like a mouthful of cereal. At the end farthest from the motel's office, a single vein of light runs between drawn curtains. This appears to be the only other occupied room tonight, two cars parked outside its door. The first is a late-'90s Neon, its rear bumper sutured in place by duct tape. Next to it is a Mustang that's in even rougher shape, thanks to its owner's novice hacks at souping it up. Rims look about as sturdy as tinsel and its spoiler, off-color and oversized, might as well have been nailed onto the trunk.

"Will there be TV?"

"You bet," Henry says, parking outside the office. "C'mon, let's go check in."

The boy presses his stomach. "Can I wait here?"

Henry feels dangerously close to the one occupied room. The stretch of dark windows and loose gravel seems to compress as if by the sharp crank of a vise. Then again, it could all be in his head. So much has been lately, and so he says sure. That's fine. He locks the truck and then double-checks the doors.

A bell jingles in the doorway, announcing Henry. A bike chain harnesses a box TV to the office ceiling. Watching it from behind the counter is a woman so overweight it's impressive. To imagine her Henry-sized skeleton submerged and supporting the weight of another two of him, along with the strength it must take to endure such a constant burden, makes her every movement a feat. Her eyes, pressed into flapjack-batter cheeks, are stunning. They are jade and gentle and empty and he would recognize them anywhere. They belong to a person used to being invisible.

"Need a room, a forty-buck one will do," he says. "And as far from that other group as possible."

"You alone?"

His throat clears without his permission. He steals a glance back, and, thankfully, the office blinds are closed. "Just my lonesome."

He lays a pair of twenties on the counter, and to them she says, "Whoa, buddy."

"There a problem?"

"Sir," she says. "You got to pay with a credit card. Security deposit and whatnot."

"But all I got—"

He pats his pockets.

"I don't have—"

Defeat tugs his sights down to the gummy vinyl flooring. What could he tell the birthday boy?

Those sad green eyes give a flicker, as if filling with understanding. Maybe she sees it in him, too. Recognizes a fellow less-than. The tip of her tongue runs over a chapped lower lip, swabbing it into a grin. "Tell you what."

He bends over the counter, closing in as if for a secret.

"Yeah?"

"If all's you got is cash, we'll call it sixty even," she says. "A deposit sort of thing."

31

He slaps down his third and final twenty onto the counter like a winning poker hand. She collects it with all the ceremony of a high school janitor.

"So I'll get that twenty back when we—when *I* check out, then, right?"

No answer. She is occupied. Engrossed in the demanding task of counting cash—one, two, three, yes, it's all there, sweetheart. Did she really not hear him or what?

"You working the graveyard shift, ma'am—miss? That's fine because I got to be heading out at seven sharp myself. Will you still be here? Or will you let the next person on know about our little arrangement here?"

The TV pulls a gray chuckle out of her. He offers up a nervous laugh, too, trying to remind her he's right in front of her, and has asked her a question that needs an answer, and now. She taps the three bills flush.

"Done misspoke," she says.

"Okay? As in?"

"As in not so much a deposit." She sets the bills in the desk drawer. Turns a key. "More like a service charge."

$230.62

As much as Papa claimed to appreciate irony, this would have been beyond him. Henry could never tell Papa that he owed his first job—and now his first paycheck—to one of the skinnies.

For whatever reason, despite having a good decade or so on Henry, Al had taken a liking to him way before this shelf-stocking gig. They met in a parking lot, the social gathering point of all towns like theirs. That first night, Al's rosy cheeks had flushed even ruddier when his hand met Henry's. He slapped away the tenner Henry offered to get in on the night's shards. It was his treat, dude. From then on out, it seemed Al derived a big-brother satisfaction in dosing Henry up with booze and drugs, dragging him along to house parties and motel-room benders like some rescue mutt Al had trained to snort lines and recite grimy jokes.

Al was hardly skinny, though. He was so swollen with girth and charisma, it was as if he'd sapped all sustenance and character from the rest of that skeletal, ever-rotating cluster of local junkies and twitchy vagrants: the skinnies. Al regarded this crowd and its transitory members as both a revenue stream and a disposable workforce for his various hustles around town. The way they came and went—what with all the ODs, arrests, and babies—there wasn't much point in remembering names.

But it wasn't as sketchy as it sounded, he'd assured Henry, believe him. The thing was that every single last one of them skinnies was already in too deep and too far gone to think of themselves as anything *but* disposable. He meant like, all the filthy shit they did for a fix? They'd debase themselves just to freebase, dude. Fun to watch, though, fucking hilarious, and, now that he mentioned it, if Henry ever needed to nut, just say the word, and Al got him. Had some favors coming his way, if Henry caught his drift.

"Dead serious, though," Al had said. "You can do literally *anything* to these skinnies, whatever your kinky black heart desires, feel me?"

The, as he chortled through a menu of sex acts and torture methods, Henry tuned him out, cringing but nevertheless grateful that he'd made a real friend.

Today Al stood where he always did between deliveries, with his rump crutched against the yellow cement-filled post at the supermarket's loading dock. This was his outpost. From here he arranged drug deals and black market trade-offs, collected bets, and coordinated a ring of meth-heads who ran liquor store errands for high schoolers across the county. If the grocery store manager hadn't been one of Al's most loyal and depraved clients, Al could never have used the loading docks as his side-hustle headquarters.

It was Friday, payday, and Al looked uncharacteristically nervous, gnawing on a Kool and clapping his flip phone like a castanet. The store manager had gotten too high, needed to come down somewhere private, and so tasked Al with passing out paychecks. He was using his gut as a desk to shuffle a deck of envelopes while a dozen workers circled tighter, tapping boots, reminding him of their last names and the order of the alphabet. A flake of ash clung to Al's sweaty double chin, his face shaken by the responsibility of distributing livelihoods. When it was Henry's turn, he saw that Al had set his paycheck apart from the stack, pinched between two fingers.

"Lap dance funds," Al said.

The envelope looked official. Its plastic window cast a sheen over Henry's name and address, printed in a mechanical, matter-of-fact font. He opened the envelope with delicate pinches, unwilling to take any chances with its precious contents. The material the check was printed on felt sturdier than the paper of classroom handouts, so flimsy and frivolous by comparison. He unfolded it and on the other side of a perforated seam were charts tabulating all the hours and wages and deductions.

Al flicked the Kool. Spat. "Don't look at what Uncle Sam's took."

It didn't matter. Henry had never held so much money in his hands. He was no math wizard, but all it took was a single shift of a decimal point to see this paycheck held more than ten times the spending power of what he'd typically been armed with for the weekend's entertainment. With this small fortune, he wasn't limited to his weekly twenty-dollar allowance, which went straight to chipping in on the night's poisons, only to peel himself off a basement floor with a mean case of comedown shakes, a skull full of wet cement, and an empty wallet. This felt like he was getting away with something. His name printed next to such a sum shot an asteroid through him, a comet tail of possibilities crackling through his thoughts. The punch clock said there were still another four hours left of his shift. Four hours of tugging pallets and stocking shelves were also four hours to devise a plan.

There were purchases to be made. He was going to deck his room out with posters and black lights, stock up his CD collection, and get a louder stereo. He would buy himself new jeans, fresh sneakers, a haircut. Then, cleaned up and cash in hand, he would be ready for the most important purchase now possible: a proper date with Michelle.

To make it happen, Papa had to spot him the truck. The old man was a permanent fixture at the dining table on the weekends. Except for his near-closing-time errands, he never left the house, so how could he refuse? Henry had done as he'd been told. He'd gotten a job, taken the bus every day after school, and never once asked for help. Even though this had all been done to keep Papa if not pleased then at least pacified, after a month of good behavior, of obedience, Henry was owed.

So what if Michelle was older. Henry wanted to pick her up, left hand slung over the wheel, the right in her lap, steering her any which way she wished, be it to the mall or Mexico. The landscape at this corner of the state was expansive and flat, lumpy at best, so parking at the edge of some cliff to enjoy rolling vistas and dig into each other alongside a row of other parked, rocking vehicles wasn't exactly an option. Maybe a fancy restaurant? He would gladly spend every last cent of this paycheck on sushi or surf'n'turf or whatever la-di-da candlelit dinner might please her, and she was more than welcome to skip off to the ladies' room and puke it all up afterward, for all he cared. It didn't matter. Nothing mattered other than the prospect of being totally alone together. They had so much to say.

The eighth crease of the pebble Michelle had snuck into his shoe was more bend than fold. As carefully as he just opened this envelope, he'd pinched the tiny petals of paper back until it was a matchbook-sized scrap. On it, in her knobby scrawl, was her email next to a heart she'd filled in with black ink. It'd taken a full two weeks after Henry's release till she finally wrote back, explaining she didn't have internet at home and could only sneak onto her Hotmail account at school when the librarians were distracted. Her messages, when they did come, were as jumbled as her handwriting, confessional and hilarious, unpunctuated except for marching bands of exclamation points. Every night after work, he would log on to the computer in the living room, muffling the modem with a sweatshirt so the dial-up tone and digital squeals wouldn't wake Papa in the next room. Even if she hadn't managed to write earlier that day, he was content to read through their previous exchanges and let his imagination spell out the slim daggers of her fingers, working their way off the keyboard and around his throat.

"I know a place we can cash these after work, open all night," Al said. He folded his check into the cellophane of his cigarette pack. "Meghan's having people over tonight, you down?"

Henry slid his check into the front pocket of his jeans. Stroking the slight corner beneath the denim set off a damn near carnal glee.

The mere thought of a night alongside the same old delinquents made quick work of this thrill. Hour after hour of smoking and boozing and jaw grinding and waiting for dawn with the skinnies sounded about as appealing as offering his scrotum to the deli counter slicer. What did sound enticing was the chance to turn this check into a lean pile of cash. He would find a way to back out last minute, a way to get back home to the computer, to Michelle, and arrange a time and place for them to get together. So, making a frown of approval, he told Al, "Cool."

"Fuck me, dude. Tonight gonna be a good one." Al was fidgety, how he always got when discussing weekend mischief or his newest get-money scheme. He went for another cigarette, but it fell from his fingers and off the edge of the loading dock. "Bet my whole paycheck I rail Meghan tonight."

"Not happening."

"Will, too, dude," Al said. "You can watch for twenty."

"Twenty says she can't find that toddler pinky under all this," Henry said, swatting Al's stomach.

"Dude."

Al was all appetite. Not an ounce to spare for something as trifling as wit, so he would never have cooked up a decent comeback, even if the Taystee semi hadn't turned the corner just then. By now, Henry had learned to cheer this delivery with the others, its cargo promising a couple hours of easy lifting. Right now, though, racks of bread and crates of pastries were a disappointment. All of it too light, bagged air, when he was roiling with this newfound power. He wished it was a meat delivery instead. He would have pushed past the forklift, marched straight into that frosty trailer, then heaved the frozen slab of a split cow off its meat hook and slung the son of a bitch over one shoulder, strutting and whistling some lovesick ditty all the way to the butcher's.

$17.41

The rooms closest to the motel office are all doubles—only twenty bucks more. Otherwise, she says, Henry is in the last vacant single, room 8, next door to the other occupied room.

As if the service charge wasn't reason enough to despise her. That unexpected expense means he'll have to find a few hours' work before tomorrow's interview after all. Lunch money plus the gas to get Junior back to school alone will leave them with pennies. And now this woman has bled him only to put them next door to whatever degenerate lowlifes—no room for doubt, he's seen their cars—are staying in room 9. No wonder she's used to being ignored. She is a hideous billboard of a woman.

He pockets the key to room 8 along with the last of his cash. Can't help but run his fingers over the slight seam the bills make beneath the denim, ensuring their safety. He wants to vomit after saying, out of habit, "Thanks."

As he smacks past the office door, the bell above gives a Christmas jingle, as out of place as mistletoe at a wake. Outside, dusk has been sheeted under a cloudy, starless sky, leaving below it a darkness that amplifies sounds, tunes them crisper. The gravel croaking beneath his footfalls. A lone cricket chirping beyond the tree line. A click. A second click hardens into a *tap, tapping*, and then a *knock, knock, knock*. A stranger's voice says, "Hey, kid."

A slender man stands hunched at the driver's window of Henry's truck, peering inside.

It happens fast. Too fast to distinguish wrath from panic. The next thing he knows, he's got the slender man's shirtfront balled in both fists and rams him into the side panel. He screams at the shadow of a face he can't see but can certainly smell: menthols, ammonia, scalp.

"Whoa, whoa. Easy now, buddy."

"The fuck you think you're doing?" Henry yells.

The man opens his hands to show Henry he's unarmed, as if that were the fucking problem. Henry yanks and slams the man against the truck again, peeks into the driver's-side window. Junior is inside, safe, hugging his knees to his chest, forehead buried in his forearms.

Even though he's half-blind with rage, Henry's thoughts flicker back to that horrible November evening—his old friend Lucius and the fire-axe; the crayons and subtraction homework; Michelle's mono-syllabic gibe and red clown smirk.

Henry can't let the boy see him get like that, not again.

But this needs settling.

Henry jerks the slender man away from his son and into the dim glow cast by a pair of curbside vending machines. The stranger's comb-over sprouts too close to his brow, giving him a shrunken, overcooked look. His shirt is silk and two sizes too big. Between Henry's fists, hanging from a gold chain, is a gem-encrusted pendant in the shape of an AK-47.

When the man tries to grin, it looks as if it hurts, his lower lip jiggering like a hooked fish.

"My dog just come up sniffing and then I seen the kid. Just checking if the little guy were okay, feel me? You watch the news? Junkie bitches be leaving they kids to roast on the daily."

Slowly, firmly, Henry releases the man. He pivots, setting himself between the stranger and the truck. No leash in the man's hands. No doggie bags poking out his pockets, though something heavy in his waistband.

"What dog?" Henry says.

"She here somewhere," the man says. "Pooping or some shit. Come, doggie!"

It's so still, so quiet that Henry hears cartilage creak as his fingers flex back into a fist.

"Come on, doggie." The man tries whistling, but only shoots a putrid gust past thin, brittle lips.

Then, in spite of all suspicion, a dachshund's head materializes under the tailgate of Henry's truck. The dog doesn't obey the man's thigh slaps and calls, instead scampers toward the service road. The man darts after it. His pants are so loose and weighed down that he has to hook his fingers into the rear belt loops, turning his silhouette into some handcuffed fugitive, waddle-jogging around the parking lot.

Henry climbs into the pickup, asks Junior if he's all right, if he was scared. The boy says yes, then no. He doesn't budge, locked in an upright fetal position. Henry pulls the truck up to room 8 but leaves a three-car-wide gap between them and the Mustang. When he slips the backpack straps onto Junior's shoulders, he sees the nape of the boy's neck is shining with sweat. Is he that sick, or had he been that scared?

Opening the door to room 8, he leans down to the boy's ear. "We're here," he says in as comforting a tone he can muster. "I'm right here."

And so is the small-faced stranger, who, through raspy breaths, now greets them.

"Hey there, neighbors." He's cradling the dachshund awkwardly, like a child struggling under a load of firewood.

Henry presses Junior into room 8 and closes the door without stepping in himself. He turns around, holstering a fist in his front pocket. "What do you want, huh?"

"Question is what do *you* want." The man winks, then wiggles two paws into a sad mambo. "She for sale."

The dog is belly up, hind legs spread, and she is clearly a he.

"We're good."

"You sure? Purebred and housebroken. A steal for an even Benny."

Henry crosses his arms. He refuses to go in with Junior until this sleazy dogmonger has shut himself into room 9 for the night. "I said we're good."

"How's about eighty?"

"No."

"Fifty."

"No."

"Twenty?"

Henry says goodnight, but makes no movement toward door 8. The dogmonger's mouth stretches to share a clenched-tooth smile, a canine capped in gold. "Fair enough. Case you change your mind, you know where to find me."

The door to room 9 opens and unleashes a surge of sound: a TV on full blast, pounding through a breaking news sound bite, sliced with woofs and whinnies. The dogmonger has to kick his way past three wet snouts to shut the door behind him.

Before entering 8, Henry doubles back to the truck for his duffel bag, holding a Goodwill suit that'd cost more to dry clean than purchase. In it he tosses Junior's present, wrapped in coarse brown paper one seam sealed by a row of yellow smiley-face stickers.

$207.55

As soon as Henry finished counting the cash, he understood why this pane of bulletproof glass had been installed: to protect the cashier from people like him. The glass was cloudy with scuffs, evidence of previous attempts to collect what had rightfully belonged to anyone on his side of this panel. What a lowdown, slumlord hustle. Charging him for his own money, skimming the dues for his sweat, his time. These scumbags banked 10 percent of any check under five hundred dollars, but only 7 percent of anything bigger—why would it cost more to have less? It was expensive to be poor, and so right here, right now, Henry resolved he never would be.

With the ten twenties, the fiver, and two singles held rigid, he troweled the three coins off the counter and into his free palm. When he flashed a sneer through the glass, the cashier raised his eyebrows as if to ask, so? What exactly was Henry going to do about it? From between the cashier's lips crowned a bubble the color of brain matter. It grew.

Henry turned to leave. Didn't have to stay to know it would pop.

The muffler of Al's Bonneville was shot, turning all drive-time conversations into yelling matches. Still, even at such a volume, lying to Al was easy. Putting up with his whining, not so much.

"But you look fine, dude."

"My stomach hurts," Henry said. "I want to go home."

"I need you tonight, Henry, c'mon. How's about I throw down for you? Bank your first paycheck, blow it on something bigger, or invest it, like on this idea I got for—but, hey. C'mon. Toot the rest of this baggie. All yours and plenty more at Meghan's."

"Not tonight."

"Dude."

"Shut up and take me home."

Al ducked, rummaged under the driver's seat. When his ham-hock shoulder brushed the wheel and swerved them into the adjacent lane, Henry dove to steer them back straight.

"Just what the doctor ordered, dude," Al said, swatting Henry away with a half-drunk bottle of rotgut tequila. "Down the hatch. That and a couple bumps will have you tip-top, hunky-dumpty-dory."

"We'll hang out tomorrow, but tonight, nah. I'm not going out."

Al huffed. "Fag."

"Fat-ass."

"Fuck you, you swishy lady-boy," Al said. "Fucking Filipino faggot."

"Right," Henry said. "The alliteration was a nice touch."

"Literate this." Al grabbed his crotch. After that nothing was said, nothing heard except the busted exhaust system, a sustained, tinny screech like a cat getting mangled into a megaphone, until Al slammed to a stop in front of Papa's house.

When Al killed the engine, a quiet fell to match the empty neighborhood street. He tracked two furry, nicotine-stained dice swaying under the rearview, as if waiting for total stillness to speak. After a final teeter, he grabbed and twisted them, showing Henry a roll of snake eyes.

"Yo dude, look," Al said. "Gorilla tits."

"Clever."

"So," Al said. "Hit you up tomorrow?"

"For sure," Henry said, climbing out of the Pontiac. "Let me know what Meghan's dick tastes like."

So much of Henry's boozing and sniffing had been made possible by the fact that Papa fell dead asleep by nine o'clock every night. His snores were a chainsaw to fresh birch, coming in husky screeches that rumbled from the bedroom and past the thin walls of their house. To Henry sneaking in at all hours of the night, Papa's snoring functioned like a siren, though it wasn't a warning. Instead, its cry promised safe passage, just so long as he steered clear.

But he couldn't hear a thing from the front door tonight. He

43

checked his watch—quarter past ten—then pressed his ear to the door. The wood was cold, as if left chilled without the heat of its typical nighttime pulse. Was it a trick of the brain? Of sobriety?

He was sober. A current of self-righteousness tickled him, rolling his shoulders back and cocky. On the off chance Papa was still awake, Henry wouldn't have to slither down to his bedroom to wait the old man out. Instead, he could look Papa dead in the eye, proving that he'd adhered to the tenets of his parole by getting a job, working every single day after school, and had done so (for the most part) sober. There was no reason to prevent Papa from forking over the truck keys just for one night, so Henry could, again and at long last, see Michelle.

Even stranger than the quiet were the lights: they'd been left on upstairs. A mortal sin in this household, where no room was lit unless occupied, no square of paper towel disposed of until on the verge of disintegration.

"Papa?"

Henry went to the living room. Books caked the walls from floor to ceiling, giving the room a subterranean, cavernous air, with unshelved stacks growing out of the ground like rectangular stalagmites. Their density seemed to be pulling all the lamp's light into the walls, casting hard shadows over the spines like rows of narrow teeth. Framed photographs sat bracketed between books. Mom had always played the role of family chronicler and so only appeared in a few of the snapshots. Not a single photo had been taken following the diagnosis. Should some future archaeologist stumble upon these photos, it would appear their family had died abruptly. It was for the best neither he nor Papa had picked up the camera in her place, hadn't captured any images of her so gaunt, so frail, so unlike herself. He preferred to remember her how she was in this one, the photo of them leaning against a magenta jeepney.

"Got something for me?"

Papa was sitting at the dining table, two neat piles before him. One was a stack of progressively shrinking papers—bills, envelopes, coupons, receipts—held down by his checkbook. The other was a cluster of tough, mustard crescents of dead skin. He drew the razor along the corns on his palm, a callus rind curling tighter and tighter till it fell to the tabletop. He swept it into the pile with the back of his hand. While this act of grooming was so quintessentially Papa, this man was not. Hardly recognizable. The severity of such exhaustion couldn't solely be the result of staying up past his bedtime.

"I asked," he said, "if you've got something for me, ah."

"What do you mean?"

Papa opened his right hand, displaying the shallow channels the razor had carved into a paler, fresher layer of calluses. "You got your first paycheck today, didn't you?"

"Yeah," Henry said. "So?"

Papa curled a finger, beckoned. "You know the tradition."

Yes, Henry did, but fuck that. "This isn't the Philippines."

"What's your last name?"

Coolly, he reminded Papa.

"Then act like one, goddamnit." Papa jerked his hand up but caught himself before hammering it down. The fist fanned open, shooed off an invisible fly.

"Sixteen years," Papa started. "Every hour of every day for the last sixteen years, I've given to you. Every meal you've ever eaten, every night you've slept in safety. I gave you my name. Whether you're in Manila or on the moon, you'll carry my name. Our family's name.

"If you're willing to spit on that, on a tradition of dignity, respect, and gratitude just to hold on to a couple of dollars, then fine. Keep it. But in that case, I'll be taking back everything else. Remember, now that you're working, you've got to earn what's yours."

Henry was quaking. He was flame, he was bile, but Papa wasn't wrong. If this—the capacity to earn his own money—was what made him independent, a man, then he would have to find a way to keep these indignant, baby-boy tears now welling in his eyes from falling. The best he could come up with was to slap the cash onto the tabletop. He even dug out the two quarters, the nickel, and smacked them down, too. A pretty little cherry on top.

Papa didn't thank him. Hardly looked at him. Just started counting.

"This is light. I thought you were making a dollar more than minimum wage? After taxes, by my math," Papa tilted his calculator, "there should be two hundred thirty—"

"I cashed it. Fuckers kept ten percent," Henry snapped. "Want that, too? With interest? I'll have it for you in two weeks."

"I hope you learned something." As Papa pressed himself to his feet, his eyes turned to the living room, the daybed.

"Know what?" Papa thumbed the fiver and two singles from the stack, set them beside the coins. "Here. Keep the change, ah."

Before passing Henry on his way to the bedroom, Papa stopped. Henry's whole body was rattling, every last tendon struggling to keep the tears from his cheeks and the snot from his lips. When Papa squeezed the nape of Henry's neck, the razor's etches tickled his skin. Papa tugged, tender yet firm, bending Henry into a bow, then placed a kiss on the top of his head. Once Henry creaked back upright, he cringed at the sight of Papa. The old man's face still looked as worn out as before. Not a hint of triumph. Was Papa not chalking this up as a victory for the old world, or at the very least some minor comeuppance against the country and culture that had so thoroughly snuffed out and discarded him? His expression revealed nothing. Just a slate of fatigue. Maybe that ache clutching his eyes was remorse. Perhaps satisfaction. Why wouldn't he come out with it and just tell Henry?

"Tomorrow you'll see," Papa said. "You'll understand."

$17.41

Inside room 8, shadows press against a single cone of light from a bedside lamp. Curled into a ball, Junior lies on top of the bedspread, his back to the glow. Too dark, too quiet, so Henry slaps on the overhead lights. When that fails to stir the boy, Henry marches over to the bathroom and flips those on, too. On a wrought iron patio table sits a phone, an ashtray, and a desk lamp. He clicks it on and aims its beam at Junior.

When this interrogation-room tactic proves ineffective, he lowers his voice into a prime time cop-thriller snarl. "Tell us. What's the birthday boy think of his surprise?"

The only answer Henry gets is a muffled woof from next door.

The corners of his mouth dip in approval. Not bad. Not bad at all. Better than expected. Sure, the color scheme is pretty overbearing. Everything from the wilting fleur-de-lis wallpaper to the bedspread, lampshades, and carpet borrows some shade from the spectrum between scab and scar. Without a doubt these corporeal tones had been a preemptive step to camouflage guests' various stains for years to come, but, to Henry, there's actually something homey about it. Even with room 9's woofs and TV din, it feels warm, cozy, and he says so to Junior.

Seems the boy is opting for the Fifth. The same legal advice Al had shouted as he got dragged through a steel door. Henry shudders. Repeats, "I said it's cozy, huh, Junior?"

This time the boy manages, "Mm-hm."

Henry steps out of his boots. Hugs the carpet by curling his toes, a small pleasure he hasn't realized he missed until now. Peeking back into the bathroom, he's delighted to find an actual bathtub, two single-serving tabs of soap, though no minibottle of shampoo. He doesn't have scissors, but maybe, if he's careful, he could give the boy a trim with the utility knife. That way he could get a more thorough scrub at Junior's scalp with the soap. He plugs the drain and twists the hot water knob. It's not only the steamy torrent pummeling his hand that warms him. It's the satisfaction of providing for his son, for the first time in a long time, like a decent father ought.

"Know what would help your tummy?" he calls from the bathroom. "Help you digest?"

"Hm."

"This nice, hot bath I'm making you. Get in here."

"No."

Goddamnit. He's dropped forty—no, *sixty* fucking dollars on this stunt. He'd internally justified this lavish risk with the fact that he would give the boy a proper scrub down, rather than yet another washcloth swabbing like they've been reduced to these last six months.

"You're not getting your present till you're cleaned up, hear me?"

The boy's head lifts, eyes narrow. "Present?"

"It's your birthday, isn't it?"

"You didn't have to do that, Pa."

"Course I did."

"Why?"

"Because what's my name?"

". . . Pa?"

"There you go."

Henry is being curt, which makes him feel bad. He turns off the faucet and joins the boy in bed, turning himself into a nest around Junior. "Let's go, bud. It'll help your tummy. I promise."

"How about you go first? I want to watch some TV."

"Junior."

"It *is* my birthday."

Smart-ass.

It's Henry's own damn fault for pointing this out in the first place. Then again, what difference would it make if he showered first? Might actually do him good, calm him down. He'd felt the nudge just now—the poke. His temper prodding him into Papa territory, or even nastier regions. The last thing he wants is to snap at the boy. Any of his attempts to make today special would be rendered null and void if he yelled, even just once. And so, to prove the scope of his benevolence, he goes to unzip the duffel bag.

Three muffled gun blasts make the paper bag–wrapped gift hop in Henry's grasp. If the shots weren't followed by a Wilhelm scream and an orchestral peal, he would have leapt and human-shielded himself over the boy. He slaps the TV on and cranks up the volume, hoping to wash out room 9's ruckus.

"Don't be scared."

"Your pa is never scared," he says, plopping onto the bed. "Here. Happy birthday."

It's beyond him where Junior has obtained such self-restraint, such patience. The way the boy turns the gift to examine it, how he thumbs the line of smiley-face stickers, then looks up to reveal a smile of his own, so full of knowing it makes Henry shudder. Junior unpeels each strip of adhesive then presses the paper back, seam by seam, rather than shredding the gift open in a squealing flurry how any other birthday kid would. There's almost a tinge of fear in the cautious way Junior undoes the wrapping, reminding Henry of the anxious, delicate technique he'd applied when changing the boy's diaper the first couple times. At long last, after such prolonged anticipation, the gift is free of its brown shell, and the look on Junior's face suggests he, too, might as well have opened up a load of infant shit.

The boy tilts the box, squints. "What is it?"

"It's special. This is, well, was, when I was your age, one of my favorites. One of my heroes. Read it. What's his name?"

"Macho Man Randy Sav . . . Sav . . . ?"

"Savage," Henry says. "Like crazy or wild, but in a strong way." He flexes his biceps, mimicking the doll's pose. "Like your pa."

"You're not this strong, Pa."

"*Oh, yee-yuh?*" Henry says, imitating the Macho Man's notorious rasp. The boy doesn't catch the reference. How would he?

"That was his catchphrase," Henry says.

"But what makes him special?"

Henry is stumped. What exactly about Macho Man Randy Savage had so appealed to him as a kid? Was it only because Randy Savage's olive skin and black hair had somewhat resembled Henry's? Had it been the gruff, prematch diatribes the Macho Man barked into the mic, threatening adversaries and lauding his own invincibility? Was it the manic, Tasmanian-devil scuttle of his grappling style, or how he churned entire stadiums into a frenzy from the top turnbuckle before slamming into an opponent's sternum with his signature finishing move, the flying elbow? Perhaps it had been Randy's devotion to Miss Elizabeth, how any slight to her reputation would launch the Macho Man into a frothy rage that could only be satiated with a merciless battering in the ring, best finished off when Randy's queen slid a folding chair under the ropes for him to clobber the offender into a gory, repentant pulp.

Such bloodlust and vengeance are no good for a child.

What a pageant of eggshell masculinity. All those glittering robes, pleather cowboy hats, and knolls of muscle packaging a man just as afraid, lonely, and love hungry as the next. Henry doesn't want any of these traits to ever manifest in Junior. He ought to be doing all he can to nurture the boy's tender core, protect it from the grindstone of reality before it pumices Junior into yet another heel-dragging blister like Henry.

"I'll tell you after I shower," he says. "Watch whatever you want now, birthday boy."

"Thanks, Pa."

"Hey. Want to know a secret?" He pinches Junior's chin. "Know how much I love you?"

The pinched chin shakes no.

Henry gives another Macho Man flex. Arms outstretched, he is Atlas unburdened but ready. "*This much, ooooh, yee-yuh.*"

The boy's giggle cinches into a wince. His hands jerk from the gift to his belly as if he's just absorbed a jab. "It really hurts."

The boy's forehead is a kiln, pink and shining. Henry hopes the worry doesn't crinkle his voice when telling the boy he's got an idea. Stepping back into the unlaced boots, he promises everything will be all right, and that he'll be right back.

$7.55

Motherfucker. The granddaddy of all curses. Henry'd always assumed the venom of the term, its knife twist, was self-evident: it dropped a floodlight on another's oedipal urge. But now he got it, had been wrong all along. Shortsighted to believe the person at whom the word was aimed would be stung by the accusation of that sick, Freudian presumption that all any swinging dick craved was to ram itself back into the slit it'd come from. Still though, that coke-addled Austrian had gotten the second part right, the patricide bit. Hatred for the father had to be more rampant than lust for the mother. By this logic, he'd overlooked the actual root of the term. Clearly it must have been coined in reference to that most universally loathed figure, both source and rightful target of any and every son's fury. The father, the original motherfucker.

Henry had been a fool to come home, cash in hand, and step right into Papa's trap. He should have gone out with Al and the skinnies tonight. He wanted to swill poison and breathe fire. Bleach and sear his insides till all that remained of him was a blind, staggering husk. There was nothing left in his sock drawer to soothe or fuel him. No bottom corner of a bottle. No baggies of dry green shake or cloudy shards. Not so much as a jar of rubber cement. As tempted as he was to hijack Papa's truck and flee into the night, the thought of Michelle spiked him in place. He didn't have her address, not even a phone number, so the only way to reach her was the living room computer. Couldn't risk losing her along with everything else. Instead, he was left to strip to his boxers and pace his room like some caged predator, rabid and famished and stripped of everything except his hate.

Even in the late-night privacy of his bedroom he refused to let himself cry, refused to grant Papa that one last satisfaction on top of everything the old man had already won. Henry couldn't give in to the urge to creep upstairs, log on to the computer, and check if Michelle had written back. Too risky. It was as if the locked bedroom door was fighting just as hard to detain him as every last fiber of his circuitry was to keep the tears dammed behind his eyeballs. The strain of containment racked him with molar-clicking shivers, and now it seemed even his body had decided to goad him, too, by reacting in a way that suggested a subzero tundra, when in reality he was volcanic.

He flung himself into his desk chair, yanked a spiral notebook from his backpack, flipped past doodles of daggers, rattlesnakes, and fornicating skeletons alongside half-assed class notes to a clean sheet, and set out to draft a letter to Michelle by hand. He would type it up and shoot it out as soon as he quit trembling, as soon as he steadied himself to a point where he could withstand the sight of Papa.

The first pencil snapped in his grip, stabbing a neat sliver into the side of his finger. Something oddly reassuring about the sight of his blood, as if the crimson ribbon was confirmation of the lava he'd felt smoldering beneath his skin. As he rummaged for a pen, language detailing his proposal to elope didn't run through his thoughts, only mental snapshots of their escape: smashing the window of a convertible Cadillac and hot-wiring its engine to life; the two of them tangled in the front seat while hurtling westward down a desert highway; the top down and a warm wind rinsing them of their pasts; a nickel-plated shotgun—raised, cocked, fired—blasting a buzzard out of a tangerine sky; their velocity reducing the whole world down to a golden smear, absolutely nothing able to stop or slow them, not until they went careening into the ocean, endless, shimmering, black.

But once he uncapped a ballpoint and set ink to page, just one word appeared in his ragged cursive, over and over along the first cyan line, then twice more on the second. He paused, huffed. He set out again, but still only *motherfucker* after *motherfucker* unraveled in a dense string of scribbles until the sheet, when held from a distance, resembled an oversized, rage-drunk bar code.

No memory of falling asleep. His skull was granite and empty, a mortar and pestle. So dizzy and scooped out, he might as well have pulled an all-nighter with Al and the skinnies. At least feeling this hollow meant the looming threat of a weeping fit had gotten flushed out with the rest of him. As he stirred awake, his brain seemed to short-circuit. Couldn't be sure if he'd only dreamt of barreling into the onyx surf, or if this was a glimpse into a future that had already happened, maybe some premonition he'd almost forgotten.

The morning was bright and the house desolate. Strange, since Papa rarely left the house on the weekend, and if he did, then not till sundown, only venturing out for errands during the last few minutes stores were open and crowds had thinned. Still though, traces of Papa's morning routine were strewn about. The Saturday paper had been retrieved from the driveway and was sitting in its plastic bag at Papa's dining table spot. The coffeemaker was off but still warm. The computer was on, opened to a MapQuest page listing the directions to a small town a ninety-minute drive away.

All the modem's buzzes, clicks, and digital groans echoed as sharply in his rib cage as they did through the living room. Once he was online, silence resumed, broken only when he dragged the arrow to his inbox—*click*.

Nothing. Empty as him and the house. When he went to compose a message, his fingers fell limp, eight pigeon feathers over the keys. He sat there, slumped, watching a slender column of pixels shade from black to white into the stripe-then-ghost of the cursor. The fan inside the machine whirred away the minutes in a resigned, continuous sigh.

The computer screen said *10:15*, which he corroborated against the analog dial on the wall. Hard to believe the clock's arms had already come full circle since last night's ambush. But after all this ticking and turning, what had changed? Papa had still won, Michelle hadn't written, and Mom was still dead and gone, forever and then some.

If Mom had been here, would she have let Papa pull last night's stunt? Seeing her face might help answer this question, and so Henry approached the wall of books. He tugged out the framed photo that had been taken in Manila during the only transpacific trip they'd all gone on together. In the photo, the three of them were leaning against a parked magenta jeepney. Papa was young and trim, a marshmallow grin eating up the bottom half of his brown face. He was holding both of Henry's wrists up in a triumphant pose that stood in stark contrast to the toddler's confused, helpless expression. Mom stood to the side, her skin as sunbrowned as Papa's, her fluffy dandelion perm frozen midsway. A gentle, observant smirk. Wrists crossed behind her as if either holding back a surprise or just restraining herself. She'd always been so much more hands-off than Papa.

She'd had one go-to joke, something about how the only sane application of laissez-faire policies was reserved for parenting. The touch-a-hot-stove, learn-from-your-mistakes approach. Because children, unlike the market, had the potential for self-regulation, and thereby needed as much freedom as possible for autonomous development in order to mature and grow into healthy, self-regulating adults.

Papa never begged, but he sure as shit differed. Mom had been right to believe that Papa's rigid, old-school expectations of obedience and classroom success would only push Henry away from intellectual curiosity, which they did, and far too early in life for him to naturally coast into an academic field of interest as she'd hoped. Instead, Henry liked Legos and professional wrestling. As he grew older, he fell into roughhousing with the other latchkey kids and building dirt-bike jumps in the woods, activities that let him be reckless with his body, as if the only research that could ever entice him was the study of his own physical thresholds.

These proclivities began emerging early, but ossified when he was in second grade. A worksheet had prompted him to describe his parents' jobs. Under the skirt-wearing silhouette, he'd written *My mother is a nakanamis*, proud that he'd managed to spell out such a long, complicated word all on his own. However, when it came back graded, the teacher had circled his linguistic achievement in red and drawn a question mark. Back at home Mom chuckled, then corrected his attempt, sounding out *e-con-o-mist* as she drew each letter, then explained an irony he didn't fully grasp about the word's origin, Greek for household management.

This was the first time an idea Henry had held with such unwitting conviction was dashed by a system to which he had no other choice but to submit. Despite previously exhibited abilities, which had earned him the title of gifted early on, this childhood mistake sparked a revolt against and suppression of the aptitudes that he'd inherited from his parents. Their fascination with the realm of ideas that had begun oozing through him was a gash to be cauterized. Theories and abstractions discussed at the dinner table penetrated him by some passive, verbal osmosis, all of which he later came to revile, dismissing them as pedantic classification games, glib tournaments of rhetoric. Schoolwork had always come so easily to him, and so he instead trained the sum of his energies on the challenges of the immediate and sensory. If he couldn't wring or caress it in his own two hands or feel it gurgling in his chest, he would forgo any speculation and have nothing to do with it. And now, holding this old photograph and shriveling with loneliness, he heard his stomach growl. He was famished.

He fried two eggs and threw them over a bowl of cold rice he scraped out of the countertop cooker. White rice was another constant. In the kitchen, Mom's repertoire had been limited but sufficient, a consistent rotation of meatloaf, lemon chicken breast, beef stroganoff, and veggie soufflé, every batch made in quantities that ensured at least two days' worth of leftovers. Whatever the dish, Papa required white rice for a side, even with Mom's spicy Bolognese. After she'd died, dinner duty fell to Papa, who dished up mounds of white rice, heavily salted and freckled with fried garlic, accompanied by either seared slices of Spam or his hot dog stir fry: chopped pink cylinders sautéed in a wok with onions and a can of sweet corn. Or, on the evenings when even just ten minutes in front of the stove was asking too much, he would splurge on a twenty pack of McNuggets, next to which he set the rice pot and a bottle of Jufran banana ketchup.

Even though Henry knew little and remembered even less about the Philippines, he still ate the Filipino way. Left hand gripping a fork to rake meat and rice into a tablespoon in the right. Over the scrape of a yolky spoon, he heard an engine grumbling outside, too robust to be Papa's pickup. Soon the front door creaked, but nobody stepped in.

"Henry," came Papa's voice. "Get out here. Now, ah."

What now? Henry lobbed the bowl into the kitchen sink, almost disappointed when it didn't shatter. Making his way outside, he didn't bother to get dressed. All dignity had been stripped from him last night anyway, so he stepped onto the driveway barefoot, wearing nothing but the boxers he'd fallen asleep in.

Parked next to Papa's pickup was another F-250, apparently the same year but free of dents, dirt, and scratches, its steel bumper unbent and shining.

Papa stood at the top of the driveway, arms crossed, chin turning from one truck to the second. "Which one?"

Henry shrank.

"Good choice." Papa handed him a key, then shuffled toward the newer of the two. He patted the hood as if it were a stallion, sentient, reliable. "Great vehicle. Real diehard. The way you were going before, it might even outlive you. Most certainly will me, ah."

Papa hadn't looked directly at Henry once. Hardly seemed to be seeing anything at all. The way he was speaking sounded more like a rehearsal than a conversation.

"Low mileage and gently used. Owner was a funny guy, admitted he'd bought it more for vanity than hauling. Not so much as a paint chip, not even in the bed, which we'll want to tar. Anything goes wrong, I can teach you how to fix it. Serpentine belt is cracked to hell, but I'll show you how to change that out tonight." He swung open the driver's-side door and to the ground said, "Get in."

Again, Henry felt emptied, only this time by shock. A queasy levity floated him down the driveway and up into the driver's seat. Tremors crawled back into his shoulders, his lips, which snapped stiff when Papa slammed the door shut. The shakes, which Henry tried to steady by gripping the steering wheel, resumed instantly. His mouth opened and closed, wordless as a guppy, until he finally managed one word, just a hair above a whisper—*Papa*.

The truck was so big and Papa so short that only the top of his head appeared at the bottom ledge of the window. His face soured with approval. After a nod, he turned to go inside. Before disappearing into the house, he called over his shoulder. Told Henry to check the glove compartment, ah.

Alone in the truck cab, Henry explored the dashboard's radio dial and heating knobs, the adjustable center console and its inner slots. The cigarette burner, ashtray, and side-door compartments. The emergency brake lever, hood pop, and then he clicked the driver's seat back to caress the smooth, gunmetal nylon of the rear bench seat. He wiggled the gear stick jutting up from the floor panel, tested the springiness of the clutch. He was ready.

The key turned and the engine roared. With both bare feet pressing the clutch and brake pedal, he was taken by the thrill of running machinery against his flesh and under his command. He eased his right foot over to the accelerator and revved the engine. The truck cab was drenched in sound, his laughter and the engine and a delirium of possibilities pistoning wildly through his imagination. He cranked it into reverse, eager to speed off anywhere, naked and feverish, and his foot slipped off the clutch. The engine burped, then died with a violent lurch forward.

In the stillness that followed, doubts surfaced. Bubbled, then simmered. Doubts about whether he truly deserved this, if he'd somehow actually earned it, or was just being spoiled. Whether he was too proud for charity, or too old for gifts. He wondered what could possibly have compelled Papa to make such a purchase, and if there was anything Henry could ever do to rid himself of this newfound gratitude, hardening over him like a welt. No thank-you or report card, no decadelong streak of sobriety or respectful deference would ever cut it. He collapsed to his side, unworthy and eye level with the glove compartment. He was scared to open it. He braced himself before gingerly guiding the plastic hatch down. On top of an owner's manual was a neat stack of cash, held together by a paper clip. After counting the bills—ten twenties—he found a Post-it clipped to the bottom. On it, Papa had written three words. Three words much more unexpected and devastating than *I love you*, which wouldn't have gouged half as deep as these.

$16.41

Nothing on earth turns down money except old vending machines. After six attempts to feed a dollar bill into the slot only to have it spat back out, then yanking it taut and rubbing Washington's smug face against the corner of the machine and then pinching the bill's edges stiff and creaseless with his fingernails, the slot accepts the single with a lethargic mechanical slurp. Henry punches the Sprite button. A can lumbers inside then clunks out, the boom of its exit cracking through an evening so eerily noiseless that not even crickets want anything to do with it. The can is cold and heavy like an iced artillery shell. The vending machines are bolted right outside the motel office, and he imagines torpedoing the can through the window and pegging that thieving billboard of a woman square in the forehead.

Outside room 8, the night's silence gets punctured again. Lifting key to lock, he can hear rushed voices, dog whines, and a TV booming from next door. The last thing he wants is another exchange with the dogmonger, but he might as well get this over with. Could be a loud, long night otherwise.

The instant he raps on door 9, the voices hush and the dogs bark. The TV volume goes unadjusted. When he knocks again, harder, someone inside goes, "*Ssshhh.*"

His patience is thinning. Before he knows it, he's begun hammering at the door with the bottom of the Sprite can, pressing a cluster of waning moons into the cheap composite wood of the door, which now pulls back a few inches, a chain snapping it into place. In the narrow opening appears a strip of the dogmonger's face. The column of light above his comb over sways with smoke. His eyes are bloodshot, his forehead glistening with a fresh coat of ammonia-smelling sweat.

"Changer mind, did you? Danny, fetch us the doggie."

A woman's voice asks which one.

"The wienie one, duh."

The voice says but that's her favorite, how come not the Shih Tzu or Labradoodle or—

"I didn't come for a dog." Henry presses his forearm into the door, leveling knuckles at the greasy hairline.

"We said eighty, right? Eighty a fucking steal, hoo-wee."

Henry can't tell whether this clown is trying to get a rise out of him or really is this stupid. Either way, he would love to watch him suffer.

"Listen," he says. "All I want is for you to keep it down. The dogs, the TV, we can hear everything you're—"

"Everything?"

"Everything." Someone lowers the TV's volume, then shushes the dogs or someone or some other people. Out of habit, Henry thanks whoever's inside.

The shrunken face wrinkles, sniffs. "So," the dogmonger says. "How's about fifty?"

Henry yanks the door shut for him.

The can explodes with a burst of sticky fizz. Henry laps it up, and the sweet tickle soothes him, at least a little. First he pinky promises, then swears—cross his heart and hope to die—that if Junior drinks the whole can, his tummy'll feel better. He'll see.

The TV is playing a movie showing a real-life piglet talking to a group of ducks. The farmland behind them is lush, idyllic, which, based on his experience, strikes him as miles more implausible than language-exchanging livestock. He turns the volume up a few more notches to dampen any later disturbances from room 9.

Next to the bathroom is a chintzy, stand-alone wardrobe, inside of which is nothing but a fluffy carpet of dust. Not a single hanger. No iron to salvage his button-up. From the plastic dry-cleaning bag, he fishes the wire hanger out of the suit jacket, then puts it through the collar of a white dress shirt to hang on the shower curtain rod. Only opens the hot water knob, letting the water gush and warm vapor waft. He tugs at the shirt's hem to smooth the wrinkles out with the steam and an open palm, but he's having even less luck with this shirt than with the one-dollar bill. After five minutes, the shirt-front's creases still look like a faded highway map. He'll have to call the billboard woman for an iron later.

He strips, turns on the shower, and intends to get his mother-fucking money's worth. A long, unrushed soak. None of the in-and-out rinses from back when it was his name on the utility bill. He is, however, conservative with the single-serving tab of soap. Would be nice to get two washes out of this one, so he can pocket the second untouched and wrapped up for later. His skin goes rosy and tender, his lungs spongy with steam, and after fifteen minutes even his bones feel soaked through, wobbly and warm. He plugs the drain to start filling the tub. The last time he'd taken a bath had been with Michelle. Their tub had been just as cramped as this one, hardly suited for one adult body, let alone a second.

Henry'd been racking up as many overtime hours as possible back at the gold-plating plant, where his PO found him a job. Coming home to their singlewide one night, after his third or fourth double straight, he walked in on Michelle dozing off in the bathtub. He'd only wanted to brush his teeth before bed, too exhausted to strip and rinse the day off him. A cigarette butt, scorched past the filter, dropped from her lips to the water's surface. Her eyelids had that trusting, lobe-like puff to them, which meant she was high. At that point, the pills had begun dulling her edges, but hadn't yet scooped her hollow.

"Come here," she cooed. "Squeeze in behind, like."

At first he'd said no, but was too tired to argue. Worse, she really did look marvelous in there, which in that moment overrode any of his frustrations or concerns about the frequency of her dosing. Always a total sucker for her. Smacked mute and dopey at the sight of her skin all shiny and suds-patched. Those little tentacles of wet hair squiggling over her collarbone. He could have eaten her with a spoon.

The water was tepid at best. First he fished out the cigarette butt. Bowled water in his palms, doused his hair and mopped it back into a single black swoop. Reminded him of their first night in this home, a pair of sort-of adults playing house, exchanging affectionate slurs, oblivious to the world beyond their bedroom. He said *hey, look* to remind her, too, but the gaze he got in turn was blank. Too far gone for nostalgia. It was fine, though, because when he wedged himself behind her in the tub, her back against his belly was slick and pulsing, which, blended with reminiscing and exhaustion, began coaxing him to sleep like some gooey lullaby. He closed his eyes.

She told him to touch her, wash her, then passed back a loofah. So tired, he grazed the loofah over the parts of her most easily accessible, the zones that didn't require stretching or repositioning himself. He let the back of his head rest against the wall's linoleum paneling, and he still remembers his thoughts wading away, coming to terms with the fact that he wouldn't be entirely opposed to drowning in there, dying just like this. She shifted herself upward and reached between his thighs. Tried gripping him, but all she got was a fleshy dumpling. He didn't bother apologizing because he was drifting off, fading away, and so couldn't even say what a shame it was that his bent knees, bracketing Michelle but poking out of the bathwater, were so, so cold.

"Why won't you fuck me?"

He jolted awake with a splash, surprised to find himself in a tub.

She repeated the question, just as vicious but twice as loud. She twisted between his knees, all her stoned lobes filed back to her daytime blades. Her voice rose as she asked what in the actual fuck was wrong with him? Huh? What kind of a man, after five years in a cell, came home to the woman who'd waited for him, like, stayed faithful to him, slaved away and raised his son all on her own, but he wouldn't even—no, *couldn't* even—

"Please," he said. "Junior's sleeping."

At that, she'd shot out of the tub and marched from the bathroom nude and dripping, leaving her angry wake to lap over him stroke after stroke, and now the memory washes away any allure a bath in this motel tub might have held. He ties a towel around his waist. When he opens the door, steam escapes then dissipates in the motel room. He tells Junior it's bath time.

The boy has curled himself back into a ball, now lying on his other side to better view the TV. "Can't I finish this movie first?"

Henry's patience is threadbare. He smears his face with both hands, kneading resolve into his forehead. "Junior."

"Please?" the boy says. "It's been so long since we watched a movie together."

The boy isn't wrong. It has been a long, long time since they've watched anything in a warm, private place. Been just as long since the boy's taken a proper bath, had a real scrub, and it is his birthday, so really, what's one more hour? What difference does it make how early or late they actually hit the lights? Really, they might as well stay up all night. Almost seems a waste to ignore this temporary comfort under the cover of sleep, so—

"Fine," Henry snaps, then corrects himself: "Yeah, of course. Tonight's your night, bud."

This will give him time to practice for tomorrow. Better now than later, while he's still half-awake. He grabs his note cards out of the suit jacket's pocket, before shedding the towel and settling into the bathwater.

It'd been nearly two years since he last saw or even heard from his parole officer. In their only face-to-face meeting, the PO was a gruff, toady man, like Churchill but black, chewing a stick of jerky in lieu of a cigar, any bulldog wit trimmed down to a sterile, clipboard script. When he turned to the computer, he punched at the keys with his middle fingers, muttering, and Henry wasn't sure if the grumbles and upside-down gestures were meant for him or the screen. After a few signatures and stamps, the PO flicked over a piece of paper with an address, clock-in time, and rusty grease stains.

"Gold plating," he said. "Temporary at best."

He warned the gig probably wouldn't last, the economy and what-

64

not, turning even good news grim, but whatever. Henry was as ecstatic to have a job as he was grateful to be spared further interactions with this warty buzzkill.

That was before the bathtub fiasco with Michelle, back when Henry was still riding the recently freed man's high. He came home from the precinct grinning. Even though Junior, only six then, hadn't quite warmed up to his pa, this new presence in their home, Henry scooped the boy into his arms and smacked a kiss on his cheek. With the boy trying to paw free from his embrace, Henry told Michelle about the new job, then went on to describe and joke about his PO, saying the acronym was short a letter. An *S*.

"Acronym?"

"Like, what letters stand for."

"So whyn't you say that then?" she said. "You and your big words, Hen."

"You and your big mouth." Which he then grabbed, kissed, and it felt so good to be back home that not even forever could scare him, not if forever meant living like this.

Forever lasted about a year. At least it was a formative stretch. Despite the long shifts, slim wages, and after-hours tumult at home, working alongside Lucius offered Henry a shred of steady ground over the course of that rocky year. His new and only friend had served two back-to-back, decade-plus sentences, and was three times Henry's age. Lucius had a face like an armadillo's back, its craggy ridges wrinkling around amber irises and cataract clouds. The agility of his fingers and the precision of his handiwork betrayed his unrushed, bum-knee gait. He possessed a hardened air of seen-it-all wisdom that he imparted via anecdotes and aphorisms over styrofoam cups of coffee. Later, when they got around to trading conviction tales, it was impossible for Henry to reconcile Lucius's double feature of grisly attacks with the levelheaded old man in the break room. Until, of course, the afternoon the plant announced its move across the border.

Whereas Lucius's reaction got him a third strike for aggravated assault and destruction of property, Henry had cowered, ignored his only friend's pleas. When it was over, he took his paycheck. Walked away. Only lost control once home. Later, desperate, he caved, emailed his old PO asking for job leads, anything, please. No reply, never a returned phone call for nearly six months, which was why the email about tomorrow's job interview—so out of the blue last week—had come as a welcome, grovel-worthy shock.

He has to get ready. Focus. Can't afford any more mental meandering. The bottom ridges of the note cards have gotten wet in the motel tub. He wags them dry before reading the first: *What are your three greatest strengths?*

"Well, sir, if I've got to narrow it down to *only* three—no, no. Too cocky, you douchebag."

"Who you talking to, Pa?"

"Nobody—I'm not talking." Henry stretches for the bathroom door. "Watch your movie."

This time, even with the door shut, he keeps his voice measured and low.

"Perseverance, loyalty, and, and hunger, as in, like, ambition . . . ?"

No. The online job forums detail the ideal, entry-level profile, and naming ambition could give the impression he's using this job as a stepping-stone. They want someone who'll stick around, stay put, someone complacent and—

"Dependable. I'm perseverant in that I never give up, no matter the odds. You see, sir, things haven't exactly been easy for my son and me these last couple months."

Stop. No sob stories. He's got to earn this stranger's trust and respect, not pity. Go back one, to the second.

"Loyalty. I'm loyal because I will do absolutely anything for my loved ones, along with anyone who's offered me their respect and trust. That goes for my employers and coworkers, too, sir. You could say my perseverance and drive are actually, like, fundamentally rooted in my sense of loyalty. And so that's essentially what motivates me to achieve and accomplish and, and overcome whatever challenges or obstacles life or the workplace might hurl my way. Loyalty."

Henry is back in the courtroom. There's Al at the defendant's table, quiet sobs folding his chin into his throat.

"Loyalty," Henry says, louder, because no more distractions. He splashes bathwater over his face. It drips.

"And dependable. Accountable, which, I suppose, goes hand in hand with the other two, wouldn't you say, sir? And as unwavering as my loyalty is to those I care about, so is my sense of duty, in that, you can, you know, count on me? When you need something taken care of, you won't ever have to think twice or second-guess whether the task or job or project or whatever will get done, promptly and to the utmost standards, as in, so long as you've put it in my hands. You know, if you trusted me—sir. Because I say what I mean and I meant what I said, an elephant's faithful one hundred percent."

Their after-school trips to the public library have clearly left their mark on Henry. After he's burned through his daily one-hour allotment of internet access on job shopping and scrambling to arrange handyman or moving or metal-scrapping gigs on Craigslist for the week, he always joins Junior in the children's section to practice reading out loud. Keeping the Dr. Seuss references to a minimum during tomorrow's interview would be prudent. After all, even Junior has outgrown picture books. But still, Henry can't help but ask himself, if he's the elephant who gets duped into climbing up a tree to sit on that abandoned egg, then does that make Michelle the mama bird? And, if so, does that mean she'll come back someday, too?

His teeth clench, his head shakes. He shuffles the deck of note cards. The next reads: *What makes you more qualified than the other candidates?*

Diddly. Jackshit. Fuck all.

His jaw lowers, accepting a reservoir of bathwater to gargle away his initial response, the truth. All the online forums say the same thing, how you can't convince a hiring manager of your talents or qualifications if you're not convinced of them yourself. How studies show flexing chest out and chin up in front of a mirror for two minutes has proven effective in generating testosterone for preinterview confidence. He spouts an arc of bathwater from his mouth.

"The scope of my experience, sir, allows for the practical application of the three strengths I've just identified."

In the whitest voice Henry can muster, he asks himself if he would care to elaborate.

"Why, certainly, sir. Absolutely. Indeed and my pleasure. I guess one could say I'm a jack-of-all-trades and a master of some."

Naked, alone, and winking at a scroll of peeling wallpaper in a dingy motel bathroom, he expels a chuckle. The sound is repulsive. The forums recommend something called *workplace-friendly humor*, a balance of professionalism and levity, but all of his hacks at it are corn syrup. These cheesy cracks along with all the courteous tags— the *sirs*, *indeed*s, and *my pleasure*s—are making him out to be some bootlicker. Lower than the run-of-the-mill employee, more disposable than the deferential subordinate—like this, he is subhuman.

Regarding previous experience, he plans to discuss his contracting work after high school and touch on his current stint as a freelance handyman, a nifty euphemism he's cooked up for unemployed and desperate. From plumbing to roofing, engine work to electrical, he's done it all. He's a quick learner and even harder worker, with time management and chummy customer service charm to boot. Zip it up with the three strengths, and then on to the next one:

What are your three greatest weaknesses?

Why, that's easy, your honor, your majesty: alcohol, uppers, and an acidic contempt for the world at large for having shortchanged, chewed up, spat out, and shat all over me, sir.

He gargles more bathwater, then sprays it up and over his moronic, self-sorry face. It drips down his cheeks, absolutely nothing like tears. Enough. Weaknesses. Three of them. Go.

"I suppose I tend to work *too* hard. I don't like leaving things unfinished, and so fine, whatever. Two. Sometimes I can get sort of impatient, especially when I think others around me aren't pulling their weight. And so, that said, I'm confident I would have a positive, motivational, even like inspirational influence on my coworkers. Yippee, huh? And third, thirdly, three . . .

"My temper. Yeah, no, I mean that I'm working on tact. Delivery? Sometimes I can be a bit impulsive. Can't help but speak my mind, which might come off as a little brash. But only sometimes, though. Like when I get upset, which isn't often, and but, nevertheless, fatherhood"—and here's his chance to connect on what the forums call a *human level*—"Oh, you, too, huh? You don't say. They grow up so fast, don't they? But so what I'm trying to say is that fatherhood, if anything, has shown me, has taught me—"

A muffled retch. Something dense spills. A gasp.

"Junior?"

Before Henry can fasten the towel around his waist, he's already thrown it over the puddle of vomit the boy has deposited onto the carpet. Squatting naked and dripping at the bedside, he swabs the towel on the floor with one hand while matting Junior's burning face with the other. He tells the boy everything's okay, because his pa is right here.

Henry's knees sink into the mush beneath the towel, as he embraces the boy with both arms. Junior's wiry frame is racked with tremors, so Henry squeezes tighter and tighter, as if he could still the rattles with pressure, a full-body stranglehold. It doesn't work. The boy keeps shivering. An icy fear plunges into Henry's stomach, and now he can hardly tell where Junior's tremors end and his own begin. They are a circuit of trembling, an echo chamber of unease, and as Henry squeezes tighter still, a thought rustles then lifts, spiraling louder and clearer with each lap it makes through his skull. If fatherhood has taught him anything at all, it is helplessness.

$300.00

"Here's your half."

Henry took his cut from Al, spread the bills into a mini–hand fan to better count them: six crisp fifties. Before folding them into his pocket, he paused. Something off. He put the fan between his face and the sharp morning sun, casting the cash translucent. Watermark, security thread, color-shifting ink. Not that he'd actually suspected they were counterfeits, but still.

"They already paid you?" Henry asked.

"Rich people, dude." Al reached for the chainsaw in the truck bed, but was barricaded by his own belly pressing into the side panel. He gave up. "Imagine having enough money to trust people."

"Must be nice." Henry stepped onto the rear tire and up into the bed. First he passed over the chainsaw, then eased a steel wheelbarrow down to Al, who let it thunder onto the pavement. Up that hill, in one of those mansions, there must have been at least one irritated neighbor, but nobody came out or shouted, and so Henry lobbed a shovel, two metal rakes, and a pair of loppers into the barrow, not even bothering to try to cushion their awful clanks and squeals.

He had to hand it to Al. There was no denying the chubby junkie's entrepreneurial spirit. Unlike the other skinnies, he didn't treat money as a mere means to a fix. All the scheming, haggling, and hustling, for Al, were ends in themselves. Always had been, from his middle school days of hawking his older brother's hand-me-down Coogis and dad's porno mags to spritzing water onto buds or cutting crushed acetaminophen into every dime bag he sold, he couldn't help himself whenever there was a buck to be made.

So, after seeing a local news story about a buckthorn infestation striking waterfront properties, Al had hit a Kinko's, then driven six towns east to stuff fliers into over a hundred riverfront mansion mailboxes, before even telling Henry he'd be needing his recently gifted pickup and a handful of Papa's tools. An extra set of hands—Henry's—couldn't hurt, either.

It was only 8:00 a.m., but the swampy broil radiating off the water at the back end of the property was so relentless that even the mosquitoes had to fight through the hot pulp of the air. This was not how Henry had imagined spending the first Monday of summer vacation.

Since this had all been Al's idea, he insisted on leading the way with the chainsaw, buzzing through the barky stalks. That left the grunt work to Henry. It was his job to gather and pile up the thorny clusters into the wheelbarrow, run it all the way across the acre-long property to the street and unload the debris into the truck bed, only to jog the emptied barrow back for another load, over and over.

The work was hell and only got harder. Every inch the sun climbed into the sky lifted another degree after it on the thermometer. Each sweep of the chainsaw brought them closer to the shore below, meaning there was that much more slope for Henry to climb back up, in order to heft the next load of buckthorn stalks and branches into the wheelbarrow waiting on the flat swath of yard above. Sawdust clung to perspiration, his skin beneath it breaking out in itchy hives. The cocktail of humidity and the two-stroke engine's exhaust had him winded, nauseated.

Still though, it was worth it. Satisfying to pause and measure their progress by the growing load in the truck bed. As much as his limbs and back burned, it was good to be reminded of the intricate machinery of tissue and tendons concealed by his skin. On each trip from back to front, and then front to back again, the huge Tudor house's shade was a cool, numbing balm. Clomping back to the shorefront with an empty barrow, he paused at the side of the guesthouse, twisted the garden hose spigot. The water was icy down his throat, magical over his scalp and shoulders. He took off and soaked his T-shirt, then hooked the cold, sopping rag around his neck.

71

Before spitting into his palms and regripping the barrow handles, he grazed the outline of the cash in his front pocket. In one day he'd made more than two weeks' worth of after-school shifts at the supermarket. Al had even managed to wring out an extra Benny on top of the advertised five hundred dollars. The Lexus, a hybrid, parked in the three-car garage had given him an idea. He'd told the homeowners that, for a small disposal fee, they could have the buckthorn debris processed at an all-green landfill for sustainable composting. The homeowners had fallen for it, and now the pile was bound for the first abandoned lot he and Henry came across on their forty-minute drive back west.

One hundred dollars for an eased conscience. Even if Henry was ever making the sort of money that would enable him to cough up a hundred bucks without a moment's thought, no way would he piss it away on garbage. Such casual extravagance was beyond him, as unfathomable as what lay inside this mansion beside him. The structure was more fortress than home, daunting in both size and design. Something unsettling about the asymmetrical arrangement of steep, pitched gable roofs and the lone conical spire stabbing into the sky, which he imagined provided vistas ideal for brooding over world domination while petting a wrinkly, hairless cat. Pressed into the khaki stucco was a pattern of exposed timbers forming X's, as if warding off outsiders, peasants. This house, along with all the others down the shoreline street, stood in audacious contrast to the dwellings just one town back west, never mind the relative huts in Henry's hometown. What on earth could these people have done to afford houses like these?

None of this changed the fact that he wanted it—all of it—for himself. There was no question of whether he had the nerve and determination to smash his nose to the grindstone, but where had discipline and a solid work ethic gotten Papa? Decades of sacrifice just to barely scrape by. To actually get ahead and stack cash apparently required a skill set like Al's, a propensity for schmoozing, manipulation, and scheming, especially since everyone else in the rat race was more than willing to deploy the same set of under-the-belt tactics.

The chainsaw motor quit and the air zippered quiet. By the time Henry got back to the shoreline, Al was a pink, panting loaf, dragging a rake listlessly over the twigs and leaves scattered down the slope. "The fuck you been?"

Henry didn't bite. Just picked up the second rake and asked about the root systems. He'd heard this shit grows right back.

"It does," Al said, wheezing. "Grab a shovel."

"You dig them out. You've had the easy part all morning."

"Dude. I ain't got boots." Al wiggled a sneaker spongy with sawdust. "And plus whose idea was all this anyway, huh?"

Henry surveyed the slope. From the hill's crest down to the water were dozens of nubby yellow stumps, too many to count. "No way I'm digging all those fuckers out. It'd take all week."

"You won't have to. Just the ones up top, close to the yard. The rest we'll cover with mulch." Al knocked his temple. "Work smart, not hard, dipshit."

But the digging was hard. Tedious. First Henry had to go around each buzzed stump with the shovel head flipped over to scrape away the topsoil and expose the root system, then diligently chip around and under each thick strand so he could stab through them with the spade, or else get down on his knees and cut them one by one with the loppers, making a slow rotation all the way around the stump, until he'd cleared enough of the upper, toddler-ankle-thick roots to dig out from under the system, then finally spear the shovel head underneath and pry the whole thing out by leveraging his weight into the shovel handle. Strenuous, slow-going work, much more taxing and aggravating than the first task of gathering and running the thorny stalks over to the truck.

Meanwhile, as he chopped and dug and stomped and cussed, Al was strolling about, flapping mulch bags like pillowcases and spreading the cedar shavings with dainty kicks of his sneakers. Whereas Henry's lungs had scalded him mute, Al had been jabbering nonstop

73

this entire time. Talking shit about the skinnies, repairs to the Bonneville, Fridays long gone. Now he was going on about his next hustle, which he was planning to start making moves on as soon as he'd stacked up a couple bands from this buckthorn shit, involving a black-market pill press and something called fentanyl—Henry didn't care. He was hardly listening. A minute into Al's monologue, Henry'd figured out the best way to relieve this strain and rationalize all this sweat and ache was to think about Michelle.

A tenacious, buried fiber refused to let go, no matter how hard Henry pried and threw himself into the shovel handle. It was the last root system left to dig out, so naturally it was determined to make things difficult. He threw the shovel down, squatted over the stump, and gripped the chopped nubs with his bare, blistered hands. He was yanking and twisting it, boot heels burrowing into the dirt, molars clenched and about to splinter, when Al asked if Henry'd heard back from that one bulimic bitch he was so obsessed with.

The root snapped. Henry fell flat on his ass, pulling the freed root system after him and into his lap. Swift with rage, he sprang to his feet and made a single, hammer-throw spin before hurling the dense tangle down at Al, who simply sidestepped the projectile. It thumped once against the earth, then tumbled into the river with a coffee splash.

"Fuck me. So sensitive, dude." Al smoothed mulch over the fresh divot. "That girl, broad, woman, lady, whatever. That better? So?"

Henry spiked the shovel into the ground. Leaned. "So what?"

"You ever gonna see her or what?"

"Yeah, no. Said she wants to hang out this weekend."

Al stopped. Looked wounded. "But I thought you and me was, this weekend, you know."

"Who's the sensitive one now?"

Al kicked at a hill of mulch. Spat. Muttered something about friendship, loyalty and shit, but Henry wasn't listening, at least not to Al. In a remote corner of his mind, there was a conversation under way. A flurry of eager whispers, his and Michelle's. They had so much to say. He recognized the vinegar pitch of her intonation but couldn't decipher her words, not even the general topic up for discussion. A drumming cut through the noon sun's swelter and lent their murmurs a happy beat—his pulse. It thumped as if from outside him, keeping time in some faraway place, cool and gauzy, where their imagined reunion was taking place, and so precisely where he wanted to be.

$16.40

A dot of copper on the boy's palm. He asks but what makes it lucky, Pa?

Henry tells him to look closely. Look at the year. Eight years ago—well, technically, eight years and nine months—Junior was the same size as this penny. Even smaller, actually.

"Inside of Mom?"

Henry nods. And just look how big and strong Junior is now. And so imagine how much bigger and stronger he's going to get. It's pretty cool, huh?

"What do I do with it?" Junior says.

"You keep it with you and," he closes the boy's fingers around the coin, making more of a flower bud than a fist, "squeeze. If something bad happens, like, if your tummy starts hurting again or—"

"It still hurts."

"It'll get better. Now, squeeze."

When Henry calls the motel office for an iron, the phone receiver offers no ring tone. He jiggers the cradle and its innards give a faint ding. The cradle shifts on top of the patio table to show the phone not only isn't plugged in, but has no cord at all. He's heard of stealing hotel towels and toiletries, had been planning on pocketing the extra bar of soap himself, but a telephone cord? Irritating, yeah, but he's also mildly impressed.

He steps into his jeans without underwear, then into his boots without socks or lacing them. Tells Junior to keep squeezing, to finish the Sprite, and that he'll be right back. When he clomps out onto the gravel, peals of dog barks yap after him, as if pleading to accompany him on this late-night stroll to the motel office. The grains of sand and dirt wedging between his toes, the woofs and whines from room 9, and now the obligation to interact with the billboard woman yet again—why, it's all rather unpleasant, isn't it? Much less than ideal, indeed, sir.

Outside the office door he pauses to collect himself. His hand squeezes into a fist, though the last of his coins remain in his front pocket. He expels a long stream of air as if this might release some of the heat broiling in his lungs.

The bells above jingle just as ghastly as before. The woman's flanks ooze and bulge in the gaps of the desk chair's armrests like a pork shoulder pressed into chain-link. She wields total power here. To get what he needs, he'll have to ooze courtesy, crank up the charm. He gulps, and bile curdles into a cheesy smile.

"Hey, just me again," he says. "How's your night going?"

She's locked onto the TV behind him. Her jade eyes flicker over then through him, settling back to the screen.

He plants his elbows into the counter, lowering his starchy grin square into her sight line.

She makes a stop sign of her hand. Must be something serious happening. When he looks back, there's a clan of tuxedoed men facing down a blond woman in a sparkling evening gown. She runs fingers along a rose stem as if cocking a toy rifle.

"Love this show," Henry tries. "So who's she gonna pick, huh?"

"Ssshhh."

"Sorry."

No roses left on the table. This is it, their last chance. Maybe Henry's, too, so maybe he should have put on the suit. The screen flashes a string of extreme close-ups on hearty, American male chins, all smirking as desperately as Henry. An orchestra mounts in pitch and urgency and—with a momentous pang—cuts to commercial break.

She huffs. At last, her gaze acknowledges his presence. "What?"

"Intense," he says. "The show, I mean."

She reclines deeper in her chair, already bored. It seems to pain her to ask if she can help him with something or what.

"Why, yes, actually. Yeah." He composes himself, smiles harder, leans closer. "Big day tomorrow. Was wondering if you happen to have an iron I could borrow right quick?"

His request is met with a throaty gust, the moan of the inconvenienced.

From beneath the desk comes a squeaky patter as a pair of Crocs chug the desk chair wheels and the planet above them in the direction of a storage closet no more than three strides behind her. The iron is perched on the topmost shelf. She casts a glance like a hatchet back at him.

"Can I give you a hand there, ma'am—miss?"

"I got it, I got it," she says, prying herself out of the chair with all the grace of a marooned walrus. The iron that she thunks onto the counter is ancient, its point spangled with rust. Looks more like a medieval hand weapon than a domestic appliance.

And, when she tells him that'll be five bucks, he imagines driving the thing—rusty point first—straight into her temple.

"Fuck that."

"You ain't pay with a card," she says. "We need collateral, like."

"Collateral? Not another one of your service charges, right?"

"Meant like—"

He wags a fiver, stiff and folded longwise at her, as if teasing a puppy with a twig. Takes one glance at the bill to see he's only taunting himself.

Five measly dollars.

Look at him getting so worked up over so damn little. After tomorrow's interview, once the paychecks start rolling in, he'll never have to suffer this crush again. He knows it, swears it, but to get to that point, he's got to—he can't. He can't step foot into this interview looking exactly how he's felt these last six months.

He flicks the bill. Snatches the iron. Warns her he'll be back for those five dollars in five minutes flat.

$100.00

This was more than excitement. Miles beyond the pre-sniff thrill while cutting lines on a pool hall toilet tank, or the happy flash of a fridge glimmering with beer bottles in a parentless house. This anticipation was charged with a kiddish purity, plus a twang of nervousness. Embarking on the drive down to Michelle's place, Henry was giddy. Sure, he'd seen and sniffed and drunk and smoked his fair share, but when it came to this—a *date*—he was a novice, a toddler love drunk on a schoolyard crush. In terms of sex, let alone the most basic rituals of attraction and engagement, he was utterly inexperienced. Anticipation had him in a frenzy. He had to get his shit together. If he didn't, Michelle was bound to detect just how flagrantly chaste he was the instant she climbed into the truck.

A bouquet of roses sat on the middle seat. Initially he'd lifted the center console to remove the barrier between him and Michelle to optimize drive-time proximity. He'd imagined her fawning over the flowers and, unobstructed, sidling across the seat and into his lap, and this made him a total fucking moron, corny and naive. He slammed the console down to hide the bouquet, which coughed a petal to the floor.

He reeked of enthusiasm and was drenched in effort, obliterating any chance of exuding an air of bad-boy nonchalance that, at least in the movies, drove girls like Michelle wild. In her email she'd suggested they *hang out*. No specifics, no potential date spots, not even a single exclamation point. Even still, he'd splurged his buckthorn earnings on preparations, casting himself headfirst into fantasies of sex and elopement. In his front pocket was a hundred bucks just for tonight, perhaps for a dinner they hadn't discussed, maybe later a movie never mentioned, and—*christ*—he'd even loaded the truck bed with sofa cushions and sleeping bags, just in case she suggested they find a private place to park and dig into each other under the stars. He'd bought and was now wearing a crisp pair of black Wranglers, black Timberlands, and a too-small T-shirt that showed off the new arms he was so proud of, bronzed and oak-sturdy from the last two months of work. Like some James Dean wannabe, he'd even rolled up the sleeves to reveal the blotchy collage of stick-n-poke tattoos the skinnies had left on his upper arms. He'd sprayed himself in a cologne he couldn't pronounce, and now cranked down the window to let the wind rinse the yuppie juice off him. After the first exhausting yet lucrative week of the buckthorn hustle, he had shaved his head, which, in the rearview mirror now, made his cranium look egg-shaped, delicate, suggesting none of the Marine Corps grit he'd been striving for. He'd washed and polished the truck, emptied out the ashtrays, vacuumed every cushion and crevice, and this was an absolute disaster. He ripped the pine tree off the rearview mirror and chucked it out the window.

Michelle lived forty-five minutes west, out in the sticks, in a trailer park set behind a new outlet mall, so Henry had ample time to stew himself into a panic. Each mile cast the landscape into a deeper shade of atrophy, as if, by contrast, to further highlight all of his infantile hacks at seduction, which were bound to snuff out any prospects of romantic success. Flanking both sides of the highway were stretches of scorched farmland, the horizon flatlining in the distance like a dying patient's EKG, disrupted occasionally by a slouching farmhouse or grain silo. Weather-battered billboards advertised hunting gear, salvation for spared fetuses, recreational vehicles, talk radio, and fishing boats. One warned that, after the next exit, there wouldn't be another McDonald's for another thirty-seven miles. When he was five miles from the outlet mall exit and Michelle, the billboards took on a new glossy retail sheen, bold fonts shouting about the designer bargains and family dining options to be enjoyed in only four miles, three, two, and exit now for savings beyond his wildest dreams.

The exit ramp overlooked the immense shopping complex. Lines of cars were worming into a parking lot so full it was shimmering, looking as if a square mile of ocean had been airlifted then stitched into the plains. The single service road running between the freeway and the mall's perimeter was clogged, bumpers inching up to bumpers, the summer air pasty with car exhaust and impatience. Everybody in everyone else's way. Henry's was the only vehicle that didn't slither into the lot with the rest. As soon as he passed the entrance, the road cleared. He floored it, making up for time lost in traffic, gunning a quarter mile down the open road until screeching with a hard right turn at the *Indigo Hills Residential Park* sign, an eggy pair of briefs sagging off its corner.

While the only suggestion of hills in the trailer park were the sharp buckles and craters in the pavement, it certainly felt blue, subdued. Its willow-shaded lanes stood in unnerving contrast to the outlet mall's previous commotion. The drone of cicadas seemed to be coming from inside the trailers themselves, every last set of curtains drawn shut. A messy network of power lines crosshatched the sky, so peering upward felt like being on the wrong end of a fishing net.

Saturday afternoons in his neighborhood, life was a constant presence. Men in beaters and flip-flops watering front yards, or hunched under the hood of some fixer-upper muscle car. Gap-toothed boys and girls playing war with tree-branch rifles and latex water grenades in the street. Mothers keeping watch from front porches, stirring glasses of iced tea with lemon wedges. But here the lanes and curbsides were littered with everything but people. Whereas in his neighborhood the refuse of home improvement projects and seasonal decorations got crammed inside single-car garage stalls, here in the trailer park, debris had nowhere else to go but out to the narrow lots, which were more landfills than lawns. He rolled past a rain-faded sofa. Buckled pallets and warped lumber. Pinwheels and garden gnomes. Tipped shopping carts. Pallid flamingos. Outdated campaign signs and naked flagpoles. Car seats. A mossy engine block. Fast-food wrappers decomposing with last year's autumn. A charred oil drum. There was something earnest about such barefaced disregard for order and outward appearances. It was so serenely desolate that it felt like a place where he could go unnoticed, unbothered, and so, for that reason, belong.

And then there was life—Michelle. Slumped in an aluminum lawn chair, she sat with her legs sprawled as if sunbathing, though she was covered in the same getup she'd worn every day back at inpatient: a hoodie zipped up to her clavicle, tattered blue jeans seemingly held together by an orthodontic arrangement of safety pins, and the same pair of Doc Martens, only now with laces running slack from their eyeholes. She'd since dyed her hair a peroxide blond, and a stripe of black roots ran like a flattened Mohawk down the part of her hair. She looked so resplendent that for the first time ever he wished he was creative, or artistic. Not for the sake of capturing this image in a painting or photograph for longevity, but to sing her praises. An ode, a tribute, a war cry, no—he wanted to write her a symphony.

He had to get his shit together.

When he beeped the horn, she stirred and shot him a grin full of that cool restraint he couldn't muster himself. Then again, she'd probably spent more time training her lips to remain pursed over her gray teeth. She folded the lawn chair flat, shoved it past the wood lattice brimming the underside of the trailer, took a bong rip, then set that behind the lattice, too. Pewter smoke oozed a hazy aura over her. As she approached, her loose-boot trot thumped with all the clunky defiance he remembered. The only flicker of timidity escaped when she tugged her sleeves past her fingernails, gnawed stubby and raw.

As soon as the passenger door shut behind her, he was slapped by her tart scent, now laced with weed. The sleeves drooping past her wrists reminded him of a praying mantis. In the bathroom mirror, he'd practiced saying *Hey*, aloof and unmoved, for a solid fifteen minutes. But now his throat was a knot, and so she spoke first:

"The fuck happen to you?"

"Huh?"

She rubbed his shaved head. "Kamikaze boy."

And that was when things went fuzzy, melty, even before they'd started drinking. She suggested they go to a place she knew just a mile down the road. Nothing special, a spot that catered to the weekend rush of out-of-towners killing time with lite beer, SportsCenter, and lap dances, while their wives and kids braved the crowds and hunted for bargains up the street. Since Michelle's older sister worked there, they could both get in and get served without getting carded. It sounded like a splendid idea, which Henry now said—*sounds splendid*—in total earnest and regretted immediately.

The foggy stupor Michelle's touch had put him in lifted, at least momentarily, when they first stepped into the strip club. The bouncer greeted her warmly, then openly snickered at Henry, calling him *kid*. Any glamor he'd imagined to be housed in this sort of establishment immediately proved to be just that: imagined. Besides the smears of flashing lights, laser squiggles, and disco ball refractions, the first thing he spotted was a long plastic picnic table lined with tinfoil dishes holding a lunch buffet's scraps, all of it glowing ocher under a scuzzy sneeze guard. A few women in plastic pumps clicked from one customer to the next, whose seated shadows were scattered in chairs as far from one another as possible. Baseball cap brims twisted after the women as soon as their backs were turned. A raised, mirrored platform jutted into the center of the space like a silver tongue. It was pinned into place like some huge, metallic specimen by a pole at its tip. The bodies of the women that strutted onto the stage were as imperfect, lumpy, and scarred as any he might have come across at a public pool, though this was his first time seeing a human being wearing neon dental floss in person. It was gloom in technicolor. He didn't want to get hard, but he did anyway.

The women all knew Michelle. With each new name and handshake, Henry made a point of staring intently at the spot right between their smoky eyelids, as if ignoring the rest of their bodies would somehow elevate him above the other men, those mere customers. Despite how foreign this place felt, he did find one familiar aspect, which did nothing to comfort him. In the eyes of every woman Michelle introduced him to, no matter how glitzy the eyeshadow or gooped the mascara, he found the same million-mile stare that dimmed Papa's gaze after a long day of work.

Luckily, Michelle's plan had been to drink on the patio outside rather than in the club, which felt like being trapped in a chain smoker's mouth. Other than the bouncer, the bartender was the only male employee. He was doing double duty, pouring drinks between playing MC, grabbing a mic to introduce dancers up to the stage. Henry felt as tense and mangled as his hard-on choking against denim. He was getting sick of small talk and nodding along while Michelle made the rounds, catching up with every last person on the clock, and, now—how marvelous—she asked the bartender about his upcoming arraignment. Henry hoped his strained smile wouldn't be taken for a cringe. He nodded and nodded as if nailing down his chin to prevent it from swiveling over to Charlotte, now taking the stage. When Michelle finally ordered a pitcher of Rolling Rock and two glasses, he made himself useful and slammed a twenty to the bar top.

$80.00

"Five bucks, youngblood," the bartender said.

"Then keep them coming." Henry left the twenty, gathered the stacked glasses and plastic pitcher, then followed Michelle out to the patio.

He really did try to pace himself on the first beer. He used each frothy ring left inside the glass to tally the rate of his progress. Thirteen sips in ten minutes. Seemed reasonable, responsible. Reaching for the pitcher, he wondered if maybe—just maybe—there might have been some logic behind the inpatient rule against patients sharing contact info.

The second slid down his throat as if of its own accord. After that he was cooled and golden and gave up counting foam rings in his pint glass or minutes between top-offs. The only measurement worth tracking was the number of inches between his knee and Michelle's, which he was monitoring through the black iron grating of the patio table.

"Dark in there," Michelle said. "Creepy, like."

"Mood lighting, I guess."

"Nah, Hen. Creepy as in morbid. You can pretty much hear them dying, strangled to death."

"Strangled? Who?"

"All them little dickheads. Getting choked out by waistbands, like. Ugly way to go."

For someone who hated the world so much that she deliberately expelled any nutrition it offered, Michelle sure had a good sense of humor. Dark, irreverent, and delivered with a tight-lipped deadpan, which only made him want to see that grim smile of hers all the more. She took a squirrel sip of beer, still her first. Henry had long lost count of how many pints he'd knocked back, but was pretty sure the pitcher—half-empty—was their, well, his second. Any lingering unease from the drive down and his first time in a strip club was ebbed away by the beer and the easy drift of their conversation.

Group therapy had been competitive, a daily pissing contest of adolescent suffering and survival, but here they could talk about their thoughts and selves without shame. Based on what she was saying now, plus the few snippets she'd ceded in group sessions or traded him in the TV room, he was beginning to stitch together a fuller sense of her history. Back at inpatient, personal milestones had been marked by traumas rather than the conventional sequence of graduation, college, career, marriage, mortgage, kids, and merrily, merrily, merrily, merrily, till death did them part. In Michelle's case, all the social workers and shrinks had made a hasty, concerted effort to fasten her two trauma milestones to bedrock. Number one: her mother had died in childbirth with her. This, she said, was what the professionals called *Bingo*.

Back when Henry first learned she'd lost her mother, a guilty thrill had rocketed through him, believing this might actually bring them closer. After group, when he'd pointed out their shared grief in the TV room, she sort of deflated. Gave him a sorry look.

"True," she said. "But at least I never met mine."

If she'd been suggesting you couldn't mourn someone you'd never known, then trauma número two made sure to acquaint her with sorrow. Her dad, like her mom, had been a gymnast. At first she described him as a walking paradox, but paused, then retracted the first half without explanation. He'd been top-heavy and toothpick-legged, kind of like a pasty, hairless Donkey Kong. Despite a racist streak and shitty grades, an athletic scholarship and persistent coach had gotten her dad through college, which later landed him a job as a high school history teacher, a post he'd only accepted so he could coach the gymnastics team. As considerate and attentive as he was with his athletes and the two daughters he brought to every after-school practice and off-season gym session, her dad was as mistrusting and bigoted. She snickered, saying he must have hated the

Civil War and the 1960s units, if not straight-up skipped them, like. Irregardless, she never got to see him in action in the classroom. The accident happened her last year of middle school.

Freak accident. A neglected springboard turned a routine vault demo into an unplanned Produnova. Lower spine broken—she could never stop herself from snapping her fingers whenever she told the story—just like that. The school district managed to eschew liability. Scrounging up the cash to lawyer up, let alone for surgery and the ensuing months of physical therapy, was a laughable impossibility. The sum of the workers' comp lasted just over a year before her sister had to start waiting tables. The three of them were barely able to get by on her sister's seventy-hour-a-week wages, even when they were supplemented by pushing some of their dad's pain pills. So, when a line chef jokingly suggested her sister put her parallel bar skills to work at the newly opened club by the outlet mall, she took him up on it. With their dad a breathing corpse in the bedroom and her older sister sleeping days and working nights, Michelle had been free to destroy herself as she saw fit.

Henry asked for one of her Pall Malls, hoping nicotine might kick him steady. This wouldn't have been the first time he'd mistaken damaged for deep. During those miserable, glaring moments of clarity, the cynic in him—the Papa in him—had been quick to spotlight his misguided tendency to romanticize anguish, as if only those bereaved or redlining in self-destruct mode had authentic, unfiltered access to the human condition, you know, like he did.

Didn't take too long to figure out that some addicts' compulsions were driven by sheer stupidity, boredom, or an utter lack of will power. Parental funds never hurt either. But as far as he could tell, Michelle was too sharp for boredom, didn't come from money, and the deliberation, resolve, and focus that her illness demanded actually struck him as a feat of the will, albeit pretty fucked up. At least before he ended up with his head in a toilet, he experienced a fleeting tickle. Some buzz or release, the nightlong vacation of an altered state of mind. Michelle, on the other hand, only got the sear of bile, the convulsions, retches, and gagging, as if streamlining the process, plowing a shortcut directly to the porcelain bowl.

She was efficient, his machete Michelle, and efficiency required intelligence, which she possessed in her own spit-shine way. Like her dad, she was a contradiction in motion. Gentle in tone yet cruel in humor, her simple prairie drawl dunking insults in marmalade. Timid with her hands swallowed in shirtsleeves, yet bold with her rod-straight, balance beam posture. Listen to her, barely eighteen but still holding her own, ping-ponging witty banter with Charlotte who, out on the patio, had introduced herself as Claudine.

"So that's it, the recipe for a sucker," Michelle said. "Testicles and a disposable income?"

"About sums it up, yeah," Claudine said. She had red hair and buck teeth and sat with her thighs wide, reclined in a pose much more masculine than Henry's.

"Lucky me—ha," Michelle said. "Hen here ain't got neither."

"Lucky you." Claudine eyed him, helped herself to the last of his beer. "It's a grind, girl. Not just shaking ass, staying in shape, moaning *daddy* into every man-child's ear like you mean it. This shit is psychology. Tell you one thing, some customers? Dudes that shell out for VIP rooms? They don't come just for ass, but ears. They'll drop hundreds just to be heard, listened to, noticed. Not as easy as it sounds. You try sympathizing with middle-age, self-sorry chumps for hours on end. And in heels."

Claudine paused, withdrew one of Michelle's cigarettes. When Henry lit it for her, he felt like he was on the right team, able to align himself with a worker taking a well-earned break. Although he wasn't on the clock and shared more biologically with the men, he refused to be seen as another customer, another sucker who had to pay not only for another human being's touch, but worse, her attention.

"I'm a therapist in a G-string," Claudine said. "But try putting that on a résumé."

"Could be worse," Michelle said, then fluffed her hair with a faux-sultry sway. "Ain't that right, *daddy*?"

Henry did not like that he liked this, that he was swooning. The Pall Mall hadn't stabilized him one bit. The sight of Michelle, the scent and sound of her, had gotten him swervy, woozy, drunk.

And the beer. Definitely the beer had, too.

"Right," he said, looking away from Michelle, the pitcher, and instead fixing his sights down to the tabletop's black iron grating. The diamond-shaped apertures started folding in on themselves like a monochrome kaleidoscope. He closed one eye, concentrated. The patterns shifted one last time, and behind their blur, right below them, Michelle's knee came into focus.

He grabbed it. Pulled it tight against his own knee, then bent himself as close to her as his spine allowed. He looked her in the eyes. He had so much to tell her but nowhere to start. He inhaled, and then it hit him.

He told her he wanted to write her a symphony.

"And I," she said, "want you to eat some chicken wings."

$43.00

The wings steadied his stomach, the cocaine his sights.

It was a night of firsts. First date, first strip club, and now, first time driving drunk. Even though the clutch had been too spongy under the dumbbell of his left foot and he'd killed the engine twice in the strip club parking lot, he was driving smoothly and for the most part straight, now that they were cruising in fourth gear. While Michelle had been navigating the way off the service road and onto an empty ribbon of asphalt slicing deeper and deeper into the plains, he concentrated on feeding the lane stripes into the bottom left corner of the windshield to keep from swerving.

He hadn't asked where Michelle was leading them since he didn't really care. Didn't even notice they'd pulled in to a drive-in theater until she yipped that he'd blown straight past the ticket booth. After the beer and wings and lines and movie tickets, he'd burned through half his budget and couldn't give half a goddamn.

The theater was a fenced-in field. Rows were marked by mellow tire ruts pressed into dead grass. He steered them up front to the spot farthest from the attendants and concession booth, windshield facing the screen. As Michelle went to dial the radio to the drive-in's AM wavelength, she suggested spinning around so they could watch from the truck bed. He cranked the gear stick into reverse.

Before backing up, he threw his elbow up to look over his shoulder and accidentally knocked the center console into its upright position.

"Ha," she said. "Lookie here."

The bouquet was smooshed flat, more paint splatter than floral arrangement.

"Who these for?" she said. "*Hhhmmm?*"

He went to run his hand through his hair, feeling all the more exposed when palm met scalp. Over the truck's radio came the voice of a cartoon bucket of popcorn, which was jitterbugging on the screen behind them. She tugged out a single flower, booped the crushed bud on his nose. Nubby fingernails pinched a petal, let it fall to the floor. Then another. Her voice was too flat to tell whether she was actually flattered or just blunting her digs when she started saying, "He love me, he love me not. He love me, he love me not . . ."

She paused at the last petal. Where she'd stopped in her fifty-fifty, to-and-fro taunt, only one petal remained between silence and verbalizing what Henry dreaded was the truth. He plucked the last petal himself, popped it into his mouth.

Chewing, he said, "Movie's starting."

It wasn't. The trailers were.

The tailgate dropped with a deep clank. When he twined his fingers to offer her a boost, she ignored it. She hopped up, both feet at once, then stretched her arms as if she'd just stuck a landing off the vault. By the time Henry'd hunkered up into the truck bed, her arms were still spread, only now in an accusatory flap. "You always cruise around with a linen closet?"

As if the roses hadn't been enough.

"So this your shagging wagon, huh?" she said, starting to pad the truck bed down with sleeping bags. "Big Henry's fuck truck."

He couldn't read her. Did she want an explanation? An apology?

She fluffed a sofa cushion, then plopped on top of it. "A pickup for picking up. Ha."

"Michelle, I'm—"

She brought an index finger to her lips. Winked. "Movie's starting."

This was a nightmare. He was plenty familiar with the agonizing rift between expectation and reality, but even his pessimistic bent hadn't accounted for humiliation of this scope. As he crawled toward the cab, he noticed the field of cars behind them, all facing him. How many strangers in all those vehicles had been watching him and his meltdown spectacle, far more entertaining than the opening credits rolling on the screen behind him? He situated himself against the other sofa cushion an arm's length away from her, since he was positive any attempt to approach her would only invite another crack.

Roses. Cologne. A symphony and a truck bed full of cozy-makings. Thank god she hadn't seen the condoms in the glove compartment. At this rate, it was only a matter of time till that embarrassing discovery was made as well. On top of it all, he'd gotten drunk, sloppy, too slogged down to even try to laugh or shrug off all his dinky stabs at romance.

"Hey," she said. "Ain't you cold?"

He was. The Baby Gap T-shirt had been ill-advised on more than one front.

"Then scooch."

She lifted the cover, and only then did he notice it was Mom's bese saka shawl. It must have been tangled up with the sleeping bags in the dark under-the-stairs closet. He couldn't back down now, so he wormed closer to her under the cover, bracing for another punch line. Almost winced when his upper arm grazed her elbow. She drew in a long, impatient breath, as if gathering steam. Here it came, but what now?

"What you doing?"

"I thought," he stammered, "you said."

She grabbed his arm with both hands. Lifted it up, over, then around her, setting his palm on the spade of her hip bone. She wound a leg over his, nuzzled her cheek against his chest. A faint patch of heat warmed his belly when she said, "Sure are sensitive, huh, Hen?"

"Am not."

"Are too." She pinched his nipple. The truck rocked.

"Maybe a little."

She was so compact in his arm. Less machete, more switchblade, and even though she scared him, it was so easy to press her tight against him. They were coiled so close it didn't matter that his question was softer than a whisper. "Promise not to tell anyone?"

"I don't promise shit."

She used a fistful of his shirtfront to hoist herself up. She kissed him. His neck was cranked into a painful angle, but relief wasn't worth screwing this up. His lips stiffened with the same mute idiocy as before, but she was persistent. Her jaw coaxed his lips to match the pace of hers. A tongue found its way past the ridge of his teeth, wriggled, prodding around almost curiously. His tongue was the only mushy part left of him. Every other tendon was yanked taut between the fear of both cleaving this contact and deciding what to do next. He held his breath, stuffing down an exhale that might waft her away. His lungs constricted and burned, his vision fogged, but he couldn't risk breathing, couldn't risk letting her go.

That held breath exploded in a snort. A gasp, then ragged coughs. As he wheezed through an apology, her hand dipped past his belt buckle and into his jeans.

A snicker escaped her. But this time it sounded more inviting, more playful, laughing with him instead of at him. Her fingers crept through bristle and lower still, then found him, strapped stiff against his inner thigh. She gave it a stern tug, as if trying to squeeze out any last hiccups of anxiety. It worked.

Scrambling blindly beneath the covers, he fidgeted at the buttons of her jeans until she helped out, wriggling her hips and stomping down rolls of denim with her boot soles. He dug past the curtain of her sweatshirt, and now, not only blind but clueless, he reached between her legs. The heel of his palm pressed against her pelvis. His middle and index fingers made exploratory strides, like a sprinter testing for traction on ice. When the pad of his middle finger found a ridge, a crease, the rest of him snapped rigid. He grazed her, as astonished by the damp heat it appeared he was provoking as he was terrified of somehow hurting her. He'd always shuddered when the skinnies referred to vaginas as gashes or hatchet wounds, but now he sort of got it, and so now he had to be gentle.

"Oh, come on," she said.

She smacked the top of his dainty hand, driving him inside her up to the webbing of his fingers. She gasped, let out a hungry groan, then bit his collarbone—hard.

He yelped. The sound went unmuffled by the movie's soundtrack since, so occupied by his earlier dejection, he'd forgotten to leave the truck's radio on.

"Puss," she said.

"Am not."

"Shut up."

She disappeared under the quilt, rummaging. An empty boot humped out from the covers, then another, and last the wad of her blue jeans. Wearing the bese saka shawl like a cape, she squatted over him, her twiggy legs so pale they were luminous. She spat into her hand, greased the head of his cock, then guided it into her. Clearly not her first time, and so he decided to pretend—no, prove—it wasn't his either.

Awe and pleasure were quickly swallowed by shock when he reached under her shirt and sandwiched her waist, his thumbnails and fingertips meeting each other over her spine and navel. She was so petite, but still he couldn't control her unruly sinew. He tried wrenching her in place to slow the hot-slick strokes she was making with her squatted hops, so he could last just a little bit longer, past the movie's opening scene at the very least. Her instinct was resistance, a rejection of his will—she pressed her hands flat against the cab's rear window for extra support, leverage, working him and herself even harder, even faster. With each thrust, she alternated between *Fuck yeah* and *Fuck me*, which wasn't exactly helpful in terms of prolonging this. As much as he hated her nickname for him, it sort of helped when she now sputtered, "Hen."

The truck bed was bobbing up and down and with it the huge screen flashing behind Michelle. A car chase was under way. To distract himself, to endure, he made a game of spotting banal details in the background of the frames, deciphering street and shop signs, or counting pores on the hero's nose during close-up, interior shots, while his abs clenched to keep from coming inside her. From other parked vehicles' radios came distant tire squeals, car horns, canned dialogue, but soon enough the soundtrack was overpowered by the creak of the suspension, coming in a delayed syncopation to the tide-like lurch of the truck bed.

"Fuck, Hen," she said. "You close?"

"T—to what?"

She moaned. "Me too."

She dropped from her squat, stapling her knees at the sides of his hips. She pressed her chest into his and clawed at his shoulder blades, while her pelvis kneaded and twisted, faster and closer and wetter and meaner, and then three loud knocks clacked against the side of the truck.

"Yo yo yo!" came a man's voice.

Henry's throat closed. To his left, a bald white man's face was floating over the brim of the truck bed. His head was turned away, shielding his view with one of those mini–battering ram flashlights. The motion had not stopped. Michelle refused to be interrupted. She buried her face against his neck, gnawing and slobbering, while her lower half kept thumping onto him, into him.

"Wait," she said.

"Y'all can't," the bald man said. "This a family establish—"

"*Wait.*"

She cupped her teeth around Henry's ear. Between pants she whispered to him, told him she was coming, that she wanted them to come together, she wanted him to come, come for her, Henry, come.

And so, staring apologetically at the bald man, Henry did as he was told. All his joy and worry exited him in a superb blurt. From deep in his chest came a bovine moan, and that, too, was otherworldly.

"Seriously, y'all?"

Something seismic racked Michelle. She shuddered, moaned, scraping at Henry as if clambering for shelter under his skin. After another shudder she collapsed onto his chest, her frame twitching with spastic giggles. He embraced her, turned away from the man and up to the sky, watching the screen's light bleaching out the stars.

"Lord Mary Joseph, y'all. I'm a have to call the police."

"Don't bother," Michelle said. "We're leaving."

$11.40

Henry spreads a towel over the motel carpet. Needs to remember the tag side is facing up and off the dirty floor, since he'll have to dry Junior off with this one later. The other is a soggy wad on top of the sick that the boy left beside the bed.

A pig is herding sheep on TV. Junior gives a pained giggle. Room 9's door slams. A new and deeper voice rumbles over the dogmonger's. Henry presses a button on the iron, unfurling a hiss of steam that momentarily washes out the muffled conversation next door. On his hands and knees, he sets to work on the dress shirt for tomorrow. The task reminds him of swiping a trowel over an inch-thick layer of sand, leveling a foundation before laying patio stones.

When he tries the shirt on, it's ironed so crisp it feels vaguely elegant against his skin. A debonair strangle when he fastens the last button under his Adam's apple. He closes his eyes to better recall the YouTube tutorial he'd watched over and over at the public library while he loops and snags the tie—a burgundy unwittingly matched to the motel room's decor—into a knot. The thinner bottom strip of fabric comes out longer than the top, so he tucks it between two buttons of the shirt. The suit jacket fits just fine, its vaulted shoulders making him feel bigger, stronger. He'd thought it physically impossible to lose more weight, yet somehow the waistband hangs even slacker at the steeples of his hip bones. His belt is too battered to wear to the interview, sweat-muddled and pocked with a row of holes driven through with masonry nails. A rough tally of every five pounds shed. If he leaves one hand casually tucked in the pocket, he can keep the pants hoisted in place. He'll have to hem them, though, so he tugs the cuffs up, steps back into his boots without socks. Before going out to rummage through his toolbox, he stops to check himself out in the bathroom mirror and is pretty sure he's never looked so handsome, so dignified.

He calls Junior to corroborate this, but the boy has dozed off.

A banged-up Astrovan, its engine still ticking, is parked between his pickup and the Mustang. Must have held a full load judging by the number of voices jabbering away in room 9. Henry unlocks the diamond-plated utility case and nothing inside offers anything in the way of tailoring. He clicks out four unclamped steel staples from the staple gun, then pockets the needle-nose pliers. Laughter snarls from room 9, followed by dog woofs of all pitches, all wet.

Even as he works on hemming the pants, he decides to keep the top half of the suit on, as if shedding it might disperse the earlier surge of confidence his reflection had provoked. Carefully he presses the staples through the folded layers of polyester, then cinches them into sharp, tiny bows with the pliers. After he irons the hem into a stiff crease, it doesn't look half bad. The beads of exposed steel are barely noticeable at the sides of his ankles. Trying them on, fully suited, armored, he's ready. In front of the bathroom mirror, he swells into the pitched cavities of the shoulder pads, and he knows that as of tomorrow, things are going to change, and this time for the better.

No more excuses. It is time for Junior to take a bath. At Henry's touch, the boy's eyes flutter dreamily, then stretch nightmare wide.

His voice is a handful of pebbles when he says, "Wow, Dad."

Henry doesn't correct the boy, because, yes. Right now, more so than in so long—if not ever—he feels like an American.

"You look," Junior starts.

Henry waits, billowing. "Yes?"

"So . . . I don't know," Junior says. "Different?"

Not exactly what Henry'd been hoping for, but it'll do. After all, what with the last six months, different can only be an improvement. Still though. Can't help but ask if Junior means that in like a good way or what?

The boy nods. "A very good way."

The bath can wait because first things first: Henry needs to hug his son. He scooches himself onto the bed, sets his shoulders against the headboard, then pulls Junior onto his lap. The boy is trembling, his neck and forehead sweat-slicked and radiating, and so Henry squeezes even tighter, this time truly convinced he can wring out this fever with his own two arms, his own two hands.

It's useless. Tremors keep rattling the boy no matter how tightly Henry twists the rope of his arm muscles. But a part of him is still coasting on that waning crest of pride, and maybe that's what helps him see that, in spite of everything, he's still got enough strength to hold the world entire in his tired arms. He squeezes and rocks Junior. His son, namesake, and legacy. The breathing token that irrefutably proves—against all odds and faults—that Henry's time on earth hasn't been entirely wasted. At least he's done one thing right.

On the TV a lanky farmer wearing a wool cabbie hat clamps the nipple of a baby bottle in between his teeth. He sits down on a sofa beside a sickly piglet, which sets its pink, runny snout onto the farmer's lap. An odd reticence between these two creatures, something like remorse. The cottage is dreary, the sofa shabby, and the snout veers away from the proffered baby bottle. Noon sun slices against the room's shadows, but the brim of the farmer's hat blocks the light, casting his face sorry, even a little scared. So quiet the shadows seem to creak. Then, with a voice like chalk, the farmer starts singing:

> *If I had words*
> *to make a day for you,*
> *I'd sing you a morning*
> *golden and true.*
> *I would make this day*
> *last for all time,*
> *then fill the night*
> *deep in moonshine.*

The farmer sings the verse one more time, his pillow-soft baritone gaining traction, conviction. A piccolo draws the farmer to his feet, both of which break into kicks, hops—a jig. Alone and exuberant, he stomps his heels, lifting dust from the floorboards and the pig's snout from the sofa. A merry swill of strings and brass climbs into a crescendo and then boom, launching the farmer into a triumphant, slow-motion leap through the air, and when his feet thud back to the floor, they plunge Henry's thoughts into a place so dark it's creamy.

Those lyrics have gagged him. Even if there were words that could make a day for his son, how could Henry ever expect to access them? Right now, with the boy shaking and sweating in his arms, it's impossible to locate even the most clichéd phrase of comfort or affection. It's been a battle to provide the barest of necessities, but now language, too? Any attempt to speak gets mangled by his lips, so instead they purse and kiss the top of Junior's head, ripe with a sour-milk musk. He embraces even tighter, tighter still, as if to absorb the boy into his chest and offer up his own health, his own heartbeat. The boy's done nothing wrong, doesn't deserve this. The boy—the birthday boy—deserves so much better, so much more. The child deserves mornings golden and true and glinting with opportunity. Nights like tonight. Nights of warmth, privacy, and safety, always and for all time, and deep in moonshine, which can't be seen—the motel room's curtains are closed.

Can't tell whether the curtains are drawn shut to keep that land of plenty beyond at bay, or else to trap him and Junior right here.

Henry is right here.

That's all he's got to offer, to promise.

That's the only truth he manages to pinpoint, then pin down. He wishes it could be enough, because it's all he can say, and so he does.

He goes to run a bath for Junior. Once the water's temperature is just right, he leaves it running to fill up while he's returning the iron. Won't be gone a minute. Again, passing the mirror, he catches himself, an impostor. The only other time he'd ever worn a suit was to Mom's funeral. Ever practical, Papa had insisted on buying a suit that was two sizes too large, so that Henry could grow into it.

In a dressing room cubicle, Papa tugged at the shoulder pads. Let them sift back down, an airy polyester shell over Henry's torso. Papa's rheumy eyes tracked pinches of the fabric, making measurements and predictions, sizing Henry up into the man-shaped mold he would eventually fill in to. Papa frowned with approval.

"See?" Papa said. "You'll be able to wear this to mine, too, ah."

Not that Papa had a funeral. In his will he'd stipulated that he wouldn't tolerate such a fatuous expense. Instead, he'd left it all up to Henry to decide what to do with his remains after being harvested for organs. But this is neither here nor there, because all that is here is this fool in the mirror, this fraud in a cheap disguise, its shoulders too vaulted, lapels too fat, the whole getup outdated, outsized, outlandishly pathetic.

Henry grabs the iron. Winds its cord like a bandage around his knuckles. From the front door he tells Junior he'll be right back and no ifs, ands, or buts about it—the birthday boy is taking a bath once he's done dropping this iron off, got it?

Out in the parking lot, he hears voices from room 9. The chatter has cranked into an argument. Too muffled to make out what it's all about. The voices are stitching over one another, a mishmash of vocal daggers. Threats. Henry will have to warn the billboard that she's got a situation on her hands. Maybe then she would move him and Junior into a different room.

Past the vending machine's dim glow, only more darkness. The office lights are off. The door is locked. No note in the window saying when she'll be back, just the see-through glint of his reflection. The face floating above this ludicrous costume is sneering, almost visibly considering taking this goddamn iron and driving it straight through the window, then helping himself to his rightful five dollars and—fuck it—whatever else he might find in that drawer.

A smack of wood. Behind him, across the way, light gashes out of room 9 and across the parking lot. Three figures dart outside and scramble into the Astrovan. From the room, dog barks join the dog-monger's screams, which are interrupted by a loud, abrupt burst. A few seconds later comes another burst, and then a final figure goes slamming into the Astrovan and slides its rear door shut. The engine chugs to life and the van peels away, barreling down the service road until the brake lights have shrunk down to cinders, then disappear.

Fear swiftly shifts into a violent clarity. A panicked focus activates Henry's legs and sends him sprinting back to room 8, to Junior, and just as he reaches for the doorknob, the dogmonger staggers out of room 9. The light behind the dogmonger is so bright, it looks like it's bending him over, both hands squeezing his knee. Henry's grip tightens around the iron, the cord slicing into his knuckles. The dogmonger steadies himself on the hood of the Mustang, then yells, "You motherfuckers!" to absolutely nobody.

Henry now spots the source of the two loud bursts. The last figure had popped a front tire on both the Neon and the Mustang, their front bumpers now slouching toward each other like a pair of last-call lovers.

At the scrape of key into lock, the dogmonger twists to Henry.

"Yo yo yo, hey buddy, hey neighbor man. Hold up a minute, just a sec. Come here."

Again, Henry barricades himself between room 8 and the dogmonger, who's hobbling closer and closer now, irises pinwheeling, the ammonia stink of him even more pungent than before. So close now, the jaw of the shrunken face jitters like a hacksaw.

"Back up," Henry says.

The dogmonger does the opposite. Another hunchbacked shuffle forward. His eyes yank wide when he tries fastening his jaw into a smile. "Hey, looking slick there. Real sharp, Mr. neighbor buddy. Say now, hey. Say, so I'm a need a favor."

"I said back up."

"I'm a need your truck a minute, see."

"Not. Happening."

The dogmonger presses himself off his knee, limping upright and closer, now only inches from Henry. The chemistry set stink of him singes Henry's eyes.

"Make it worth your while."

"Back up."

The dogmonger's voice lowers. "Give me them keys, bitch."

The rest of the dogmonger's body is sawing like his chin. Stench and loathing are boring a crater square into Henry's forehead. The drilling churns all his marrow and gore, heating him, ratcheting his grip around the iron. For whatever reason, Lucius slashes through his thoughts.

"Let's not get nasty. You don't want that. Your boy don't want tha—"

"*You don't talk about my son,*" Henry barks. "Now back the fuck up."

The dogmonger steps back. Shrugs.

"Hey, fine," he says. "Okay. All right."

Then, turning, the dogmonger reaches for something in his pants. Henry snaps.

It happens so fast that the crunch of steel into skull melds with the crumpling of body into gravel.

When Henry releases the iron, the bandaged cord keeps it swinging right below his fingertips. On the ground, the dogmonger's eyes stretch with shock. Black blood spills fast from a deep, crescent-shaped wound under the dogmonger's temple and begins trickling into his mouth, spattering as the man gasps. When he tries to stand, his limbs skitter like a crab on ice.

Panic claws Henry. He worms his fingers free of the cord, and the iron thumps to the ground. He squats over the dogmonger, shakes his shoulders, saying, "Look at me. Look at me."

The dogmonger's eyes dribble wildly, the rest of him twitching in weedy, erratic spasms. A female copy of the dogmonger, small-faced and hair like silly string, steps out of room 9. Her unblinking gaze springs from the gash to Henry to the iron and back to Henry. "Jesus," she says. "The fuck you do?"

"Call an ambulance."

A cough speckles red onto his suit sleeve.

The woman's pupils quiver in a rapid lateral motion, as if various interactions with the authorities are playing out right in front of her. She blinks, having reached a decision:

"Fuck that."

She disappears into room 9 and in seconds charges out with a plastic grocery bag tucked under one arm, the dachshund in the other. Room 9's door hasn't shut all the way, and now a pit bull's nose presses through the gap. The dog scuttles after the woman and manages to hump its way into the driver's door of the Neon before she closes it. Now comes a German shepherd, then a golden retriever. A Labradoodle. A Pomeranian. A boxer. A Shih Tzu. A Yorkshire terrier. A pug waddles out last, approaching Henry and the dogmonger. It takes a lap at the wound. Unimpressed, the pug trots off into the night with the others playing in the darkness, skittering out of the way as the Neon peels out, its flat front tire thumping over the gravel, then drumming down the service road.

When Henry props the dogmonger onto his side, a pistol slips from his waistband to the gravel. Henry kicks it away, then starts swabbing at the blood with the back of one hand, trying to reroute the black stream away from the dogmonger's mouth before getting Junior.

Inside room 8, the hammer of the bathtub faucet is deafening. The tub has overflowed, a film of water rippling over the linoleum and inching across the carpet. Junior is sound asleep. With his clean hand, Henry shakes the boy much rougher than he'd meant to.

First recognition then terror flashes over Junior, suddenly locked in Henry's grasp. Before Henry can apologize, the boy says, "I'm ready for my bath now."

"We have to go." He picks up Junior's backpack, wagging it like a TV lawyer would a damning piece of evidence. "Is this all you brought? Is this everything?"

When the boy nods, Henry lifts him by the armpits, sets him on his feet, straps the backpack onto his shoulders. It's quick work gathering his own belongings now that he's already wearing the suit. He shoves crewneck, socks, undies, and jeans into the duffel bag, and when he splashes into the flooded bathroom to shut off the faucet and rinse his bloodied hand clean, in this frenzied clarity he even remembers to snag the unopened tab of soap. He scans the room one last time, his own heartbeat replacing the thrum of the bathtub faucet. Their everything is so little and they've gathered it all, and so he lifts the boy up, pressing Junior's face into his collarbone, chest, pulse, telling him not to look, okay? Everything's okay, because Henry is right here.

"Don't look at what?"

Henry muzzles the boy's face against his chest. "Nothing."

Outside the gasps have twisted into a soggy wheezing. Still twitching, lying on his side, the dogmonger reaches for Henry, watching him open the suicide door and ease the boy onto the bench seat. After tossing their luggage over to the passenger side, Henry tucks the boy in, pulling the covers up into a full-face blindfold.

"What's going on, Pa?"

"Junior, listen to me."

"What's wrong?"

"Just close your eyes and keep them closed, okay?"

"Pa?"

Henry doesn't want to yell, and so through clenched teeth hisses, "*Please*." Runs a palm tinted pink over the boy's face, then drags his eyelids shut.

The inside of room 9 looks exactly as expected. Crushed Coors Light cans used as ashtrays line the TV stand. Any vacant surface is clouded white and smudged by fingerprint swirls. Bleachy smoke hovers by the ceiling. Gnarled bedsheets whiskered with fur. In the corner is a mat made of torn-out Bible pages drenched in dog piss. He finds the telephone on top of an upturned terra-cotta pot. Dials 911. Only rings twice. A woman's voice answers while Henry is still deciding whether to disguise his voice in a high or deep pitch, so his voice yo-yos when he tells her he needs to report an emergency. There's been an accident. A head injury. Bleeding really, really bad. Unresponsive. It was an accident, he swears it was an accident. No, he doesn't have an address, doesn't even know the street name. It's a motel off a service road about maybe three miles after exit four if you're coming west off County Road O. No name, just a sign that says motel and $39.99 and hurry because it's serious, it's bad.

"And your name, sir?"

"It was an accident," he reminds her, then hangs up.

Before darting to the truck, he peeks around the doorframe to check for the billboard woman. Across the way, at the rim of the vending machine's glow, the pug has mounted the Pomeranian. The boxer sniffs after their clumsy friction. Henry pulls the suit sleeve past his fingertips before lifting the iron off the gravel. When he tries wiping the iron clean on the dogmonger's pants, the blood smears thinner but not off. Frantic, frustrated, he lobs it into the truck bed to sterilize, dismantle, and dispose of later, somewhere far, far away.

$8,722.04

Everything, everyone had a price, and so this was Papa's. If this life insurance check amounted to the dollar-cent sum of nearly six decades of breathing, a solid four of which had been spent working, Henry didn't even want to know the heartless arithmetic that would one day crunch out his own price tag.

Even though it was Saturday, his body clock had still dragged him out of bed by 5:30 a.m., no matter how badly he wanted to sink back into sleep. He was turning into Papa. Before climbing out of their cozy nest, he sealed the covers over Michelle, ran a palm over the bulge of her tummy.

Rather than flip on the TV for the day's forecast, he watched the coffeepot fill drip by drip until it grumbled through its finale. Then, with the life insurance check clasped against a mug of black coffee, he toed the screen door open and took a seat on their singlewide's wood-latticed steps. Dawn's citrus matched the tart, sulphur smell of the gravel pits in the distance, the horizon line spliced by angling stalks of cranes and conveyor belts.

There'd been little time to grieve. Papa likely would have appreciated the bypassing of mourning rituals. The single-page, handwritten will, drawn up shortly after Mom had passed, simply named Henry sole executor, who could do with Papa's assets and ashes as he saw fit.

What he picked up from the med school's crematorium wasn't an urn. Just a container. Plain, cylindrical, white, slightly bigger than a Folgers can and much heavier than it looked. When he gave it a shake to assess its contents, his papa, he heard a little thump from within. Chunks of bone, he was told. Its label, printed in a mechanical, matter-of-fact font, spelled out Papa's name and three dates: birth, death, cremation. But before he could dig up the phone numbers of family members he'd only met once as a three-year-old visiting Manila, other phone calls started coming in.

A swarm of indecipherable legalese and not-so-subtle insinuations. The banks and collection agencies were demanding Henry take over Papa's unfinished payments and settle his debts, threatening repossession, probate court showdowns, and garnisheeing his wages. They were relentless, seething, foaming. Their persistence would have made even the most shameless, derisive, and downright slimy of the skinnies blush. After a twenty-minute conversation with an estate lawyer (billed the full hourly rate of $150), all the logistics and ciphers got distilled down to more comprehensible terms:

As executor, Henry was legally obliged to set his neck to the chopping block.

It tuned out that, following Mom's diagnosis, Papa had refinanced their mortgage into a home equity loan, the distinction of which Henry didn't understand other than that it now permitted lenders to collect payments from him, the estate's executor. Signing away his childhood home at a gouging loss was only the beginning. The lawyer had also explained that theirs was one of thirty states with something called a filial responsibility statute, which saddled Henry, the surviving adult child, with all of his parents' unpaid medical bills. This figure was mountainous. Mom's diagnosis had made Papa desperate, rash, and so no expense had been spared. Even after refinancing the mortgage, he'd signed off on tens of thousands of dollars, which he didn't have nor could ever repay, for whatever cutting-edge, experimental treatments were suggested by one referred specialist to the next. And now, on top of Mom's expenses—even though Papa had been pronounced dead on arrival—Henry owed another two grand for the ambulance that had transported Papa's still-warm carcass from a job site to the hospital.

After an estate sale, all that remained in Henry's possession were this check, the plain container, and his parents' library. The life insurance payout the collectors couldn't legally claim, the ashes and books they hadn't wanted.

The sun had climbed higher, rinsing the grapefruit dawn into a cloudless cerulean. The coffee had gone lukewarm. He gulped back half the mug. Sighed. Having survived the initial blitz of post-mortem duties that had distracted him from grieving, it only seemed right to dedicate this quiet, undisturbed morning to do just that. But when he wrenched his head space in the direction of nostalgia, fishing for memories and finally permitting himself to entertain all those hypothetical, never-to-be moments, he wasn't overcome by the same vacuum of despair that had sucked all color from the year following Mom's passing. Instead, what came was a pucker of guilt. Didn't seem right. The discrepancy between the degree of loss and anguish he'd felt for Mom compared with Papa's death now was so vast that his thoughts practically echoed inside him, like a penny down a well.

The problem was that Henry was happy.

In spite of Papa's death and the ensuing onslaught of digits relaying sums so unfathomable that Henry couldn't help but disregard them as nothing more than abstractions—impossible statistics like lightning strikes or lotto winning—the last three, four years of Henry's life had been, in a word, good. So much of this improvement was owed to the gradual mutation of the dynamic between him and Papa. The softening, Henry liked to call it.

The softening even had a start date: that May morning Papa had given him the truck and returned the first paycheck. Papa had even gone so far as to write three words Henry had never imagined he deserved, let alone would ever receive from the old man.

Proud of you.

The year after the buckthorn hustle, which had been clipped by a park ranger and a five-thousand-dollar illegal dumping ticket that exhausted all their earnings, Henry managed to graduate from high school. Even bumped his GPA up to a C average—insufficient to earn Papa's praise, but evidence of Henry's efforts, a gesture of gratitude and respect. Once he was available to work full-time, Papa got him a job with the contracting firm, under the condition that, come autumn, Henry would enroll in classes at the local community college.

The first two months of work had been the most time Henry and Papa ever spent together, at least actively communicating. Nine-, ten-hour days of Papa teaching him the tricks of the trade.

Before every demo, Papa would say, "Like this, ah."

And now, reminiscing, Henry finally found something specific to grieve. He'd never told Papa what a good teacher he'd been.

"Like this, ah," Papa said, showing Henry how to lift the guard and run a table saw to make quick notches in floorboards, to spare himself from unloading and setting up a jigsaw. How to feel for the copper twine between the teeth of a wire stripper, and to leave at least two inches of slack as a courtesy to the next guy who might be tasked with changing a light fixture. How to measure and set drywall quickly, without losing track of a stud's position. The seven-eleven rise-run rule for building staircases, and how to measure for a banister's bends and bracketing. How to safely connect and test gas, electrical, and water lines for stoves, laundry machines, fridges, toilets, and sinks. How to balance a level on top of a trowel, angling the grade until a third of the bubble was split, so that rainwater would run off a patio's surface and into the lawn. With his audiobook paused and headphones hooked behind his neck, Papa spoke to his hands, describing the technique and logic behind every step of a process, only to dismantle his work or fetch a fresh piece of material in order to let his son try carrying out the new task himself.

Working with his back and hands kindled embers of satisfaction in Henry, and not only on payday. Shifts at the grocery store had been a thankless monotony of restocking products in order to ensure perpetual convenience and commercial order. This work, on the other hand, turned his hours and efforts into final, tangible products. And nothing frivolous, either. The crew's and his own labor transformed dead space into havens of utility. Kitchens for feeding children. Balconies and patios for hosting friends. Sturdy roofs furnishing shelter from the elements, and under them airy bedrooms for listening to the rain. All of this motivated him to refine his craft and knowledge, inspiring an ardent concentration for Papa's demos and lessons.

Henry was a quick learner, always had been. Strong for his size and attentive to his coworkers, always there to relieve someone of a heavy load of concrete bags or offer a set of hands to clamp or press or give leverage for a tricky cut or awkward fastening. The foreman took note. Plus, since Henry had a truck of his own, he could be counted on to help with loads, disposals, and errands, and so, by that August, he was sent to work on other projects, away from Papa.

The crew usually took lunch on-site. If wheelbarrows hadn't been used for mixing concrete earlier that morning, the crew raced to claim one as a makeshift break-time recliner, their asses cupped in the buckets and heels kicked up onto the handles, half-napping as they ate bologna sandwiches, bruised bananas, and beef jerky, then washed it down with Red Bulls to motor them through the longer, hotter half of the workday.

That last Friday of working together, Papa hissed at Henry, who'd been making his way toward the others opening Igloo lunch boxes under the shade of an enormous white oak. Papa tipped his chin toward his truck and mouthed, *Let's go.*

They went to a sports bar situated at the end of a decrepit strip mall, seemingly the only establishment still in business. Exactly the type of place he figured Papa would have hated. Inside, the glare of noon was confined to the single front window, leaving the rest of the bar dark and stuffy. All the customers were men, workers on lunch taking thirty minutes to let the AC wick the sweat off their necks while staring up at muted televisions playing sports recaps and daytime talk shows.

"Long time no see, mister," the waitress said to Papa, pinching his upper arm. He almost smiled, blushed.

The waitress's left cheek was swollen, and in the fissures of her taupe foundation were slivers of plum, a bruise, yet her voice was melodic, upbeat, and perfectly suited to her pear shape and corn-yellow bob cut. Such affability after such abuse suggested a resilience that Henry both admired and envied.

"What're we drinking, gentlemen?"

Papa ordered a beer, which was odd. He rarely ever drank. And if that wasn't enough of a surprise, he then said, "My son'll have one, too."

A penciled eyebrow arced. "Just need to see the young man's ID right quick."

Henry stammered, but Papa was too engrossed by the slim menu and its three lunch options to vouch for his underage son.

"Teasing, sweetie." When she winked, her mascaraed lashes clamped like the teeth of a Venus flytrap.

Halfway through the beer, the softening was on full display. Papa's sallow cheeks tinted. A bashful grin escaped him whenever the waitress came by to check on them, and he'd begun speaking freely to Henry, stringing together sentence after sentence into complete thoughts, a full-fledged conversation. Initially, Papa stuck to his typical instructive mode, giving Henry tips for the first couple weeks of working with the other crew. Which guys deserved and would return respect, and which ones to steer clear of. When to ask for a raise, and which projects and met deadlines to mention in order to justify it. After wiping burger grease onto the lap of his work jeans, Papa paused to observe his palms. Then Henry's.

Though still instructive, Papa's tone cushioned. He began talking about how Henry needed to enroll in night classes. It was the only way out, an education. Yes, a lot had happened in high school, Papa understood that, but so long as Henry took care of his generals and got decent grades, he could later transfer to a state school, or maybe even somewhere somewhat prestigious to complete a bachelor's.

"And in something practical, ah," Papa said. "After all, you're pretty good with numbers, right? Imagine. My son an architect. An engineer. Perhaps something to do with computers, technology. The present, the future—relevant."

A wistful air settled over Papa. He twiddled with the headphones hooped behind his neck. Childlike, lonely. It then occurred to Henry how out of place the old man was in a joint like this, even while disguised in the sweat-stiffened denim of all the other working men's uniforms. How hard and dreary it must have been to stay here, stranded in flyover country now that the lifelines of companionship and his own aspirations had been severed so long ago. Among these plains of quiet, bite-your-tongue complacency, Papa was a cultural castaway. It seemed these hopes for Henry's future were the last shreds of driftwood that he could cling to as he waded along, then floated away.

Papa twisted his glass counterclockwise on the tabletop. Gave a gloomy chuckle, then said, "You don't want to end up like me, ah."

Michelle clacked the singlewide's screen door open. Her bare feet padded behind Henry. She bent, embraced him from behind, and two droopy sweatshirt sleeves flopped onto his chest. She smelled like sleep.

"What you got there?" she asked.

"Life insurance check."

Cheek against his, she squinted. "Almost nine g's, huh? Not bad."

"A drop in the bucket."

"Better than nothing." When she pressed herself upright, her belly grazed the back of his head.

"Yeah, no," he said. "Nothing."

Time to start shaping this morning into their day. The air inside was musky with Michelle's buttery farts. Pregnancy had made her gassy and irritable, and by now he knew better than to comment on either. With one fist pressed into her kidney and arching her back, she went through the kitchenette smacking cupboards open and closed, saying she was hungry, fucking starving, like, but they ain't got shit to eat so's they'd better head to the grocery store before she killed somebody. Then they could swing by the bank, too. It'd be a good idea to deposit that check and to, she didn't know, maybe talk to someone about investing it, like.

"Invest?"

She sniffed. From the side, her stomach swollen with their daughter had the same curve of a sickle. "Did I stutter? Take money to make money, and look who got some now, right?"

"All I got is debt." He waved the check like a white flag. Looked from the digits to their home, crowded with a fortress of brown boxes holding his parents' books. The maple two-by-ten planks that he'd cut, sanded, and lacquered last weekend were leaning against the wall next to a dense bundle of black pipe and couplings. "Debt and things to do."

"This your chance to get out of both, Hen."

He ignored her, started counting the hours it would take to finish the shelves this afternoon.

"You hearing me? You got to take risks to get ahead, Hen. Smart risks, like. Stock market, feel me?"

"You have no idea what you're talking about."

"More ideas than you. Just saying. Ask the bank." She grabbed the truck keys and her phone, then started heading outside. "Ask your friends."

"What friends?" he said, and the screen door slapped shut.

It wasn't that he didn't trust her. Far from it. Five months ago, when she'd told him she was pregnant with his baby, their little girl, he came here, straight to the bank, to add her name to his account, granting her full access. Not enough in there for a diamond ring or a wedding, but he could offer his trust and transparency and whatever his biweekly paychecks permitted, at least before the collectors finished bulldozing the nest egg he'd been assembling over the last couple years. Soon enough, all that would be left were twigs. Debris. Spittle. Not even that come this time next year, if he were to actually keep up with the monthly sums they were demanding. It was imaginary money. Digits on screens, ink on paper. And so that was precisely why he now decided not to deposit the life insurance check, but instead cash it. Not because he didn't trust her. No. It was just that he needed to hold it, needed to feel the dollar-cent weight of Papa in cold, hard cash before it was all gone, along with everything else the man had spent his life working for.

The bank teller had that impostor polish of a poor kid trying not to look poor. The type who'd been duped into believing good behavior and strong grades might get him a rung higher on the ladder, maybe even transport him to either coast someday, to anywhere other than the scorched quicksand of these plains he'd been so unjustly born into. The tilt of his pimpled chin and suspicious squint said it all. He really believed his clearance-rack tie and gelled hair made him better than Henry.

The teller made neat sprouts of the cash, hundred-dollar bills grouped in bushels of ten across the countertop. As he counted, his breath escaped in quick gasps, as if he were alone and talking himself out of a bad decision. Henry hated how willfully blasé the teller's expression was, as bored and aloof as the kid always seemed whenever Henry stopped by to deposit a paycheck, each one worth less than a tenth of the cash now getting stuffed into an envelope. The kid was acting as if he handled this amount of money on a regular basis with the impenetrable pomp of some high-roller, Monte Carlo casino dealer. The only hint of strain came when the punk struggled to wedge the four pennies into the bulging packet.

Henry paused to weigh the envelope in an upturned palm. Thought of the white cylinder holding whatever was left of Papa. Probably didn't weigh much more than this cash. Hard to know for sure, because a terrifying force seemed to be crushing down on it, down on him. He mumbled something.

"What was that, Mr."—the teller glanced at the computer for a surname, then went with—"sir?"

Henry unlatched his gaze from the envelope and aimed it, at the teller. He thought back to the time he'd gone to cash his first paycheck with Al. No bulletproof glass in this bank. There was a door made of steel bars like a jail cell, only cleaner, which he assumed led to a safe. It was open. He didn't own a gun and never wanted to, but his toolshed was stocked with all sorts of potentially menacing, life-threatening contraptions. A nail gun, hatchet, crowbar, or sledge-hammer would do—why even go that far? He'd heard of bank robbers armed with much less, like a candlestick to a guard's neck, a cell phone with a manager's kidnapped wife on the other end, even a deposit slip with handwritten demands. Turning to leave, he used the envelope to swat away such silly fantasies, and was still flapping it haphazardly when he joined Michelle in the truck.

He loved her for not saying anything. She took his hand into hers, releasing then regripping whenever he changed gears along the way to the supermarket.

When they parked, his field of vision took a nosedive, turning the supermarket's entrance into the precipice of a canyon. Didn't think he could bear the bombardment of products and bargains down below. Wasn't as brave as the other shoppers descending so casually after their empty carts.

He heard his voice shakily ask Michelle if she wouldn't mind running in there on her own. She agreed. When he pinched a Benny out for the groceries, her face showed a blend of awe and appreciation, and he felt slightly more steadied, centered, and loved her even more. She didn't say a word, though. Just flashed that mischievous grin of hers, the one she made whenever scheming something, but he was too tired, too emptied to ask what was lurking behind it today. She teetered over the globe of her belly, kissed him on the cheek, and took the bill.

$8,622.04

Minutes poured over Henry as if through a sieve, left him to dry, alone. Either time was lost on him, or Michelle had sprint-waddled through the entire supermarket in a flash. By the time her shopping cart came rattling up to the tailgate, the only thought he'd managed to process was that nothing short of bank robbery or a Powerball miracle could save them.

The way Michelle spent money certainly didn't help. Looked like she was planning a banquet. In the bags he began loading into the truck bed, along with eggs, bread, hot dogs, and other staples, he spotted a fresh-baked apple pie, three porterhouse steaks, and all the fixings for her homemade mac'n'cheese. If she hadn't pointed out the cart's bottom rack, he would have missed the case of beer, which he set reluctantly beside the rest.

"Any change?" he asked.

"Oh, right." She grinned and charged back to the strip mall, leaving him helpless against the automatic mental calculations of the groceries' total price. Even swollen with their daughter, she still marched with her shoulders curled back and mighty, ready to plow through crowds using her stomach like a cowcatcher, one hand resting on top of her belly while the other swayed behind her like a rudder. She disappeared into a tobacco shop, and after she reemerged, whatever she'd bought was kept stuffed in her hoodie's front pocket. When he asked, all she said was, "Something for Daddy."

"You mean Pa."

"Tomato, to-mah-to, motherfucker."

Henry wrangled all the grocery bags and clamped the case of beer under one arm to haul her entire score inside with a single trip. When he set everything onto the kitchen floor, Michelle went straight for the apple pie and a sweating tub of Cool Whip. She warmed a quarter of the pie in the microwave and plopped on a hearty dollop of cream, which immediately started melting down to a creamy puddle. Leaning over the sink, she attacked the pie with a tablespoon, nodding in approval. She rubbed her tummy, as if asking the baby inside if she were enjoying it, too. Watching her eat with such gusto made him feel as if things were just right. It was a feeling that, when he did encounter it, he wanted to last forever.

Seeing that Michelle had recovered from the illness that had brought them together in the first place, he wondered if she felt something similar whenever he passed on an offered drink or hit or line. Then again, those offers didn't come too often anymore. The two of them didn't go out a whole lot these days.

And why would they? Look at the home they'd built together over the last couple years. Even though they were only renting this singlewide in Indigo Hills, they'd put a lot of work into sprucing it up, using leftover materials from Henry's job to make it their own. He'd ripped out the stained gray carpet and replaced it with a patchwork of hickory, walnut, and mahogany floorboards. He'd swapped out the original fridge and stove for appliances that had been headed for the landfill after a flip. Sure, they weren't state of the art and didn't quite match in color, but were still a major step up from the smoke-stained, Sputnik-era appliances that had come with the place. He'd salvaged a beautiful slab of granite that had cracked during delivery to replace the Formica counter that had run between their kitchenette and living room. They'd painted the walls and decorated them by hanging up a splash of antique Salvation Army mirrors, not out of vanity but for the illusion of extra space. From the ceiling they'd hung a battered yet intricate chandelier that reminded him of a hockey player's smile. In the summer, he loved leaving the screen door propped, opening a direct sight line to a pergola made of cedar four-by-fours coiled in rope lights and the new flagstone patio, next to which he was already planning to build a swing set.

There were times he doubted whether he deserved such comfort. Like the bank teller, a poor kid trying not to look poor, Henry also felt like an impostor, merely posing as an adult. His history of self-harm didn't seem compatible with the innocent glee he drew from the tasks of domesticity, from picking out bedsheets and testing out new recipes to all their home improvement projects or falling asleep side by side without even having sex. Couldn't help but see them as a pair of kids playing house, a game he'd never previously played, let alone expected to enjoy.

But the ruse was over now. They'd been found out, and his old resolution to never be poor was dissolving. The collectors had snatched off their big-kid masks and come to levy all the dues of adulthood—plus interest.

An avalanche plunged through him. This frigid blast was either grief or terror or probably both. Michelle was scraping the last of the pie jam off the plate so intently that she didn't notice him shivering right behind her.

Losing Mom so early in life had taught him the impermanence of things, of people. Despite the ferocity of his love, it was never enough to turn the transient eternal, to harden flesh into forever. And so losing Michelle and all they'd built together wasn't merely possible, but likely. Recently, their daughter's approaching due date seemed to coax this natural fact, which had always lurked in the shadows of his mind, more and more often into his daytime thoughts.

He had to brace himself, fasten his grip against the odds, and so he now embraced Michelle from behind. One hand ran over her thigh, while the other began pawing for their daughter, to see if she might greet him back. Gently, he stroked Michelle's belly until it was met by a slight pressure. He was reduced to pulp. A stew of gratitude. Soon, very soon, once he could actually hold their daughter in his own two hands, he would be in possession of everything he had ever wanted, could have ever dreamed of—shelter, warmth, sustenance, company, purpose—and it was all so simple now. Only one thing to do: share this wealth with their daughter. She would want for nothing. She would live her entire life cushioned in all his tenderness, wading happily, forever and then some, in this abundance.

He used his forearm as a barrier between the baby and the edge of the counter as he reached into the elastic of Michelle's pants. He began kissing the nape of her neck and the sweaty, salted-caramel curlicues along her hairline. They made love like that, with her bent over the kitchen sink and his arm wrapped around her front, shielding their baby from themselves.

There was still work to be done. Michelle started on the mac'n'cheese, and Henry went for the sawhorses in the toolshed. Last weekend he'd prepped the maple two-by-tens, so all that was left for today was to bore holes through which to run the bookshelf's metal pipe legs. He placed the sawhorses behind the truck to hide himself from the street, even though the sound of the drill would attract the same handful of weary neighbors to lean on the truck's bumper, scratch under baseball caps, spit tobacco juice, and comment on whatever tool Henry was using. He locked a spade bit into the hammer drill, measured and penciled a plank, then began drilling, releasing a spray of chunky, faintly syrup-smelling confetti. It was warm for March, and he took off his shirt to sun his winter-paled back.

A moving truck hunkered past the driveway and deeper into the park. He hadn't realized it was already the thirty-first. Eviction day. Now with the hammer drill paused, he could hear a distant Harley, its engine working from a grumble into thunder as it drew closer. When the motorcycle rolled past, there was Sandi, the park manager, riding on the bitch seat, where she belonged. She and Henry traded scowls before the bike disappeared to join the moving truck.

All Indigo Hills residents were familiar with this routine. Soon enough they would take to the streets to hunt down the moving truck, trailing it like a flock of vultures. They would claim a spot along the curb, watching the movers, targeting the prime scraps, hoping for a showdown between the fresh evictee and Sandi, until they were given the green light. The instant the moving truck pulled off, they pounced. They rushed and scuttled, yanking at and bickering about the leftover belongings of a person—a neighbor—who'd just been ripped out of her home. Such brazen scavenging disgusted him, mostly because he understood the instinct so damn well.

Henry grabbed the boards to bring inside, and a passing neighbor waved. An unlit ultralight 100 bobbed in her lips as she commented on the getting's still being good. He wished her a pleasant day and let the screen door smack shut behind him.

The holes he'd bored out were tight around the pipes, making the work of leveling the planks with careful twists to the coupling pieces tedious, but after an hour the bookshelf was upright and set in place against the wall. When he told Michelle, "Hey, look," she shushed him. Her phone was shouldered into her ear to free her hands, busy slicing a tomato. She said something about nine stacks. He asked who she was talking to, but she ignored him. Brow furrowed, she said fine, she could come pick up whoever it was on the other end of the line. Would be a good chance for them to figure out just how exactly they ought to go about all this, like.

"All what?" Henry asked.

She folded the cell phone shut. Looked at the bookshelf and said it looked good. Banquet platters sat under hand towels on the counter, and a peppercorn of a fly somersaulted above the raw porterhouses. "Thanks," Henry said. "So what army you got coming by tonight?"

"Just Al." She took her car keys. "I'm a go pick him up now. Bonneville at the shop, brake lights busted—again."

He surveyed the feast. "Sure we'll have enough?"

After Michelle took off, Henry set the TV into the gap he'd built for it on the shelving unit, then began unpacking the boxes of his parents' books. Not that he or Michelle would ever read them, but they'd been his parents' most cherished possessions. There was something authoritative and smart-feeling about their presence, and they went well with the living room's look. Just decorations for now, but maybe one day their daughter would page through them, fill her head with facts and histories. A book fell to the floor, its pages open to the ceiling. In the margins were both his parents' handwriting, logging different responses to the same text. He kissed the page, felt silly, and so set it back on the shelf. He turned on the TV so he would feel a little less alone.

On the spines were the names of storytellers and thinkers Mom and Papa had studied, admired, and probably hoped Henry would too one day. He found one of the peer-reviewed journals that had published an article by Mom. The margins of every article except her own were ribboned with her tight, balloon-animal cursive. Knowing Mom, it'd probably been ignored out of embarrassment, similar to hearing your own voice recorded on tape. He read through the abstract and introduction, combing the scholarly jargon for a single glimmer of Mom's patient, sunshower voice, but to no avail. He closed the book and set it on the top row, where the fancier ones belonged.

By the time all the shelves were filled, there were still another two crates left to unpack. Henry sifted through the boxes, trying to remember if he'd seen any of these dust jackets forked in front of his parents' faces. There were too many. Again he scanned the names already on display, hoping these were the right ones, those who had inspired or challenged his parents the most besides each of their all-time favorites: Keynes, Marx, and Rawls for Mom, then Baldwin, Nabokov, and Bulosan for Papa.

It occurred to him what was missing. A name that merited a prominent place for display. Next to the academic journals holding Mom's work, he tugged out four hardcovers. In this fresh gap, he placed the white receptacle holding what was left of Papa, carefully turning the cylinder so his name appeared alongside all the others.

Michelle and Al clomped inside, laughing. Al wore a shiny red tracksuit that hung baggy off every inch of him except where it strained over his stomach like a sunburnt manatee. The pant cuffs were tucked into a pair of yellow, unlaced Timberlands that had seen better days. To conceal his receding hairline, he'd shaved the rest of his dome. Almost gave him a tough, thuggish look, but from eyebrows down, his face was as rosy and earnest as ever. He framed his stubby teeth in a smile before booming Henry's name.

Al hugged Henry into the damp cushion of his torso and took a deep sniff as if reveling in the scent of sawdust. "Fuck me, dude. Been a minute, huh?"

When Al released him, Henry saw what he'd suspected: Al was strung out. Couldn't stop fiddling, couldn't stop jabbering, saying how awesome it was to see Henry, the both of them, he meant, duh. How it'd been so long, way too long and, hey now—lookie here—that bookshelf was new and sure looked good, real good, dude, and then he flopped onto the couch while his eyes zipped around the singlewide in search of other recent projects or touch-ups, the game he played anytime he came over and—

"Goddamn, them steaks!" Al hefted himself back to his feet, wiped his nose on a sleeve, tonged up a porterhouse, and told nobody in particular to fuck him if these weren't the biggest motherfucking steaks he'd ain't never seen.

"Who wants a beer?" Michelle said.

"No thanks," Henry said.

Al side-eyed his friend, then corrected him. He used a Bic to pop open both bottles. Henry looked from the beer to Michelle, who gave him a go-ahead nod.

She sent the boys out to the patio to catch up and get the grill going. After Henry unfolded lawn chairs, Al crashed into one. He squeezed the armrests, reconsidered, and popped back up to thump a slab of flagstone with his boot heel. He lit a Kool, paced, sniffed, coughed, twisted a pinkie in his ear, inspected it, then flicked. All the fidgeting was making Henry anxious, so he did his best to look occupied as he poured coals into the Weber's gullet. After a few sips of beer, he realized he hadn't put anything in his belly all day besides coffee. With his stomach empty and alcohol tolerance at a virginal level, he welcomed the boozy glow. Even took a hit of Hennessy from the fifth Al offered to help speed things up.

It'd been months since they last saw each other. The two had drifted apart when things heated up with Michelle, back when Henry traded his old habits for this new and all-consuming addiction. Other than the occasional crack about being pussy whipped or getting old and going square, Al didn't appear to resent Henry's withdrawal from the skinnies, plenty distracted by all his side hustles and comedowns. Whenever they did get together, Al chatted and laughed with Michelle in the same easy, goofy way as ever, and Henry was glad the two got along so well. But once the nights got late and Al's eyes went from glazed to bloodshot, sometimes Henry would catch Al staring at him with an odd melancholy, which stood in queasy-making contrast to his otherwise jovial dopiness.

As for now, it was still early and Al was in full swing. He drained his first beer quick and called up to the kitchen window for another. Henry tensed, knowing all too well how Michelle responded to taking orders, from men especially. However, she not only obeyed, but also came out with a second for Henry, as if encouraging him to drink. He accepted it, even though the first was still half-full. Shrugged, because fuck it. Might as well drink. Didn't look like he'd be getting a word in edgewise anytime soon.

Alternating between pulls of beer and the fifth of Henny, Al was all revved up and blathering about his newest hustle with a skinny named Rodney, a stuttering, shifty-eyed bastard whom Henry felt he could sure as shit throw a lot farther than trust. The one time Al had brought Rodney here, every one of his stammered comments about Henry and Michelle's home seemed laced with a bitterness that struck Henry as a nasty breed of envy. Al and this Rodney had a pickpocketing thing going, working the commuter trains into the city. Al served as lookout and emergency muscle for Rodney, who slithered his hand into purses and pockets. Decent take from the cash, plus the gift cards they spent on electronics and whatnot to pawn along with the pinched cell phones across the state line. But the slow burn, the long-term investment, Al explained, was selling credit card numbers for these bid coins on the internet or something—Henry hadn't quite made everything out, his attention already ebbing from the alcohol. He rubbed his eyes as Al joked about still being broke for now, since whatever cash he made from the wallets or pawnshops went straight to rent, into his belly, or up his nose, and but, hey, come to think of it, did Henry want a line?

Al swabbed the film of grime off the truck's hood, then poured a tiny white hill from a vial the size of a bullet. Right then Michelle kneed the screen door open, carrying the platter of steaks and a bottle of beer. Henry cleared his throat, sidling between the powder and her sight line.

"Go ahead, Hen," she said. "Deserve a treat after all this month's shit."

Then Al began saying fuck, over and over, and flung his arms open for a second hug. Said he was so sorry about Henry's old man, and even more sorry he hadn't said anything yet, condolences and shit. He lifted the fifth to pour one out for Papa, paused, then spilled out some beer instead. He called Papa a damn good man, said they sure didn't make them like that anymore, that was for goddamn sure, and Henry himself wasn't exactly sure if he'd been nodding or shaking his head as he approached the truck, twisting a Benny into a tube.

The line produced a gust of clarity, like a hairdryer to a steamed-up mirror. He tipped his head back and let the numbing silt drip from his nasal passages down into his throat, passing the tubed bill to whoever wanted the next sniff.

Michelle manned the grill. Al was making a commendable effort to cede some stage time, asking about the pregnancy and all, saying if she hadn't asked the ultrasonic technician nurse lady about the sex, then how come Michelle kept calling it their daughter?

She flopped a steak over, spurring flames. "I can just feel it, Al. A woman got a sense about this sort of thing. Instinct. Not that you'd know anything about that."

"Okay, but hypothetical speaking—just asking—so but what'll you do if it's a boy?"

"Then that's Henry's problem," she said.

"But seriously, though," Al said. "You got a backup boy name just in case?"

125

"I don't know. Name it after Hen for all I care, but it's not happening anyway, so shut up." She took a sip, and only then did Henry realize the last beer she'd brought out had been for herself.

"The fuck, Michelle?" he said, snatching after her beer.

She peeled away, middle finger lifting off the bottleneck. "It's fine. Relax. Just one."

"For real, dude. Chill," Al said. "My ma was toe-up the entire time she were pregnant with me and look how I turned out."

"My point exactly."

She looked from Al to the bottle, set it down, then netted smoke with the grill's lid, covering the meat and flames.

Once the sky settled from blue to bruise, the rope lights glinted like chubby fireflies caught in the grain of the pergola beams above. Henry'd given up counting the bottles and lines, letting himself unwind and chuckle at Al's stories about close calls and long nights, and when the steaks were ready they all agreed it would be best to eat outside for the first time this year, even though Henry hadn't gotten around to building any patio furniture yet. He had an idea, though. He'd been collecting leftover retaining wall blocks to eventually install a raised garden at the front end of the singlewide, so he made laps from the pile behind the toolshed and carried one sixty-pound block at a time back to the patio, until he'd stacked four into a rudimentary table in front of each of their lawn chairs. It felt good to move and sweat a bit before sitting down to dinner, made it feel earned.

The steaks were so big they barely left any plate space for sides. Al balanced two dinner plates on his block tower, the first dedicated entirely to the porterhouse, the second loaded high with mac'n'cheese, a dinner roll, and a few leaves of lettuce. A hush fell among the three of them as they all began eating, the sound of their chewing and swallowing indistinguishable from the spring evening's thrum. The bloody muscle char was so delicious it had an almost stupefying effect on Henry, dulling the crisp awareness the lines had brought him. He slouched against the backrest to take a break between bites, bummed a Kool off Al, who then skipped back inside to load up on more macaroni, the lettuce untouched.

The full-belly serenity was disrupted only by an almost audible sense of gratefulness, a crackling, electric current that threatened to bolt through Henry all night if he didn't channel it toward the appropriate recipient, and soon. Reclining, he listened to his own voice thanking Michelle for the wonderful meal, as well as Al for the company and cocaine. Sure meant a lot to him, the world to him, to have everything he could ever ask for and, most importantly, these two beautiful people to share it all with. He was the luckiest son of a bitch that ever lived, he told them, and hearing this self-evident truth stunned him into silence.

While his mouth had been motoring in autopilot, his thoughts had been meandering unchecked, off to somewhere murky, dark. A jumbo screen ignited against the black of his eyelids. It glared and pulsed and scrolled through the inventory of his friendships, accomplishments, and hopes. Smack center he saw himself, minuscule, earthbound, but nevertheless a man. A man who had everything, which sure was a whole lot to lose.

He shuddered. Blinked himself back to the patio. Shakily, he rose to collect the plates and start on the dishes, but Michelle took them from him.

"I got it, Hen. Stay out here. Al got something to tell you." When she leaned in for a kiss, their baby brushed against Henry's arm.

Al was in Buddha mode. Lips drooping in moronic bliss, a hand stroking the red planet of his stomach. Michelle kicked his shin. "Right, Al?"

"Right right right. Leave one a them plates out here, though." Al mopped the grease up with a roll, popped it into his mouth, then poured out another white hill to gun them through whatever it was he had to say.

"Drink up," Al said, and so Henry did.

The fifth clanked back down to the concrete table. Lines were sniffed. Al dabbed a finger into the puddle of meat juice and across the dust, then swiped it along his gums. Leaning forward with his elbows on his knees like a football coach, Al made a spearhead of his hands. His voice lowered even though there was no way Michelle could hear them over the thrash and clatter of water and dishes, even though it'd seemed she already knew what Al was about to say.

So Michelle had filled Al in about the debt, this whole responsibility statute bullshit. She'd also told him about the insurance money, the nine bands. Now, see, there was an idea he'd been working on since forever and, if Henry was interested in chipping in on a down payment, they could turn it into something serious.

Henry's teeth were sawing. He pinched his jaw still. "How much we talking?"

"Dude." Al lit a Kool. "By my math, I'm thinking like a hundred."

Henry snorted. "How?"

And now Al inflated, drum-rolling his thighs. It was all about the downers now, dude. Kids were dropping the same amount of cash on a single oxy that would get them a half gram of smack, but everyone was all fuck needles now, fuck the '90s. Nowadays smack had the same rap as meth or crack, but literally everyone was down with pills, from trailer rats to suburban brats and all the way on down to their bored-ass moms. Motherfuckers couldn't get enough of them, but the scrip game only got you so much and demand was high, sky high, fucking outer space status, and so what Al was trying to say, long story short, was that he'd finally gotten his hands on a pill press. Ordered it off the Silk Road. Been tinkering around, mixing up a recipe to color the inositol—just this white vitamin B powder base—so the pills were like that Lucky Charms marshmallow green. Finally got it down to a fucking science, dude, last batch turned out exactly, and he meant like *identical* to, eighty-mil oxys. Windshield wiper fluid and yellow food dye, who'd a thought, right?

Thing was, Al didn't have the cash to pick up the substitute, filler drug, fentanyl, at least not weight. Already got a plug up in Canada who could hook up a quarter kilo for just ten bands. That was half the going price, typically eighty k a kilo, and the craziest part was—he

128

meant, but did Henry have any idea how many pills that would make? Only took ten mcg's, twenty-five for the long-gones—and that was mcg's, not milli- but *micro*grams to match the punch of one oxy. That would come out to oodles, dude, a fucking butt ton of merch. And plus he'd heard of a heavy hitter in the city who was always looking for bulk. Nobody to fuck with, though, otherwise Al would a just fucking gone for it, sold a load of blanks and run away to Mexico or some shit. But this fentanyl shit fucked you up just as good as any oxy or codeine or morphine or whatever, actually probably even like better, so this guy wouldn't never be getting no customer complaints, feel him? All this was fail-safe and foolproof and now was the time to get the ball rolling, Al said, then sent a stream of menthol out of his mouth.

"Only coming to you with this because I love you, dude."

"And because I got eight bands in my pocket."

"Michelle said nine?"

"Almost," Henry said. He thought of the dissolving resolution, of the nest egg in the bank, and accidentally told Al it could be ten if need be.

"Fucking a." Al raised the fifth.

"No," Henry said. He moved the plate from Al's block tower to his. Sniffed another line to keep his head straight and mind made. "Not doing it. Thanks but no thanks."

"Why not?" Al's voice tweaked into a child's whine.

"You joking?"

"You see a clown nose? A water-squirting flower on my shirt, here, dude? I'm dead-ass serious and want to know why not."

"It's illegal, for one."

"Says the slope ex-meth-head," Al snapped. "Sorry. Too far."

The faucet inside had stopped. So had the clank of plates and jangle of cutlery. Henry turned away from Al, sick of this fat bastard's racist cracks and half-baked get-money schemes. Michelle stepped out, watching from the steps with her arms crossed on top of her stomach, standing in the exact same spot she'd found Henry drinking coffee this morning. Felt so long ago now. A faint recollection, the kind you couldn't be sure was true to what had actually happened, or was just the memory of the last time you'd remembered it, tones embellished by nostalgia, edges smudged by time. At this point, all he wanted was for Al to shut up and fuck off, so he looked up to Michelle as if for permission, or backup. Her posture straightened. Although she bore no resemblance to his mother other than the wet-cigarette color of their skin, the expression she made now reminded him of Mom. Of the sad-stern tilt of her head whenever Papa was lecturing or yelling at him, her way of silently telling the boy to be patient, to please just wait and hear the man out.

Al reached over, squeezed the top of Henry's leg. Drew a zero with his thumb on Henry's inner thigh before letting go, sighing.

Who did Henry think Al was, huh, dude? He ought to know by now that Al would never, ever do anything to put him in danger, because, duh. Al got it, knew Henry wanted jack shit to do with the game, and Al didn't blame him one bit, what with a baby on the way. And that was exactly Al's point. He wanted to do this for his friend—his best friend—to get that little family of theirs going on the right foot and forward, and so Al would take care of everything and still split the score right down the middle. Fifty-fifty, because fair was fair. He would drive all alone, all the way up and back from Canada to pick up the gear on his own, no biggie. Would measure and press every last pill himself, if Henry weren't cool with helping out with that either. Al would even make the drop-off over in the city solo if he had to. All he needed was the cash to get things going, but from then on out he could keep this shit moving along on his own, unless, of course, Henry ever wanted back in at some point later on down the road. But for right now, one step at a time, dude. Baby steps. Little baby-girl baby steps.

$11.40

The Astrovan, the Neon, and the dogs have all fled into the night, so what's stopping Henry? Truck at a standstill. Engine gurgling in neutral. Right boot eases off the brake pedal. The truck humps over the slope's network of tire ruts as it crawls toward the service road, toward anywhere but here, and then his boot stomps back into the brake.

A lurch, a wobble, stillness.

Henry tilts the rearview mirror, aiming it over by the Mustang where he's left the dogmonger. Too dark and far to detect any sign of movement, and so he angles the mirror to check the bench seat behind him. A heap of blankets, shadows. Hooded in Mom's shawl floats the pale oval of Junior's face, all dreamy and feeble. Henry reaches back to stroke the boy's hot cheek, tugs the shawl over his mouth like an outlaw's bandana. Not sure whether it's the thought of Junior seeing him do what he's got to—what he can't not do—or if it's the sight of the boy's face itself that Henry can't bear. Could be both or neither, and either way he throws the gear stick in reverse.

The truck hobbles, backing up the slope. When it swings around, the beams spotlight the dogmonger, sprawled under the Mustang's front bumper. Everything that'd happened in the heat of the night and smear of the shadows takes on a garish veracity, a beyond-a-reasonable-doubt lucidity.

Only a matter of minutes till sirens cast everything in a strobe light of crimson and cobalt, cobalt and crimson. Questions and handcuffs and Henry promised he would never, ever go back. But something won't let him leave. Won't let him flee like the dogs and the others, like he should, like he must.

A stomp, a creak, and the emergency brake meets the floorboard.

He can't step out till this grisly scene, rocking in the headlights' glare, steadies.

He can't soften his footfalls against the gravel. The blood so black before, now illuminated, is a fire truck red, and there's so, so much of it oozing from the divot in the dogmonger's gored face. The eyes of this sticky red mask are stretched into white ping-pong balls that lock onto Henry. Pupils dilate when each attempt to speak only escapes as a retch. No language needed to articulate this shade of fear.

Something rustles.

A hand lifts. At first Henry recoils, expecting a punch or throat snatch. But the fingers are spread, weak and trembling and almost pitiful, working through the air toward Henry's. As if to say please— please don't leave me. Not like this, not alone.

The dogmonger's hand hovers there, quivering, imploring the comfort of his assailant's touch. Henry sighs. Tugs a sleeve past his fingertips.

Cuffed in stiff cotton, his hand is a dull, cumbersome pincer. It pokes into and rummages through the dogmonger's pockets. First it finds a Bic. A crumpled comet of receipts and gum wrappers. A flip phone. A smartphone, too. Careful to keep his fingertips covered, he rolls the dogmonger onto his side. The dogmonger is beyond protest. Just makes a weak gavel with his heel against the ground, and then a second pistol, a snubnose, slips out of his boot. Henry can't risk touching it let alone taking it to pawn tomorrow. No wallet square in the back pockets. First one empty. In the other he finds keys latched to a severed rabbit's foot dyed clover green, then a single dollar bill rolled into an unfurling tube, which is the only thing he takes before leaving.

$50,000.00

Didn't seem fair, didn't seem right. Not the legal implications, or compromising some sense of integrity. It was the ease of it that rattled Henry.

He and Al were back in the truck, safe, unscathed, pulses slowing and palms drying. A minor victory when the trembling key slid into the ignition and the engine turned, its grumble melding with the crinkle of paper as Al reached inside a brown grocery bag.

"Here's your half," Al said, and that was that. With this commonplace gesture, like passing a diner menu to a stranger, Henry's callused hands cradled five bands of hundred-dollar bills. Fifty stacks. Half a hundred grand. It had heft. Girth. A paperback Bible cut in half.

And it'd been so easy.

He and Al had put in the hours but hardly the sweat. Maybe a few icy shocks of adrenaline, but not a drop of the tarry perspiration of manual labor. After he talked it over with Michelle, it hadn't sat right with him—making Al do all the prep on top of running all the risk—and so every day after work and over the last two weekends, he'd gone over to Al's to help measure and press the counterfeit oxys. All twenty-five hundred of them, and then some. Even though Henry hadn't been able to work up the nerve to drive to Canada and then cross back over the border with a quarter kilo of pure, powdered fentanyl, packed in a catalog envelope with a strained red string, he hadn't been able to let Al make tonight's handoff in the city alone. Despite the risk, or perhaps to protect their investment, Michelle had assured Henry it was the right thing to do.

The trap house was a ninety-minute drive away, set on the farther, eastern edge of the city. From the elevated freeway that bypassed downtown, the distant skyline was jagged, inflamed. The spires at

Mom's old campus were hangnails, the stadium's low dome a wart. Girdling them were buildings that didn't quite scrape the sky, just chafed it. All together they formed a carbuncle, a sawtooth horizon ready to ooze.

Henry locked the truck's doors before taking the exit into the industrial rim, where all-glass condos gave way to smokestacks and long-abandoned factories. As they rolled past block after crumbling block of row houses, Henry imagined their previous punch-clock inhabitants. Lifelong careers on assembly lines. Secondhand staring monotony. The daily shuffle toward obsolescence. This must have been why Papa had wanted Henry to study, then later see his son in an office wearing a suit instead of a tool belt, sipping from a logo'd mug instead of a thermos, working on a laptop instead of on his hands and knees.

But Henry would never have traded the serene desolation back west for a life in this concrete hive. Here, packed so dense, contagion by the parasitic more—more assets, more status, more brand-name validation—would have been inescapable. Even if off-the-clock lifestyles varied, labor was universally in service to the insatiable pit of industry and commerce. Same difference in the end. Whether by shovel or spreadsheet, everybody had to dig.

Duplexes ran in columns as uniform as a military parade. The trap house was identical to the others except for a white Escalade bulging out of its tight driveway. Al winked at Henry before poking the doorbell. An immense, pasty man wearing a beater and a blank expression let them in. He was so big that the double-barrel shotgun looked almost toy-like in his grasp. A second glance confirmed that it'd been sawn short, and Henry's ass went swampy.

Al, on the other hand, was a mellow bulb, entirely unfazed when his hand went un–high-fived. On the drive into the city, he'd insisted on sampling their product yet again. Quality control, dude. The dose had left him so calm that when a pat-down revealed a .38 in his waistband, he practically purred when telling the pasty man to keep it safe for him.

The duplex was unfurnished except for some folding chairs circling a stack of wooden pallets. That was where the pasty man set Al's piece, after he'd opened the chamber and tipped five rounds into his baseball mitt of a palm. All the while Henry was busy flexing and straightening himself to come across as hard and crime savvy as humanly possible, though he was fairly certain the rest of him was as visibly mushy as his boxers.

But once they took a seat, the exchange had been painless and quick. Professional, even. As daunting and ruthless as Al had made this urban drug lord out to be, the man who joined them on the folding chairs was, in a word, ordinary. No jailhouse ink, battle scars, or gold-capped canines. Just another white guy in an oversized polo and flat-brimmed baseball cap. Might as well have been headed to the ballpark, where he'd order a hot dog, plain, with a Diet Coke.

While another guy counted the pills in a back room, the ordinary drug lord offered each of them a Corona, which he failed to open after a number of whacks against the pallet. Al got the bottle caps off with a lighter and began chitchatting about the weather, mutual acquaintances, gas prices. In no more than ten minutes, Al was handed a paper grocery bag that looked suspiciously light, but, sure enough, held the ten bands, all in Bennies, and so that was that. He clapped, chugged the beer, and said it was about time they got on their merry way, gentlemen, but it'd been a pleasure doing business with them. With that (and Henry cowering at his side), Al sashayed to the front door and wagged the still-empty snubnose in a wave good-bye.

The palm now on the steering was as slippery as the other tucked in Henry's lap, squeezing his half of the cash and leaving a slimy patch on the bills' edges. Al turned the radio on full blast, lolling his head as he dispatched cackles and whoops. Henry eased off the gas, coasting them back under the freeway's speed limit. As he came to terms with this new reality, this abrupt prosperity, a strange urge rose inside him. Over the music's blast, he asked Al if he could hold it.

"All of it," Henry said. "Just to, you know, feel it."

For the full religious effect, he pressed the other five bands tight against the cash already tucked in his crotch. Blood rushed to meet it. He was racked by tremors of pleasure, of power, and—as if catching a scent—Al drummed the truck cab's ceiling and released a sorority-girl squeal.

It was still more than an hour's drive back home, and so Henry accepted a white bump off Al's house key. Little to no effect, since he was already gunning it in celebration mode. A night in wouldn't do, so he flipped open his phone, texted Michelle, told her to put on something nice.

At the beep of the horn, Michelle stepped out onto the front steps and into the headlights. She never wore makeup or heels or her hair down, but tonight her eyelids were dusky, her feet perched in stilettos Henry'd never seen, and her hair swept over one shoulder in a lush cascade. The way the shoes arched her back, extending her huge, pregnant belly, pressed her into a regal stance. She looked like a movie star. Better. She looked like Christmas.

To accompany her properly, Henry dashed inside to change. Unfortunately, Papa's suit measurements had been off, way off. Henry had long outgrown the funeral suit he was supposed to have grown into, and so the most formal thing he owned was a once-white button-up. It was veined with wrinkles, which flattened smooth where the fabric clung to his sprouting potbelly. Unwilling to part with the cash, he stuffed the five bands into the front of his pants, pressing a row of ledges into the shirtfront.

They went to Red Lobster.

By the time they got there, the dinner rush had cleared out, imbuing the empty franchise with a note of VIP exclusivity. Before even reaching the table, Al told the hostess to send over a bottle of their finest champagne, which was out of stock, and so they settled on martinis. Those glasses were plenty fancy, Al assured them. They draped themselves over the chairs like they owned the place, their chatter loud and their laughter swilling in the air like burning butter. Too riled up to read their menus, they simply agreed to everything the waitress suggested, and by the second round of cocktails they were gorging on peppercorn-panko calamari, mozzarella sticks, jumbo coconut shrimp, buffalo chicken wings, two servings of crab legs, three rock lobster tails, a twelve-ounce New York strip each because why the fuck not, and then washing it all down with gin and olive brine and a bottle of whatever the white wine was called that the waitress had said would complement their spread. Peering over the debris of crushed shells and chicken bones, Henry didn't say anything when Michelle sipped from Al's martini glass. Not even when she accepted Al's vial and waddled off to the ladies' room, because tonight was a celebration. Tonight they were invincible.

When dessert came, Al leaned back into his vinyl throne and lit a Kool. The serving staff paused from divvying tips to watch as the manager approached. The bill was delivered with a nervous rap on the table, and they were told there was no smoking, please? It was well past closing time, and, as much as their business was appreciated, maybe they could settle up and finish their evening somewhere else? If they wouldn't mind?

Al's eyes floated up to this disturbance. The butt corked his smirk into a pucker. He sucked, dragging till his cheeks folded in over his molars and the cigarette smoldered down to a teeny elephant trunk of ash.

Blew.

Ash fell to the floor without a sound. Behind the cloud, Al's cheeks were stoplights.

"Okeydokey." The cigarette hissed in a cone of gin. In a British accent he said, "Shall we?"

"Let's."

Henry stood up and immediately collapsed against Michelle's chair. This gave him the idea to help slide her chair back from the table, but the unexpected chivalry sent her straight to the floor. The three of them erupted, cackling like senators, tycoons, gangsters, and, as he peeled her off the ground, Al withdrew a drum of cash. He flicked bills into the air and over the plates, shells, and bones. Henry paused, watching a bill drift and twirl, a dead leaf in the breeze. His thoughts leapt to his sixteenth birthday, the twenty-dollar bill for bus fare a sudden anvil in his lap. Then to his hopeless appraisal of Papa's dollar-cent weight, after he'd cashed the life insurance check. Something new was blazing inside him, a power. The strength to incinerate their burdens, to reduce doubts to ash. Cinders. Soot. Bone. But before he arrived at an idyllic locale to finally spread Papa's remains, Henry's elbow was hooked, and the trio stagger-strutted their way outside.

After a pit stop at the liquor store, they stormed into the single-wide with a bottle of Dom Pérignon and one of Jack Daniel's. Al offered them each a pale green pill. Only Michelle accepted. She smacked her mouth and dry-swallowed before Henry could send a protest through the haze of seafood and booze, but really, what did it matter? One little pill of basically the same shit the doctors would be pumping into her veins once her water broke couldn't hurt. Even though he'd passed on the downer, he was greedy with the lines, after Al pulled a mirror off the wall and whitewashed their reflections with the rest of the vial's contents.

They popped the champagne and drank it out of jelly jars, still gauzy where labels had once clung. The bubbles disappeared as quickly as the pill took hold of Michelle, making putty of all her edges and pressing her deep into the couch. Her head bobbed to and fro, and she smiled, giggled, and then, almost timidly, asked Henry if she could see it. Touch it, like.

"Can I watch?" Al said.

"No, you perv," she said. "I mean the money. The cash, like."

To see the exact same urge take her confirmed everything for Henry. They were made for each other. They were puzzle pieces.

"Of course you can."

Henry slid down to the floor, kneeled at her feet. Pride boomed in his chest as he lifted his shirtfront and stacked the bands on top of her belly with the sort of hushed reverence that the pimply bank teller could never understand.

At first the tremors that rocked Michelle worried him, as if she were shivering with fever, but soon came a dreamy snicker. Past droopy lids she peered down at the flat bricks of cash. She took one, fanning the bills so they grazed the tip of her nose. A long sniff. An even longer sigh.

Still kneeling, he set his ear to her belly, listening for a heartbeat amid the gooey hum of incubation. His arms snaked around her. Again, she sniffed. He asked her what it smelled like.

"Like," she whispered, "kind of . . ."

She was molasses. He was combustion. He was roiling, scalding, aching to hear her say the same words that were swimming through him. Words like *freedom* and *power* and *love*. How beautifully they would ring in her voice. He closed his eyes and amid the darkness came a thumping. Their daughter's pulse. A slight pressure pawed into his cheek.

Al made a hog's snort and his head ricocheted from the mirror's surface. Plugging his nose, he forced a sneeze into a retch. "Probably smells like fucking money, dude, duh."

"Yeah," she said, her voice receding, a rowboat coasting into still, black waters. "Money."

Eventually the Jack overpowered the lines and caught up with the pill that Al had popped. The three of them were slumped together on the couch, Henry in the middle, drunk but still drinking, since at this point there was no point in stopping till oblivion. The only light came from the muted TV, supported and encased by rows of book spines looking like some foreign, upright masonry. Thousands of pixels flashed in tandem to assemble a man in an all-white suit with skin the color of a football, flapping fistfuls of gold necklaces so frantically it looked like he was gearing up to take flight. The yellow cords transformed into a treasure chest overflowing with cash, a phone number flashing over it like a distress signal.

A flint scraped. An orange tulip appeared at the tip of Al's cigarette.

Michelle was snoring lightly. Her geometry fit perfectly against all the happy slabs and hinges of Henry's own body. Here in the warm confines of his home, with his best friend beside him, the nine bands of cash heaped on the coffee table, and the tenth tucked into his waistband for safekeeping, he was complete. He wanted nothing, absolutely nothing, and what a luxury that was. A blessing he couldn't wait to share with the baby, whenever she decided to come join them. Should be any day now, really, and for the first time since learning Michelle was pregnant, he truly felt ready for their daughter's arrival.

A new weight met his shoulder. Al had shifted, slumped closer. A woozy, almost smitten expression dripping over him. He mumbled something. Only the second time around did the mutters take shape. Twice now he'd told Henry how much he loved him.

"Love you, too," Henry said. It hung funny in the air, and so he added, "man."

A meaty hand, still pinching a Kool, slid over to Henry's knee. The cigarette was jutting upward when the fingers dipped, squeezed into Henry's inner thigh, then caressed.

Henry didn't recoil. Didn't speak. Maybe it was the sense of completion that relinquished his will. Let come what may, whatever. Maybe it was the booze or drugs or money or their combative chemical reactions that fired a rush of blood below his belt, where he again stiffened against the brick of cash in his front pocket.

Al's fingers had begun crawling deeper into Henry's lap. They met an obstacle, the cash, and paused, as if rallying to mount this inch-high hurdle. Henry shifted, neither closer nor away, just deeper into the sofa, lowering the threshold. Al's fingers took their cue, stepped onto the brick one by one. They stroked the cash beneath the denim. When they met the slight rift between the brick's edge and Henry's cock strapped rigid against it, they tittered, playfully tracing this rousing boundary. Al nestled closer, released a sigh pumiced hoarse by exhaustion or longing.

"This what rich must . . ." Al started. "I mean, fuck."

Henry waited.

Al gathered himself by kneading the cash and Henry, the rift between them imperceptible now. "Just saying," Al whispered. "This is what it must feel like to be rich, huh?"

Henry scoffed. He reached for Al's head and pressed his own back into the cushion. Eyes shut, chin lifted skyward, he said, "Nah."

"No?"

"No," Henry said. "This is what god must feel like."

$12.40

A night without sleep.

From the motel, Henry had driven miles and miles, sinking the gas gauge needle into the red to bring them to this remote riverside park. Its parking lot sits at the bottom of a steep wooded gully, blocking it out of view from the main road. After mummying Junior in the covers, as if to both entrap heat and subdue the tremors, Henry took off the suit jacket. Hung it on the handgrip over the busted-out passenger window. A headless ghost hovering in his periphery over the course of all these stretched-thin minutes that keep compounding into one hour after another. Hours meant and needed for rest instead wasted away on squirming and writhing and souring the truck cab.

He needs to be rested, sharp for tomorrow's—today's—interview. But when he clicks the backrest one notch closer to Junior in the backseat, the hoods of his eyelids invite carnage. All of last night's gore replays even more vividly than when it'd been floodlit by the headlights. Steel into flesh. Human weight meeting gravel. Blood blacker than red. Pupils soggy with fear. Wheezes unable to flee with the dogs into the night. A hand quivering, reaching, ignored.

At least he'd paid in cash. No digital trail, let alone a receipt. Sure, the billboard lady wouldn't have any trouble spotting him in a lineup, but Henry shakes that possibility out of his head, because it's never going to get to that point in the first place. He's got things to do, a promise to keep.

The fever has Junior drifting in and out of sleep. Whimpering, mumbling, now saying please to someone Henry can't see.

It's a full nelson. A stranglehold wringing his larynx into a stir stick. He wrangles his torso as if clamoring in a straitjacket, and humps onto his right shoulder. There it is again, the suit, headless and hovering. His jaw is sore after hours of clenching to contain whatever it is that's broiling inside him, maybe a bellow, or a plea.

The dream starts with a rustle. A squirming beneath the polyester, a scrambling for escape. Michelle's chin jabs up then hooks over the shirt collar. She peers straight through Henry, wearing that same drained, faraway expression she assumed after all that had happened happened. Foggy and bloodshot, blind to what's right in front of her. Just a mask of herself, its sharp chin now thawing, bloating into jowls. Strand by strand, her hair sweeps then falls, a final breeze uncovering a scalp, hairless and the color of an undercooked pork chop. The expression remains distant, but now dims with dejection. Even after all these years, Al still can't bring himself to look at his friend. There's no forgiving Henry—not after what he'd done—but even still, he thrashes awake and clears his throat so he can apologize, out loud and in total earnest, to a thrift store suit, here in his truck.

Dawn glints in the cracks of the foliage above. As Henry opens the door, crisp morning air rinses the sour stink from the cab but not off him. He drapes a washcloth around his neck and makes his way down a winding footpath through the woods leading to the river. If this park wasn't a two-gallon drive from Junior's school, they would spend more nights here. On top of the slim chance of getting caught trespassing after hours, it's so isolated that the DNR doesn't bother padlocking a concrete shed with stainless steel basins for the night. A rare 24–7 bathroom. Don't bother cleaning it too often either, but privacy and running water are a fair trade for disinfectant. Inside, it's dim and damp and reeks of wet leaves and tart urine. No mirrors, no toilet paper, and today no hot water knob. Broken off since their last visit. The stripped, exposed bolt won't turn in his grasp, so he splashes frosty water over his face and neck until his skin prickles firm and numb, before soaking the washcloth for Junior.

Back outside, his muscles go as taut as his skin. He is not alone. A presence, someone watching. He swallows his breath as he creeps along the path, peering between trees to scan the parking lot. The truck waits alone. Behind him, still nobody. He tells himself to quit being so paranoid. Get it together. Breathe in, and then a fierce bleat sends him jumping.

A crow announces itself with a caw. It slaps out of the branches and into the sky. Next thing he knows, he's craned his neck and begun jogging after its airborne trail toward the river. The bird's beak stabs straight forward, never dipping to check for its own reflection in the water's surface. By the time Henry gets to the muddy banks, the crow has flown so far it's a freckle, shrinking off to someplace Henry can't but wants to follow. He crumples to his knees, panting, his chest blistering. Abandoned. Earthbound. Landlocked. His breath and temperature cool according to the river's flow. Its churn is soothing, inviting, and so—this time absolutely certain he's alone—he screams.

Motion resumes. The river is flowing, the crow keeps shrinking, and Henry is still right here.

When he turns the engine, the gas gauge needle floats up only to sink back into the red. He turns the heat on full blast. Drapes the soaked washcloth over the vents. As it heats up, he leans back, nudges Junior. Says it's time to get ready for school.

"Mommy?"

"Just Pa."

Henry takes the rag, not quite hot but better than the faucet's ice, then kills the engine. Reaches over the backrest and under the covers to unearth the boy's face. Flushed. Gaunt. The fever sheen exaggerates the valleys under his eyes. Working the tab of motel soap into a lather, he asks how his big eight-year-old boy is doing this fine morning.

"I didn't finish my homework."

"Uh-oh. Can you get detention for that? Suspended, or—don't tell me—expelled?"

The boy is unamused.

"C'mon. Let's get you cleaned up." Henry reaches for Mom's shawl, but Junior pitches back.

"I don't think I can go to school today."

"Why? Because of your homework?"

"I'm sick." He tugs the covers up. "I'm sorry, Pa."

"Junior, buddy," Henry starts. "You know how important today is for your pa, right? For both of us. You got to tough it out and go to school, so Pa can do what he's got to, too, okay? And I know you can, because you're tough. Know how I know how tough you are?"

The boy shakes his head.

"Because you're eight now, that's how."

The boy is trying not to cry. Before he can say anything, Henry beats him to it, snatches something off the floor. He lifts the boy's birthday present, arranging its plastic limbs into a bodybuilder's flex.

"Need you strong as Randy Savage today. I mean, do you think a little cold ever stopped the Macho Man, huh? C'mon. How about showing me those big-boy muscles?"

Two twigs creep out from the covers. Bend.

"There's my tough guy." He grabs a wrist before it can retreat again and shucks the covers aside. The boy's cotton pajamas are darker, sweated through and vacuum-sealing his frame. A damp stain on the bench's nylon might pass for a shadow, except it doesn't mimic its corresponding body's shivers. After pulling the boy into the front seat and peeling off the pajamas, he drapes his withered, naked son across his lap. Lathers Junior's hair first, massages his scalp, then squeegees the suds down his neck to scrub his back. Finds an odd tension when extending the boy's arm, limp yet trembling. He hands over the rag, so much of its heat already lost, telling the boy to get his feet and weenie while his pa fetches some clean clothes, okay?

Skull still reeling from the night. Has to steady himself against the truck bed, and then he sees it. He's shocked that his thoughts haven't once whipped to the iron, sitting right here on top of their garbage-bagged belongings. The fog of dawn has lifted. Maybe the morning sun has shed some light and restored rationality. If rivers are good enough for corpses chained to cinder blocks, then this one's got to be as good as any for this potentially incriminating domestic appliance.

A soaked-dog shudder. Imagination running wild, galloping para-noid and pessimistic. The dogmonger will be fine, he tells himself. He'd called an ambulance. It'd been an accident.

Still though. Always smart to play it safe. He tugs the crewneck's sleeve into a mitten over his fingertips. Then, just as he grasps the handle, a Subaru comes rolling down the dirt road and into the park-ing lot. A haggard stranger carrying a clothing iron down to the river at the break of dawn would look pretty weird, so he stuffs it under a Hefty bag full of clothes. Across the way, a white man in mesh run-ning shorts steps onto the hatchback's rear bumper, dipping into a stretch. While waiting the jogger out, Henry goes through Junior's bagged wardrobe, sniff-testing T-shirts. They all smell of play and grass and Royal Pine air freshener.

As Junior dries off with a blanket and starts getting dressed, Henry pretends to be looking for something in the truck bed, steal-ing glances at the jogger, willing him to get on with his workout and disappear down a trail already. Time is tight. They've come a long way from town and still need to get gas before heading to school. But the jogger has traded the bumper lunges for some Caucasian version of tai chi, so ditching the iron will have to wait.

They stop at the first gas station they come across. After send-ing Junior to brush his teeth in the bathroom, Henry toggles the pump, putting exactly five dollars into the tank, which, at $3.23 a gallon, only gives him another twenty-two miles or so on the high-way, about eighteen in town, and the trip to school alone will sink the gas gauge needle right back where it started this morning.

Stepping into the Spee-Dee market is a tie-dye shotgun blast, all the posters and packaging an assault of colors. Every last pack of chewing gum and bag of potato chips, on down to each single-boxed condom and jug of windshield wiper fluid, is nauseating. Junior shuffles out of the bathroom, toothbrush in hand and looking shell-shocked. He turns to a rack of prewrapped breakfast sandwiches, lured to the heat lamps like a moth. When Henry approaches, it's as if he can actually smell the maple bacon, the pepper of spicy sausages, and the biscuits' buttermilk seeping through the greasy wax paper—one for $2.50, or two for $4.00. Can't swing it right now, not if he's got to pump another couple bucks into the tank later. Still hasn't forked over the boy's lunch money either. The spit of bacon in a skillet cracks through him. He flinches, twists, then spots a case of ninety-nine-cent muffins and doughnuts, but even one of those can't quite be justified right now. Puffs of enriched flour and granulated sugar are just empty calories, when what they really need is some nutrition. Vitamins and protein. He steers the boy from the heat lamps and toward the counter, before asking if he's hungry.

Junior grips his tummy. "I don't know."

On the checkout counter is a basket holding red apples and over-ripe bananas. Henry sifts for the two plumpest bananas of the bunch. When it's his turn to pay, he reconsiders. Returns the second to the basket.

"Big enough for ya?" The teenage cashier is wearing eyeliner and enough hairspray to style every male head in this buzz-cut county. His voice is gentle, lonely. Something like pity jabs at Henry, thinking about this kid growing up out here, like this.

But he's got no flirt in him at this hour. Just reaches into his pocket and says, "Never is."

$0.01

It was enough to put the world on pause, moments like these. Their two-month-old baby boy sleeping belly up, caterpillar fingers dabbing after dreams, tucked between Henry and Michelle. The two of them were a pair of parentheses, an afterthought tag team devoted to guarding this miraculous comma born of their own flesh and love.

A hiccup of calm, of clarity. A merciful respite from the mental and emotional bedlam brought on by these new responsibilities, this new life. Besides these crystal moments, few and fleeting, the thrashing was constant. Henry was drowning in a vortex of dearth. Never enough money, then never enough patience, energy, or sleep needed to scrape together a pinch of the last. Not so much a vicious cycle as a perpetual toilet flush.

So this was parenthood.

He had to check himself. Catch himself. Clog this whirlpool before he was fully submerged in angst and self-pity like he'd been as a teenager, before meeting Michelle, and well before becoming a pa. After all, for the first time in his life, he had a damn good excuse, if not a full-blown reason, for being. Their baby fattened his days with meaning. But even though he'd found his purpose, he still hadn't located his place. All his griping for more and never having enough—he was asking too much. Because, pretty much certainly, acquiring an external and objective purpose was way more than anyone could rightfully demand, let alone expect. Who on earth didn't want more money, more energy, more sleep, more everything? He had to remind himself this was already far more than he deserved. Had to shut up and get to the task at hand, just like everyone else.

Still though, there was a bone to pick—then snap—with the nature of time. These days, every glance at his watch was a slap. All the hours spent at work and away from his family stretched into a vast and arid grassland for him to crawl across. But once he did make it to the other end, precious minutes at home were reduced to winks.

After each sleep-starved night of infant rocking and feeding and cleaning, leaving for work in the morning felt like fleeing. A man on the run with a price on his head. Constantly looking over his shoulder had begun robbing him of immediacy and presence, whether at work or at home. Tasks as simple as leveling base blocks and fastening diaper straps were now a foreign arithmetic. Hammers and baby powder containers leapt from his grasp. He was overlooking steps as innate as penciling tiles before cuts, or turning on the coffeemaker after he'd loaded a fresh filter. Withered minutes meant a withered him.

Today he hadn't gotten home till seven. After dumping his wallet, phone, and a splash of change onto the nightstand, he'd flopped facedown in bed without undressing and—just his luck. It felt like a teaspoon was stabbing into his thigh. He'd missed a single coin in his front pocket but was too dead to fish it out now. Evidently, Michelle was just as beat. Not a word, not even a reproachful squint, when her eyes fluttered over his sawdust-stiffened outfit on top of their new baby-safe duvet.

Even wrung out by the day, she looked lovely. Hair bunned into a frizzy tumbleweed. Palms folded under her cheek as if in a sideways prayer. He asked about her day.

"*Ssshhh*," she said. "Baby's sleeping."

He pointed his chin to the crib, offering to sneak the baby into it. She shook her head, and he was glad. Didn't matter if this moment wouldn't stretch to his liking. However short-lived, the bounty on his head—all those robbed hours and dollars due—was forgiven here, for now. This bounty, in the other sense, was something to revel in. Here was the sum of his efforts—his family and home, his world entire—all right here and within arm's reach.

The crib was a fresh artifact of their recklessness. After Red Lobster, they'd let the good-times boulder keep rolling. They continued splurging, because they'd earned it. First, they'd forgone the local Walmart and instead driven three towns east to pillage a Target's baby department. They filled two carts with a wardrobe of onesies, booties, and bibs, to be washed separately with a jug of odorless, infant-safe laundry detergent. A breast pump, milk storage containers, tubs of organic milk-based formulas, and a stockpile of cold-pressed, additive-free produce purees. An on-the-go changing bag made of leather finer than any purse Michelle'd ever owned, each of its suede pockets to be stuffed with ointments and creams, disposable wipes, and a portable changing pad. A plastic bathing tub for the kitchen sink, a soft-bristled hairbrush, and microfiber towels. A bulb syringe, mini–nail clippers, thermometer, and pacifiers. A state-of-the-art stroller, to which they could mount its accompanying and equally sophisticated car seat. A crib worth five times what they'd paid for their own bed. Then Henry'd told the cashier to charge him for and send out a pallet of Huggies in ascending sizes.

Next they'd gone to replace Michelle's clunker. He'd initially wanted to get her a convertible, but the reality of potential catastrophe changed his mind. Michelle and their daughter would need a tank, maybe an Escalade like the heavy hitter's back in the city. But after she'd refused to drive anything bigger than their home, they settled on a gently used Saab, which the dealer swore had a frame reinforced by freight train–grade steel to protect Swiss drivers from two-ton reindeer wandering onto fjord-side highways and all, believe him.

Neither of them had health insurance, so they did their research and set aside five grand for the delivery. Then they hit a casino to scrub the remaining stacks down to two halves. The first was a bundle of cash in less-conspicuous denominations. The second was a cashier's check, which, within forty-eight hours, had vanished as a five-figure scoop into his filial responsibility–statute dues. With the last of the cash in smaller bills and so larger bands, Henry'd been scheming a visit to the park manager, Sandi. But just as he'd finished counting out enough to both catch up on back payments and pay off next year's rent in a fat, fuck-you wad to plop onto her desk, Michelle's water broke.

The it's-a-girl cigar hadn't been the only surprise.

Nothing could have prepared Henry for such horror and gore. Right before his eyes, Michelle was being split from the inside out. It was torture. As she panted, pushed, bellowed, shrieked, and cursed his very existence, he was utterly helpless to assuage her pain, or steal it away to endure in her place. And worse, in the delivery room he was only an obstruction, always in somebody's way. Like a buffoon, his contributions consisted solely of echoing the nurses' orders and squeezing Michelle's hand when it wasn't clawing him away. Not only was he useless and impotent, but all of her suffering—*Look what you did to me, you rat bastard!*—had been entirely his fault.

If guilt and futility hadn't sufficiently crushed him, then a new word made quick work of sending him to the floor, down where he belonged. At hour twenty-two, a nurse said something about an episiotomy. Briefly, he wondered how any theory of knowledge could reconcile such prolonged physical torment, until a pair of shears was handed to the nurse. She gave them a test clip in the air, ignoring Henry's pleas for just a minute, a second, a definition, and then—*snip*—he fainted.

The fall resulted in four stitches, a CT scan, and a moderate concussion. The following day, after coming to in a hospital bed next to Michelle's, he had to determine the runner-up for most flagrant shock of this ordeal. A toss-up between the internal wildfire emblazoning a new and horrifying capacity that'd been sparked by the first time he held his baby ("A *boy?*—a boy!"), or the hospital bill.

The miracle of life was as gruesome as it was pricey. After Michelle'd braved twenty-six hours of labor, an emergency caesarian, and an extra night for recovery, they were well beyond their researched budget. Exhaustion did nothing to blunt her anger for Henry in the next bed, whose pansy ass had not only missed the birth of their son, but also blew up their hospital bill with his little tumble, like.

An abandoned laundry bin gave him an idea, not even quarter-baked, but he was desperate to make it up to her. Late the next night, he threw on soiled scrubs and a stolen surgical mask, eased Michelle and Junior into a wheelchair, then began tiptoeing them down the hall.

His escape plan was foiled when a billing clerk road-blocked the wheelchair, diverting them from the fire exit and into his office. The clerk's voice was an abacus ticking through the sprawling catalog of charges incurred. When he began laying out various payment plans, Henry shushed him, asked him to just please, please stop talking. Even post-concussion, his mind was made up and firm. Not a chance in hell would he let his son start life with even a penny's worth of debt, and so, within an hour as promised, Henry was back in the clerk's office with the last of the cash. He held it like an un-labeled dumbbell, unable to gauge its weight. He plopped it onto the desk, leaving it to the clerk to make sense of.

Fifty stacks, half a hundred grand, that biblical girth had come and gone in a matter of months. They were back where they'd started, before Papa's insurance check, before the porterhouses and pill press. On Junior's first morning home, Henry'd woken up before the alarm for work. Kissed Junior's forehead and Michelle's lips, then climbed into his truck. At the horizon, the June sun was an extension of himself—a blister, chafed and glaring. Out of options, and so he'd called Al. No answer. Two months ago now. Still no response.

Whatever, though. At least now Henry knew what he was sup-posed and had to do. It was his job to keep his eyes forward, to keep looking up, and they would manage. How couldn't they? All of it was right here, in this bed and within arm's reach, and—oh, he couldn't help himself now.

He uncurled and inched his fingers toward that black satin soft-ball of their baby's head.

Michelle smacked his hand. "Don't."

She was right. Always was, but still. He locked his hands between his knees to restrain any other late-night cravings for a quick touch that might reaffirm his recently bestowed purpose. He mouthed *sorry*, but her eyes had already shut. Whether feigning or forcing herself to sleep didn't matter, since exhaustion like theirs made one effort indistinguishable from the other. And while touching Junior was off-limits, he got away with stroking her cheek with the backs of his fingers, which she kissed. Happily, he reclamped his hands, took her lead, and closed his eyes.

The phone squawked from the nightstand. Its ring was belligerent, and its vibrating jingled the coins into angry sleigh bells. No telling how much time had passed since he'd fallen asleep—if he had at all—only that Junior was crying, Michelle was cursing, and the phone was determined to evade Henry's grasp, jittering off the nightstand before he could strangle it silent.

It was Al. He was here, right outside, and sorry it'd been so long. Just that shit'd been bonkers lately, couldn't press these pills fast enough on his own, and but could he come in quick? Finally meet his basically like nephew?

"What time is it?" Henry said. "I mean, no. No way."

"Late, yeah. Fair enough. But you, though. Get out here, dude. We got to talk."

Henry pressed himself out of bed, conveniently already or still fully dressed. Michelle was cradling Junior and offering him a nipple that was swollen into a flushed chessboard bishop. "The fuck you going?"

"Al."

"Hen, no. It's so late," she said. "Come here."

And so he did.

He kissed her lips and Junior's cowlick and knew precisely what he had to do.

The instant Henry slid into the Bonneville, it was obvious Al was in a bad way. The stink alone said it all, the day-old pot roast of Al's sweat mingling with the chlorine of scorched meth. The glossy pouches under his eyes begged for rest, while his irises quivered in bloodshot puddles. He went to pat Henry but recoiled as if zapped. Shuddered, then said, "Looking good, pops."

The compliment hung funny in the air. As if needing to anchor himself, Al's hand clenched the gear stick then threw it in reverse.

"Where we going?" Henry asked.

"Fucking nowhere."

Al whipped out of the trailer park, away from the strip malls and freeways and city to the east, and instead steered them westward, hurtling in the direction of the cornfields, the plains, the pines. Henry was stewing. All he wanted was an answer. A date, even a rough time frame for when they could get to pressing and pushing the next batch—whether in a single delivery back in the city, or just selling baggies, even single tabs, to friends, coworkers, neighbors, schoolkids, whatever. The last two months of these fifty-, sixty-hour weeks of flipping kitchens and digging holes were breaking him in two, but nowhere close to even. And now with a baby to feed, and so, yeah. In this case, the ends absolutely justified the lowdown, junkie-hustle means. Then again, when didn't they? The means, he meant. Not that he could turn this question to Al, who'd been blathering non-stop this entire time, pausing only to bring the pip's stem to chapped-scabby lips and set a Bic's flame under the charred glass orb, inside of which shards tinkled and smoldered, and Henry was so goddamn exhausted and frustrated that he didn't turn down a hit.

The smoke was chillingly familiar. A frigid chute down his esophagus and into his lungs that detonated microscopic crackles of lightning past the pores of his skin. The meth kicked in quick if not instantly, and soon enough he was bobbing along to the anxious rant streaming out of Al. Yammering on and on about none of it being his fucking fault. He weren't losing any sleep over it, not on him to spoon-feed or babysit. Grown-ass men ought to know their own doses, and but none of this couldn't get pinned back to him—to *them*—right, dude?

"Yeah, no," Henry said through gritting teeth. "Course not."

His chin went back to nodding in vigorous accordance to everything Al had to say, because Al had something Henry wanted, needed for his family, and so he had to time this just right. Patience. Tact. Cunning. He clamped his jaw, resolute, solid. Then Al hushed mid-sentence as if choked. At last a wordless moment, and so this was Henry's chance.

When he said Al's name, he got shushed. An index finger went from Al's lips to the rearview mirror. A pair of headlights was growing, closing in from behind, and, rather than overtaking the Bonneville, lights suddenly rinsed the cab in crimson. Then cobalt. Back to red, flashing over and over. Al slapped on the right-turn signal, cranked down the window, stuffed the pip into the seat cushion, eased onto the brake, then started telling either himself or Henry or nobody in particular to fuck him, fuck him, no—be cool. It was cool. Everything gonna be fine, okay? Right? He took Henry's hand. Squeezed. They hadn't spoken since or about the night after Red Lobster, and then the Bonneville stopped.

In the driver's-side window appeared the torso of a police uniform, asking if Al was aware he had himself a bum brake light? No biggie. Still needed a peek at his license and registration and—a sniff. A ruddy face lowered into view, its nose pruny. A second sniff, a click, and then a flashlight beam was scampering over them, the dashboard, the backseat.

"Whyn't you step out for a quick sec. And pop the trunk while you're at it."

"Sure thing, officer," Al said. Then, to Henry, he hissed, *"Run."*

In as much time as it'd taken Al to throw open and lunge out the door, he'd tripped and skidded across the asphalt. The cop dove and drove a knee into Al's back. Beside Henry, a pistol and a second cop had materialized, yelling, "Hands—hands where I can see them!"

It all came in snapshots or sound bites. Al slammed against the hood. Cuffs clicking around Henry's wrists. The squad car trunk against his cheek. The right to remain silent. Smacks up his ankles, his thighs. And will be used. Smacks at his hips. Against you. The single coin went undetected. The cops' asses in the air while their top halves rummaged inside the Bonneville. Gathering on its roof, one by one, discoveries. Evidence. First a half-drunk bottle. The pip and crumpled baggies. A yellow catalog envelope. The trunk popped open. Spare tire lifted. A gallon ziplock of pale green. In the backseat of the squad car, Henry blinked, and when he opened his eyes, the crimson light now shrieked white—a camera flash. Mug shot. Turn left. He turned left. A second flash, then he was shoved into a plain square room lined with plain steel doors. The space was fully lit despite the hour, freezing despite the season. Walls layered clumpy with paint like cinnamon icing, while recent carvings and graffiti awaited a fresh coat. Mold and turpentine and tequila breath. In each corner of the ceiling was a round fish-eye mirror and a security camera monitoring a dozen metal chairs facing the same direction, like a classroom or DMV waiting room. Al's roast-beef musk. He leaned into Henry, telling him these fuckers ain't got shit. Whatever they asked, just say he didn't know nothing, and they'd be out in no time flat, back home for breakfast, it was all good and gravy, and then a guard grabbed Al and began dragging him toward one of the steel doors. Over his shoulder, Al shouted the Fifth, the Fifth, the Fifth, and then steel clanked shut. Henry waited. Nothing to do with his hands shackled to the floor. Nothing to see in this beige cube. No clock or calendar. No windows or screens. Not even a no-smoking plaque or digits marking the doors, but from behind them came the occasional muffled sob, shout, or cackle. Henry couldn't sleep, not after the meth and dread, but he could blink for as long as he pleased, or bear. Most times, when his eyes reopened, the room was just as he'd left it. Other times, he'd find a new guest. First a vagrant who smelled exactly how he looked, sprawled across three chair seats, snoring. A guard made a lap around them, nodding into the camera lenses above. Later, a scraggly white kid, cussing and spitting, acting hard and looking mortified. In the movies people always got a phone call, and so when the guard reappeared, Henry asked for his but just got a snicker. He blinked for seconds or hours or days, and then a man with a flattop and an accordion folder strode through the room and into the same door Al had disappeared behind—or was it? All the doors were the same. They seemed reserved for the drunk and threatening, or else the strung-out and foaming. An Asian woman floated among the chairs, her makeup a fiasco and coral-tough fingers interlocked over the small of her back. While the others sat slumped, she took her seat with poise, her spine rigid and thighs crossed. He thought of Michelle's thighs. Of what the nurse had done between them. He heard her screaming. Saw her laughing. Saw her rocking, nuzzling, cuddling Junior. It was his turn. His turn to hold their baby, but he couldn't—the cuffs. When he jerked his wrists, a fist gripped the chain, yanked him to his feet, and tugged the chain even higher to fold him into a penitent pose as he was steered toward one of the steel doors himself. The next room was smaller, colder, darker, one wall half-covered by a mirror. A metal table with a steel ring for the cuffs. The man with the flattop was reviewing the contents of a manila folder, too focused to acknowledge Henry's arrival. The man looked from the file to the mirror and delivered an expression so lax and self-assured that he seemed bored. Sounded bored, too, entirely unfazed when each of his questions was met with the same response. How long had Henry known Allen? Lawyer. What had he known about the contents of the trunk? Lawyer. And how they'd been manufactured? Lawyer. Was he aware of the overdoses linked to this particular batch? Lawyer. Or that two had resulted in death? Lawyer. Which meant a manslaughter if not second-degree murder charge, and did he have any idea how much time that carried? Lawy—Thirty minimum, and exactly how old was he again? The man checked the file. Right. A sentence potentially longer than all the years Henry'd spent dicking around before landing his punk ass right here. Thirty years was a long time, but didn't have to be. Things could be worked out, negotiated, and the man yawned. Now, look. His buddy in the next room had a rap sheet longer than a donkey's cock, whereas he, Mr. Henry, on the other hand, was somehow squeaky clean, which could go a long way in a pickle like theirs. A lot of time could be saved and tears spared, especially Henry's. His family's. Already plenty enough evidence collected suggesting Allen had been the brains of the operation. Black-market pill press and an ounce of pure fentanyl had been recovered from his home earlier this morning, and he meant, c'mon, kid. With all things pointing to Al, Henry shouldn't have to

157

take the same fall. Didn't he agree? Three decades, possibly more, just for being in the wrong place at the wrong time? The man didn't know about Henry, but that sure seemed steep to him. However, if Henry played ball, cooperated, signed a plea bargain, and testified in court, they could bring a lifetime down to ten—maybe just five, with good behavior—for possession of a controlled, Schedule II substance. This was the best deal he was gonna get, and a one-time offer. A lot on the line. Too much, what with that Chatty-Cathy next door. Sure liked talking, didn't he? Lots of good times together, between them two, huh? Even mentioned Henry'd recently had himself a kid. A boy. Little Henry Junior, wasn't that right?

"Don't you talk about my son."

The flattop man rose. Went from one wall to the next, leaning on each as if testing their sturdiness just for something to do, circling Henry like some crewcut buzzard.

"Think about your baby," he said. "Where you're headed, you'll be meeting plenty of young men who grew up fatherless."

In the one-way mirror, Henry's reflection was vaguely opaque, as if evaporating, already beginning to disappear. Still not entirely convinced that his presence would actually help his baby in the long run, but still. Five was bad, but thirty unimaginable. By the time he got out, Junior would be older than Henry was today. The man rolled a folder into a chubby baton. Thwacked it on the tabletop. As he turned to leave, Henry said, "Wait."

He wanted his phone call.

When Henry stepped back into the first room, it appeared that Al had made new friends, the other detainees now gathered in a tight orbit around him. He was sweating, gnarled by a comedown, yet laughing at his own punch lines. Even the guard was chuckling from the sidelines. When Al turned at Henry's arrival, his expression wilted.

"What'd I tell you?" the flattop man yelled. "I said to keep these two separated. Get that fat fuck in a holding cell, now."

The guard fumbled past the audience and grabbed Al. As the

guard lugged him away, Al reminded Henry that these fuckers ain't got shit. That he and Henry were golden. Him and Henry, forever, dude. He loved him.

And Henry loved him, too, in whatever muddled-up, brotherly hate kind of way Al deserved after ruining their lives. Henry couldn't go through with this. He had to. One day Al would understand, would forgive him. After all, Henry'd forgiven Al for what happened between them, no—what Al did after Red Lobster. It was whatever. Things happened, and some things were best kept secret, locked away.

Henry swallowed. Forgiving himself would be harder, which he now told Michelle, after sniveling through everything that had gone down since the phone rang last night. He hammered the pay phone. No coins rattled inside. He stuffed his fist into his pocket and clenched the stray coin, a penny, as if for luck, as if that could change anything. With the receiver against the skin of his teeth, he whispered, confessed that he didn't know what to do.

"What you got to, Hen."

"But."

"But what?"

"But Al."

Michelle cleared her throat. But nothing, but whatever, she said. The fuck had Al been thinking? Picking Henry up all twisted in the middle of the night, and with merch in the trunk? And plus hadn't it been Al himself who'd offered to take any and all heat in the first place? Remember, Hen? Only thing Al had asked Henry for was the down payment. Far as she was concerned, anything—any of Henry's, like, involvement had been a favor. Innocent, like. Apples and bananas, what them two had done, and that weren't no excuse for him to be facing the same kind of time as Al, no way.

Henry was in a hallway. A linoleum tunnel. One end led back to the main room, then a door, behind which was Al, while the other end must have led outside, homeward. Even when Henry trained his mind's eye down the hall and past the steel, he couldn't picture Al. Maybe already gone, already a ghost. "I can't, Michelle."

"You better," she said. "You got too much to lose."

"Yeah, no."

"And what Al got, huh? Bad habits, worse breath, and a bust-up Pontiac. This some two-plus-two shit, Hen. Might not be easy, but sure as shit's simple."

Michelle and her guillotine logic. One clean chop. She wasn't wrong, but she wasn't here either. Would she have been able to see Al behind that door? Henry still had no idea what time it was. Didn't know how to tabulate the time that had passed, let alone measure for the future. If he couldn't track seconds or minutes, how could he ever conceive of thirty years? How could he consign either or both of them to a fate so immeasurable? He began tapping then hitting the receiver against his forehead, making a metronome to reacquaint himself with the drum of seconds, to summon Al's likeness from the still, black pool of his memory. Not so much as a ripple. Just heat. A warmth blossoming above his brow. It went from a sizzle to scalding. Among licks of Michelle's voice and white-hot flames, in this place where Al hadn't resurfaced, Junior emerged instead, and so that was that. That was plenty enough.

$6.41

The toothbrush, dangling from the boy's hand, drips a trail of foamy blots onto the asphalt, marking his path from the Spee-Dee market to the truck. He ignores the door, instead clambers up into the truck bed. Starts sifting through garbage bags until he finds his puffy black winter coat. When he cinches the bag shut, his face raisins. Asks how come Henry'd stolen the iron.

It's early June and sure feels like it. The sweat beading at Henry's neck will have glazed into a soupy wet suit by the time this morning's work is through and he's headed to the interview. Even still, the boy zips the coat up to his chin, pulls the hood over his head, then reaches for the dashboard, the heat knob. Henry swats the hand away and says, "No," which remains the only word exchanged between the two during the gallon-long drive to school.

Only two nibbles of banana disappear behind the hood before the fruit flops onto the center console. Still, Henry doesn't bother ordering the boy to eat more. As if scared that opening his mouth—even to simply encourage the boy to eat—might unleash something rash, even hurtful. Lucius had told him to look out for number one. Instead, Henry unpeels the banana all the way. Despite having trained himself to chew with monkish patience, he gobbles it down in two orangutan chomps. The substance seems to dissolve inside his stomach rather than fill it.

Along the sidewalk, a row of yellow buses expels swarms of children, scrambling and grabbing at one another as they buzz down the walkways and into the building. The approach of summer vacation has charged the schoolyard with a sunny urgency, an almost palpable anticipation. Lawns combed tidy. Green leaves swaying plump. Sun high and bright, casting stark shadows inside the truck cab, so grim they're viscous. The truck is idling outside the main entrance. Henry waits for Junior to move or speak. Maybe even wish his old man luck on this very important day.

Not a budge. Not a peep. Not so much as a glance past the hood's furry brim.

Henry clears his throat.

Nothing.

"Well?" he says.

Just a sniffle, and so Henry's done waiting. He twists Junior toward him by the elbow and just like that the boy spills. A gush of snivels and ratty whimpers. Junior pleads with Henry, saying he's too sick to go to school, his stomach is killing him, he thinks he might pass out, really though. It isn't right to force him to go to school when he's practically dying, like. Just look at him. He needs rest and medicine and please, Pa. *Please.* Why can't he just stay in the truck during the interview? He'll wait. He'll hide. He won't make a sound and promises nobody will ever notice him. Swears it, just—please?

"You done?"

"Please, Pa."

Henry inhales through his teeth. Got to hold firm. Can't sway the slightest. If it weren't for that damn service charge, the boy could stay, but now there's no way. He can't pull up looking for a half day's work with a kid in tow—no. His answer is final, his head already shaking, reiterating. He exhales. "Get out. Go. Don't you make me say it again."

"This is crazy!" Junior says. "What is wrong with you? I'm sick. I can't. You can't make me—"

"Enough!" He punches the steering wheel. The honk startles a cluster of children and sends them skittering inside, where Junior belongs, too.

"You are going to toughen up and get your ass in there this very minute."

Not a budge, but a peep. A mutter. A grumbling from behind the hood. Henry isn't sure, but this little shit better not have said what Henry thinks he did.

"What'd you say?" he hisses.

"Mom would never do this to me."

In a flash Henry is out and on the other side of the truck, ripping open the passenger door and shaking the boy by the shoulders. He shoves the hood down and screams, demanding the boy look at him—now, goddamnit.

"You look at me when I talk to you, ah."

The boy does as he's told. His eyes lift, cloudy with hate or fear or defeat—whatever. Henry doesn't care.

"Do you see your *mother* here? Or anywhere? Have you even heard from that bitch since she, since she—*no*. Not once, not ever. But tell me. Tell me who is here, huh?"

The boy sneers but caves. "You."

"And what's my name?"

The boy squints. "What?"

"What is my name?"

". . . Pa?"

"You're goddamn right." He digs into his pocket, counts out four singles for lunch. "And you see this?"

The boy doesn't respond, so Henry repeats the question, this time bellowed.

"I see it, I see it."

"Sometimes a man has to do things he doesn't want to, and today it's your turn. Today it's your turn to man up and show Pa and everybody else just how tough you are, got it?"

Tears have begun branching down the boy's flushed cheeks.

"I asked you a question," Henry says. "Now tell me: you got it?"

"Pa," Junior whispers. "Please."

He's fucking had it. He crams the cash into Junior's hands, then wrenches the boy out by his armpits. Junior's knees buckle when shoes meet pavement, but the boy manages to stay standing, head dipped and chin nestled in the hood's fluff. Henry stomps his way back to the driver's side. It doesn't feel finished, though, doesn't feel right, and so over the truck bed, he points at his son. "Do the right thing, ah. Make me proud."

$0.00

Rot had a sound. Isolation and biology colluded in the audible disintegration of these caged men. A strangulation sustained over the minutes made hours, the hours made days, the days made weeks, the weeks made months, the months made years, the years made decades, the decades made rot.

Those sentenced to life without parole lived every day knowing the exact place of their death, but not the time. Henry couldn't understand how they carried on, let alone carried their padded lunch trays. Didn't they feel it, too? How the rage and shame and regret festered in the air of this place, lacquering them in a scuzzy coat of futility? Could they not hear the same static buzzing in each cell and through every last corridor? It was the fizzle of human decay, which, if he held his breath, sounded like his own molars gnawing raw meat very, very slowly.

Over that perpetual chewing came interruptions. Rubber slipper soles grazing concrete. Conversations compressed into side-eyed grumbling. Jeers. Kissy sounds. Guards doling out commands like asides about the forecast. Buzzers and clanks and the languid tick of a clock's second hand.

Such a wealth of time. A fortune of hours made a famine for company, a drought of affection. After lights-out, his cell flooded with a tremendous loneliness, a shade of gloom so impenetrable that it threatened even the prospect of morning. The sort of darkness that robbed sight but heightened touch and hearing. But with nobody to tickle or stroke, no one to offer or absorb secrets, what else was there to do before falling asleep other than listen to the concrete? Lying on his side, he let the scent of ammonia and dried perspiration envelop him, while he focused on whatever was teeming deep inside the pores of these cinder block walls. Even though the faint droning was constant, he had an urge to sift through it and locate the source of that clandestine rhythm. A pulse. A beat. Some echo of a lullaby to rock him—on top of this creaking plastic mattress—into sleep, into a dream, before he resurfaced into another tomorrow and more gnawing.

Tonight a new sound came chiming in the distance, bright and spritely, growing louder and nearer. A gleeful thunder. It was the sound of yellow, of sunflowers, of laughter—Mom's.

He found himself hog-tied and belly down in a lush meadow. Through the swaying grass and cattails he saw her, Mom, wearing her best saka shawl like a cape. It fluttered gold and phosphorescent in the breeze. She swayed to and fro, cradling a child—his baby, perfect, pink, faceless. She dipped her head. Blew a raspberry on Junior's tummy. After the silly wet note, the plush honeycomb of her hair swooped back up so she could dispatch more laughter, shame-less, radiant, reverberating like daffodils.

There was so much to ask her, to tell her, but when he tried call-ing out to her, a cascade of sand poured from his mouth. Panic seized him. After so many years, this was a betrayal. She was too distracted and happy to notice him, her own baby, writhing at her feet. Then his baby giggled, too.

All of a sudden Henry was engulfed in the same flames from the hospital bed, when a nurse had first lowered Junior into his arms. A near weightless bundle, a feather boulder. From the baby's lips to his toes, all his shrunken-down features were so irrefutably human, so terrifyingly fragile. Then four teensy monkey fingers had clamped around Henry's index finger. Just like that, an ignition. The itchy gash on his scalp and the post-concussion fuzz were cleared by a great scald-ing, as a new and horrific knowledge seared over and through him like a bucketful of boiling tar. This love defied logic. It was beyond reason, obliterated self-interest. This blinding devotion to this itty-bitty per-son was absolute to a dangerous degree. In an instant, he learned of a horrifying capacity and total willingness to do anything—no matter how base or vicious—for another human being.

Ungreased metal on metal squealed. A rusty axle. At the horizon, pushing a wheelbarrow up a hill, was Papa. Whereas Mom, here and now, was a spring coiled tense with health and youth, Papa was weathered, old. Sunbaked hide sagging off a whittled frame, his black hair a charred bushel. Over the wheelbarrow's brim dangled four limbs, pallid and porky. One of the wrists lifted, went to wipe snot dribbling down Al's upper lip. He was still weeping, had probably never stopped. Still couldn't bring himself to look Henry in the eyes. Neither Al nor Papa seemed to notice them in the meadow below. Instead, Papa pressed on, chugging the wheelbarrow to the hilltop, where a lavender fog had settled over its crest.

Once the mists swallowed Papa and Al, Mom finally peered down at Henry. Floating over Junior in her arms was that sad smile of hers. Seeing it almost felt like forgiveness.

She asked Henry if he would tell the baby about her.

More sand gushed over Henry's tongue, so he nodded frantically— yes, yes, of course he would. So much to say, so much to ask, but the grains of sand coarsened, clumped, and now chunks of gravel splintered his teeth and shredded the roof of his mouth.

"Will you tell him about me?"

Yes. Every last memory and everything she'd ever taught him, he would share with his son. How could he not? Any ounce of tenderness he possessed was owed to her, which his son—her grandson— deserved by the barrel. It didn't feel like a true promise if he couldn't verbalize it, but how could he with all this gravel shredding him from the inside out? All he could do was squint up at her and try to transmit this oath via their gazes, but she kept asking the same question, again and again, and then he woke up.

Every morning in this cell was half nightmare, half miracle. Either way, it was surreal and hard to believe that after such a night, the sun had returned and motion resumed. He'd gotten into the habit of verifying this seemingly improbable cycle. First thing every morning, he would crane off his bunk to peer out the envelope-sized slot in the concrete, double-checking if daylight was still shining and life beyond still happening, possibly even waiting for him.

A second envelope-sized slot in the cell was cut into the center of the steel door. The tip of a baton entered it and clanked against its rims, the preamble to individual messages.

"Visitor," a voice said. "Hands."

Henry pressed his back to the door and slipped his wrists through the slot to be cuffed, before being led to the visitation hall.

In the yard and corridors and mess hall, all the inmates' papery navy jumpsuits were propped by chests ballooning with don't-fuck-with-me pomp. But here, in the visitation hall, spines jellied and curled into question marks. Shoulders huddled into phone receivers as if they were prayer beads. A despondent gravity tugged a row of forgotten men into panes of bulletproof glass reinforced by a thin wire chain-link that crosshatched visitors' likenesses into chunky pixels.

Once locked inside a booth, Henry was uncuffed. On the other side of the glass, Michelle was an ice pick. Gaunt from exhaustion, crusty with poverty. A wet stain over her left nipple made a black thought bubble above their baby's head. Junior was sound asleep, a beautiful nugget wrapped in a mangy bath towel. That snarl of suspicion still hadn't left Michelle's glare. It had hardened over her gaze ever since he'd climbed into the witness stand.

Henry took the receiver in one hand, flattened the other against the pane as an invitation to Michelle's. Hers were occupied, though. One was holding their son, the other at her mouth as she gnawed on a cuticle. She cauterized the raw fingertip with a lick before readjusting her grip around Junior and clutching the phone against her shoulder.

Though his mouth was still a desert, this time *Hey* fell out instead of sand.

"Hey," she said, just as arid. "Holding up in there?"

His hand, unmet, descended, streaking four smudges down the pane.

"Yeah, no. I guess." He had nothing to report other than the sound of rot. "How about you? Holding up out there?"

"Ha," Michelle snorted. She shifted, squaring up like a linebacker. Her head swiveled, her neck cracked, and then she got right to it. The fuck did Henry think, huh? All she could say was thank shit her sister worked nights and had been able to watch Junior while Michelle went to work herself. Not like that changed much of anything, like. Just weren't no way to make ends meet on her own. Their home was falling apart. Kitchen sink clogged, air conditioner busted. Not that she could afford to keep it running. Her nipples were chomped raw. And who'd a thought diapers would be so fucking expensive, and this little shit factory weren't helping none, burning through them like it was his motherfucking job. And she never slept, Hen. Felt like she ain't had a wink since back before he got took. Did he have any idea what that was like? Working overtime and watching a baby and cutting coupons and squeezing pennies and keeping alive but not living—and all on zero fucking sleep? Impossible. She weren't going to make it. She was so tired, Hen, so tired that everything felt heavier, like. Everything far away, on mute, and moving slower. The days, the time. And still a whole another nine years of this shit?

"Five with good behavior," Henry said.

"Fucking splendid, Hen," she snapped. "You ain't let me finish. The last time we talked? I was right. We really are gonna have to file for bankruptcy. Got any idea what that means?"

His fingers climbed back up the smudges. He lied, telling her he did and that everything was going to be fine. Reminded her how long it could have been. Five years was a drop in the bucket compared to, well.

She hadn't heard. Hadn't wanted to listen, it seemed, having tipped the receiver away from her ear.

"It's just I can't," she started.

"Can't what?"

There was no budging that glass, no getting through. The sinew of his forearm quaked and burned as he pressed harder and harder, but he couldn't reach her, couldn't touch his family. All he wanted was to encourage her, to celebrate her. Way back when they'd met, she had come back from the dead, put meat on her bones and sunshine in her chest, and so he knew she could do absolutely anything she put her mind to. His faith in her was so resolute that he couldn't get his head around it, couldn't believe her saying she couldn't. "But what, though? You can't what, Michelle?"

"I can't stop thinking about Al."

His hand fell because neither could he. He saw Al sobbing in the wheelbarrow, sobbing at the defendant's table. While the plea deal and testimony had kept Henry's sentence local and limited, the manslaughter charges got kicked up to second-degree murder. That plus the smuggling of merchandise over state and national borders faced Al with decades in a federal penitentiary. Throughout the scripted questioning and cross-examination, Al had stared at some point beneath his trembling orange county jumpsuit, as if watching all his tomorrows sluice down the drain of a slaughterhouse floor. Never steadied, never once looked up at this treacherous, self-serving rodent—his best friend—in the witness stand. When it was over, Henry looked past that whimpering pumpkin to Michelle seated in the back. Whereas Al's eyes were locked on the floor, hers were unflinching, terrified, and drilling straight through Henry.

Into the receiver, he stammered through things he wasn't sure were true or mattered or comforted her, but anything was better than the silence that would fall otherwise, and the gnawing that would follow. He heard himself say he'd done—no, they'd done what they'd had to. Just like she'd told him to, remember? For Junior, for their family.

The baby awoke with a fragile yelp. Beady black eyes tried making sense of the bleak monochrome of stainless steel and waxy paint. Michelle sniffed, then cooed sadly. Rocked her arms before the baby got to crying. She dipped her head. Asked if he wanted to say hello to Daddy.

"Pa," Henry said.

She rolled her eyes. Set the receiver to Junior's ear.

Henry muzzled himself with the mouthpiece and into it said, "Happy birthday."

The baby's eyes widened, awed by this bodiless voice. Henry leaned into the glass, willing his son to look at him, to see him. He thought about the it's-a-girl cigar, Michelle sweaty and raging with her legs splayed, the horror of watching her body split and gush, how helpless he'd felt to help her then, exactly a year ago today. How helpless he'd felt the very first time he cradled Junior. How helpless he felt now, unable to smash through this glass and scoop his family into his arms and carry them off, sprinting up the hill after Papa and into those lavender mists.

Since Michelle couldn't hear what he was saying now, it was like telling Junior a secret. Remembering the note Papa'd left in the glove compartment, he told his son how very proud he was of him. How beautiful he was now, and how strong and smart he would grow up to be. How sorry he was that he couldn't be there with him right now. It was just that, sometimes, things happened. Papas made mistakes, too. Even though Junior might not understand this till much later on, papas were just people, scared and confused as everyone else, but trying their hardest. He told Junior that he loved him, he loved him so very much, and before Junior knew it, his pa would be right there with him, forever and then some. He promised.

$2.41

There is free coffee at the contractors' entrance of Home Depot. At the far end of the parking lot, a dozen day laborers sit on lunch pails, picking at caulk stains and craning their necks after passing trucks. A few stand when Henry rolls by, and those who recognize him turn away.

The store is empty. Too early for the stay-at-home-mom gardeners or the after-work DIY-er crowd. Henry squirts weak coffee into a styrofoam cup. Recently he's been taking it with sugar for the extra kick and calories, and so now bites the corners off three packets. Pours. Stirs. A muddy vortex. He should not have yelled at the boy. Should never have opened his mouth in the first place. The first sip scalds his tongue. When he blows, the burnt scales rustle like the last of autumn's leaves, and he needs to focus. He will make it up to Junior tonight, but no point in beating himself up now when there's nothing he can do, not when there's so much else on the line.

Sipping quick so he can get a refill on the way out, he wanders the wide aisles of building materials, looking for an empty slot, an out-of-stock item to name in case he gets stopped by an employee. As he passes the lumber and rounds into a lane full of bagged cement, the logic behind the division of inventory dawns on him. The contractors' half of the store holds all the fundamental elements for building a home, all of which later get concealed by the ornaments for sale on the other side, all the paints, light fixtures, moldings, carpets. While the construction of a home adheres to a sequence—the structural first, foundation and framing; next the functional, plumbing and electric; and last the aesthetic, decor and color schemes—it's by no means a ranking of importance. A shelter might only require the first two, but all three are essential to create a true home. If given the materials and a patch of land, he knows he could build one for his family. Not that he's entitled to that, but still. Doesn't seem too much to ask for, either. Before his imagination pours the foundation's concrete, he takes note of an empty slot here in the irrigation and drainage aisle.

Hunger has him cavernous all over again, the pangs reverberating through him like his footsteps in this warehouse. The caffeine and sugar spur a riot of worries—Junior, money, the dogmonger, iron, and interview—in his brain, but deliver no strength to his limbs. Just a hot sputter in his gut. He flicks the stir stick to coax the slug of dregs and sugar into his mouth. The grains scrape over his tongue and down his throat as if he's swallowed a shot of sand.

All the gore and panic after last night's bath has left him greasy. It's early enough that he can shit in peace, then scrub himself down with the men's room's green industrial-grade soap, even though it'll dry out his skin and leave him less clean than sterilized. Might help.

It doesn't. The skin of his face gets papier-mâché brittle. He uses saliva to moisturize the flaky patches under his nostrils, then stops for a second coffee before exiting. Only decaf left, so he doubles up on the sugar. A burnt-down candlestick in an orange bib rounds the cash register and starts approaching. Asks if there's anything he could help Henry with today.

Yes, Henry thinks, loads. He spits six sugar packet corners into his palm. To the coffee, he says, "Looks like you're fresh out of drain tile."

"I could check out in the yard for you," the candlestick offers.

"No need," Henry says. "I'll live."

The doors slide shut behind him. Out in the parking lot, June's steam is halitosis, promising to make the morning's work grueling and messy. This hadn't been the plan. He'd wanted to stay fresh and review his note cards all morning, but the surprise service charge plus the unrecovered five dollars for the iron have secured the slipknot. He needs cash. Bad. Not even enough for gas to get him to the interview, let alone for tonight's dinner or an I'm-sorry treat for Junior.

As he drives up to the day laborers, those who recognize him make no effort to hide their vinegar, and Henry can't exactly blame them. The two one-ups he's got on them—his truck and English—get him picked up first without fail. As a courtesy, whenever he doesn't have a job slated for the day, he drives to different towns so he's not screwing the same guys out of work on a regular basis. But after six months, he's made the rounds. He's a familiar face. Competition. A two-legged challenger in a cripple's race. Only the one-eyed man Henry'd tarred a roof with back in March nods to him.

Henry kills the engine. Cranks down the window. Clicks the seat two notches back and blows steam off the coffee's surface. Doesn't bother with the note cards. For now, he extends a hand to shake an invisible one.

"The pleasure's all mine, sir.

"Can't thank you enough for setting aside the time to speak with me today.

"Why, just fine. Just great, sir, and yourself?"

He rehearses various chuckles, gauging which most effectively radiates health and plenty.

"You have light?"

The one-eyed man has appeared beside him, pinching a bent cigarette. His nose comes up to Henry's elbow on the window's ledge. Same height as Papa, with similar straight, tar-black hair. The curtains of an unbuttoned flannel shirt flank the man's belly, tattooed with a foggy calligraphy spelling out *Amor de Madre*. No patch over the missing eye. Just a slack eyelid drooping over the pearly pink of the socket, a permanent wink at the world's saddest joke.

Henry pushes the cigarette burner into the dash. They wait.

"So," Henry says. "How you been?"

The man nods. Apparently hasn't picked up any English since they'd last worked together. Silence bakes between them, and so Henry points to the sun. "Gonna be a hot one, huh."

"Yes," the man says. "Much."

The burner clicks. Unwilling to take any chances with their indispensable dinnertime appliance, Henry holds the hot coils down

173

to the cigarette's tip. Smoke lifts between them, clears, and the man says, "Sank you."

"De nada."

A dump truck engine grumbles in the distance. It comes lumbering and squeaking into the parking lot, hauling a New Holland skid loader in its trailer. First it slows, crawling past the waiting laborers, who rise and roll back their shoulders, before it stops alongside Henry's truck, trapping the one-eyed man between the two driver's-side doors. The driver is as fat as Al had been, but these forearms suggest a boulder-rolling sturdiness. Freckled skin looks as scorched as the top of Henry's tongue, except for a pasty bandit's mask striping his eyes and temples. "You two coming?"

"Depends," Henry says. "Only got time for a half day."

"Lucky you. Ripping out a driveway. Done by noon if youse two haul ass like me."

"What you paying?"

"Hundred." The fat man must have caught Henry's eyebrows hop. "For the *both* ya. Fifty for three hours' grind is more than fair."

Henry's done a lot more for a lot less, and so he nods. The one-eyed man looks from the fat man to Henry, waiting for a translation. No pen and paper, so Henry's index finger scrawls *3hrs/$50* upside down in the grime on the truck's door. The filthy fingertip points to the two of them, as he tries mustering some high school Spanish. "Yo y tú—I mean, sorry. Usted."

The one-eyed man tilts his head at the numbers in the dust. "Okay."

$12.22

Before pulling out of the Home Depot lot, Henry'd had to ask the fat man for gas money. A pair of dark sunglasses dropped from forehead to nose, landing perfectly over its pale outline like a manhole cover. From the passenger seat, the one good eye followed a twenty getting passed between the two trucks. Henry mimed an explanation by pointing from the bill to the gas gauge, then giving a thumbs-up.

A rickety pump spat an extra nineteen cents' worth of gas over the five-dollar mark. After breaking the twenty inside, he handed the one-eyed man two fivers, his fair share. Not without reluctance, but it was the right and honest thing to do. The good eye went from the gas gauge to the cash then back to Henry. The man folded one of the fivers longwise, then gave it back.

The offer of gas money lands like a haymaker. These extra five dollars break Henry back into the double digits, providing an abstract sense of security, a mattress under the gallows. The weathered look of the man, which suggests five dollars weigh just as heavy in his wallet as in Henry's, doesn't make enduring charity any easier. Not like he's got enough pride left to turn it down either. This kernel of dignity and its wordless acceptance are wringing his tear ducts. It stings.

Henry huffs. He has got to get his shit together. He rubs his nose. "Muchas gracias."

"Gracias a ti, güey."

"By the way," Henry extends his hand, this time reaching for a very real one. "I'm Henry."

The name of this man, who might be the closest Henry's come to a friend all year, is Jorge.

Rush hour has clogged the three-lane freeway to a stop-and-go crawl. The sun above cooks the tarmac below, pressing a sweltering haze into the truck cab. Still though, he doesn't want to burn any extra gas by running the AC, and just as this crosses his mind, Jorge points to the dashboard.

"I can?"

Jorge reaches past the AC knob for the radio's, tuning the dial to a mariachi station. The dump truck leading the way comes to a stop, and the motion lulls Jorge's head into a bob, trailing the song's beat. His lips mimic language but release no sound. He starts drumming against his lap, and soon enough Henry takes his lead. The good eye peeks over, asking permission. After Henry nods, Jorge grins, then begins singing along, word for word. Between verses the two exchange hushed giggles like kids with a secret. The band's accordion and brass lilt in a melancholic, minor key, following the *one-two-three* of a dragged-out waltz. While the singer's voice warbles cheesy and melodramatic, Jorge's sandpaper croon seems a far better fit for this forlorn melody. Then again, Henry isn't sure it's actually a sad song, since the only lyrics he can actually make out are the refrain's *para siempre, para siempre*. Can't remember what that means either. *For something*, he figures, then wonders for what?

The song ends with a crash of brass and yodels. Henry applauds against the steering wheel as Jorge bows and blows kisses to adoring fans in the glove compartment. When he sits back upright, he's beaming and got his phone out, its case patched with frayed duct tape.

"Look," he tells Henry. "My family."

Traffic ahead comes to another dead stop. Boot pressed into the brake, Henry brings the phone screen up close. The photo looks like it'd been taken in one of those sun-bleached villages where stray dogs gleefully roam unpaved streets, snouts chasing after children playing soccer and food carts' barbecue smoke. The family is lined up in front of a stucco house, the roof's terra-cotta tiles faded to the color of gums. Jorge is wearing the same shirt, only in the photo it's tucked in, buttoned up, and ironed crisp. He has two eyes here, both fixed firm and proud and straight into the lens. His wife is almost a head taller than him, her skin a healthy maple syrup against the lime of a cotton sundress. In her arms, a baby. To the other side of Jorge are three boys descending in height, their matching flattops making a black stepladder.

Jorge thumps his chest. "All boys."

"That's one good-looking family you got there, Jorge."

"You have?"

Henry does, one boy, eight years old, but not a single photo at hand. Guilt bites him. Even though he hasn't loaded minutes onto the cell phone sitting dead in the door's side pocket, he could still use it for snapshots. Never occurred to him to do so till now. But what exactly would Junior want to remember from these last months anyway? Henry certainly doesn't want any souvenirs from this shameful stretch. Soon as he's back on his feet and living respectable again, the only value that memories of these hungry months might offer is a lesson in gratefulness. Like the starving-kids-in-Africa line, just a card to play if Junior ever gets whiny. But how many photos of them are there from before, back when they'd been a family? There'd been a few disposable cameras getting clicked and passed around, right after Junior was born and before the shit hit. But that's it besides a few school photos out in the utility case, as far as he can remember. Had Michelle kept documenting the boy's growth? And if she'd ever bothered to develop the film, where had those prints ended up?

Last December, circumstance and desperation had put all their possessions—even those dripping with sentimental value—out in the frosty yard with masking-tape price tags. Henry'd come up with the rule and stuck to it: If it didn't have a practical function, it didn't get a spot in the truck bed. Clothing and tools. An iron skillet, a boiling pot, cutlery, and a bundle of cooking utensils. School supplies and books. Only the most cherished and educational of Junior's toys. The sole exception to his functionality standard had been a plain white cylinder. The urn merited a space in the diamond-plated utility case, locked away with other essentials and irreplaceables like power tools and their birth certificates. A shame that he'd never located a meaningful place to spread Papa's ashes and pass a solemn moment. Then again, this spot would have suited Papa as fine as any.

Nothing else from the bookshelf made the cut. While a neighbor bought their TV only minutes after Henry'd set it on the driveway, all the books went untouched. Once cleared, the bookshelf he'd built reminded him of a rib cage. Got fifteen bucks for it, not even a quarter of the original cost of its lumber. The following day he loaded up and took his parents' entire library to a secondhand-book store. Most were turned down due to all the marginalia. Fifty bucks for about five times as many books. Whatever possessions Mom and Papa had left on this earth, Henry heaved, stack after stack, into a dumpster out back.

He can't remember what he'd done with the photo of the three of them in Manila. Can't piece together the topography of Papa's visage. Can't be sure whether it'd been a dream or a ghost that had relayed a question from Mom, a favor, let alone if he has ever fulfilled it. The boy has never asked about Henry's parents, and why would he? It's Henry's responsibility to tell Junior about the boy's grandma and *lolo*. It's up to him to provide more than food and shelter, but also moments worth remembering, memories to preserve, retrace, and one day share.

"Go," Jorge says.

Henry stirs. Traffic has crept ahead, exposing a band of freeway the length of a basketball court between them and the trailer's tailgate. Jorge tries humming along to the next song, but Henry doesn't join him this time. He's thinking about the iron. He could ditch it in the dump truck.

They park along the curb of a house as huge and pristine as all the others in this development of flawless lawns and wide curving streets, free of pedestrians and other debris. Henry and Jorge go to unload and mount the two steel ramps for the skid loader. The ramp is a five-foot ladder of solid steel. It yanks down his arms and out of his grasp, thundering against the pavement as he hops backward to save his shins. Either it's heavier than normal, or he's flimsy with hunger. Either way, he's embarrassed. Jorge has already locked his ramp's clasp onto the lip of the trailer and is piling shovels, a pick-axe, and a sledgehammer into a wheelbarrow by the time Henry shakily deadlifts the second ramp off the ground and into place. Only a minute's labor, but sweat is already pricking at his back.

Up the slope, the garage door opens and ejects a squeaky-clean BMW. It pulls up beside the dump truck, and the homeowner steps out. He's got hair groomed tidier than his lawn and a young, clean-shaven face that only addresses the fat man. As they chat, the home-owner fists his hips, mirroring the fat man's posture, speaking in that nervous, almost apologetic way that white guys take when get-ting chummy with the help. Likely to start dropping *ain't* and hock-ing loogies if he hangs around much longer. Henry rests the handle of a twelve-pound sledgehammer across his shoulders, making like a rolling pin over the tense meat of him. When the homeowner even-tually registers him and Jorge, he sees brown and so forgoes English. Instead gives them a two-finger salute like a pilot.

It is grunt work, but Jorge doesn't make a peep. Doesn't even sweat by the look of it. Industrial logic reveals itself through repetition, and within a minute Henry and Jorge are a two-man disassembly line, having wordlessly fallen into a mindless, muscle-searing rhythm. First Henry slams the sledge into the asphalt, hobbles a foot back, then swings again, leaving a web of fissures and craters through which Jorge spears the pick-axe then pries loose, so that the fat man in the skid loader can scoop all the slabs and rubble into its bucket and over to the dump truck.

Now that he and Jorge are working totally in sync, a sirloin pen-dulum, it's too easy for his worries to frolic and mosh unchecked. He drowns out Junior's feverish whimpers and his own impending job interview blunders by focusing on the minutiae of this back-breaking procedure. Each rotation begins by dipping into a slight squat that simultaneously lowers the hammerhead like a cocked cata-pult and generates the force that now presses from heels to toes then extends his knees and blasts through his hips and spine, as his arms begin heaving the sledgehammer up from behind him, arcing over his shoulders and head, and as it reaches its apex and curves into its descent, his right hand slides down the handle to meet the left, and together they give a final tug to drive the hammerhead faster and harder than a freefall, until—*thock.*

It reminds him of that carnival game where you hammer a lever in order to ding a bell at the top of a plywood pillar. Soon he's thinking about games, youth, Junior, and he clamps down a wheeze and swings even harder.

Thock.

The diesel fumes and limestone dust steep into a sepia filter over the driveway. Amid the amber haze, something is twinkling. A Ferris wheel's lights. There's the peppermint swirl of a circus tent. Rows of stalls selling rigged games and deep-fried treats, and here comes Junior, a tuft of cotton candy blocking his face from view. Beneath the sugary cloud, the stick starts stretching, growing so heavy that Junior has to support it with both hands. He grimaces, struggling. Next the fluff starts congealing, condensing in on itself until it's a stout, solid cylinder—a hammerhead. The boy looks solemn, resigned, as if dealt a sentence he doesn't deserve but can't contest. In his hands, the sledgehammer is so oversized that it's clownish, except there's nothing funny about how it's tugging the boy down to the ground.

Henry should not have yelled at him. Can't remember the last time he had before this morning. Whenever he gets frustrated with the boy, he feels himself wadding up and shrinking down into Papa. He wants none of that old-world, Filipino-father's-word-is-law horseshit to come between him and Junior. The boy shouldn't have to wait until he comes of age, like Henry had, before understanding the scope of his own papa's terrifying, stupid-making love for his son. He much prefers Mom's laissez-faire approach, wants to implement it, too, though with perhaps a pinch of regulation if Junior grows up to start making some of the same choices Henry had after Mom's death. But parental sanctions don't have to be delivered via yelling fits or head smacks, like Papa had done before the softening. At least Papa had never struck the mother of his son, let alone raised a finger to her. If not a better father, he'd been a better man than Henry. Whenever Papa got frustrated with Mom, he always caught himself, corralling any runaway lashes of anger and rerouting them toward Henry, rebranded as discipline. But discipline is more than bellows and denigration. The boy is too sensitive for what Henry'd endured as a child and unleashed on Junior this morning. The little softie hadn't inherited a pebble of Henry's grit nor an ounce of Michelle's acid, and Henry adores that about his son. He wants to shield the boy's tenderness, keep him callus-free. At only eight, the boy is already more thoughtful and perceptive than both his parents combined. So attuned to Henry's expectations that—even racked with fever—Junior obeyed and soldiered into school, because he'd known what today holds for his pa. But does the boy understand what today holds for him, too?

Henry wheezes, heaves, then slams the hammerhead into the earth. Easing himself upright, he resolves to do something special for Junior tonight. And he will apologize. He takes off his T-shirt, mops the sweat from his brow. His chest is full of embers. Other than one trickle streaking from Jorge's hairline into his empty eye socket, like some physics-defying tear, the man appears dry, unscathed, as he hefts a slab of asphalt the size of a refrigerator door into the skid loader's bucket.

Now that they've cleared the first strip of asphalt abutting the street curb, the machine's bucket can pry and crush the rest of the driveway, leaving Henry the task of hammering oversized wedges into more manageable chunks, while Jorge works to clear the edges by hand. The work is moving along faster than Henry expected, and the possibility of wrapping up before noon relieves him, at least a little. Hunger still has him lightheaded and dog-tired. Each strike feels like he's depositing some waning and unrecoverable portion of himself into the crushed rock.

The skid loader rolls down to the dump truck. As the bucket cranes upward and the unloading rubble bellows, Henry props himself on the sledgehammer's handle as if it were an old man's cane, and his thoughts flit to Lucius. Breathless after his one-man ambush, Lucius had made a crutch of the fire-axe. Slung his grizzled head. Begged for Henry's help.

When the skid loader engine quits, a summer breeze whistles, whisking an almost unnerving levity over Henry. Even the fat man's stride has a new bounce, now that he's squeezed out of the skid loader's pod and is walking toward his truck.

"Back in forty-five," he tells Henry. "I'm a run this load to the dump."

The landfill—the iron. In the dump truck's open-box bed, the iron would be a needle in a thirty-two-ton asphalt haystack, forever a quark among acres and acres of demolition wreckage.

"Wait," Henry shouts.

His empty belly is now an advantage. He is quick and nimble and darting for his truck bed, soon rifling between and under all the Hefty bags—*where had Junior put it*?—until eureka, land ho, hallelujah. He pauses, awed and frightened, observing the iron as if it were a pair of dice he was about to throw on a double-or-nothing roll.

And then the dump truck rumbles off, disappears.

Henry is a void. The iron clunks back into the truck bed. Famine has twisted him ditzy and oblivious to time, and so he opens the driver's-side door, starts digging in the side pocket. Like he'd done with the sugar, he gnaws the corners off two ketchup packets and one relish, then squeezes them into his mouth. The silt blooms sweet over his tongue, fires a dart of sugar to his brain. He smooshes the morsels of pickle against the roof of his mouth before swallowing it all in a measured gulp. Flavor is a tease. Now that it's trickled into him, his belly gurgles for more, for sustenance, eventually yielding to silence with the rest of him.

Only takes twenty minutes for him and Jorge to finish clearing the last of the asphalt edging the lawn and concrete of the garage floor's foundation. They gather the remaining debris into a tidy heap so the skid loader can scoop it up in one go, and then they could load up, sweep up, get paid, and get going.

Until then, they'll have to wait. They sit on the dropped tailgate, watching their work boots sway. Fingers drum an aluminum din against the truck to muffle their language barrier. He's not quite sure what time it was when the dump truck rolled away, but it sure feels like it's been a good forty-five minutes by now. He turns the ignition one click for the dashboard clock—*11:42*. He has to get going soon. Anxiety starts crunching dollars and minutes in his head, and among the frantic calculations emerges a voice, his own, bumbling through a goulash of digits and cusses and snippets from his note cards. He jogs over to Jorge.

"Think we'll actually get out of here by noon?"

Jorge shrugs, unfazed by his lack of comprehension. Henry begins mentally counting in Spanish, hoping the momentum of the sequence might swing him past *ocho, nueve, diez, once*—

"Doce," Henry shouts, tapping his watchless wrist.

"¿Ya?" Jorge says. "¿El tiempo se va volando, no?"

"No, I mean," Henry starts. "I mean, tú y yo . . . nosotros, uh, vámonos at noon, twelve, doce, right?"

Jorge squints. "Pues, yo me quedo hasta que me pague, güey."

Henry smiles, nods, because this is going fucking nowhere. He has to get cleaned up and out of here quick, and so grabs the nub of motel soap then sprints to a garden hose. The first splashes are tepid, stale, but after the coils of resting water clear, it's freezing. He scrubs at his shoulders and back frantically, then reaches into his jeans to flush the bayou out of his crotch. The soap disintegrates once he gets to his face and armpits, the vital parts of him he would have prioritized and lathered down first if he wasn't starving, if his brain wasn't in a blender. He finger-combs his hair back in a sopping sweep, remembering that—along with everything else that has gone straight to shit—he never got a chance to give his or Junior's mops much-needed trims.

After toweling off with the sweaty T-shirt and sniffing his pits—still tart, musky—he hurries back to the truck. He scrambles for the stick of deodorant, which at some point had abandoned its home in the glove compartment for the floor and damn near launched him into a delirious fury. And then, when he uncaps it, the last chalky crumbs of it fall to the street.

Henry screams.

"¿Estás bien, güey?"

Henry dabs into the plastic plunger of the deodorant stick and rubs the scant residue under his arms, but it's no use. He cannot go to the interview reeking of decay and diesel fumes.

Using the open passenger door as a makeshift dressing screen, he steps out of his jeans and into the suit pants. Smears the dust and grime off the boots with the wadded-up T-shirt, then tugs the hem over the laces. All the while he keeps glancing through the windshield, willing the dump truck and the fat man to reappear. Again, one ignition click—*11:54.* He gives up knotting the tie, yanking at it like a backward noose in frustration. He needs a pen and paper. There is no pen and paper but—back on the bench seat—a red crayon. He holds his breath, steadies his grip, then prints his name and the number of his dead cell phone onto the paper liner of the McDonald's ice cream cone.

"Órale. Que guapo, güey."

"Here." He hands Jorge the paper liner. The gesticulations his hands are flapping and folding into are ridiculous but he doesn't care. He needs Jorge to understand.

"Yo necesito to go—va, I mean, yo voy, right now. Ahora, okay? But so when the fat man pays you, you take mi dinero, too, and then call me at this número. Mi número, got it? Fifty dolares. No, wait, after the gas, it's forty. Forty. Cuatro-cero, para mi, okay? Comprende?"

Jorge nods. Shakes Henry's hand, wishes him *buena suerte*, tells him *que vaya con dios*. Henry can't help looking from the good eye to the socket. In that fleshy recess he detects a definitive loneliness, and so fears this could very well be good-bye for good.

Henry is driving recklessly. Blasting past and swerving around other vehicles, all of which seem to be occupying the road for no reason other than to delay and aggravate him, until he comes screeching to a stop outside a CVS.

Henry storms through the entrance and startles a dozing rent-a-cop. All the products and displays smear as he power walks in search of the deodorant aisle, still fiddling and failing with the necktie. He pivots, now facing a multicolored wall, each of its hundreds of bricks promising a unique scent or odor-combating technology, none of which are on sale. He reaches for the Old Spice, full price $4.97. Given what's left in his front pocket, this is extravagant. Still has to buy dinner for Junior, and, after this, there's no way he'll be able to purchase some sort of penance for this morning's outburst. Plus, if he wants to get that call from Jorge for the forty and later hear back from the interviewer, he's got to load the five dollar minimum onto his prepay phone—yet another expense he's been putting off, because who the hell is trying to get ahold of him, who the fuck is he supposed to be reaching out to?

Farther down, before the shaving gels and creams and razors and trimmers, are sample bottles of cologne, tethered to a shelf by thin metal cables. He sniffs at the nozzles, not sure what to be smelling for. He settles on the Drakkar Noir, its French-sounding name seeming more refined than Adidas or Playboy. He untucks the shirt-front and stuffs the bottle under the fabric, blindly aiming the nozzle at his left armpit.

"Don't move."

The rent-a-cop has assumed the self-seriousness of a real cop, posing at the end of the aisle. Thumbs hooked in his utility belt, he approaches Henry, who is now shocked frozen in this compromising position. To make things worse, the panic and embarrassment twitching over his face can't possibly help him look less red-handed. He goes ahead and degrades himself even further when he tries explaining himself, the situation—just a little mixed-up misunderstanding—by calling the man *sir*. Like a fugitive spotlit, surrounded, and setting his weapon to the ground, he slowly withdraws the cologne, showing it's still secured to the shelf.

"I'm not—I wasn't stealing, wouldn't steal anything, not ever, sir. Just testing it, I swear—sir? Just, please?"

The security guard deflates like a fisherman, his line snapped by the first keeper all week. Instead of *sir*, he refers to Henry as *bud*.

"Had to check. Saw you and you looked, well," he says, wiggling a walkie-talkie antenna at a black plastic half sphere screwed into the ceiling. "You know."

Henry does know. This means the rent-a-cop has probably been watching Henry from the moment he'd stomped in, which also means Henry isn't fooling anyone. Even in this suit, he must look like some deadbeat. Loser. Degenerate. Grifter. Like a fool, he thanks the security guard before shuffling away to grab Junior's dinner, a can of Chef Boyardee spaghetti and meatballs. He sets this and a Snickers for himself onto the counter. Without looking up, he tells the cashier he needs to put five bucks on his prepay. Gets five digits in only to get thinking, only to reconsider. Jorge won't call. Those forty dollars are gone, which makes these five all the more precious.

"Never mind," he says.

"Need help?"

The cashier's skin is the color and texture of a pecan, imbuing her with a windblown yet sturdy air of knowing. The curls of her weave sit in a lush purple nest on her shoulder. Her question has only one answer, but all Henry manages is, "Huh?"

"With your tie." She points at the ribbons dangling from his neck. "My ex never got the hang of it either."

She comes around the counter. Toe to toe with Henry, she smells wonderful. A clean, earthy aroma. Manicured nails make tiny clicks against each other and the buttons of his shirt. Her knuckles graze his chest. He's so hungry that he's made a moron, made feeble, and it's been so long since a woman last touched him. As she cinches the knot up to his clavicle, the top of her hand warms the length of his sternum. She pats his upper arm, gives it a squeeze. Tells him now that's better. Very handsome.

Blood rushes to his cheeks, makes him lurch as if by a tide. To her hands, those gentle, delicate hands, he says thank you. Can't quite bring himself to look directly at her, as if doing so might change her mind about him. He turns to leave before he says or does something to embarrass himself.

"Sir?"

"Yeah?" he sputters, twisting back to her. "I mean, yes?"

She is beautiful. Exquisite. He wants to empty the cash register and run away with her.

"You forgot to pay. Total is three eighteen."

$1.75

Two hours and twice as many buses had passed before Henry gave up. Michelle wasn't just late—she wasn't coming. Turned out he would need the bus fare he'd so proudly waved away. He turned from the open road, shuffled under the watchtowers, back through the prison gates. Buzzes and clanks. Inside, the same guard who'd discharged him earlier now gave him seven quarters. Then a wry smirk, which Henry found oddly reassuring, as if suggesting he wasn't the first to have come crawling back for spare change.

When the next bus pulled up, the driver clapped a hand over the coin slot. His forearms were thick and smudgy with tattoos. He nodded, then told Henry, "Welcome back, son."

Wanting to put as much distance between himself and charity as possible, Henry went to the last seat and huddled against the window. In its frame scrolled the watchtowers, windowless complexes, chain-link perimeter, and razor-wire curlicues, until the prison and five years gave way to combed farmland and October fog.

Michelle had better have a good fucking excuse. Even Papa'd remembered to come scoop Henry from rehab, nearly a decade ago. As dejected as this abandonment left him, the feeling still got leavened by the movement of the bus, its steady charge through the sprawl. It was bewildering how, for his entire life, he'd taken such velocity for granted, if he ever considered it at all. Back in his cell, after lights-out, the walls narrowed with each exhale, closing in on him, suffocating him. Gag ball. Straitjacket. Drowning. Every night his aches and memories had engorged him into an animal too big and scared for that concrete box, but now—out here—he was downright puny.

No latch to open the window, but there were worse things than imagining his breath as a prairie wind against the cold window. He blew a gauzy patch onto the pane, obscuring the plains beyond. A fingertip blotted a penny-sized aperture into the frost, and through it he saw everything he could ever ask for. A pinch of land would do just fine. After all, now that he was so minuscule, who was to say itty-bitty Henry couldn't chisel out a little nook for himself and his family? This time around, he wouldn't bother anybody. He would keep out of everyone's way, keep his head down and eyes fastened to the task at hand, he swore it.

It took three transfers and a twenty-minute walk along the shoulder of a county road to reach the Indigo Hills sign. Night fell without ceremony, as if dusk had forgotten him, too. No sunset pyrotechnics for his return, just the sad confetti of brown leaves beneath charcoal clouds.

Five years had done a number on the trailer park. The rougher, western end's neglect had spread to their side, what used to be the nicer half of the park. The years had smashed beer bottles on the streets, chucked bald tires into front yards. Coughed away paint and sneezed mold onto aluminum siding. Put up and forgotten campaign signs, let them soak and prune along with the garden gnomes, folding chairs, pinwheels, and flamingos. As he approached his truck in the driveway, he thought back to picking Michelle up for their first date. Pulling in and seeing her slung over an aluminum lawn chair in a heroic slouch. How she'd marched through the bong smoke, her Doc Marten stomp somehow bellicose and blasé all at once. How her grin was almost cruelly cool as she eyed him like a midnight snack, which she could savor as easily as spit out.

Bone rapped against wood. The knocks were coming from behind his truck, ratcheting quicker and sterner against the front door. A gravelly voice told Michelle it knew she was in there.

It was the park manager, Sandi. The name had always suited her. Virginia Slims had sizzled her face into a shovelful of dry soil. An aging biker groupie, she loved nothing more than gossiping with the leather-vested, Santa-bearded tenants, and climbing onto the backs of their Harleys, whose exhaust pipes were far less menacing than her voice. She'd never liked Henry, and now reminded him of this with a sneer.

"I want my money," she told him.

"Nice to see you, too."

Her face knotted in thought. As if only now registering his prolonged absence, or, more likely, determining the appropriate racial slur for him. She made her way down the steps, the lattice facedown over coarse grass. As she passed, she reminded him she wanted her fucking money.

"Yeah, yeah," he said. "Don't get your diaper in a bunch."

Michelle didn't answer until Henry said Sandi was gone, c'mon, it was him. The door creaked back, a chain strapping the narrow gap steady. In it appeared a sliver of Michelle. "Hen?"

"Yeah."

Once the door opened, they just stood there, took a moment to measure each other against the molds of their previous shapes, the templates of their younger, former selves. The Michelle before him looked shaved down, as colorless as autumn drizzle. Unkempt in loose shorts, fleece-lined boots, and a hoodie. Her chin was working its way toward words. Maybe a greeting, preferably an apology. Whatever it was, it seemed to be eroding whatever dregs she had left.

The martyr in him hated how easily he forgave her. All it took was reaching into the drapes of her sweater and tugging her close. The joints of their bodies creaked into place like a snaggletooth zipper. Latched tight and warming, he shushed her when she said sorry, and something surged inside him. He was tremendous and terrified all over again. Had to close his eyes. Settle in, calm himself. From the darkness came a loud burst that stunned him back into the living room.

The burst hadn't been in his head. It was the bathroom door clapping shut. A child had just dashed inside.

"Junior?"

When they unclasped, Henry shrank back down to more familiar proportions. Michelle stretched back the skin of her face with both hands, then started patting at it like a mound of clay she was trying to arrange into a sturdier composition. She bent into the bathroom's doorknob and told it that daddy was home, and he was really, super excited to see his big boy, like. Didn't Junior want to come out here and say hello?

Henry couldn't altogether blame the boy. He was essentially a stranger, little more than an acquaintance to the boy. The obligatory nature of their previous encounters made those visitation hours terse, strained, like submitting to sweaty, distant-uncle hugs at a family reunion. Only he hadn't received even that—an embrace. Not so much as a touch or hello. To Junior, he was just a birthday card sender, a specimen behind glass, begging into a telephone receiver so that the boy might reach up and press his palm against the pane, too.

He told Michelle to forget it. Let the kid be. It was fine.

The park's spreading decay had found its way into their home as well. Every surface was coated in grime so dense it was more scab than filth. All the mirrors hung crooked and dusty, and the black pleather sofa was pocked with rips, releasing wisps of white padding from tiny, rabid mouths. Their trailer was a one-bedroom unit, so the corner by the living room bookshelf had been designated as Junior's space, marked by a bare mattress. On it lay a plum sofa cushion for a pillow and Mom's bese saka shawl, twisted and worn translucent like a shed snakeskin. A bicycle against the wall. Lego pieces scattered across the Frankenstein floorboards, sticky under his boot soles. He squatted to examine the object the boy had been assembling before fleeing for the bathroom. It was a simple, square box. He was impressed by how the boy had shaped it into an even-sided cube, the corner pieces alternating, interlocked to ensure structural integrity. It showed promise, potential. Imagine: his son an architect, an engineer—relevant.

Planning. Future thinking. Dreams curdled by an awareness of the self-delusion necessary to even momentarily entertain such fantasies. But this cube, constructed with such meticulous technique by a kid of only six, was actual evidence of potential. It vindicated

Henry's otherwise misguided hopes, and indicated this boy could do so much more, could be so much more.

Henry twirled the bese saka shawl into a fabric nest to properly display the Lego cube like some priceless artifact in a museum. He peered at the bookshelf, up to the most prominent slot: Papa's urn, the journals with Mom's articles. He gave them a frown of approval. Wished they could see this exhibit for themselves. Even though he'd never lived up to his parents' expectations and would never realize the potential they'd mistakenly seen in him, the fact that his own son was bound to surpass him in all respects seemed to one-up all his parents' efforts and hopes for him.

"Hen," Michelle said. "Think someone wants to say hello."

Behind her birch branch legs was Junior. He was a paler version of Henry at that age but already more handsome in a disturbingly adult way. On Junior, the faint hint of Michelle's edges compressed Henry's features into a bust of stoic dignity. Squatting, Henry extended the top of his hand, as if coaxing a stray puppy, and instantly felt stupid, patronizing.

"Hey, bud," he croaked.

Nothing.

"Saw the box you made. It's really good."

The boy said something too hushed to make out.

"Speak up," Michelle said. "Whyn't you get closer, give your dad a hug?"

"It's not a box." The boy came around Michelle to retrieve his creation. "I prefer container."

"That's a much better word," Henry said.

The boy, turning the container in his hands, said *yeah* with academic boredom.

"And so what's it for, though? What's that container contain, huh?"

"It's a secret."

"Can't you tell your pa?" Henry asked. "You can trust me, you know."

The boy looked him dead in the eyes. Henry was sure he would up and die if he didn't get to hug him soon, but he locked his arms into planks at his sides. Couldn't force this, couldn't rush it.

"Wouldn't be much of a secret if I did, would it, Dad?"

Evidently Michelle hadn't listened, had clearly continued referring to Henry as *Dad* in spite of his singular, do-re-mi simple request. In time he would teach the boy, but right now he didn't want to skewer this fragile exchange with a correction. He knew better than that, had to dam this deluge of emotions behind an anodyne smile. He did, however, want that hug. He did his best to wring the meek out of his voice when asking the boy if he could please, pretty please, have one?

The boy looked back at Michelle. She nodded like she'd done to Henry years ago, back when this magnificent creature had been growing inside her. Go ahead. The boy shuffled, knee by knee, across the mattress and into Henry's arms.

The levy snapped. Henry spilled. He squeezed the boy tight, desperate, as if clawing after everything that was suddenly gushing out of him. He sobbed and gasped and moaned and laughed, because, at long last, he'd finally made it home.

After the boy and Michelle had pried themselves free, it didn't take much to get Henry drunk. She hadn't even asked if he wanted a drink. Just went ahead and filled two old jelly jars with Jim Beam, clanked them, said welcome back, then got started in the kitchen. Before the first sip, the fumes alone sent him reeling. He steeled himself, mentally promising Michelle and Junior just this one. He deserved just this one.

Conversation was sparse, the living room dim. After failing to eke out any information about kindergarten or the boy's favorite games or animals or colors or movies, Henry took down the bourbon in a single gulp, fiery and delightful. While debating a refill, he joined Michelle in the kitchenette. She was slicing hot dogs on the countertop with a meat cleaver. Next to a box of store-brand mac'n'cheese, blue flames stroked a pot of water.

The booze and the sight of her got him giddy, simmering, aggressive. He thought back to when she was pregnant, bent over the kitchen sink. Swelling against his inner thigh, his hard-on pressed past the seven quarters in his pocket, each ridge a caress. With one tug, her hoodie was on the floor. He pressed up to her from behind. All of her twined, tensed. He lapped at her ears and neck greedily, huffing in this new musk of her, a blend of cut grass and polyurethane. She was thinner than ever, her ribs a xylophone, her hip bones spades, but his famine overrode concern. The elastic of her shorts was loose, a worn-out rubber wavelength inviting his fingers inside. When his hand dove into her shorts, she lurched.

"Not now, Hen."

"C'mon. Dinner can wait."

"No."

Henry reached. Shut off the stovetop flames. He stroked her stomach, and again groped south. "C'mon."

"No, Hen."

"I'm starving here." He clawed into her panties, their threadbare cotton almost moldy to the touch. Just one yank would rip them off her. "I want—"

"*I said no, motherfucker.*" She snapped away, wielding the cleaver like a battle-axe. Her irises were jittering with a familiar strung-out current, though one he'd never seen coursing through her. His hard-on curled up like a frightened hedgehog, shriveling beneath the quarters in his pocket. His feet drew the rest of him back, away. Junior watched from the mattress, crouched tense as if on starting blocks, at the ready to pounce should he be called to protect his mother from Henry, the stranger.

"Easy, easy," he said, pushing air as if warding off bonfire smoke.

"You can't, like." The cleaver clanked against granite. She massaged her face again. "Like, like, have your cake and eat it whenever the fuck you feel like, feel me?"

He didn't, but fuck it. If he couldn't have cake, then bourbon would have to do. He filled his jar, shot it, then poured a third serving to nurse. Michelle turned her back to him and resumed chopping hot dogs, her shoulders flexed and edgy. Junior glared at him, tracking his every step from the kitchen on over to the TV. Henry smacked it on, rummaged through wrappers, papers, and empty cans on the coffee table for the remote, then flopped onto the couch. The rabid mouths wheezed in unison under his abrupt weight. Michelle's rejection and outburst had gotten him lightheaded and cold-sweaty, a feeling that seemed to match the static he found on every channel. Of course. Hunky-dory. Fine and dandy. Fuck.

"Cable's out," he announced.

"Really think we can afford cable?"

"Ask Al to get one of the skinnies to come hotwire this shit."

The blade clattered into the sink. She stormed out of the kitchen and into the bathroom. The TV's snowstorm sustained the silence after Henry's slip of the tongue, as if to make him dwell on his mistake. As if he hadn't spent half a decade wallowing in the shame of what he'd done, so the last five years hadn't been fifty. His molars started grinding to fill his skull with another noise, a different thrum, one that wasn't quite loud enough to wash out his mental pleading and whining or, now, the *knock knock* on the front door.

Henry lasered a look that was meant to send Junior to the door, but the boy was absorbed in fastening a lid to the Lego container.

"Who is it?" Henry yelled.

No answer. Peeling himself off the couch, he imagined gripping the jelly jar and driving its rim square into Sandi's front teeth. The impulse was so great and his hate so large that—to keep himself out of trouble—he backhanded a clearing among the coffee table's debris to leave this potential weapon. The toilet flushed. Michelle came out, clambering her shorts up, humping over and barricading herself between Henry and the front door, saying move already, christ almighty.

On the front step was a man in white overalls, a white T-shirt, and white paint splattered past his wrists. A grin for Michelle vanished when he noticed Henry, who now crossed his arms to bloat the meat of his forearms. In the yard, he'd avoided eye contact at all costs, but here, in his own home, he was alpha.

Michelle said it was cool, she fucking got it, then shoved Henry aside.

Seemed if Henry wasn't screwing things up, he was getting in her way, and so to spare them all yet another showdown, he shuffled off to go stare at the pot of water, to make it boil. Over the hiss of gas and the water's simmer, he heard Michelle thank the painter. She told him to come on, relax. Ought to know she were good for it by now, like. Her hand stuffed itself into the hoodie's pocket, where it remained after she shut the door and returned to the stove, making a show of ignoring Henry.

No milk, no butter, so the three of them sat side by side on the sofa pushing spiral noodles and hot dog chunks through bowls of orange broth. The bourbon sank Henry into a divot in the cushion, as if lowering himself rather than lifting the bowl in order to slurp down the salty juice. He thought back to the last time there'd been three sitting on this sofa. Instead of the sprig of his son carefully blowing on a spoonful of noodles, in Henry's periphery had been Al, chuckling and swiping a credit card across the surface of a mirror. The TV, switched on but soundless, was now tuned to the only channel that came in, a grainy, public access something. Two white men sat across from each other at a round table. The set behind them was pitch black, so dark and shapeless that gauging its size was impossible. Could have been filmed in outer space or a coffin, for all Henry could tell. No way to know much about that place, and that's why there was one thing about it which he was absolutely, 100 percent, totally certain about. It was the exact same place where, at this very moment, Al must have been.

The boy tipped his bowl and drank the last of the neon soup. He used the heel of his palm to napkin his lips. Smiled, gave a full-belly sigh. Then, when he rose, Henry snatched the boy's arm—harder than he would have liked.

"Forget something?" Henry said.

The boy looked scared. Henry held firm.

"Mom?"

"Hen, let go. You're hurting him."

He pulled the boy close. The spoon rattled, then fell to the floor. "Your mother made you a nice, warm dinner. Now what do you say?"

"Mom?"

Henry made a nightmarish, game-show buzzer screech. "Wrong. Try again."

"Hen, what in the fuck do you think you're—"

"Teaching our son manners. Etiquette. Respect." He drew the boy closer still. "Now, Junior. After somebody takes the time to do something kind for you, what do we say?"

"Thank you?"

"Thank you, *who*?"

"Thank you, Mom?"

"Thank you, Mom, for what?"

"Thank you, Mom, for dinner?"

"And how was that dinner?"

"Henry."

"Dad, I don't—"

"Pa. My name is *Pa*," he said. "Now. Thank your mother for the warm, delicious dinner. Compliments are important. Courtesy, it's called. Gratitude, see? Now let's hear it."

The boy looked down at the spoon. It lay still. The boy was shaking.

"Now."

"Hen."

"Now."

"Thank you for the warm, delicious dinner, Mom."

Henry roared, exultant, proud. At last, he released the boy's arm to applaud him with a stern clap on the back. He raised his jar to Michelle, a toast to this feat of parenting.

She mouthed *asshole*, then scooped Junior up and into the kitchenette with her. Henry was impressed with himself, having found his stride as a father—a papa—in mere hours. To think this very morning he'd woken up on a stiff plastic cot in a prison cell was surreal. This was an achievement worthy of celebration, like the night at Red Lobster, when for a night he'd been rich, when for a moment he'd been god.

He wanted a marching band, fireworks, cocaine, and champagne, but the bottom corner of the Beam was all that was left and so would have to do.

Facing a corner, Michelle dug into the pocket of her hoodie and slapped a palm to her mouth. Dry swallowed. Shook her head. Leading Junior to the bathroom to start getting him ready for bed, she paused in front of Henry, who was sprawled spread-eagle on the sofa. She fingered a gnarled plastic baggie out of her pocket. Pinched out a red circular pill and gave it to Henry.

"You need this more than me," she said. "If that don't chill you out and shut you up, then I don't know what."

Far cry from champagne and the exact opposite effect of coke, but, like the bourbon, the Oxy would have to do. He popped then chased it down with the last of his jelly jar's amber.

Soon enough, a match was struck—a blissful wick glowing and growing in his belly. This radiance worked through all his goo, cell by cell, past membranes and around tendons, until it met the final barrier of his skin. Serenity leaked out from under his fingernails and undulated up into the air of the living room, where it unfurled and dispersed and had taken hold of Michelle, too. She was toweling Junior dry with an air of peaceful vacancy. The jitter of her irises had been subdued, netted by a silky droop to her eyelids. A muffled, faraway memory of this afternoon reminded him of how strange and fucked up a day it'd been, so much so that it now seemed to be playing out in front of him like a soap opera rather than from his own perspective. As if through a sniper's scope, he watched himself whimpering at the bus stop. She'd forgotten him, left him stranded and waiting on the day he'd believed—hadn't for a millisecond questioned—was going to be monumental for the two of them. Sure, he'd gotten a bit pushy with her, but in the name of passion. A little hard on Junior, but in the name of parenting. He was sorry. He was trying. But what more could they expect? He was a caged hyena now released, famished and slobbering after his appetite, only to get tranquilized and succumb, and quite happily at that.

His muzzle stretched, drawing in air for a howl or cackle, but instead he yawned. His tongue lapped over his lips and teeth, prodded the indent of his canine and dislodged a morsel of hot dog. He swallowed.

It was a fight to get to the bedroom. Five years had leveled his tolerance. What had been a serene fuzz while he was seated now gelled into a damp morass he had to wade through, the floor squishy and teetering under each step. Skull full of helium but shoes turned into anvils, he lost his footing and began stumbling until the doorframe rescued him. It eased him upright. He hugged the carpet with his toes, steadying his sights so he could decipher the mirage rippling inside the bedroom. By squeezing one eye shut, he managed to superimpose the two opaque, Michelle-like shapes into the single, actual, marvelous her. Michelle. His machete and everything, his all that and then some. She gave a low, understanding chuckle, and he returned a high, dimwitted snicker, and just like that, the two of them were shucked clean of any lingering anger or guilt. Just like that, they forgave and forgot this very strange and fucked-up day.

A slow, careful game of undressing each other. Plenty of time-outs to rest, moan, kiss, giggle, then giggle at their giggling. Either he'd slithered under her or she'd somehow scaled him—the trail of their progress was muddled, erased, but so was everything that wasn't right here on their skin or in their mouths. All that mattered was that they were belly to belly, their minds tiptoeing the edges of sleep, while the rest of them melded into a single, tender hide.

While Michelle pittered in and out of sleep like raindrops off pine needles, Henry didn't want to give in to oblivion, not just yet. He wanted this to last, and thought sharing it with someone else might help sustain it. He eased Michelle off him, their naked, gummy pelts peeling like cling wrap off lasagna. When he stood, he found that the pill had worn off a bit and restored some solidity to the floor, which was now less seesaw, more diving board. He opened his drawer and was stroked with reassurance, seeing his clothes untouched, folded as neatly as he'd left them five years ago. He stepped into a pair of gym shorts, then went to the living room where a blizzard was scrolling on the TV, right above Junior. The boy slept in the same pose Henry found himself in every morning: face up, spine rigid, hands in a funereal stack over his sternum. Unwilling to risk waking or scaring the boy, he lay down on the floor, propping his cheek on the corner of the mattress to better observe.

Sure was something. What exactly, though, he didn't know the word for, if such a sensation had ever been located and named before now. Didn't need a word. This was simply a moment, an opportunity—his. This was his chance to tell the boy things he could explain, as well as the others he was still figuring out. No perfect place to start, so his breath unraveled into sentences similar to those he'd fed into the phone back on the boy's first birthday. Tonight was different, though. Without a pane to separate them, his message would surely reach its intended recipient. He told the boy secrets and praise, made promises and oaths, then very gently took the boy's hand into his. The last thing he said before drifting off to sleep, too, was sorry.

$9.04

All the online job forums said if you're not fifteen minutes early to an interview, you're late. And so, by this count, Henry is already five minutes tardy.

The address has taken him to an industrial park on the outskirts of the next town east. The blueprints for these buildings hadn't sought inspiration any further than their most fundamental building material: the cinder block. At the perimeter of each concrete container after concrete container are wide black moats of asphalt poured over burnt-up and bought-out farmland. He accelerates past parking lots designed with higher turnouts in mind, much more than this scattering of midsized sedans and minivans, their windshields glimmering with tin-foil accordions to deflect the nine-to-five sun. He is six minutes late when he brakes, coming up fast behind an eighteen-wheeler that's crawling ten below the speed limit.

The semi's brake lights now flare as red as he feels, and the trailer creeps to a complete stop in the middle of the road. Reverse lights blink silver, a beeping rings out, and so Henry's got to throw his truck in reverse to let this tortoise son of a bitch back up into a shipping company's loading zone. Again, this fuckwit turns too sharp, has already jackknifed the trailer twice, and now trudges forward to straighten out for a third attempt, apparently hell bent on delaying Henry and ruining his life.

Eight minutes late. In the rearview mirror, the road behind is empty. He peeks between the trailer's axles, and the coast is clear ahead as well. He cranks the wheel left, throttling hard to hop the curb. The truck bed fishtails, tires spinning over the grass until catching traction, and he goes squealing around and past the semi. As soon as the front tires thump back over the curb, he floors it, rocketing down the road for another thirty seconds before screeching up to the address. It looks like any other warehouse along the way, but up this close he can see a black glass door pressed into the middle of its khaki facade.

Whether nine minutes late or six early, he's still going to need two. The forums advised a full two minutes of posing like Superman in a mirror. There's no reason whatsoever, they assured, to be embarrassed about verbalizing words of self-encouragement. This will boost confidence, testosterone. Not enough time to scramble in search of the men's room inside, so he marches right up to the black door. In its sheen he is met by his reflection, cast dim as if through sunglasses. Together, they twist knuckles into their hip bones. Roll their shoulders back. Their chests expand, their chins lift then tilt, and he wonders which, if he even has one, is his good side.

The mirror trick actually works. Holding himself with such authority seems to shrink his outdated suit down to more modern tailoring standards. The pant cuffs show no sign of last night's jury-rigged alterations. The flush of his cheeks isn't the toast of anxiety but pure vigor. After the Snickers bar's sugar and protein, he's still hungry but not famished. The hunger is good. It will sharpen him, file him down to a predatorial focus. So lean, he keeps the waistband from falling with his left hand in the pocket, lending him a casual air and freeing the right for hearty handshakes. Only his hair is in need of adjustment. As if preparing to grab a retaining wall block, he spits into a palm, then rubs both together. He molds the black pouf down, to the left, and it doesn't just do—it looks good.

He's no impostor, no fraud. He is an American like everybody else, and so entitled to everything else. Summoning this morning's homeowner—white, clean, easy-go-lucky free—Henry shakes his hand with the self-assuredness of a man with nothing to prove, for they are equals in both capacity and worth. A pleasure to meet you, truly. Most certainly. Super.

He flaps into one last flex. With the heel of his fist, he traces a wide *S* across his chest and fastens it with a pound. Ribs don't give an inch and he is ready. The door swings open and right inside is a security guard, slouched against a counter, smirking. "Looking mighty sharp, Mr. Kent."

"Henry, actually."

"It's a joke, kid."

"Yeah, no." Henry tries chuckling into focus, normalcy. "I, uh, got an interview. It's over at Hor—"

"Horizon Lines. Right." The guard makes a finger pistol, fires it to the right. "Last door thataway."

As Henry makes his way down the hallway, the security guard tells him to go get 'em, champ. A gunmetal carpet absorbs his footfalls, allowing the old, linear lightbulbs set in the checkerboard of asbestos ceiling tiles to hum uninterrupted. Right outside the entrance, he's fine, just great indeed. He grits his teeth into a high-beam smile and pushes through the door.

"You must be Henry. I'm Alex."

The extended hand belongs to a person quite the opposite of the homeowner. Alex is a stocky black woman, her hair cropped short and dyed yellow, a wig of microwave popcorn. She looks tough but understanding, the sleeves of a man's oxford shirt rolled past forearms like chimneys. Her Nikes are spotless and have a boisterous, Las Vegas color scheme. Henry slackens with relief. Her he can handle, see things eye to eye. Even her bone-crushing handshake is better than strained chitchat about airline preferences or golf handicaps.

Henry's greeting enters the air perfectly naturally, exactly as he's rehearsed.

"Pleasure is all mine, Henry. Right this way."

Alex has the sturdy, bow-legged gait of a shot-putter. Past the reception area, the space opens into a sprawling factory floor striped with a series of desks and men arranged as neatly as a tractor-plowed field. All the rows dart and shrink toward the same point—a mirror-paneled cube in the center of the floor, as if it's there to force the men to watch themselves being watched. Bulky male necks and shoulders stiffen as Alex and Henry pass from behind, though not a single head turns to greet or even peek at them. The employees sit shoulder to shoulder, speaking into headsets and staring at computer monitors, wearing polo shirts the same traffic-cone orange of county jail smocks. Despite the vast spread of this office, its ceiling feels oppressively low, amplifying the collective din of voices, keystrokes, mouse clicks, and that ceaseless lightbulb drone.

The center cube is Alex's office. Inside it is neat and sparse. Reminds Henry of the interrogation room, except here the one-way mirror is reversed and on all sides, turning him into an invisible spectator in the center of a sold-out arena. Alex falls into an ergonomic, micronetted desk chair with spacecraft-worthy lumbar support. The chair Henry sits on is a stiff, unwelcoming contraption, like a bear trap caught mid-clamp. When he sits, the backrest bends him to attention. He shifts, settles, then shifts again, kicking an ankle onto his knee. His fingers interlock, then sink to rest over his belly button. Having found an arrangement of limbs he hopes showcases a balanced blend of poise and affability, he gives Alex a frown of approval. This is her cue. She may begin.

"I'm sure you're familiar with what we do here, but legal makes me give every applicant this same rundown before the interview itself, so bear with me, k, Henry?"

"Sure thing," he says, certain he's never uttered those two words together. The chin dip now dispatched is meant to convey how thoroughly versed he already is in all that she's about to relay, as well as how sympathetic he is to the nuisance of legal's insistence on such tiresome protocol. So, yes, by all means, Alex. Proceed.

She lifts a laminated sheet of talking points though doesn't seem to be reading off it. Her tone is bored and almost apologetic, explaining how here at Horizon Lines, it's essential they're upfront, transparent about the fact that they're a privately owned corporation that gets considerable funding from the state's correctional department due to the training and hiring processes they practice, k? Reintegration, they call it. Yeah, yeah, she ain't exactly wild about the term either, believe her, but hey. Essentially, Henry, the company is interested in cutting labor costs while the state wants to get ex-cons trained and employable for a modern, service-based economy. All the gentlemen he can see around him start off in this call center, and they're getting themselves invaluable, firsthand customer service experience. Learning how to accommodate clients' needs and getting familiar with professional jargon. Every last one of them gets to study the ins and outs of all kinds of businesses' policies, everything from credit card companies and hotel chains on down to loan servicing and retail. That sort of stuff, all right? Pay ain't stellar but he's guaranteed his forty. Decent healthcare package, matching 401k option, but the potentially life-changing benefits are the biweekly, on-site workshops that Horizon Lines puts on. Cover things like marketing research, sales techniques, even management strategies, and all that whatnot. Fact is, if he asks her, it's good, meaningful work they do here. And, boy, he ought to see some of the fellas she's got over the years. He's one of the lucky ones, best believe that. Still young. Had a short sentence, less than hers—she winks—but there's plenty of guys out there who'd done thirty, forty, fifty years plus. They stepped out and into one scary-ass, brand-new world that didn't give half a goddamn about them, specially since all they got to offer workwise, more often than not, is either skills for jobs that'd been sent to China, or the same shit—stuff, she means, the same stuff that'd got them locked up in the first place. End-all be-all of what she's trying to say here is that, if all this sounds good, fair, upright, and all, well, then they can move right along to the interview. All's Henry's got to do is initial here, there again by that sticky tab, then sign and date on the last page.

He adjusts his tie. Tells her it all sounds stupendous. She sure must be proud of doing such good, meaningful work. She nods, then rolls a pen over. He initials twice, writes down the date, then draws his signature as sharp and deliberate as a skyline.

Though Alex doesn't look like the type who would say *cool beans*, she says just that. She reviews the contents of a manila folder, and then asks the most horrific of all interview questions:

"How's about we start with you telling me a bit about yourself?"

"Yes, gladly, Alex. Absolutely." He clears absolutely nothing from his throat.

It's an out-of-body, out-of-his-mind experience. The answer he gives (or at least hears himself giving) is earnest, tactful, and glossed with sterilized workplace elocution. He manages to cover the scope of his work history, seaming his own real-life, firsthand experience to the relevant, transferable skills he'd memorized from the job description. He touches on his *time away*, then expertly segues into a condensed meditation on what he'd learned from prison rather than the experience itself. He calls these lessons *takeaways*, the most important of which, Alex, was the importance of family. The value of commitment and devotion to his own, to be there for him—them. To provide them a safe, comfortable life full of the opportunities that maybe he'd once had, but had been too shortsighted or just plain scared to pursue himself.

This whole time he's been tracking Alex's nods and eyebrow scrunches for hints of suspicion or boredom, neither of which, by his measure, he's provoked, even after speaking only about himself for such a long, unbroken stretch of minutes. In fact, she appears to be really listening, actually seems interested in what he's saying, maybe even in him as a person.

This must be why rich people go to therapy. What a delight to be heard, to be understood and matter. Nearing the end of his monologue, he's overtaken by a soothing wave brought on by something more than the successful delivery of his abridged life story. Instead, he can't help but suspect this foreign balm might simply be the attention, perhaps even sympathy, of another human being.

By the end, he's so depleted that he can't assemble anything but a cliché to close on, telling her that's him in a nutshell.

She jots something in the folder. And when she thanks him for sharing, it sounds like she really means it.

The rest of the questions are all pretty standard, basically word for word off his note cards. No curveballs about the number of jumbo jets currently airborne around the globe, or grains of sand in the Sahara. Nothing about desert island reading material, or previous workplace role models. She does sneak in one cutesy question about what kind of animal he would be, and he says dog. Though a number of reasons flutter about him, the only two he catches and now releases are loyalty and caring, which appear to satisfy her just fine. How great. Swell.

Otherwise, it's all:

Why should I hire you?

Why do you want this job?

How do you deal with conflict?

And stress?

He even nails the three biggest weaknesses question. Impatience, stubbornness, and unrealistic expectations, he tells her, then briefly touches on how he's working on each one, overcoming them, maneuvering his answers into not-so-subtle suggestions that these ostensible shortcomings might actually be virtues when considered from a different perspective. Impatience, from another angle, could be punctuality, or a demand for efficiency, right? Stubbornness reflects a firm belief system, a solid moral foundation. And another term for unrealistic expectations is ambition. Some might call them dreams.

He should not have yelled at Junior this morning.

"Henry?"

He shakes himself back into the office, snaps back into the bear trap. "Sorry."

"No problem. We're almost done." She makes another quick note. "So, last but not least: Where do you see yourself in five years?"

His mind's eye shrieks white. In the pale expanse, he sees a speck, a faraway silhouette. It is approaching, crystallizing into focus. It is Junior, not only nearing but actually growing. He is older here, has filled out into a young man—a robust, laughing version of Henry himself at that age yet unsapped by grief, drugs, or malice. A brick house sprouts then settles, clean and built into the earth. Inside is a kitchen with a full pantry, a fridge brimming with a cornucopia of produce—bundles of green asparagus and lettuce, yellow lemons and bell peppers, red tomatoes and apples, purple grapes and onions—and a window above the sink gives onto a blue-stone patio and a grill of industrial proportions. When he lifts the lid and the smoke clears, he sees steaks the size of his head, sizzling and squared by char lines, next to a chain of swollen sausages that wind around juicy chicken drumsticks dripping fat and barbecue sauce into the flames. He's seen plenty enough.

"With any luck," he says, "right here."

Alex's head tilts, an invitation to elaborate.

"And, hopefully, in a higher position? Right. More responsibilities, new challenges, you know? Suppose I could see me doing something like what you do. Helping others get their good foot forward. First things first, though, I got to concentrate on getting *this* job, and then doing it good and right. Take it as it comes. A step-by-step, day-by-day sort of thing."

She writes a longer note this time. The manila folder closes without a sound. She rises, extends an open hand across the desk. "Thanks for coming in, Henry. That was great."

"Really?"

"Really."

"So does that mean I'm good? I got it? I mean, I can start tomorrow—right this very minute if you want, just say the word."

"Technically speaking," Alex says, waving the folder, "I got to run all this by my boss, protocol and all. But let's just say, between you and me, I got a hunch you'll be getting a call from somebody upstairs by the end of the week."

Jubilation. Fireworks and champagne and orgasms. By the time Henry makes it to the truck, he's dizzy from clenching all his gristle in order to have stopped himself from pirouetting out of Alex's cube and cartwheeling down the channel of desks and heads, then leaping out the front door and into the sun. Alone now, he can let loose. He squeezes the steering wheel to anchor his torso, bucking and thump-

208

ing on the driver's seat like a rodeo steer. No crow, no river, but still he screams and screams.

All he's got to subdue this thrill are his fists, flattening elation against the steering wheel, the dashboard, pound after pound after pound. He's got to collect himself, has to get back to thinking what's what. First things first, he'd told Alex, and so first of all, he's got to figure out what that first thing actually is.

The phone. He's got to get it charged with juice and minutes. After all, Alex said *by* Friday, so—who knows?—they might be calling him sooner. What if they called him later today? Not a minute to lose. He digs the flip phone out of the door's side pocket, then unwinds the charger's cord like some mangled yo-yo. For safekeeping, he stuffs the cigarette burner into his front pocket, then plugs the charger into the dashboard and sets the phone in the cup holder. The instant the engine turns, he's flooring it, racing out of the industrial park and into the first gas station he can find.

The gas station shop's window is a collage of cigarette and energy drink posters, their colors as bright as shouts. In a strip of glass between two ads, his reflection flashes. It stops him. No doubt about it: he is visibly stronger, bolder, sharper. He is radiant. He loosens the tie and undoes the shirt's top button, lending him an air of chic nonchalance, and in this condition an idea comes to him as if by a breeze, because in this condition there's no way, nohow, anyone could tell him no.

He goes directly to the back corner, the fridges. Twenty-four ounces of the Champagne of Beers for $2.99 is a fair price, well worth it, because it's very much deserved. Anyway, he's already bought that can of Chef Boyardee for Junior's dinner. The beer along with the five bucks' worth of minutes for the phone, he assures himself, are an investment. Not just to remain reachable for the call from Horizon Lines, but also for Jorge with this morning's forty dollars.

Henry steps into the checkout line, rolling the can of Miller High Life in an open palm as if it were the grip of a javelin. The cashier is a mousy, angry little thing, the sort whose spite blinds her to how lovely she really is. She catches him staring. She glances up again, catches him again. When he winks, pink percolates out of her dimples and over her cheeks.

He hands her the can in a way that ensures their fingertips touch. Her cuticles are crescents of scabs. She asks how it's going—*beep*.

His elbows plant into the countertop. He leans in, squaring himself in her sight line. "Been a day. Hell of a day. Figure I'll need another ten of those to cope."

A grin curls her lips. "Tell me about it."

This he decides to take literally.

"You wouldn't believe me if I tried," he says. "First of all, I got robbed."

"No shit?"

"Yes, shit. Fuckers pulled a gun on me. Got off with my wallet and phone, right outside my office."

"Oh, my god," she says. "Full-on stickup status?"

"Full on. And that's not even the worst of it. But I'll spare you the boring details and come out with it." He sinks lower to the counter, even closer to her. "Just cut straight to the part where you come in."

"What do you mean?"

"I'm going to need a favor from you. A tiny one. Just a crumb of compassion from you on this terrible, no good, very bad day. Think you can help me out?"

He grins. She grins. "What you got in mind?"

He fans the five and four singles between them. "I managed to scrape this out of my glove compartment and seat cushions. Nine dollars should cover this very necessary beverage along with five bucks' worth of minutes on my backup, prepay cell."

"Okay . . . and?"

"Thing is, my tank is empty. Running on fumes, and I still got to pick my kid up from school two towns over. Now, I hate to put you in a compromising spot and all, but just hear me out. I was thinking maybe you could ring me up for this beer and the phone minutes, plus an even twenty bucks on pump número dos out there. I got plenty of cash at home, and I promise you—on my mother, my son, cross my heart and hope to die—that I'll come straight back here with two crisp twenty-dollar bills: one for the till, the second for your pocket."

Pink goes gray. "Dude. I believe you and all, but."

"How late you working until?"

"Pulling a double, here till midnight, but."

"I'll be back in an hour, tops. That means your register will only be short for not even sixty minutes, that's it. What's the difference, right? And plus another twenty for you. I mean, look at me. You seeing me? You honestly think I'm trying to pull one over on you, hustling a pretty young thing for a squirt of gasoline? C'mon. Give me a hand here."

And so now he takes hers. "Please?"

She peeks behind her. They are alone. He gives her spongy hand a squeeze. She grins, shrugs, then says yeah, fine. Okay. He stops himself short of kissing the top of her hand and instead draws it up to his crown like a blessing.

After running through the phone number to put the five bucks of minutes on, a new idea comes gusting. Why doesn't she go ahead and keep those ten digits for herself now, too? She can call him whenever she wants, for anything she wants.

"And I mean anything."

Her eyes roll, pink reheats, and the cash register rings out at $28.66.

On top of the fiver and four singles, he places one penny, a copper cherry on top. Gets one quarter and two nickels in return. He jingles the change at her. "Hey."

"Hey, what?"

"These thirty-five cents, no," he unpockets his last three pennies. "Excuse me, these thirty-*eight* cents wouldn't cover a Black & Mild, now would they?"

"You're the worst," she says, reaching up to the shelves.

"Wine."

She groans, delighted. She chucks the tobacco twig at his chest. "Now get out!"

One quarter, two nickels, three pennies, and a cigar slip into his front pocket. He grabs the beer then bows, pushing his way out of the door with his ass, telling her she's the best, a lifesaver, an absolute angel. He'll see her soon. Real soon. And she better not forget to call him, okay?

$576.17

Michelle was in a bad way, had lost control. Over the last year, the pills had hollowed her out, leaving in her place a gaunt, greasy shell of the person she'd been. She was using daily—that went without saying. The real question was how many times a day? How many hours had she squandered stoned comatose, or writhing through a comedown? How many precious dollars had she pissed away on pills? And if not cash, then what else was she trading for a fix?

Several times now, Henry'd threatened to strip her name from their joint checking account, but couldn't. In spite of all the broken promises, yelling matches, and castaway ultimatums, he was still too scared of losing whatever fragments were left of her. After his time away, he owed her patience. It was only fair, a score to be settled by compassion. It wouldn't be right to carry out any of his post-argument caveats, such as changing the locks or cutting her off financially, not even from these scraps.

And these were the last of them, the scraps. This paycheck. The final paid eighty hours of his life, after taxes. A year ago, the PO had warned Henry that this gold-plating gig wouldn't last. Places like these were closing left and right, so Henry had better keep an eye out for other job options before the day came—probably a Friday, a payday, now that they'd dismembered the union—when management announced a move across the southern border or to the other side of the Pacific.

Still cushioned by the initial shock of the news, Henry hadn't detonated just yet. With the paycheck dangling at his side like a white flag, he stepped out of the truck and crossed the parking lot to the bank. November was slicing into his jacket, trying to cut him down. He fought to stay upright, even though he couldn't work up the nerve to cut Michelle loose, just like he hadn't been able to work up the nerve to join Lucius, not even an hour ago. Too meek, too scared to pick up that second fire-axe and swing.

The bank teller with the impostor's polish had apparently escaped the plains, had probably moved on to bigger and better things. Henry was still right here. Here in this beige-walled credit union, here in this beige fucking town. Even this replacement teller was as beige and unremarkable as their surroundings. Henry didn't bother with a greeting. Didn't say a word about Michelle's access to the account, either. Just signed and slid the check across the counter. The printed balance statement read the exact sum of the check itself: *$576.17.* Michelle had not only cleaned out their account down to the very last cent—there was also a pending thirty-dollar overdraft fee, which he couldn't afford to approve paying off right now. To keep track of his worth, down to the penny, he carefully folded the statement and slid it into his front pocket.

Calculations crunched through his mind like a mouthful of gravel. It was time to go home. Time for household management, not so much economics as damage control.

The first paycheck of each month went straight to Sandi for lot rent and to chip away at the late fees accrued from when he'd been away. The one he'd just deposited, the month's second, was to be divvied up among the rest of their debts and the barest of necessities. There were still dues on court fees, a good chunk of the bondsman's fee and its accrued interest, as well as old phone bills from the Department of Corrections, which had charged $1.86 per minute, turning Michelle's voice scant by the start of his second year away. Winter had come early and biting, but the thermostat was off-limits. Putting food in their bellies and gas in the tank overrode the inconvenience of wearing layers indoors. They were spread so thin and shivering that any little bit would have helped, but because Michelle had walked out on her last gas station gig, she was disqualified from unemployment benefits.

Getting his head around Michelle's addiction was arduous. His old habits paled on the depravity scale. He'd never been host to a single parasite, never at the mercy of a specific substance's claws. His teenage weekend benders of meth and liquor and pills hadn't been so much a way of life as they'd been a distraction, a vacation from his natural adolescent state of mourning and global disdain. Sure, he'd struggled with limits, doses, and had viewed oblivion as the weekend's ultimate goal, but the resulting hangovers and come-downs were plenty enough to deter him from heavy, habit-forming use midweek. The truth was his own recovery had actually been sort of easy, at least once his relationship with Michelle began.

The doctors had said bulimia was rooted in a need for control, but back when they first met, their healing was a collaborative, even playful act. They upended self-pity with sarcasm, repackaged trauma in the bubble wrap of their mutual, hearse-black humor. They ran constant experiments on each other's sexual and emo-tional machinery, drafting operating manuals for a fully functional and feeling human being. And through that process, qualities like Michelle's curiosity, meticulousness, and machete wit resurfaced and crystallized, suggesting even to her that she might actually de-serve tenderness, too. Oblivion lost its allure once she convinced Henry and eventually herself that they were both capable and wor-thy of love.

And so it was only fair that he returned the favor now. It was his job to revive her, to refill this Michelle-ish vessel with all the steamy pulp and verve that he'd fallen for in the first place.

But loving her like this was grueling. That none of his efforts to heal her had succeeded, let alone been acknowledged, lacquered him in a tarry resin of frustration and inadequacy. Every night that she came stumbling in, too pilled-up to speak or open her eyes, another ounce of his apparently finite patience burned away. Recently, its fumes had begun steeping into something bitter and vindictive. It took all his strength to quarantine what remained of his sympathy away from this new and burgeoning scorn, festering and spreading through him like a cancer. In an attempt to replenish his affection and patience, he forced himself to review the reasons to endure, to salvage her.

Naturally, the first was Junior. Michelle remained the mother of their son, whom Henry refused to let suffer a motherless childhood.

The boy was at the kitchen counter wearing two fleece sweaters and a red flannel scarf when Henry got home from the bank. Junior sat hunched over a splash of papers with a crayon jiggering in a gloved hand, his tongue jutting out the corner of his mouth like a cartoon thermometer. Henry asked if Mom was home.

"Went out."

"She say where to?"

"No," the boy told the crayon. "Just out."

A familiar, exasperating drill. Henry was furious that she'd up and left the boy alone yet again, and even more furious that she might be right—Junior was such a good boy, she'd insisted, that he didn't need their constant surveillance. But the boy was just that—a child, a second-grader—and where the fuck else did she have to be? If she didn't have a job, then she didn't have an excuse not to be right here, right now. He imagined her staggering in later tonight and their ensuing inevitable skirmish. How her eyelids glossed like boiled shrimp whenever she was high. How she was reduced to curbside slush, all her movements dwindled down to an April thaw. How coolly she deflected all his pleas and recriminations with her almighty *ha*.

Besides Junior and the debilitating fear of failing and losing Michelle forever, Henry's list of reasons to endure was short, restricted to memories. There were sporadic moments when a resemblance of the person she'd been would flicker over the husk of what was left. A rare, earnest slice of her shadow smile. A note of her falsetto chuckle. A stomp of her tough, clunky stride. Those occasions when she whispered *sorry* with such fragility that he actually believed her, even if only for a second.

Recently these glimpses didn't reinforce but instead shattered his resolve. It was devastating to witness how the enthralling, complex spectrum of her former self—the one he'd loved, the one he now so missed—had been cleaved in half, leaving only two modes: violent or vacant.

There was no reasoning with either.

Just last week, the boy had been doing homework at the counter, in the same pose and place as he was right now, tongue jutting and brow furrowed. He ignored Henry, who'd already asked him to get ready for bed twice. Henry clenched fingers into a fist. Watched his knuckles go white. Thought of Papa, then exhaled.

"Junior. Don't you make me a say it a third time."

"*Don't make me say it a third time*," Michelle said, her voice toady and mocking. The front door smacked behind her. She made a hawkish strut across the living room, then propped herself against the hallway wall. This blocked Junior's escape route to the bathroom, where he usually waited out his parents' nightly showdowns.

"Or else what, huh, *Hen*?" She smirked, gray yet bloodthirsty. "What you gonna do about it?"

His molars were at the verge of splintering, grinding down a retort. He refused to bite.

"That's what I thought, ha."

She winked at Junior. She folded her wrists into her armpits, turning her elbows into bony wings, and flapped.

When she called Henry chickenshit, she lit the fuse.

When she made the predictable sound effect, he exploded.

Their opening jeers collided in the air of the living room, sending them into a tailspin of screaming. They raged on and over each other, and Henry didn't care if Sandi came to threaten yet another 911 call or eviction—let her come. He didn't even care that Junior was trapped between them—let him watch, let him see what his mother had become. The boy slid off the kitchen stool and made a run for cover. When he tried squeezing past Michelle's legs, she squatted, bracketed him between her knees.

Then she hushed. A lower decibel, a new tactic. To secure victory, she used their child as a human shield. Voice wrung saccharine, she asked the boy to hug her, come hold his mommy, like.

The boy reached up, just as helpless to her call as Henry'd been what now seemed eons ago. Down on the floor, rocking their child back and forth, she leveled a weedy grin at Henry, then started cooing a lullaby into a torpedo.

"It's okay, baby. Daddy's just angry. Daddy's just angry."

Since that night, she'd spent this last week clocked into her second, vacant mode. Things were quieter but no easier. Whenever he tried speaking to her, his sentences traveled as if through saltwater, edgeless and sinking. On the rare occasion she happened to notice his jaw in motion, she would tip her head to one side, gawking at him as if he were a guppy in a fishbowl.

After nearly a year of defeats and humiliations, that metastasizing contempt had manifested in a voice. An appalling, secret wish came hissing from a dark corner of his mind: that she would just get it over with herself. That she might follow the lead of their shriveled-up, empty-eyed neighbors and either run away, or just up and OD already.

Today, Henry didn't think twice about opening a beer. The first gulp put half the can in his belly and his ass on the stool next to Junior. Now that the checking account had been temporarily replenished, he dug the checkbook and a flurry of overdue bills out of the junk drawer. The papers wouldn't lie flat, each sheet warped by palm sweat, every envelope tattered like a trout gutted by fangs rather than a filet blade. The second was a more measured sip. He flipped past the onion-peel carbons to the first blank check, then paused. Peered up to the white container on the topmost shelf. Set down the ballpoint. He asked what the boy was working on and tussled his hair.

"Dad!" The boy yanked away. His Forest Green Crayola resumed coloring in rectangles on a worksheet.

"Hey. Your pa asked you a question."

The crayon stilled. The boy turned a sneer to him. "Mom calls you *dad*. Everyone at school calls their dads *dad*. Why do you want to be so, so . . ."

"So what?"

"So different."

The beer was gone.

"Well?" The boy's sneer crimped into a familiar smirk. His mother's. "Your *son* asked you a question."

Henry didn't have much of an answer. Whereas Papa had a direct tie to his fatherland and a genuine, culture-reinforcing motive for his insistence on being called Papa, Henry was far removed from this half of his heritage, its bonds dissolved by geography, its traits diluted by Mom's genetics. It'd been even further washed out of Junior by a second coating of Caucasian from Michelle. All Henry knew of Tagalog was *mahal kita* (I love you), *putangina* (son of a bitch), and how to count to five, maybe ten if he chanted out loud and let the sequence's rhythm swing him all the way through *anim, pito, walo, siyam*—but what did it matter? He crushed the can's sides.

"Because papas are different," Henry said.

"How?"

"Because papas do what they have to."

"What?" the boy said. "So you're saying regular dads don't?"

"Nope." Henry flattened the can into a medallion, then rose for a second. "Not like papas do. One day you'll see, ah."

The green rectangles were for math class, a subtraction exercise. The boy moved on to the next equation: *$20.00 – $11.75 = ?* Next to the question were a dash and two decimal points over a horizontal line, a template for children to fill in by stacking the budget on top of the price, and then show their work. The boy skipped carrying the ones and instead went directly to coloring eight rectangles green and one of the four circles silver. Henry knew he was supposed to feel proud at the sight of his young son clicking through such calculations in his head, but his vision was shaded, gone grayer than the boy's Timberwolf crayon. Along with the living room's colors, sound got muted, too. He took a gulp and watched the boy breeze from one problem to the next. After finishing the second beer and grabbing a third and doing some arithmetic of his own, Henry asked how come they didn't read a book instead, how about?

On the coffee table were empty Pall Mall packs and burnt-down tea candles, each tin cup sprouting a bouquet of cigarette butts. At the edge nearest to Junior's mattress was a stack of library books, by now so long overdue that Henry was scared to return them and face the late fees. He plucked through the stack, pulling out his personal favorites.

"What do you say? We could do the giver tree, or the love you forever."

He heard himself slurring and he didn't care.

"Also got Horton and the egg, and here's the give a cookie a mouse, too. Where's the Alexander and his no good, really bad day one, huh? Your pick, bud."

"Those are *kids'* books. My teacher wants me reading chapter books." The boy lifted a smaller book, fanning its pages into a taunt. "See? All words, no pictures."

"Well, hey. Look at you. Come and read it to me on the sofa here."

"I have to practice reading in my head." The boy's tone suggested only an utter moron could be ignorant to such a glaringly obvious duty.

The last of the third beer was lukewarm and sour and so was Henry. A red-hot wire was coiling around him. Constricting him, searing him. The little shit. How dare this uppity brat take such a condescending tone with his father. His pa. Yeah, sure, Henry might have done his fair share of questionable and flat-out stupid things, but he sure as shit didn't deserve such derision, such contempt—especially not in his own home, especially not from his son. Yeah, sure, he might not know much, but even an utter moron like him knew that snatching the book—the *chapter* book—out of the boy's hands and thrashing it against the wall, which he did just now, was rash.

The boy startled but shrugged it off. He retrieved the book, then locked himself in the bathroom.

Alone now, Henry threw the stack of kids' books against the wall. The problem wasn't merely an issue of anger, but the lack of a repository in which to unload it. He was mad at Junior, even madder at Michelle, but knew taking it out on either was unfair. He shot two columns of heat from his nostrils, the steam too wispy for the wild-fire inside him. He'd flicked through all the packs but couldn't find a stray cigarette. Not that he smoked regularly or even really wanted one now, but either way their absence felt intentional, deliberate, yet another slight on this terrible, horrible, no good, very bad day.

$0.38

Things finally looking up and it's all pretty much magnificent. Been a long time coming, and in this buzz of delight Henry can't even decide where to begin: the cold, heavy can of High Life or the delicate sprig of the Black & Mild? The cigar's cellophane crinkles like wrapping paper, a tiny gift for himself. He's earned both, deserves it all, but, really, he shouldn't let himself get too distracted just yet. Really ought to gas up and get going.

Two doors open, first the truck's gas tank flap, then the gas station market's, out of which steps the cashier. Henry starts pumping gas, peering past the hood of the truck to track her. In the crook of her elbow she's got a bottle of Diet Mountain Dew and a chili dog, freeing her hands to fidget inside a pack of Camel Crushes. She's so pretty, so enticingly mischievous, that the grin she flashes him is a lasso, its cord going taut and trailing after her as she rounds the corner by the dumpsters. A tug at his throat. The glee of surrender. It would be stupid not to follow her. No time to waste. He's already taken care of the phone and can finish filling up on his way out. After just a gallon, he racks up the nozzle, shuts the gas tank flap, and saunters after her.

The dumpsters are wedged between the market and a car wash stall, offering a shaded enclave. Almost cozy if it weren't for the stench, so ripe it's candied. The cellophane tube floats down to the asphalt and his teeth clamp the cigar's plastic tab. He asks if she's got a light.

One hand hides a joint behind her back as the other lifts a lighter to the tip of the Black & Mild. Smoke rolls sugar over his tongue before he exhales a thick, syrupy cloud. He's breathing fire and conquest. He is monstrous and regal and so, with a slight bow, he says, "Mind if I join you?"

"Free country."

He cracks the High Life open and motherfuck champagne—cold beer is exquisite and everything. An electric fizz rinses his insides. That first gulp gets him feeling so mighty that he could shoulder press this dumpster and hurl it over the car wash stall, just because. He is capable of insolent and supernatural feats, like walking on water or bringing back the dead. Maybe he already has. He adjusts his stance, compressing the inches between them down to a switchblade tension. A nervous chuckle escapes her.

She lifts the joint. "Want a hit?"

He's always been a sucker for uppers, so weed isn't really his thing. However, feeling this immense and powerful and owed a celebration, he accepts.

The hit he takes is overzealous, greedy, and the exact opposite of the beer. A volcanic skunk blast scalds the branches and capillaries of his lungs then sputters through the rest of him. Holding his breath, he is a clogged exhaust pipe. The trapped fumes syphon into a blinding pang, before clawing out of his throat and nostrils in a fit of smoky snorts and coughs. When his knees buckle, he's brought eye level to this pretty little devil.

She drags then swallows a hit elegantly. Her voice sounds submerged when she asks if he's all right.

"Never better," he gasps.

"Fooled me."

By the time the ember reaches the card stock filter, their eyelids sag ruddy. The gas station, vehicles, streets, power lines, plains, and people waiting beyond their shady corner all cease to exist. The world entire is here and her and him.

Yet their talk is itsy-bitsy. Their laughter is bashful, their chemistry pure. Cozy and cool in the shadows, they now inhale and sigh in perfect unison, and it's fucking hilarious. They rattle with delirious mirth. But when she plugs her cackles with gnawed cuticles, a chilling recognition fires barbs down Henry's spine. Right before him, a ghost takes flesh—Michelle.

His senses backfire with a resplendent boom. His skull reels as the world beyond their enclave yanks back into being, everything deafening and suffocating so tight against him yet just out of reach.

How Henry's missed Michelle. Grieved her. Her shadow teeth and grindstone voice. Her citrus scent clinging to their bedsheets. The gentle stab of her shoulder blades into his chest. All their secrets and stories and jokes. Their home, their refuge of warmth and plenty. Plenty enough they'd gathered and shared to keep their family safe, fed, and warm, and so plenty more than he'd ever deserved.

So long ago now—seven, almost eight months—it's like November never happened at all. More a memory of a dream than an experience, or a scar. Everything they'd toiled for and built together demolished in a rash instant. Or perhaps that was what they'd been wading toward all along. Over the course of the years, they'd both grown up and—however gradually—apart. They drifted so far apart that when Michelle needed his help again, he'd been too puny to return the favor. The egocentric prick had taken her self-destruction personally and let all his fear, resentment, and rage fester and scar, fester and scar, until that voice hissing in the darkest corner of his thoughts got what it wanted. It—he had wanted to be free of her, wanted her gone. Since he couldn't cram her into the mold of his expectations, he'd opted for the easy way, the coward's route. Too chickenshit to fight for the only woman he's ever loved and who's ever loved him. Instead, when the mother of his son had cowered in need, he trampled on top of her, used her as a soapbox for his self-righteousness with an audience of one.

But in the end, she was right: he is a monument of such inadequacy that he isn't beyond merely purpose, but also function. He was and remains a failure. First he'd failed Papa, then Al, later her, and so naturally it's only a matter of time till he fails Junior, too.

Their son. Michelle was and remains the mother of their son.

His hands lift through the dumpster's fumes, palms upturned, reaching for her, gingerly. Can't she see? He's unarmed. Swears he won't hurt her. Just hear him out, just—please?

He tells her he's so, so sorry. Let him—he'll do anything. Please.

But Michelle is as gone as ever. It's the cashier who takes a step back before his fingertips can stroke her cheek. She peeks at her phone's clock. "My break's over. You, uh, take care. See you in an hour, right?"

Palms drag over his face. He offers an apologetic chuckle, tries explaining it's been a long, long time since he's smoked. Hit him too hard, got him way up in his head and all, but yeah. Thanks, though. What time is it?

"Three forty-five."

"Fuck."

School lets out at 3:30 p.m. and he's still a fifteen-, twenty-minute drive away. He sucks the Black & Mild and guzzles the beer, hoping nicotine and carbonation might clear the weed's fog, but by the time he's gunning down the street with the windows cranked down and summer chugging over him, he realizes two things: one, the beer has only further thickened the haze, and, two, in this frenzy, he forgot to pump what was left of the twenty dollars' worth of gas. Just over a gallon in the tank, a puddle in a cave, about as empty as his belly. He crushes the accelerator to the floor.

It's more freefall than flight the way he's barreling through traffic, careening into the shoulder and over the median as he plummets past other vehicles. His nerves are jitterbugging in all his pores. He tries quelling the panic by swatting the steering wheel as if it were the wet black nose of an insistent mutt. Down, boy. Down. It does as much good as the language he releases into the truck cab, telling nobody but the fog that it's okay, it's all right. Everything's going to be just fine, buddy, he swears it. He's coming, he's right here, and by the time the truck squeals into the school's drive, the building and its surrounding lawns and walkways have the vacant calm of a graveyard. All the children have been hauled off by yellow buses or minivans. Even the teachers' lot is almost entirely cleared out. Once the truck humps over the curb closest to the entrance, slamming the brake pedal is like pulling a ripcord. He sprints into the school, the tail of his suit jacket billowing behind him absolutely nothing like a parachute, let alone a hero's cape.

Inside the elementary school everything is shrunken down pint-sized. Bulletin boards at knee level, ceilings low and corded with colorful construction-paper chains. The dairy-like smell of children at play still lingering in the halls. When he goes for a second whiff, the scent curdles, turns putrid. The gutter musk of cigar smoke and the bite of his malnourished body odor overwhelms him. And, judging by the secretary's narrowed eyelids, she must certainly smell it, too.

"We've been trying to get ahold of you for over an hour."

Even after loading the five dollars onto his phone, he was too distracted by his twenty-buck conquest, then the beer, tobacco, weed, Michelle's ghost, and traffic to check if it'd charged and turned on. He apologizes profusely, repeatedly, explaining his phone had died and but where is Junior? Where is his son?

The secretary pulls car keys from her purse, jabs a tiny dagger toward the nurse's office, then leaves.

Unlike everything else in the school, these half dozen cots are not miniaturized. Each one has the length and volume of an adult-sized casket, sheeted in the same fleshy material of a whoopee cushion. On the last one is Junior, tucked fetal, back turned to the door. Even from across the room, Henry can see the tremors racking the boy's entire frame.

Henry drops to his knees beside the cot. Down, boy. Down. He wraps the pretzel of his son into an embrace, whispering the same things he'd told the fog during the drive over here, and to the same effect. He lifts Junior, light as a bundle of kindling, off the cot. When a papery blanket slips off and to the floor, he notices the boy isn't in his jeans, but has been changed into a pair of oversized gym shorts, the drawstrings looped into two long bunny ears hanging from his emaciated navel. The boy's left hand is balled into a fist, and between two fingers is a ridge of copper. The lucky penny.

Henry turns to leave and is met by the school nurse. There's an anxious, maternal crook to her as she retrieves the blanket from the floor and sets it back over the boy. Behind her, leaning against the door frame, is the school principal, his tree-trunk forearms crossed over a knitted tie.

"What happened to his jeans?" Henry asks.

"Little Henry had an accident," the nurse says, nodding at a heavy-looking bag in the corner. "Poor guy's got a fever through the roof. We've kept a close eye on him, but couldn't administer any meds to help. We didn't have a signed authorization form on file from—well, you know."

"I'm sorry, I just must've forgot, but you can now. Give him anything, whatever will fix him. He said he felt kind of bad this morning, so has he been here all day, or?"

The principal says they've been trying to get ahold of Henry for—

"Over an hour, yeah, I know. But is he . . . ?"

"His teacher told us that every time she'd asked if he was feeling sick, he said he was fine." The nurse strokes Junior's flushed cheek. "Been toughing it out all day. Until the accident. Gym class, last period of the school day."

"So what should I do now, huh? What you think's the matter with him?"

"Not really my place to diagnose, but I'd guess it's a stomach flu. But with that fever and mean cough of his, could even be pneumonia. Best get him to a doctor for antibiotics, just in case."

The nearest hospital is over thirty miles away, an impossible distance to cross on fumes. Not that either of them has health insurance, anyway.

"No, yeah, but is there anything I can do or give him in the meantime?"

"Main thing is to keep him hydrated," the nurse says. "Lots and lots of water. He emptied himself out and hasn't been able to keep much down since. Got to be starving, so some soup would do him good. Ibuprofen for the fever, too. He's burning up."

"I'm cold, Pa."

"Think you could give us some, save us a trip to the pharmacy?" Henry says, tucking the blanket tighter around the boy. "You got my permission, right here and now."

The nurse tenses.

"Nope," the principal says.

"Hey, but. Please? Just look at the kid. Help us out here."

"School policy."

The nurse looks from Junior to Henry. With her back to the principal, she mouths *I'm sorry.*

"School policy?" Henry yells. "Look at my son. He's fucking dying here."

"You're going to need to calm down." The forearms flex. "Now that you, the child's legal guardian, are in custody of the student, his well-being is entirely your responsibility. We can't be held liable for any medical complications if—"

"Fuck this."

Henry lifts the boy over his shoulder, freeing a hand to rifle through the cabinets. Boxes of bandages, rolls of gauze, and a jar of cotton swabs come tumbling out, but before he can locate any pills, the principal reaches under Henry's free arm and crushes him into a half nelson. Henry totters and leans into the hold, struggling to keep Junior from falling.

"Get the fuck off of me, you—"

The principal squeezes a yelp out of Henry and tells Dottie to call the police,

"Fine, yeah, no. It's fine. Everything's cool, I'm sorry. Just please, please let me go."

Henry submits. Goes limp. When the hold loosens, he wriggles free and collapses to the floor. Somehow he's cushioned Junior from the fall. He refastens his arms around the boy, peers up from the ground.

"I'm sorry, sir. Worried about my kid is all, you know how it is. You get crazy, right? But, please. No need to get the cops involved."

The principal's stance is wide.

"Don't make me beg, okay?"

A heel lifts, a grappler toeing the line, eager for the whistle. "Dottie?"

"I'm begging you."

The telephone clacks onto the cradle. Dottie flashes the principal a silent plea.

"Enough," the principal says, broad chest heaving. "About time you got your child back home. Where he should've been hours ago. Where the rest of us who've been waiting for *you* to turn up would like to head as well. What do you say?"

Nothing. Henry says nothing at all. Not even when the principal stops them at the doorway to reclaim school property, the thin blanket, which he peels off Junior, only to toss it over a desk chair. Not even when Henry trudges through the low halls, sensing the principal tailing them on their way out, as if Henry were some disgruntled, freshly fired employee scheming a parting vengeance of vandalism or theft.

The truck sits akilter on the curb, matching the wobble in Henry's field of vision. Standing at the passenger's-side door, he wraps the bese saka shawl around Junior and rubs the boy's shoulders as if trying to spur a spark with a twig. The boy's head lolls. He has Michelle's boiled-shrimp eyelids and beneath them irises skitter up and down the blanket's pattern. A firm blink. Recognition steadies him, and abruptly his head cocks back to fully take in the figure above him, his pa. The boy's eyes shimmer, then narrow into slits. Henry's wrapped the covers so tight that Junior has to squirm in order to free a shoulder, an arm, an elbow, until, finally, a hand with which to slap Henry.

The boy's got the strength of a noodle. It doesn't hurt, but still. It's a surprise.

"You fucking asshole."

Never heard such venom out of the boy. These words, the runoff from his parents' fights, must have permeated his vocabulary, but Henry would never have expected such proficiency, such jugular-slashing accuracy. He's stunned. Needs a moment to generate a response, torn between reprimand and apology. Then, just as he starts tipping toward the latter, a small fist connects with his chin.

Then another. Again and again, until the thuds hammer into a tempo for Junior's sobs, insults, and the list of his father's crimes and deficiencies. His pa had forced him to eat that ice cream cone, even after he said he couldn't, even after he said he was sick and too full. Dragged him out of the first bed he's slept in in months, in the middle of the night, before even taking a bath. Kicked him out of the truck and into school when he was like this, Pa, like *this*. Humiliated him—yelled at him in front of the whole school. Hadn't answered the nurse's calls, not even the principal's. His pa had forgotten him, abandoned him.

The punches stop. The spot of Henry's chin where he's accepted thump after thump is glowing. All of Junior clenches, channeling the dregs of his energy into one final wail. A weak, slobbery roar. At last, he crumples, exhausted. Through the trickle of sobs, he mutters something else, but it gets lodged behind his teeth.

Henry leans into the little furnace. Gently as he can, he says, "What was that, son?"

"You killed Mom."

Not even a second to turn air into a rebuttal or denial. The boy's already begun repeating it over and over—*you killed Mom you killed Mom you killed Mom*—spinning a mantra of flames. Henry accepts these lashes, like the punches, without a word until the chant starts losing steam, each lap softer, cooler than the last, almost coaxing the ravaged child to sleep, tugging him into a slump against the center console.

Henry's got no idea how far they can get on that squirt of gasoline, or what they can do with one quarter, two nickels, three pennies. He cups the boy's forehead. A teakettle. Whimpering, shivering, sweating. Henry uncaps the water jug and sets it beside Junior, who either doesn't notice it or flat out ignores it.

Before turning the ignition, Henry holds his breath. At first the engine sputters but eventually does catch. The gas gauge needle bobs up, then floats down to an ambiguous zone over the red. About ten miles from here, across from the Walmart, is a strip mall with an urgent care clinic. If they run out of gas on the way—so fucking be it—he will carry the boy, sprinting down the shoulder of the road.

A stroke of cosmic mercy gets the truck to the strip mall. The lot here has a loose scatter of dented sedans and a lone squad car, but across the way is a dense multitude of windshields, glimmering with oceanic calm before the Walmart. The store dominates the horizon, lurking so formidably that it resembles a battleship.

Henry turns his back to the Walmart and jogs to the clinic with Junior his arms. Instead of merchandise or mannequins, the clinic's broad strip mall windows showcase purgatory. A drab waiting room with plastic chairs and pallid faces. Inside, the faint smell of blood charges the air with something metallic, more flavor than scent. There's a sniffle. Then a groan. As Henry passes the ailing and the seated, their expressions are all caught between pain and boredom. A man in dusty coveralls waits with his injury elevated, his hand wrapped in a towel on top of his head like a damp maroon turban. A woman cradles a trembling a child whose ankle is cocked in an impossible bend. A teenager wearing only gym shorts and high-tops wheezes pitifully, his neck, chin, and lips swollen to blimpish proportions. Henry sighs. Such communal anguish soothes him.

Until he sees the cop. Leaning against the receptionist's counter is a policeman with a push-broom mustache and the complexion of watermelon meat. Henry can't make out the cop's words but detects the cadence of rural flirtation. Meanwhile, the receptionist moves her mouth inaudibly around a lollipop, perhaps deflecting the cop's come-ons, or else speaking to a caller on the opposite end of her headset. Her gaze drifts between a pair of computer monitors, until noticing and floating up to Henry and Junior.

"So," she says, left cheek bulging. "What's up?"

"My son." Henry angles his back to the cop. "He's sick, but like really sick. Got a fever, stomach bug, maybe even pneumonia?"

"A fever, huh?" She claps a clipboard onto the counter. "Here. Fill out your insurance info, and, yeah. Probably be a little while."

"I don't got insurance."

"Then just a billing address. And answer them medical history questions on the second page there, then sign the bottom of the third."

Rather than admit he doesn't have an address either, he just says thanks. Pokes the chained pen at the forms before working up the nerve to ask this stranger for a favor, a tiny kindness, then taps the pen to get her attention. He tells her all the kid really needs is some ibuprofen or something for the fever. Maybe she could, if it isn't too much to ask, just give him a couple pills while they're waiting and all?

"We can't really." She plucks out the lollipop. It is brown and slimy and receiving more of her attention than Henry.

He pounds the counter. "You can't really what?"

"Administer. Can't administer anything till we got him processed. Fill that out, wait if you want, but really, the Walmart's your best bet—hello? Yeah, this is urgent care. What's up?"

And just like that, Henry goes invisible right before her eyes. A nothing, a nonentity occupying neither space nor time, let alone anybody's thoughts or concerns. But before he evaporates entirely, something starts brewing. Some formless, weightless thing recognizes another formless, weightless thing—a voice, a word, a sentence. The boy in Henry's arms is asking for his mom.

As quickly as Henry'd been deleted, he erupts back into flesh and sensation. Sulfur and ammonia crank him into a state of focus so sharp and immediate that he can hardly hear, as if his vision is drawing extra strength from his auditory function's neural reserves. His legs have begun moving so fast that perception gets delayed. Somehow, at some point, he's gone around the receptionist's desk and begun charging down a hall. He's wound past a gurney and a white-coated woman, and his free hand has lifted to stroke his son's face, then turned it toward a nurse who's just stepped out of a room, reaching for the plastic flags at the doorframe. It seems whatever he's said has stunned her hand between the green and red flags. Even muffled, he can tell it's his own voice that's started pleading, explaining, and so it must also be his voice that's repelling her. She's taken a slow, measured step backward, warding him off with her stethoscope, as if a coin on a rubber string could ever deter him. She's facing but not seeing him, instead peering over his shoulder.

"What the fuck are you looking at?" Henry yells. "Look at me, look at my son. He needs help. We're right here."

Another step and her back meets the wall. Cornered. She looks from Junior to Henry, then over his shoulder again.

"Look at me!"

Pressure. A tug. A freckled hand has fastened around Henry's bicep and now slowly turns the rest of him and Junior around. It's the cop. His grip holds firm while the other hand buoys in a gesture meant to suggest peace. A lip worms under the thick bristles, and the cop says he's going to need Henry to calm down, okay? Take her easy, sir.

"Sir?" Henry says. "I'm a man—not *sir*."

"Alrighty?" Brow and mustache furrow. "Well, man, whyn't we pump the brakes? Got a little one myself. Know good and well how scary it is when they're hurting, but easy does it."

Manic and trapped, Henry swivels his sights away from the cop's rosy cheeks and searches for an escape route. Up and down the hallway, nurses peek past doorframes to view the commotion. Even the receptionist has wheeled back from the desk, reclined and gawking, and behind her, past the broad strip mall windows, is the squad car. A ray of sunlight glints ruby in its light bar's reflector. Henry's thoughts flash cobalt then crimson then back to the passenger seat of Al's Bonneville. He clutches the nape of Junior's neck. While an officer of the law physically restraining Henry should have been plenty enough to cinch him compliant, it's a memory, a promise that stun him into compliance.

He hangs his head. Lifts Junior higher on his shoulder. He lets the cop lead him down the hall, through the waiting room, and out to the parking lot. All the while, the cop talks in that hasteless farmhand way, relaying platitudes about parenthood and perseverance so earnestly that they vaguely ebb toward wisdom or solace. He even checks the squad car's glove compartment for Advil. When the bottle turns up empty, the idiot tells Henry he's in luck and happily points to the Walmart across the way.

One quarter. Two nickels. Three pennies.

For absolutely nothing, Henry thanks the cop.

"Why, sure thing," he says, straightening his posture. "And don't you worry none. Seen with my own two eyes that this little guy is in good hands. Y'all gonna be just fine."

Setting Junior in the passenger seat, Henry notices the phone charger cord dangling down to the cup holder like a lifeline into a well. By now the phone has got to have charged some. Just a little life. A desperate thought occurs to him: What if Jorge has called about the forty dollars?

Holding his breath, he reaches into the hole. He flips the phone open, his teeth grinding as it boots up, and a blocky animation welcomes him to the device. Only one bar of the battery icon has filled in. Besides four voicemails from the school, nothing. Call log as blank as before. Not a single text. He'd been a reckless fucking moron to have trusted Jorge, to not have even thought of taking down the stranger's number.

As he folds the phone shut, its screen flickers as if turning off, but then the signal icon sprouts a second bar. The phone vibrates once. Twice. Now a third time.

Three texts, all from the same unknown number, dated two weeks back. A 415 area code. The first word he reads is *Hen*.

A nostalgia wallop. His intestines tangle. Before actually reading the three-bubble-long message, he's transported back to nights spent on the living room computer, reading Michelle's emails like a detective combing through old evidence for new clues, parsing her run-on sentences and scrutinizing their every last word in search of some hint that might reveal she was secretly as smitten as him.

But these messages are curt. Clipped phrases. Abbreviations and acronyms strip away any trace of possible concern, let alone affection. Michelle had run off to California. Finally made it to the ocean. Overrated. People too happy. Weird. She burned through the money in a week. Then OD'd the next. Now at a halfway home. Working part-time. Saving up. Wanted to come home. Soon. She even wrote that she was sorry, for everything, but still, *fuck u*. She wasn't sure about the two of them, but knew she needed to see Junior. Asked him to tell Junior she was sorry and that she would be back as soon as she could and that she loves him very, very much. Promised she would make it up to him. To Junior, she clarified. Doubted she could ever really forgive Henry. They would have to talk.

During his second read through, he does a better job of conjuring her voice. No way she would ever forgive him, but, maybe someday, the boy could. He strokes Junior's head, slicking his hair into a handsome, sweaty swoop.

"Mommy's coming home," he whispers.

The boy is quaking and mumbling but doesn't stir from his fever dream.

Michelle is coming home with no home to come back to. Even still, right here in Henry's hands is the one and only reason she's coming back. The only one who matters, the only one who's worth anything. Worth everything. He thinks back to December, back when they'd left their home and hit the road for good, and it's all so clear now, again and right in front of him all along. He's only got one job: that which he's got to. Whatever it takes to keep their child safe, happy, and healthy.

And lucky Henry. The medicine his son needs is right inside that Walmart, and so that's where he's got to go, and it feels pretty damn good to know at least that.

$576.17

Henry'd lost control. Really shouldn't have snatched and thrashed the boy's book, but whatever. He'd lost count of beers, too, and so helped himself to another, because fuck it.

He cracked open the can and threw the refrigerator door so hard that the entire appliance danced. There was a fifth of vodka in the freezer. Might help cool and lube him free of the coil, wound skin-tight and scalding around his neck. The freezer's inner walls were caked in pillows of frost. He plunged his head into the box, set a red cheek against frigid crystals.

The cold cell whisked his thoughts back to the gold-plating plant. Earlier this afternoon, after the announcement, only one employee had lost it. The last one he ever would have expected.

"Name's Lucius," he'd said, back on Henry's first day at the plant. "You can call me Lou or Louie. Some like Cool-heart Luke, others just do Juice."

Over this last year of working together, Henry stuck with the man's given name, appreciating its peculiar mix of the noble and sinister. Anyway, it felt silly to fall back on a nickname for this old man who really did speak and move like some icicle-bearded master from a kung fu flick. Lucius, on the other hand, never bothered using Henry's name, referring to him only as youngblood, which Henry didn't mind one bit. The moniker instilled a sense of belonging in their two-man tribe and sounded like a genuine term of endearment from a modern-day sage to his apprentice.

That first day, Lucius had ignored the shift manager's initial buddy-system pairing for Henry's training, waving off the pudgy white man and leading the rookie away for a tour. As Lucius shuffled ahead, he aimed a knobby index finger at the rectifiers, rollers, hoists, and racks, explaining each contraption's role in the electroplating process. In a husky murmur yet vivid detail, he described how electric currents running through vats of cyanide dilated the pores of the metal to be plated, into which the gold salts were deposited and fused. He pointed, saying that right there was the lab where technicians converted the gold bullion—real pricey-ass shit—into pure salts. And over there, just behind the control furnace, was the safety station, emergency shower and fire kit and all. But what he really wanted to show Henry was down this way, here by the delivery dock. Lucius lifted a plain crate's lid as if it were a treasure chest. Inside were hundreds of inch-wide nickel bands stacked into neat columns. See now, normally they just plated computer parts, circuit boards and all that, but not this week, nope.

"Okay," Henry said. "So what's this week?"

The old man's lips crinkled into a grin.

"This week we gilding high school graduation rings."

Under Lucius's guidance, Henry caught on quick despite the lack of verbal instruction. Out on the floor communication was patchy, their mouths gagged by respirators and chat buried under the incessant percussion of heavy machinery. During lunch, though, their conversations were crisp and edifying. Lucius loved dedicating those daily thirty minutes to disclosing post-prison tips over styrofoam cups of coffee. How to save money, find extra work, and prioritize. How to cut ties with the streets without burning bridges, or turning old friends into new enemies. Strategies for rebirth. The virtue of humility and a clean, simple life. How to know when to cash out and kick back. How much was enough, and then how much was plenty enough. The two traded stories about their families, jokes about their mistakes, and Lucius taught Henry how to learn from the latter. They were friends. They were honest with and confided in one another. Although Henry never worked up the nerve to tell Lucius the whole truth about what had actually happened to Al, Lucius was the only person he'd ever told about Michelle. Six months ago, he muted his voice as if that might also subdue his hurt, to tell

Lucius about what she'd been doing to herself, and so, in turn, to her family.

Lucius took it all in, his milky cataract gaze locked onto Henry. Once Henry finished, Lucius just nodded slowly, as if ceding to a raw deal, then sighed.

"When everything said and done, it all come down to her wanting to change. Her wanting to get her shit right for her own self. Till then, though, it's all on you to stay focused and do work. More than anything, you got to look out for number one."

"You mean, like—me?" Henry asked. "Myself?"

Lucius smacked the back of Henry's head, much harder than Papa ever had. "Now I know you're young, but not even you is *that* stupid. Think."

"Yeah, no," Henry said. "But number one?"

"The boy, youngblood."

As always, Lucius had been right six months ago, and so, maybe, his reaction this afternoon was the right one as well.

Earlier today, ten minutes before quitting time, the shift manager had snapped a padlock onto the lab door. Then, flanked by two policemen, he stepped into the middle of the plant floor. A megaphone gave one siren whoop and rendered his voice robotic, ordering the guys to wrap up and circle up for an announcement.

Barrels were hoisted, cyanide trickling then dripping off the raised racks. Rectifiers were deactivated, leaving the tanks to simmer, then still. Last the workers gathered, peeling off rubber gloves, safety goggles, masks.

The shift manager rapped a stack of paychecks against the megaphone's cone and spurred a screech of feedback. He then announced that, effective immediately, the plant was closing, just as Henry's PO had warned. The two dozen workers circled tighter, huddling into a fearful denim amoeba. Soon shouts of protest and disbelief ruptured the membrane of shock. One man, enraged beyond language, simply spat. The phlegm smacked the very spot on the floor where Lucius had been standing right beside Henry only seconds ago.

When Henry looked up, he saw Lucius at the far wall, cocking his torso and throwing an elbow through the pane of the fire extinguisher case. Glass shattered and heads spun. Lucius toppled the extinguisher to the ground, then reached back to where two fire-axes formed a tall red X. He came out swinging, cracking the axe head against the control furnace with futile pings. When the cops closed in, Lucius sent the axe in wide horizontal sweeps to ward them back. The swings whooshed through the air, and their momentum yanked the old man forward, making him hobble after each of the axe head's plummets. Between swings, he screamed.

"It ain't right, y'all can't—"

A whoosh. A clank and hobbling.

"This our livelihood—our lives."

Through ferocious sobs, Lucius screamed for justice, dignity, mercy. He chopped and staggered and bellowed. And then, for the first time all year, he cried out Henry's real name, howling for backup, for his friend's help.

Henry was paralyzed from the nose down, voiceless and helpless to watch as one of the cops crept up from behind Lucius. The cop was visibly unimpressed, as if bored by the task of waiting for this pitiful geezer to wear himself out, which, after a few more growls and swings, Lucius did. The axe head gave a final toll against the floor's trough, then bounced into the cop's ankle. The impact was harmless but physical contact nonetheless—a green light for force.

As Lucius struggled to stand, crutching himself upright with the axe handle, the cop kicked it out from under him and threw him to the floor in a choke hold.

Inside Henry crumbled, but outside he was placid. Another worker charged toward Lucius, who was retching under the cop's aggravated weight. As ashamed as Henry was that someone else had launched to his friend's defense first, it didn't matter. That would-be working-class hero was thwarted almost immediately, frozen midstride when the second cop reached for his holster.

Cuffs locked around Lucius's wrists. He was either refusing to walk or incapable of getting to his feet. His wiry frame went flaccid as the cop dragged him toward the exit. The way Lucius's head lolled, strands of tears and saliva draggling from his chin, he looked like a child drained to submission by his own playground tantrum.

A slab of flagstone now wobbled under Henry's boot.

At some point he'd made it out to the patio. At some point he'd pulled both his head and the vodka out of the freezer. At some point he'd finished the beer that'd been in this empty can, in his cold, chapped hand. He set the can down, stomped it flat, then squatted to shim it under the loose patio stone. One way to get things steady, restore balance, now that it was too late to join his friend, grab the spare axe, and swing. With his knees against his chest, he'd folded his whole body into an earthbound cannonball, and in this position he allowed the coil to twine around his entire body, even tighter now, hotter now, barbed and scalding. Shame compressed him into a singular urge, an impulse to destroy.

A set of headlight beams swung in and stunned Henry, who was still squatting on the patio, incubating his freshly laid egg of remorse and fury. Blinded by the glare, he heard a car door open, a sludgy chuckle. The clap of the door restored his vision, and he caught a glimpse of a Mustang backing out and peeling off. Michelle was a windblown twig, eyes glazed over and gone, shuffle-swaying toward the front steps, seemingly oblivious to Henry on the patio.

"The fuck you been?"

Her head sagged in his direction. Freewheeling in mode two, she swiped at the air as if to scrub him out of sight, before staggering up the stairs and into their home.

The front door slammed shut behind Henry. He barked her name. When he ordered Junior into the bathroom, the boy stayed on his mattress and armed himself with two long, sharp Legos.

Henry and Michelle began screaming in unison as if by cue. Their voices snarled and churned into a molten ore, spattering fiery blurts of demands, insults, and accusations. Even through the smokescreen of his rage, he kept a crosshair locked on his primary objective: to make her feel as wretched and worthless as possible, before breaking the news of the layoff. He wanted to drive her down so he could climb on top of her, above her, to bellow and gloat. He wanted to scream and stoke all his labor and sacrifices into a wild blaze, next to which her miserable, rat-like proportions and disgraceful behavior would be torn from the shadows, finally floodlit and indisputable.

She was selfish, reckless, pathetic. Again she'd ditched her son— *their* son—so her junkie ass could go off and get high with whatever lowlifes could put up with her sorry excuse for company. And while she was god knows where doing fuck knows what, where'd he been, huh? Out there, at the crack of dawn, busting his ass for hours on end. Slaving away, day after day, for her and Junior, for fucking pennies, for fucking nothing. What had he been thinking? What had he been waiting for? He should have just gotten it over with, should have done it himself and—and then her fingertips speared his sternum.

"Oh?" Her voice went chilly. "And so getting piss drunk and shouting and cussing in front of the kid is *so* much better, like. Real role model material. Dad of the century, ha."

"At least I'm here," he hissed. "Least I'm trying."

"And about goddamn time—ha." An arm flopped instead of shooed. "*Ha.*"

Then came the slurring, her hot spittle diatribe. Going on and on about how it was her turn now. It was about motherfucking time Henry put in the work and the hours, so that she could finally get hers, like. Finally relax a little. Live a little. Five years she'd done, doing every goddamn thing, and all on her own. A miracle they'd made it. A miracle. Day in and out, grinding away to turn fire into wine, sweat into bread, like—and but for what? What the fuck for, huh, Hen? For him to come back out of the blue, out of prison, suddenly all high and mighty? For him to come and guilt-trip her for living a little, just for having herself some fun and a little life, like? For what then? No, she really wanted him to tell her because all she saw was this, this, this preachy, shit-for-brains faggot too busy feeling sorry for himself because they hadn't thrown him a homecoming party, because there weren't no marching band banging after him on the way to work every morning. He weren't doing nothing more than what he was *supposed* to, just what he *got* to, just like what every other grown-ass man in this country got to. Really, though. Really must have thought he was something special. Some sort of hero, like. As if anyone here needed saving. And even if there ever had been, it weren't like he could have done jack shit about it—ha. Weren't that a hoot? A riot. Mr. Jesus Henry Christ had come a-strutting down the mountain to *save* them. Honestly. Who in the actual fuck did he think he was? Don't tell her he actually believed he could save them, let alone provide for them, like a real man, like.

Michelle shoved spittle off her chin. "Ha."

A pause.

It was his turn now, but he couldn't lift his head.

He looked at the boy on the mattress, then back to his boots.

He told her she was right, she was absolutely right.

Told her he'd been laid off today. Let go.

Told her she was right, yet again. Right as usual and all along.

Told her he'd failed them. He was sorry. He was so, so sorry.

A canyon of silence. To ever work his head back upright seemed impossible. Eventually he managed, and when he did, he caught a spark. A flicker of the person she'd been, the woman he'd loved. He wanted to hold her, to be held by her. Could this be their rock bottom, their turning point? She absorbed the news and the apology with a slow, gentle sip of air, and then released it—"*Ha.*"

She peered behind her, checking if anyone else had gotten the joke. Junior looked down.

"Ha," she said.

She twisted toward Junior, asked how come he weren't laughing— didn't he get it? His daddy was a joke. A loser, failure, bum. And a fucking snitch. Brainless, dickless, and now jobless, too, and but did Junior even know what that meant? *Useless*, baby. It meant his daddy was totally fucking useless, like—ha.

She approached the mattress, stooping down to the boy. Said but seriously though, baby. Pay attention. She needed now more than ever for the boy to listen to her. Pay extra, super-duper close attention to Mommy, cause he really ought to remember this moment and what she had to say forever and ever, like.

She crouched lower and so did her voice, telling the boy he'd better do everything he possibly could so that he wouldn't end up like his daddy—no, excuse her—his *pa*.

Yeah, yeah, yeah. She knew nobody in their right mind would ever want to turn out like that. Course not. Duh. And so that was why Junior had to use today as a lesson. A real-life example of what would happen to him if he weren't a good boy, weren't a smart boy. Otherwise, well, all he had to do was look—right there, see?

She jabbed a thumb over her shoulder.

"Right there," she said, then released a fleet of mirthless chuckles that rolled her into a sort of trance. She shuddered midsway, blinked, started coming to. She looked around as if trying to locate herself, then noticed her own thumb. Seemed it was pointing to something. Her head turned, slowly, curious as to what it was signaling right behind her. And when she turned and discovered Henry, he swung the back of his fist into her mouth.

The blow twisted and threw Michelle, sending her rag-doll splayed and facedown on the floor. A hand quivered up, reaching for Junior, only inches from her fingertips.

The boy's face went stony. From the corners of his eyes came four streams of tears, streaking down his cheeks and meeting under his chin in a dewy bow. An agonized squeal escaped him, more animal than child. The boy seemed too scared to move, even to protect his mother, who was now pleading for him, calling his name. When he looked up to his father for either an answer or help, Henry didn't care. Towering over this scabby rat bitch, he felt immense. He felt godlike.

Michelle's lips were smeared red like some horror show clown's. "Ha."

"See, baby?" She spat blood. "What'd Mommy just tell you?"

Henry ordered Junior into the bathroom. Now.

"See what your *pa* just did? You saw that."

"Now, Junior."

"Know what kind of man hits a woman? A mommy?"

"Don't you—"

"The selfish, tiny kind. You saw what he done to Mommy, but do you know what he done to his best friend? And so what he could do to you, too?"

"It was *your* idea. You're too far gone and fucked up to remember the truth, what you told me to do. Didn't even think about it, Michelle, just—*snap*. Your mind was made up and Al's fate sealed."

"Ha—"

"You asked me to, and so I did. For us, for our family—Junior, in the bathroom, *now*!"

"Look at him, your pa. Dickless, useless, and a liar, too. You don't want to end up like that, do you, baby?" She crawled across the mattress, embraced the boy around the belly. "Come here. Come hold your mommy, baby."

The next part was easy. Shockingly, shamefully so.

Henry snatched a fistful of Michelle's hair and dragged her to the door. She was so light, a dried-out crust. No matter how madly she flailed or loud she screamed, it was so easy to heave her out the front door and smack it shut after her. The deadbolt and chain locked in two swift, easy swipes. He pinched the house key off her keychain, then threw the Saab keys and her winter coat out the window. She tried clawing into the opened window, but it was easy to slide it shut, sealing out her screams and the November wind. Her fists whacked and rattled the front door in its frame. He pressed his back against it then slid down to the floor, leveraging his weight in case the locks didn't hold. Let Sandi come, he thought. Let her call the cops. Let them have their pick, they could take either Michelle or him away, all three of them for all he cared, because nothing mattered, not anymore.

The boy had never made it off the mattress. Had been right here.

Had seen it all. Over the bangs and shouts from the other side of the door, Henry couldn't hear the boy's voice but had no trouble reading those lips, begging him, *Pa, please.*

Henry looked the other way. Couldn't let the boy see him like this, doing this.

Eventually Michelle gave up. At the sound of her storming down the front steps, Henry pressed himself up to watch her through the window. He couldn't spot her until she reappeared, rising from a squat, having pried up a football-sized hunk of flagstone from the patio. Cradling it against her hip, she waddled over to his truck, then drove it through the passenger's-side window. Broken glass crunched under her feet. She slammed into her car and blasted its horn. The engine turned, revved, and then she was gone.

$0.38

Henry is right here, in the driver's seat, fists at ten and two o'clock, steering them toward the sea of parked cars and the Walmart cresting its iridescent surface like some colossal marine predator in the distance. They coast past a Winnebago setting up camp for the night, then turn into a wide channel of rear bumpers. The closer they get, the larger the blue and gray building swells, growing and growing until it towers over and sprawls around them in the truck, which he parks by the crosswalk, just steps from the entrance. The gas gauge says fumes, but he leaves the engine running. Got to take his chances. Might have to make a quick escape.

When he steps out, the asphalt gives under his boot like a trampoline. He lunges into a wobble, crawling his palms along the truck bed to keep himself upright. Really ought to dash inside and get this over with, but something tells him that a parting good-luck embrace from the boy will stabilize and center him.

But opening the passenger door looses an abyss. In Junior's place is a dark pit, howling with the threat of finality. Before Henry gets pitched into the chasm, he clutches the grab handle, heaves himself up and into the truck, and it's so silly. All his melodrama, his inane bent for the hopeless and finite—come on. He's seen plenty enough to get it by now. Deep down he understands that the end of one thing is just the start of something else.

Then again, no.

Leaning over the boy, he knows at least this right here is unending, unwavering. This love is the exception, his sliver of forever. He tucks the bese saka shawl tight around Junior, huddled and shivering against the center console. Can't be sure if he's said he'll be right back or not, but it doesn't really matter because he will, because that's his job. One last look, a silent promise, and then he closes the door, gently.

The cling-wrap cobweb of the passenger window offers no sheen, so he angles the side mirror to survey his reflection. He buttons and smooths out the suit jacket, tugs the tie's knot all the way up, then arranges the two ribbons into a perfect arrow pointing down. He doesn't bother squatting to check his face. Wouldn't want to see himself like this, doing this, and so instead just unbuttons the shirt-sleeve at his right wrist like a magician backstage, gearing up for the evening's sleight of hand.

Glass panel teeth slide open sideways, more swallowing than wel-coming Henry into the shopping cart atrium. A tongue of scuffed linoleum, a low ceiling pulsing above, and past the second set of doors stands the gatekeeper to these vast, fluorescent entrails: a toe-nail clipping of a man donning a blue vest and a vacant grin, a roll of smiley-face stickers held out like a collection plate. A train of shop-ping carts crackles and clacks and seems to cue the store's thrum, ceaseless and otherworldly. No telling whether elysian or infernal, but it's undeniably eternal. The promise of so much plenty is dizzy-ing and instantly shrivels Henry down to humbler proportions, a morsel he can only hope might go totally undetected.

He's got to focus. Get to the pharmacy, get the meds, and get the hell out of here. Determined to hide in plain sight, he offers the greeter a solemn nod, struts past the proffered yellow sticker, and immedi-ately makes his first mistake. No cart. Not even a basket. Might look suspicious to the black half globes above recording his every move, but doubling back for either would probably call even more atten-tion to himself. Got to act casual, natural, convince himself and everyone else that he belongs here as much as anyone else. He feels a sort of magnetic tug coming from the right, in the direction of the pharmacy department, but he lets himself coast straight ahead amid the trickle of empty carts and shoppers, hoping that rerouting his plan of attack might lead the hounds off his scent. To the greeter's back is a row of nipple-high pallets. It forms a barricade before the cash registers and funnels the incoming flock into the supermarket. The first pallet is a cube of Vlasic pickle jars, cartoon storks laughing at him from every last cylinder. Next, Jack Daniel's barbecue sauce. Then Lay's potato chips—yellow Classic, green Sour Cream & Onion, red Wavy—followed by Pepsi, all Pepsi, until the last one shared by Corona and Corona Light, and in the rafters above the Mexican beers, an American flag dangles from its side, turning its stripes into prison cell bars. In the main lane is a rug of fake grass stapled in place by a cast-iron fire pit, a portable grill, and bags of Kingsford charcoal. After the Fourth of July barbecue ware comes a table holding crinkly plastic containers of dinner rolls, cinnamon rolls, lemon tart cupcakes, bear claws, cornbread, and *Everyday Low Price*—only $3.98 each. He pivots away from the empty-calorie pastries and toward nutrition, the produce, and trips into a shelf of scrotal avocados. He charges ahead, resists the nourishing lure of green grapes, red grapes, tubs of precubed watermelon, mango, honeydew, apple, pineapple, strawberries, hubcap-sized party trays of celery, cherry tomatoes, cucumbers, baby carrots, broccoli, cauliflower, alongside vats of guacamole, ranch, mayonnaise—low fat, regular, zesty—and it's too much, too tempting. Rubbing his eyes, he bumps into a man in a mesh tank top and apologizes to a plastic crate that's either half-empty or half-full of cantaloupes the color of brain matter, and his own brain is swelling, about to pop like bubble gum as it absorbs and processes this barrage of stimuli. His vision muddles, smears the organic section into an Amazonian array of greens, until the shelves stop at an endcap freezer full of Eggo waffles and Cool Whip. It's notably cooler in the frozen food aisle, humming like a choir in a seashell. Along the upper trim of the freezers are green signs labeling the sections to his left: *Dinner Breads, Breakfast, Breakfast, Breakfast, Dessert.* He misses the dinner breads entirely after a glance at the glass doors flashes back a chump in a floppy suit whose face is squeezed by fatigue and guilt. At the far end of the aisle is a cluster of shoppers bent over their cart handles, a herd of metallic cattle. Henry decelerates to a trot, and slowing down along the first quadrant of

Breakfast brings the boxes of Jimmy Dean breakfast sandwiches into focus. The glossy photos of croissants with sausage, bacon, poached eggs, and melted cheddar tantalize him in a way the produce couldn't. Just imagining the scent of spiced lard and fluffy buttermilk biscuits stirs a shudder of famine as all-consuming as lust. How he'd wanted to suck the CVS cashier's pretty pecan fingers knotting his necktie, wanted to give the athleisure-wearing mother at McDonald's a horizontal workout worth remembering, wanted to turn the mousy gas station clerk out and into Michelle—no, to this day nothing roars as feral or insatiable as his hunger for Michelle. Even now he would forgo a thirteen-course orgy for a nibble of her earlobe. He is ravenous. He has to cool off, hurry up, and so the waffles, biscuits, breakfast burritos, canned Minute Maid juices, and Sara Lee pies all smudge into a frosty technicolor before he slices past the shopping cart herd and breaks back into the main lane, lightheaded and short of breath. Junior is waiting, the truck is running, the seconds are ticking, and so he prays nobody is watching as he interlocks his fingers and tips his face to the halo glare above, proposing a silent deal to the rafters: make this lap through the supermarket a successful diversion, and he'll gladly turn over whatever little he's got. He swears it, just— please. Amen. Even though Papa had been raised Catholic, he and Mom had always sneered at organized religion and the idea of an omnipotent, benevolent god who nevertheless subjected its creation to such rampant suffering and injustice. Still though, at Mom's funeral Henry'd spied Papa thumbing the beads of a beechwood rosary, looped over the tops of his fingers like brass knuckles. Papa's lips squirmed but released no sound, perhaps bidding his wife a silent farewell, or else positing a secret bargain to the void, just like Henry, right here, right now. He thought he'd ironed out the conditions of this absurd pact only in his mind, but now he hears his own voice muttering as he turns into another wide thruway that leads past the women's clothes. The pharmacy awaits at the end of this stretch, but there's an obstacle course of sluggish customers and huge racks clogging the lane. He dips into a slight squat, greasing his knees limber for this sprint. He zips past the Energizer and Duracell display, around another wishing him *HAPPY SNACKING* before he dodges a rack of empty DVD-sized slots and a cube tiled in gift cards for websites and restaurants like Applebee's, Chili's, Hooters, Red Lobster, and there'd been a time when he was rich, a moment when he possessed a Bible's bulk of cash and the divine power to purchase any damn thing in this godawful bazaar, whatever trinket, gadget, or treat that might please or sustain Junior and Michelle—his family. They'd been a family back then, but what are they now? The question rips him to a standstill. He doesn't have an answer, just thirty-eight cents in his pocket and a glass jewelry case to his left. A yellow *CLEARANCE* banner runs above the velvet-lined clams, all their jaws locked open to show off their synthetic pearls and pendants and gems and chains and rings and at one point he'd wanted more than anything to marry Michelle. To pamper and spoil and devote his every last everything to her. To write her a motherfucking symphony—ha. And in the end? *Ha*. In the end, the boy was right: Henry killed her. He'd taken it upon himself to thunder all high and mighty and strike her down. He hit her. He hit her. He hit her. Assaulted, attacked, laid out, sucker-punched—there's no way to rebrand the violence into something forgivable. If not entirely well, at least she's alive somewhere in California, but whenever she comes back for Junior, she would never have anything to do with Henry— not after what he'd done—and so her absence from his waking hours would only augment this ocean of alone, this high tide of remorse doomed to never recede. A wave crashes in his mind. He struggles against the undertow, anchors himself to a rack of beach towels rolled into terry cloth scrolls alongside Banana Boat, Hawaiian Tropic, and Australian Gold oils and creams. All this landlocked beach gear, thousands of miles from either coast, but still a shoreline begins unfolding itself down the main thruway so goddamn vividly that it has to be a memory. There's Michelle walking across the sand, her naked frame opaque and glinting like a dust-coated diamond. The surf sweeps over her feet and leaves cappuccino froth around her ankles.

He hustles after her and into a perpendicular lane that cleaves both this made-up memory and the jewelry section. The lane is a bridge to the men's clothes, its corner rack showcasing Independence Day paraphernalia. Cotton T-shirts of white, blue, and gray depict bald eagles gazing stoically at unoccupied armpits, while others fly the flag, Old Glory either flattened into a rectangle or else curled by an unseeable breeze. *Born Free. Freedom Isn't Free. FREEDOM*, plain and simple. *God Bless America. 1776.* No mention whatsoever of any truths held self-evident or rights unalienable, but that's hardly the cause of the horror that's birthed directly above like a boulder on a string. It's what shimmers in his periphery, there, across from the men's clothing section: the pharmacy department. He's here, right here, steps and seconds away from what he's come to do and better get done quick, because he doesn't have much of a choice one way or another, or a million. Just has to reach out and take it, but his grip is a liability. Can't afford another mistake. He wipes his hands over the jacket, but the polyester more squeegees than absorbs the moisture. He passes three teenage girls in the makeup aisle who crane their necks at a high mirror, smacking their lips. Signs at each and every endcap down the way promise a new *Everyday Low Price, Everyday Low Price, Everyday Low Price.* The next aisle is shopperless but cramped by vitamin boxes' yellows and purples, greens and reds, blues and oranges striping the shelves with no regard for chromatic sequence like a disgruntled rainbow. Facing it are headless male bodies, seemingly carved out of oak, plastered onto plastic vats of whey protein and energy powders. The shelves clear into an opening before the pharmacy window, beside which is *Allergy Relief,* across from which is *Pain Relief.* He pauses to regroup at the nearest endcap, pretending to examine ingredients on a package of Neutrogena Makeup Remover Cleansing Towelettes while covertly surveying his surroundings. He forces out a yawn, squinting and arching his neck as he scans the ceiling for security cameras, trying to pinpoint a blind spot on the ground. He peeks past the serrated ridge of the periwinkle packaging to track the customers' paths as they mill from one *Everyday Low Price* to the next. They're all potential witnesses or whistleblowers, possibly even secret shoppers with handcuffs hidden in their jorts, for all he knows. None of them walk. They trudge and shuffle down the main lane, as if their rickety shopping cart wheels were propelled by some hidden motor that was actually towing them along, like a tractor hauling off a felled rodeo steer. He comes across a stray cart. Might help him blend in. He casually takes its handle, lets it tug him forward as he studies the shoppers for more camouflage pointers. Every man, regardless of age, race, or size wears a baseball cap, so Henry looks down. Clunky orthopedic sneakers. Once-white socks gone Dijon. A prosthetic leg. Varicose veins. Crisco oozes out of cargo shorts and into flip-flops. Torsos defy elastic waistbands. Bra straps floss into blimpish shoulders. Arms so roped with muscle they look nautical, others so flabby they look edible. Collars stretched into frowns. A trache-punctured throat. Cranberry psoriasis. Lopsided goatees. Wrinkles like gashes or dragonfly wings or survival. Irises like May mornings. Irises like despair. Zigzagging cornrows. A gray cotton candy perm. Hair like braided honey, hair like wisteria, hair like Michelle's. Pigtails like two chutes of motor oil sway at the back of a girl's head as she wags a Super Soaker, begging her mother for permission to place it in their cart, which they now realize is missing. The mother spins and catches the culprit, the thief, Henry. His back goes slimy but his throat is parched. Can't muster an apology. Just crumples into a penitent bow and surrenders the cart. Doesn't seem right, doesn't feel fair. Whatever he owns he must inevitably relinquish. Wherever he goes he is universally rejected. He doesn't belong because he can't. His exile is everlasting. But is it really too steep an order to be equal to, or simply among, these people? Yeah, he knows he's done terrible, shameful things, and still does them here and there, but on accident, like last night with the dogmonger, as well as a few sort of bad things, like what he's got to do now. But this is for his son. The end justifies these petty means, right? Shouldn't stealing for the sake of his son's health balance out the ethical seesaw? No denying his three gravest trespasses have sunk the immoral end of the scale deep into the playground muck. He'd attacked and banished the mother of his son. He'd betrayed and effectively locked away his best friend. He'd ignored his last friend's pleas, let the police trounce and chain and drag him away. He can hardly bring himself to mutter any of their names, but he's been trying, he's been fighting, and if he truly is beyond redemption and all hope of ever becoming a good person, is it still too much to ask to be a regular one? While he did something treacherous, he's never done anything treasonous, nothing against the country. His life sentence to the status of an untouchable seems both cruel and unusual. All he wants is to be like any one of these people, these Americans doing the best they can with the itty-bitty they got, one day and purchase at a time. It's all right here, right in front of him, mere inches from his fingertips, and so he stretches them into five points and slaps himself across the cheek. The smack sizzles. Flames catch and spread. It's entirely up to him to put himself within arm's reach and take it, and so he marches straight past the pharmacy window, his body ablaze and its trail of smoke be damned. The shelves are brimming with options, and Junior deserves the absolute best. An eye-level stream of orange: Equate Daytime, DayQuil, a combo box of Day- and NyQuil, then plain old purple NyQuil, followed by the lime green of Mucinex boxes before the shelves end and give way to a row of metal prongs, shish kabobs of Carmex, ChapStick, Burt's Bees, below which are boxes with circular tins of balm. Oh, to be more than the boy's shield but his balm, a salve to alleviate and comfort and—more shelves, more medicines. Pink boxes of Benadryl, blue boxes of Allegra, a grassy knoll for Claritin, and the final half of the aisle is dedicated to *Pain Relief*: red for Tylenol, navy for Advil, emerald for Excedrin Extra Strength, crimson for Excedrin Migraine, sky blue for Aleve, yellow for Bayer. Each brand name and color comes in a dozen different sizes, varying counts and doses, extended release, instant relief, liquid tabs, gel tabs, and all that matters is that he take the very best one, the most expensive yet in the smallest package, which he can fit under his unbuttoned shirtsleeve. But first things first, he's got to outwait this lady who's just parked her cart right next to him. Under a silk hijab, her face turns from a box of Claritin to another of Equate Loratadine. Time is tight. Each second burns another drop of gasoline, every minute hoists Junior's fever further up, further deathward. Still though, this permits a respite, a moment to breathe, browse, compare. Advil turns out to be the most expensive, which he can only assume is owed to its superior quality. His left hand goes for the largest box, three hundred 200-milligram tablets for $19.98, while the right helps itself to two of the easily concealable Advil Pocket Packs. Two decoys, one target. It's now or never and he's ready but needs this lady to make up her goddamn mind and leave him—despite how desperately he craves company, understanding, touch—alone. Waiting, imploding, he feigns concentration and draws the fine print under his nose, mirroring the woman beside him. A full minute passes. The thermometer climbs. The box descends in her hands, and so does the one in Henry's. She squints, he squints. She sighs, and Henry is broiling. His rage is frothy, savage, but with no turnbuckles to climb or folding chairs to hurl, all he can do is shake the pills into angry maracas, as if that might shoo her away. Instead, it prompts her to examine the Benadryl. As the pills go from maracas to a can of mace, a Molotov cocktail—something, anything repellent or explosive—she looks up and catches him scowling. They exchange the timid smiles that retail decorum demands of shoppers who've made eye contact, and he wants to scream. Assessing his options, he knows he's too racked with anxious twitches to stuff the pills under his sleeve while he's walking, and moving to another unoccupied aisle totally defeats the purpose of the two decoys that he intends to return oh so innocently to the shelf. Maybe doing it here with this lady right next to him would be the slickest move of all. The sheer audacity of shoplifting in plain sight and only inches from a witness just might clear him of all suspicion. Since he first stepped inside, his every movement has been charged with a furtive, guilt-ridden quake, so this isn't only the timeliest tactic, but also the most prudent. If it's now or never, he chooses now. Now—*go*. He sniffs. A knob in his forehead twists and his focus goes telescopic. A sold-out stadium, its collective breath held, bracing for flying-elbow impact. Now. He sniffs again, clears his throat, and expels a few raspy, hollow-chest coughs to muffle any pill clicks as his pinky presses one of the Pocket Pack vials up his wrist and into his sleeve. It settles in place, secured, unnoticed. It was so easy, went so quick, and relief fizzles through him, because it is done. The tricky part at least. To keep the small box in place, he's got to keep his right hand folded into an awkward, arthritic claw at his side, and so he uses the left to return the decoys. Apparently the lady beside him is impressed by his shrewd consumer resolve, because she now nods to him, and the smile he deploys in turn is celestial. Even after their gazes detach, the sense of completion stays with him. Turning to make his escape, he forces out another cough to cloaks the pills' clacking when he lets the bottle slide into the suit's front pocket. A sigh gusts him out to the main thruway, sailing him down the homestretch past home decor and straight toward the cash lanes, the exit, Junior. This propulsion doesn't belong to him. It's as if all that's left is the chore of treading water, keeping his head surfaced while the flow of *Everyday Low Prices* and carts and shoppers and white linoleum and even whiter lights carries him closer and closer and he's so close now. Happily, he defers to the current, a piece of driftwood with purpose, a destination. Merrily, merrily, merrily, merrily, and life is but a nightmare—he's become a walking, tone-deaf tambourine. Step after step, the pills shout, *clack* and *clack* and *clack*, merrily, merrily, merrily announcing his escape. He tries whistling over the noise, but his lips are too dry since his nervous system has dispatched all water caches to cool the rest of him down. The checkout area is a minefield looming closer and larger now, and he hasn't devised a strategy for navigating past all these eyes, all the black half globes, one staring down at every single cash register. He dips his head to watch his boots flashing left-right-left-right-left over the floor and immediately realizes this evasive tactic is a fucking flare, a crackling, ruby-red comet tail spotlighting him as he flees a crime scene. Slathered palms mold his face muscles from panic to staid, before he presses his chin up and his shoulders wide, as if strutting back into the job interview for round two. Only a criminal would weasel out through one of the unattended cash lanes, but he's no novice, he won't rush into this trap. He opts for the brazen route, dissimulating among the longest line of carts and beneath his faux-bold veneer. Wheels squeak. Items thud onto conveyor belts. Buttons click. Scanners beep. Receipts print. The boom of his heartbeat makes a dance of his skips and side-steps past the shopping carts, baskets, customers, and cashiers. He's prepared for any gaze that might hook his own, at the ready to deal counterblows in the form of courteous nods. He's so close now, so close that he can see a sliver of dusk beyond the sliding doors. A frail old lady struggles to lift a paper bag into her cart. She is the final hurdle and he is so close. In a swoop, he wrangles the four remaining bags off the counter and into her cart and gives a neighborly salute, before breaking free of the checkout lanes and into the airy clearing by customer service. He gulps down a yip. He crams his hands into pockets to restrain them from outstretching as if crossing a finish line. He has to check himself. Take her easy. Down, boy. He breathes in, smooths his lapels like a businessman, exhales. Done deal. Gravy. Triumph. He's close, even closer now, so close that through the glass doors he can see the rear bumper of his truck. The air beneath it is woolly—exhaust—and so the engine is miraculously still running. Twined so tight, so ecstatically zeroed in on the target, he only notices the security guard after fully rounding the corner and striding sternum first into a stiff extended palm.

"Sir," the guard says. "A word?"

"Please."

Animal instinct elects flight. Henry pumps left, then rockets off to the right. The guard wobbles but manages to grab the back of Henry's jacket, tearing him to a stop. Duty overrides the impulse to squirm out of the jacket, because Henry will not abandon the medicine in its pocket. Thrusting both arms frees the fabric, and he sprints past the first set of doors, through the shopping cart atrium then out to the pavement, and he's so close now, so close that he can just about reach out and touch the passenger door, behind which is Junior, and when he looks behind him for the guard, a second one spears him into the side panel of the truck.

The second guard pins Henry facedown on the sidewalk. Henry thrashes and screams until a knee slams square between his shoulder blades, zippering him silent, scraping his breath out of him as if with a rusty spoon. He gasps and gasps, swallowing heat but no oxygen. The guard's knee is a stake, forcing him to writhe like a salamander nailed to a board. The concrete is a cheese grater against his cheek. He can't breathe, can't move, can't fight, can't think. The thrashes ebb down to squirms, the gasps down to whimpers. As his limbs deflate, his wrists get wrangled into a set of zip-tie cuffs over the small of his back. His bound wrists are used as a lever to hoist the rest of him to his feet in a way that keeps him bent over, head down, submissive.

Oxygen returns to him in tiny, emphysemic straw sucks. When his chest gets pressed against the truck bed, he turns his gaze to the tailgate, away from all their garbage-bagged belongings and Junior, and instead looks back to where they'd come from, as if searching for the point where they'd made a wrong turn. A foot kicks the inner arch of his boot and spreads his legs. Questions are asked but nothing is said. Hands pat up and down his ankles, waist, and sides. Whatever strength he's got left is spent on twisting his shoulders and hips just to make things difficult. Puny spitballs of resistance.

They find the Advil first. Henry spits air. A threat to call the police turns into a call to the police. A hand digs into the front pocket of his pants, withdraws his driver's license, job interview note cards, and the dashboard cigarette burner. The one quarter, two nickels, and three pennies remain in place.

While waiting for the police, they ask more questions. To each one, Henry shakes his head no, because fuck them. His mouth is shut, his eyes are shut, and he concentrates on transmitting instructions to Junior in the truck cab, willing the boy to do the same—don't give them a thing, not a word. Shopping cart wheels clatter out of the entryway, and he can feel the shoppers' stares boring into the back of his neck. He is a specimen. A less-than to be quarantined, dissected for science.

Tires grind up to the truck's rear bumper. The tissue of his eyelids is illuminated, glowing pinkish red, pinkish blue, over and over. When a car door shuts, the truck's engine hiccups, stammers. After a few strained chugs, it finally burns through the last of the gas and shuts off. As the engine cools, it makes a ticking sound, like someone snapping their fingers to summon a misplaced memory.

"I know this fella."

That bucolic drawl. Henry doesn't have to open his eyes to see the cop's mustache and ruddy jowls. After glancing at Henry's license, the cop leans against the truck bed and dips into Henry's sight line, as if to better share this expression of paternal disappointment. "Say, Mr. Henry. Whyn't you fill me in on what all's going on here, how about?"

"Suspect was caught stealing these."

Pills rattle.

"Tried to flee the scene."

"And assaulted me in the process."

"Left us no choice but to apprehend and restrain him on the premises."

"Refusing to cooperate."

"Won't say a word."

"That sound about right, Mr. Henry?" the cop asks. "Anything else I ought to hear, you know, from your side a things?"

So much to say and even more to ask but no way or where to start. Henry's tongue is a desert, his mind barren yet bedlam. When his lips part, nothing falls. Not a word, not even sand.

"Okeydokey, then." The cop flicks the license. "Let me run this right quick."

Within five minutes, the cop is out of the squad car and saying exactly what Henry knew he would. He makes some dated, buckaroo whistle, then starts telling the guards it turns out Mr. Henry here got hisself a record. Felony drug charge. Boy done five years down-state, only a year or so out on parole, and so, yeah. He drops a re-cycled campaign-trail catchphrase about recidivism, replacing the *v* with a second *d*, before asking if either of the guards has taken a look-see in the truck.

The cop makes a rudder of Henry's wrists to steer him over to the squad car. Presses the back of his head and then the rest of him into the backseat. The door slams. Inside it's airless. Burnt coffee and old vomit. Henry wriggles forward, crushes his forehead against the di-vider's metal grating to peer through the diamond-shaped apertures.

The cop approaches the truck with a John Wayne gait and an im-becile's jaw. He steps onto the rear tire and begins sifting through the truck bed. He knocks on the utility case, then turns an invisible key in the direction of the security guards. He reaches under and rum-mages inside garbage bags, the first one full of Henry's winter clothes. Then he squints.

The cop lifts the motel iron. He picks at a rusty freckle with his thumbnail and seems to stiffen before setting the iron down. The second bag is full of Junior's dirty laundry. He unfolds a pair of the boy's underwear, frowning as if it were a particularly tricky Sudoku puzzle. He peeks into the cab's rear window then startles back, ap-parently seeing and only now remembering the sick child. He slaps his forehead and scuttles over to the passenger side.

All this time, since blurting that last word when asked for one, Henry hasn't managed to assemble and expel another. Even though his silence had initially been the only means of defiance left to him, he can't be sure he hasn't actually gone mute for good. Diaphragm drops, lungs swell, vocal cords flex, and tongue cocks, but nothing sounds. Then again, what would he ever need to say now? What good were words if they couldn't make a day for Junior, could never sing him a morning, golden and true, and for all time?

Then the cop opens the passenger door. Leans into the truck cab.

Henry shatters. He ruptures and floods all at once, and rediscov-ered language—at least one word—comes blasting out of him: *No*.

He screams it, bellows it, furiously helpless, over and over in the echo chamber of this squad car. His howls ricochet and gnarl his frame. He rams his shoulder into the door, bangs his forehead against the cage. The entire vehicle rocks, teeters with his anguish, but nobody notices him. Exile. Pariah. Nothing. Nobody. Nobody sees him weeping. Nobody hears him begging, "Don't touch my son. Don't you take my baby."

When the upper half of the cop reemerges, four limbs sway limp from his grasp. The cop presses the backs of his fingers to Junior's forehead. Cups the boy's chin, gives it a gentle, terrified shake. The cop's rosacea cheeks flush redder yet as he speaks into the radio on his shoulder. He hails a security guard, who now hands him the evidence, the Advil. Balancing Junior in one arm, the cop rips the packaging with his teeth and tries palming a pill into the boy's mouth.

It cannot end like this.

They'd had so much more to do together, so much more to learn. Ground to cover and inches to grow. Secrets to share. Memories to make and keep safe. It isn't his fault. He'd needed so little but asked for too much. It is all his fault. He'd had so little to give but would surrender it all, every last cent and scrap for just one more chance. One last chance. Maybe he'd already been given one, so perhaps this is it. And so there's nothing left to bargain with, nothing left to offer. No more promises or tomorrows. No more stories or hugs. No more failures, disappointments, or dreams. No more lies. Not even the one he's muttering right now, aiming it past the cage to his son outside, out there.

"I'm right here," Henry tells him. "I'm right here."

$195.70

The end of one thing just meant the start of something else. It'd taken years for Henry to come to terms with this apparent truth. Back when he'd been an angsty, bereaved teen, the fact that motion continued (nor ever paused) during his fits of despair always seemed such an insensitive, even cruel perpetuation, as if the world owed him a moment of stillness and silence to accommodate his personal tragedies. Still though, no matter how dark it got, the sun always turned up. Eventually. Just like it had the morning after Mom passed. Like it had after every death-tempting bender. Like it had after his first night in county, and then every following morning over the next five years in the state pen. There in his cell, he used to start each day the same way, craning off the top bunk to peer through that envelope-sized slot in the concrete, double-checking the world was still there, still going, and of course it was. Even that morning after the plant closed and he hit Michelle and ended their family— there it was, right there, grinning gold and new in the east, crawling imperceptibly higher by the minute.

What today's end might be the beginning of was as uncertain as any. All he knew was that it was coming soon. Any minute now it would be kicked off with a knock on the front door. Then, as soon as it opened, and he and Junior stepped out of their home and into the truck, that something else would begin.

For the time being, though, all Henry could do was wait.

All he knew about Michelle's disappearance was that, one, it was his fault and, two, she'd withdrawn every last penny from their shared account, before going off to wherever she'd gone.

And motion resumed.

There'd been no time to wallow in remorse. Henry was Pa now, and so had things that needed getting done, first and foremost of which was to figure out how to replenish both funds and the pantry. After a week of asking after openings in shops and garages around town, landing an on-the-books job proved hopeless. At the bottom of every application was the box, the motherfucking box: *Have you ever been convicted of a felony?*

Getting a call back was as unlikely as it was later impossible to scrape together enough money for rent, food, gas, and bills by scrapping metal or taking odd jobs around town. He'd even gone so far as to beg Sandi—just short of falling to her feet—to let him work off the month's rent by doing repairs and upkeep around the park, the same sort of deal she cut for her geriatric biker pals.

Sandi spat tar.

"As manager, safety's my number one priority, boy," she'd said. "Really think people don't talk none? Think us all don't know where you been the last five years, huh? Got shit for brains to think I'd ever let your ass into other residents' homes."

Electric and gas had been cut earlier this month, the last, December. Their lantern burned through D batteries at an unaffordable rate. After going through a box of tea candles, he'd picked up a cheap case of white dinner table candles and found that bowling their longer wicks and taller flames with aluminum foil radiated even more light and warmth. He now positioned himself over one of these mini–tinfoil torches now, toasting the ache out of his knuckles. Even though it was cold enough inside to make his breath visible, the top half of his coveralls hung loose at the back of his waist, trailing him like a canvas shadow. His bare forearms pressed into the countertop while his hands rearranged all the money he had left to his name—nearly all of it made from a frigid, frost-dusted yard sale—into four stacks: three twenties, seven tens, nine fivers, twelve singles. A neighbor on his way to the laundromat had traded thirty-three quarters for Henry's dresser. The quarters were stacked in eight stumpy cylinders. These stacks along with the stray quarter, a dime, six nickels, and five pennies put him at exactly $195.70. No matter how many times he recounted or arranged the bills and coins, the sum never changed. And it wouldn't last long.

The only piece of furniture he hadn't lugged out to the snowy driveway was Junior's mattress. Had to let the boy sleep as comfortably as possible these final nights in their home. Other than that, where the boy was sitting now, their home was completely empty, so hollow that all sounds and talk reverberated at a louder, lonelier decibel.

Junior was wearing long johns and his black parka. The hood was pulled over his head and he'd wrapped Mom's bese saka shawl into an oversized scarf around his face and shoulders. A tinfoil-bowled flame cast the once vibrant shawl into a muddle of amber and shadows. All Henry could see of the boy's skin were his hands clicking Legos into a complex, asymmetrical structure that could never be balanced upright to stand on its own. Ever since Michelle had left ever since Henry'd struck her and thrown her out—the boy had grown stingy with his eye contact. Henry tried willing the boy to look at him now. If the boy did look, would he catch an echo of what Henry'd seen in Papa years ago? A worn-out man at the dining room table, huddled over a checkbook, bills, receipts, and a calculator, diverting all his hours-turned-dollars from one account to the next, calculating subtraction after inevitable subtraction required to maintain a home, to sustain a family.

The boy wouldn't look up, and so Henry said, "Hey."

The boy ignored him. Henry repeated himself, louder.

"What?"

"Never mind."

The boy finally looked up, only to catch his pa looking down. For a moment Henry considered setting the stack of snow-warped envelopes and the eviction notice in the candle's flame. As if smoke and ash could change anything, as if they could ever amount to something more than their charred weight. The eviction notice had arrived mid-December. Sandi made a theater of staple-gunning each corner into the front door, Henry all the while cowering inside, pretending not to be there, even with his truck parked right out front.

After her knocks and jeers stopped, he slipped out to snatch it before Junior got home from school.

NOTICE
You have been evicted from this property by virtue of a
Court Order served by the County Sheriff's Office.
YOUR PRESENCE ON THIS PROPERTY WITHOUT
THE EXPRESS PERMISSION OF THE LANDLORD
AS OF DECEMBER 31, 2015, WILL BE CONSIDERED
TRESPASSING AND MAY RESULT IN YOUR ARREST

Sandi's eagerness to rub his face in the news turned out to be a slight, accidental mercy. She'd given them a full two weeks to make the necessary preparations. Seemed inhumane to have benefited from witnessing Sandi evict some of his previous neighbors. Still though, he'd learned a lot by joining the gawkers at the curb, watching in silence as one of their neighbors got stripped of home and worldly possessions. By now he was familiar with and prepared for Sandi's eviction drill. Her tobacco juice smirk as she thumbed to a moving truck and asked, "Curb or truck?" Did the evictee prefer their things to get dumped in the lawn, or else hauled off in the truck to a storage warehouse that held a fifty-dollar-a-month ransom on each four-by-four pallet of personal belongings, on top of a two-hundred-dollar moving fee? If forced to choose between having a stranger charge him for his own shit or leaving it to get picked through by the buzzards, then he was damn well going to make a couple bucks off whatever they wouldn't be needing for life on the road.

The yard sale wasn't only a last-ditch effort to make some cash. It also denied Sandi the satisfaction of seeing Henry as trounced as all the other evictees as they watched fat men in back braces ransacking their homes, cramming their lives into a truck, or else tossing them out to the lawn. And in spite of all the acid he held for Sandi, he refused to burn this bridge by unleashing whatever was stewing inside him, sure to exit as an eruption of either screams or weeping. Instead, he would set aside pride and spite and swear to pay off all his dues, so they could move back into this park. He was determined to go out with whatever dignity a naked man can muster. He had to.

The thing was that some gerrymandering quirk had landed Indigo Hills in what had become, thanks to the outlet mall's tax revenue, one of the best school districts in the state. It wasn't like he would ever be able to afford a stand-alone home anywhere else in town, at least not anytime soon. And even if he had the money to afford rent elsewhere, there was no way he'd get a chance to sign a contract, let alone be invited to a house viewing. Word was that the state judiciary had recently developed a phone app that put a comprehensive database for background checks in the front pocket of every hiring manager and landlord out there. His status as a felon not only forced him to check the box and out of the voting booth, but also barred him from getting any form of state assistance—welfare, food stamps, Medicare, housing—as well as ever clearing a background check for a decent home. Regardless, it was essential to keep Junior enrolled in this school, as much for the quality of education and all the door-opening opportunities it could bring as for the boy's emotional well-being. The kid had been put through enough. Had already lost his mother, was soon to lose his home. This school was the last sliver of stable ground beneath the boy's feet.

And so walking away with his tongue bitten in a charade of poise was Henry's only option. Not only would he make amends with and promises to Sandi, he would even be doing a favor for the movers, who, just like everyone else today, would be itching to join friends and family, pop bottles, watch the ball drop on TV, then kiss their special someone at the stroke of midnight.

After the gas and electricity had been cut, all their dinners had to be prepared on the grill outside. A few nights Henry'd had to shovel a path through the snow to get to it, where he stood bundled up to his nose, turning hot dogs and stirring a pot of rice, watching his breath swim away with the smoke and steam. But once they hit the road, parking lot barbecues wouldn't be an option. Impractical, dangerous, sending literal smoke signals to child services. And even though he'd seen chutes of barbecue smoke drifting up from the Walmart parking lot, he refused to join their ranks and raise his son in a mobile shantytown. He didn't know if that made him an arrogant prick, didn't care if it did, and so never gave it a second thought.

That first afternoon of preparations, right after the eviction notice posting, had been spent devising a way to cook dinner in the truck cab. He didn't stop tinkering when he heard the school bus outside, not even when Junior walked in. Henry was sitting cross-legged on the floor, using a pair of pliers to crimp and bend a wire clothes hanger into a contraption that looked like some junkyard crown, sized for a house cat. When the crown was finished, he jogged out to the truck and sat inside it, shivering and waiting for the cigarette burner to warm up, then pop. He ran the tube of hot coils back into the living room, inserted it into the center of the crown, then balanced a can of chili in its wire prongs. It took about fifteen minutes and two more trips to the dashboard, but the maroon goop nevertheless reached a temperature more palatable than lukewarm.

"It'll be like camping," he told Junior.

"Whatever," the seven-year-old said with a teenager's scorn.

Wasn't as if Henry'd ever gone camping himself. By now he'd adopted Papa's low opinion of the pastime, which he shared one night after Mom suggested they all go on a camping trip.

Through a mouthful of rice, Papa scoffed. He swallowed, then called it preposterous. It was absolutely ridiculous to intentionally deprive oneself of civilization's amenities. Nothing more than a bourgeois simulation of scarcity, turning true struggle into whimsy. And, in that way, it wasn't just asinine but an insult to the world's poor, who actually battled hunger and the elements on a daily basis. He shoved more rice onto his tablespoon and said if Mom was so interested in experiencing dearth and poverty firsthand—and he meant real, abject poverty—well, then any money for tents and tin cups would be far better blown on another trip to Manila. She could spend a day or two scavenging in the slums. Wouldn't that be fun, ah.

Mom's lips pursed as if she'd taken a sip of coffee, charred and bitter, before they bent into her sad smile. She reached across the dining table and took Henry's hand.

"You don't have to come," she told Papa. "Henry and I don't need you. It'll be just the two of us, braving the great outdoors and the world at large."

"And bears," Papa grinned. "Just the two of you and grizzlies, ah."

At ten years old, Henry had been intoxicated by the thought of being alone with Mom, the two of them an intrepid duo taking on whatever creatures and conditions they might meet in the depths of the wilderness. His imagination ran wild, constructing a scene so vivid and frequently retraced that to this day it remained stored as a memory never experienced.

The forest was dark. The scents of moss and pine needles mingled with the sounds of birds chirping and deer foraging. He couldn't know what other beasts might have lain in wait in the shadows, but he was with Mom, and so never felt scared. She led the way, winding around tree trunks like the ankles of giants, pointing out the best footing for scaling stony ravines, picking and passing him back wild berries, until the woods gave way to a sunny clearing on a cliff top, where they could safely set up camp and keep a lookout for whatever else might be coming their way.

Recalling this unrolled a nauseous surf as he poured the chili out of the can and into a bowl. That memory never lived had incited a great vortex now churning him earthward, as if both light and mass had been guzzled by the sequence of Mom's actual fate and the macabre taunt of all that might have been.

Henry dipped a teaspoon into the chili, looked up at Junior, and went bedrock steady. The boy took the bite. Gave a frown of approval. Meanwhile Henry was swelling with all that could be, all they could be—he saw it as lucidly as he'd seen Mom stepping into the sunny clearing. This something else, this new thing slated for December 31, was his chance to make up for all the time he'd lost and things he'd done.

Wasn't too far-fetched a fantasy. After all, Papa had undergone the softening. If he'd managed to change, then certainly Henry could, too. Despite withholding all affection and praise throughout Henry's youth, Papa eventually shed his rancor and granite and redeemed himself by the time Henry was a young man. And so this actually gave Henry a head start on doing the same with Junior. Sure, he knew grueling, hungry days were coming, but he'd heard that shared struggle reinforced bonds, fostered trust and solidarity. This ending would be the beginning—their beginning.

Then again, Papa had never hit Henry's mother. Never sent Mom to the floor, then boomed righteous and terrible over the person who'd gifted him both a son and purpose. Never dragged her by the scruff and thrown her out, never expelled her from their lives with his own two hands. No, nothing even close. Toward the end, Papa had been devotion incarnate. A walking sacrifice, a martyr preimmolation. He'd risked his job and taken unpaid leave through the entirety of Mom's last year so he could take care of her at home, as well as chauffeuring and accompanying her to all appointments and sessions. He racked up thousands on flights and hotels to visit specialists around the country in spite of his shoestring pragmatism, in spite of the odds, in spite of the statistical certainty that he was doomed to spend the rest of his days robbed of his dearest companion and entombed in debt.

That night, after Henry'd done what Papa would never have been capable of, Junior sobbed so violently that Henry thought the boy might never stop, might wail himself to death. Gasps and screeches so vicious they threatened retching the boy's lungs out of his chest and onto the floor, onto the very spot Henry had sent Michelle only minutes before. The boy clawed and slashed Henry away, telling him he hated him, he hated him, over and over, until he'd depleted himself entirely. As he withered, Henry inched closer, then embraced him. In Henry's arms, the boy convulsed with weak, erratic spasms.

During that first lull, Henry would have done awful, heinous things for mere access to the right words. Words to soothe, to console. There must have been some vault, an armory storing the appropriate language to heal or at least ease the boy. Some verbal balm to remind him that however impossible it felt now, morning would come.

"Mommy's very, very sick," he'd said.

"Don't you worry.

"She'll be back. In the morning. You'll see.

"It's okay. Everything's going to be fine, just fine.

"Mommy will be back."

Henry's breath petered out before he could remind the boy of where his father was in time and space. Regardless, the fact that Henry was right here wasn't likely to provide any solace. And in that moment he felt so small that he couldn't be sure if he wasn't actually elsewhere, somewhere airless and remote, so far away that anything he might do or say would instantaneously dissipate into the vacuum of these lonely miles between them.

One more squeeze, then Henry's embrace went slack. His shoulders slumped and fell, dragging his eyelids after them. It was dark and mossy and quiet and cold and he was scared and then, in the distance, a flicker. Something yellow.

He remembered a daffodil, a promise. A favor Mom had asked of him.

Exhaled air began curling into more recognizable sounds seemingly of its own accord, unraveling off his tongue and past his teeth where they sewed themselves into meaning, braving that impossible distance between his lips and the boy's ear pressed against him. At first the sounds were more brushstrokes than rhetoric. Oily drips that, when combined, suggested an impression, a loose description of Mom—Henry's mom, the boy's grandma. She was the one, Henry explained, who'd given him and Junior all their good parts. All their curiosity and tenderness, all their smarts and discipline, and then Henry stopped. Reconsidered.

"Yeah, no," Henry said, correcting himself.

That was when it sank in. All of Mom's goodness had lain dormant in himself and instead skipped a generation, having waited patiently to set its roots and flourish in a worthy host: Junior. Did he know that, huh? Because Henry did. He got it now. Could Junior see it, too?

The boy shook his head.

"Have I ever told you that my mom was very, very sick, too? Back when I was little, almost twice your age, but not even half as brave as you. I know how scary it is to watch your mom—your heart and whole wide world—get so sick and weak and not know how to even start helping her, how to help fix her."

It seemed his voice had stilled the boy's tremors, and so Henry continued, telling the boy that his grandma had been like a sunflower. Tall and yellow and strong. Her face always tipped up to the sky, absorbing the warmth so she could share it with everyone else. And Junior, he did the exact same thing on sunny days. Really, though, they were so similar. How the simplest treats or tasks—like a nibble of chocolate, or tending to a scraped knee—put Grandma in a sort of trance that was way beyond focus. More like reverence, or awe. Just like Junior. And so what Henry was trying to say was that Junior had somehow, so luckily, inherited all of Grandma's good qualities. All her strength and sweetness and smarts. That was for sure. His grandma always knew exactly what to do and say to help Henry, keep him from crying. Because the truth was—and now this was a secret, could Junior keep a secret? Okay, because the truth was that when Junior's pa had been his age, he'd been a total crybaby. It wasn't funny. It was true. A real wimp and, in comparison, actually kind of stupid, too. Nothing like Junior, so dang smart. So smart and strong and sensitive and that was exactly why his pa needed him right here, right now, always and forever, and then some. He needed Junior's help because he couldn't do this on his own.

It was true.

"The thing is, Junior, you've got no idea how proud your grandma would be of you. Really, though. Know why? Do you want to?"

The boy nodded.

"Because Grandma was smart enough to understand that only you've got what it takes to help your pa, to help fix me."

A quiet spread. Henry shuddered. Had to resituate himself in time and space right there, right here, embracing his son on the floor of their home.

After such sobbing, the boy's voice was a rash. "But, Pa?"

"But what?"

"Isn't that? I don't know," the boy said.

"It's okay. You can ask Pa anything."

"Isn't that a lot of responsibility? You know, for a seven-year-old?"

Henry remembered he'd chuckled, which had both surprised and worried him. Humor had seemed impossible in the wake of such violence, such shame. And as much as he'd hoped that he possessed the basic tact to tell his son, yes, it certainly was a lot, but Henry believed in him and was so very proud of him and absolutely certain that the boy could handle even the scariest situations or unfairest responsibilities, he couldn't remember what he'd actually said, because, now, the memory got cut short. Interrupted. Snipped like a joke before its punch line, or a vow of silence to a forgotten secret.

In an instant, six weeks whipped past and then yanked out from under Henry. A *knock knock* on the front door had thumped him back here, back to now, 4:32 p.m. on December 31.

It was time to go. Time for this to end so whatever that something else was could begin.

"You ready, bud?"

The shape wrapped in the bese saka shawl rocked into a full-body no.

Okay. Henry raked the cash into a single stack. Folded it, pocketed it, then splashed the coins in after. The knocks grew faster, harder. From outside, Sandi said she knew Henry was in there and would call the police if she had to, goddamnit, don't test her. She wasn't playing around, and it didn't agitate Henry at all. Ignoring the knock's tempo for his own unrushed shuffle, he passed one final time through the husk of what had once been their home, this space where they'd once been a family. He reached down and lifted the boy to his feet. While their eyes roamed loose and nervous, hunting for any stray memories that might have crawled into a vent or gotten caught in the radiator's grating, their hands held firm. Together and steady now.

The chain dropped, the deadbolt swiped, the knob turned, and the door pulled back from Sandi's mittened fist. The wind was pushing whorls of snow through a deep lilac dusk. Behind Sandi, at the bottom of the steps, stood two men wearing ski masks and back braces over gray sandstone duck jackets.

"Hey there, Sandi."

"Curb or . . . ?" Her question fizzled as she peeked inside the trailer.

"I took care of it," Henry said. "Figured I'd spare you the moving costs."

That brought back her spark, gave her something to bite.

"Spare *me* the cost? Ha. That's all on you, boy. Still gonna owe them two the minimum for driving all the way out here. And plus it's a holiday. Might be extra, time and a half, you got that?"

Henry swallowed. Sure, he said, that was fine. That was perfectly fine, just throw it on his tab. Oh. And he supposed she'd be wanting these, huh.

The house keys jingled and dropped into her mitten.

Sandi stammered, apparently furious that Henry wasn't as well.

He was, though. Of course he was. But rather than cave to this urge to either brawl or weep, he just swallowed it down one more time, then smiled.

"If you wouldn't mind, Sandi." He took a dainty sidestep past her, nodded to the movers, then led Junior by the hand out the front door and down the steps.

Detecting a weight, a reticent lag, Henry cranked his and Junior's fastened hands behind them, then gave their arms a stern swoop forward, as if trying to swing the boy up into the air and launch him over the parked truck. Henry looked down, the boy looked up. Henry winked, the boy grinned, and then his little arm tugged Henry's bigger one back for a final pendulum lunge before they detached, splitting ways for their respective sides of the truck cab.

"Oh, and so, Sandi," Henry said, pausing at the truck's door. "One last thing."

Junior sprang into the cab. He straddled the center console and started rubbing the frost on the rear window. After buffing a porthole into the cold gauze, he set his chin to the backrest, settling in to watch.

Sandi joined the movers' steaming silhouettes, now a row of three human smokestacks. She crossed her arms. Her head cocked as if to ask Henry, huh? What now?

"Just want to make it clear that I don't got no hard feelings about all this. I know it's just business. And, like I told you before, you'll get your money. We'll be back. That said, we sure would appreciate it if you tried keeping this one vacant and ready for us."

A burly scoff. Sandi barked through the inventory of his debts: three months back rent, association dues and sanitation bills running back till June, move-out cleaning fees, and Henry'd best not forget about these here moving guys. She made a hatchet of her mitten to chop at syllables, saying his punk ass wouldn't be getting back into any one of their properties without settling all that up, with interest, on top of first month, last month, and a security deposit—in cash and up front.

He gave a distrait wave. "I know, I know. Every last cent you'll be getting. You got my word. You haven't seen the last of me."

The door slammed shut after Henry. Ignition turned, engine growled, gas gauge needle swung up, then floated down slightly to show a full tank. He'd prepared. They were ready. The dashboard vents were gusting cool air and because it was warming by the second, the breeze felt like a living breath, a sustained whisper rinsing him in an unexpected satisfaction, like affirmation from a total stranger.

Henry stepped onto the clutch and cranked the gear stick into first. He turned to Junior, still straddling the console. Told him to sit normal. Forward, and buckle up now, please.

"Wait, Pa. I want to see this. Remember it."

Fair enough.

Henry eased onto the gas pedal, and now they were really leaving. This was really motion. Ending that and starting this. The open, snow-sheeted plains were spliced by the wire of a county road, darting straight and shrinking, chasing after the flush of lavender steeping deeper and darker as it melted behind the western horizon. Out here, there was and always had been plenty enough space between them and that point where the road vanished up ahead. Plenty enough space to chisel out a nook for the two of them to keep fed and warm. They wouldn't bother anyone. They didn't need much. Plenty enough to go around.

Under the headlight beams, wisps of snowdrifts shimmied and swirled over the pavement like paints that wouldn't mix. Junior didn't see the dance. He'd stayed put, right there, chest pressed against the seat and looking back. Henry let the boy be. Might actually be a decent idea for one of them to keep track of where they'd come from. What they'd done and who they'd been. They were a good team. The intrepid duo that hadn't been then, but could be now. When his fingers wrapped around his son's ankle, the contact was like closing a circuit—an electric sense of completion charged through him, through them. A jolt. A joint shudder. Whether triggered by dread or anticipation of the sprawling freedom that was now closing in on them, it didn't really matter. Didn't need a name. Fear or joy, doubt or opportunity, either way it had sparked the same current. Then again, all that had mattered, did matter, and could ever matter was right here. Within arm's reach and his to hold tight and keep safe, from here on out, forever and then some.

And then night fell. It pressed the last of dusk's light below the windshield and the scent of spring into the cab. Gasoline, cut grass, fresh asphalt, and a daffodil. Henry swallowed, smiled, and was whole. Complete. Finally had it all figured out. With such a wealth of certainty, there wasn't a single question left, because all that mattered was this little boy. All that mattered were his heart and mind and health, all his potential and tomorrows. Everything right here and so, so easy. All Henry had to do was keep his promise, with his hands steady on the wheel and eyes on the road, because it was his job to keep looking forward, to keep looking up.

Acknowledgments

This book wouldn't be here if it weren't for the support of those in my life. To retrace so many acts of compassion and generosity throughout the years absolutely floors me, and so—from right here, down on my knees—I extend my most humbled and heartfelt thanks to:

¢ My parents, Mi Wikström & Gib Pellet and Nilo & Zoe Guanzon, who taught me a dollar is measured by sacrifice, as well as how to sift love from life's rubble.

¢ Chris Clemans, whose grit and vision found this vagabond story the finest home imaginable.

¢ Steve Woodward & Fiona McCrae, for their unparalleled artistry and guidance.

¢ Katie Dublinski and the Graywolf crew, for all their hard work and astounding care.

¢ Pia Wikström & Nilabja Bhattacharya, who first gave me shelter in this city, and keep me warm and fed to this day.

¢ The earliest readers of this book, for their incisive notes and nourishing friendship:

    ¢ Miguel Alonso-Lubell

    ¢ Ellie Anderson

    ¢ Simon Guanzon

    ¢ Tate Halverson

    ¢ Mina Hamedi

    ¢ Cat Powell

    ¢ Anthony Ray

    ¢ Sarah Timmer Harvey

¢ The faculty, staff, and students at Columbia University's MFA Writing Program, whose patience with me is beyond compensation, not to mention comprehension. A special thanks to my four work-shop professors:

    ¢ Elissa Schappell, who trained my crosshairs on the jugular

    ¢ Ben Marcus, whose lessons on form helped inspire this book's budget-chapter conceit

    ¢ Mark Doten, who gave me the green light to write weird

    ¢ Ben Metcalf, who taught me (among many, many things) how to read

¢ The sociology and English departments at Hamline University, in particular Professors Kristina Deffenbacher, Veena Deo, Martin Markowitz, Navid Mohseni, and Sharon Preves, who were the first to suggest to me that a story like Henry's could matter.

¢ Jacob Thomas Kelly, who always pushed me to the furthest limits of my abilities, whether at a job site or on the page.

¢ Aliza Lalani, whose benevolence I strive to one day match, and thereby earn.

¢ Mi familia madrileña, por aguantar todas mis tonterías y su amor sin fronteras.

¢ Anchorage, for life.

¢ WU LYF, for telling fire to the mountain.

¢ A.C., for you can guess what.

¢ Debbie Petschl and the crew of Twin City Landscape, who instilled the work ethic that keeps me digging to this day.

¢ Michelle Alexander, Matthew Desmond, and Shaka Senghor, whose writings on mass incarceration, eviction, and life after prison were integral to my research and remain vital to the cause of human dignity.

Jakob Guanzon was born in New York and raised in Minnesota. He holds an MFA from Columbia University's School of the Arts, and lives in New York City.

The text of *Abundance* is set in Adobe Garamond Pro.
Book design by Rachel Holscher.
Composition by Bookmobile Design and Digital
Publisher Services, Minneapolis, Minnesota.
Manufactured by McNaughton & Gunn on acid-free,
100 percent postconsumer wastepaper.